Michael was born in Portsmouth in 1948. He discovered books at the age 11, at Woolmer Hill School, and had an active mind in English composition but didn't write his first book until 2002.

He moved from Surrey to Berkshire to study sciences at Slough College of Technology, and worked for I.C.I. as an Experimental Officer.

Michael moved to West Yorkshire in 1981 to attend college and now lives with his partner, Jennifer, near Leeds and their spare time is spent visiting properties owned by English Heritage and The National Trust. Michael also does voluntary work locally.

Also by Michael Sutton

A Widow's Passion
Published 2003 (Vanguard Press)
ISBN 1843860201

Just Imagine
Published 2004 (Vanguard Press)
ISBN 1843861453

No Mind Any Man
Published 2006 (Vanguard Press)
ISBN-10: 1843862557
ISBN-13: 978 1843862550

Begging For Words
Published 2006 (Vanguard Press)
ISBN 1843862573

In the Heartlands
Published 2006 (Vanguard Press)
ISBN 1843862565

On The Crest Of A Wave
Published 2006 (Vanguard Press)
ISBN 978-184386-349-6

An Enchanted Gentleman
Published 2008 (Vanguard Press)
ISBN 978 184386 421 9

Miranda

Michael Sutton

Miranda

Vanguard Press

VANGUARD PAPERBACK

© Copyright 2008
Michael Sutton

The right of Michael Sutton to be identified as author of
this work has been asserted by him in accordance with the
Copyright, Designs and Patents Act 1988

A CIP catalogue record for this title is
available from the British Library

ISBN 978 184386 464 6

*Vanguard Press is an imprint of
Pegasus Elliot MacKenzie Publishers Ltd.*
www.pegasuspublishers.com

First Published in 2008

**Vanguard Press
Sheraton House Castle Park
Cambridge England**
Printed & Bound in Great Britain

DEDICATION

For Angela and Simon, a very special couple. May
they know much happiness in the path ahead.

And as always, to Jennifer.

Michael

Chapter One

Tears slid silently down Miranda's cheeks as her whole body was wracked with grief. She had been this way for the last four weeks.

Amos, Miranda's father, had sent her to Spain to El Estancia, her father's villa. It was a white painted house with a balcony and red shutters to the windows under a smart red tiled roof. El Estancia, as the name suggests, was more than a plain villa, it had land to the rear with a stable. In the villa Amos had arranged for Maria, who was a Spanish maid, to stay and Amos thought, company for Miranda.

It was a beautiful day: there was a cloudless azure sky, a gentle breeze, and a clear view of the sea and rocks below. Miranda sat at the balcony window and couldn't see the view. In her misery, in her mind's eye, she saw a handsome young man, rugged, full of life with an enchanting smile and a shock of red hair.

Maria came to check on her.

"Miranda, you haven't touched your coffee, it will be cold now."

"I don't want it, I want to die," said Miranda, through a tear-streaked face.

"It's been four weeks now since Edward's accident, you must come outside with me, the fresh air will do you good. Your father, Amos, made me promise to look after you."

Dazed, Miranda allowed Maria to lead her to the bathroom to wash her face and comb her hair.

Now Edward, 25, was killed in a road accident by a runaway lorry. The doctor said because of the massive impact Edward had died immediately. Miranda and Edward had only been married four weeks and he was her first true love. Such a tragedy. Miranda thought she would never recover.

Miranda under more fortunate circumstances was beautiful. She had long shoulder length, shiny black hair, generous kissable lips and flaming emerald-green eyes. In a nutshell, she was beautiful. Her father, Amos, was a Methodist, and so raised Miranda chapel-wise. Miranda was sensitive, loving and considerate of others. She loved her father deeply, which is why she decided to summer at El Estancia on the Spanish coast.

Maria took hold of Miranda's arm and led her down the twenty-nine steps to the beach front. They were greeted in the little rocky cove with sand leading down to the shoreline by screeching whirling seagulls, which was normal for Maria, for the local gulls knew she brought a basket of bread pieces.

Miranda's hair blew in the breeze and the sun shone on her bright red, sleeveless dress. From a short distance she looked like any young lady taking a stroll. But on Miranda's face, and over her hair and mind, no sun shone. Only a black cloud descended as she clung to a small photograph of Edward.

Maria steered Miranda down to the shoreline where the seagulls waited to be fed.

"Here, my pretty boys!" called out Maria as she threw the bread in the air.

She loved to watch their aerial acrobatics as they swooped down catching the bread before it landed on the sand.

"Come on, Miranda, you throw some bread."

"I can't!"

"Why can't you?"

"I can't let go of his photograph."

"Oh Miranda, it is right to grieve, but your father sent you to me to forget about the accident. He wants you to get on with your life. Edward would want you to be happy again, to get on with living. Take one day at a time. You can't stay in your room all the time it's not healthy."

"But I love Edward."

"Yes, dear, you do, but love his memory. Carry with you happy times. Do you believe in the spirit of man?"

"You know I do."

"Then take your sandals off and walk out in the sea and let the tide take the photograph, let go, let Edward's spirit be at peace."

"Will you come with me?"

"Of course I will, Miranda. I promised your father I would look after you."

They did it together.

"Goodbye, Edward, I shall never forget you. Goodbye my love."

Nestled in the rocks was an artist. They didn't see him, but he was busy with his brush on canvas capturing two beautiful ladies: one obviously Spanish, and the other of a fair complexion, probably, he thought, English. Robert, 37, a professional painter, often came to Seagull Cove, for that was what he called it. He enjoyed the peace and solitude of sky, sand, sea and rocks. He had never been married and it wasn't that he was a confirmed bachelor, it was just that he was sensitive. He, over the years, was a late starter; he used to be very shy, and now at 37 was full of bruises. His problem was he fell in love too easily and his romances ended when he got hurt. He learnt the hard way that women weren't as sensitive as him and that they were 'users' and 'takers'. If only he could meet a young lady who was happy with the simple things in life and not the 'plastic world'.

Maria sat Miranda down on a rock and watched the waves lapping the shoreline.

"I like it here, Miranda, because it is so peaceful. Nobody to disturb the natural beauty of the sky, sea and sand. I consider the seagulls my friends."

"How often do you come down here?"

"Oh, once or twice a week. I can't afford to feed the seagulls everyday."

Robert, the painter, sketched furiously on his drawing pad, catching the outline of 'The Girl On The Rock', as he called it. With his pencil he wrote, 'red'. He sketched her outline, the curve of her neck showing above her summer dress and the full tresses of her hair as she arched back taking the sunshine full on her brow. Robert didn't continue to sketch Maria, just the English woman. Luckily for him he had binoculars, which he used to capture details usually of birds feeding or nesting. But today he wanted to capture the 'lady-in-red'. He was fortunate in that he had both good short sight and long sight. In his time, Robert had painted several portraits, those of his girlfriends. He just loved to paint beautiful women. He just wished one would fall in love with him. He was able to capture a woman on canvas, but he couldn't capture a woman in his heart.

"How do you feel now?"

"Like a grey veil has been lifted off me, but I shall always love Edward."

"Shall we walk?"

"Let's paddle in the sea," said Miranda with a slight smile.

"You know, Miranda, when you smile, you light up the sky."

"Thank you, Maria. Maria?"

"Yes, Miranda?"

"Have I been terrible these past weeks?"

"The answer is, terribly upset. You haven't eaten much. You need to eat to keep your strength up."

"Actually, I'm hungry today."

"Good, that is a sign that you are getting better. Let's go back up the beach to El Estancia."

Maria's mother, Meralda, was taken ill the following week.

"I have to go to my village, Sigma, in the hills. I'll catch the bus tomorrow; it only comes twice a week. Cecilia, my neighbour here, who has come to fetch me, will stay the night in the guest room."

It was time to repay some of Maria's kindness over the past month thought Miranda.

"Nonsense, my father arranged for a hire car for me, which I haven't been well enough to use. It's still in the garage. I will take you both now."

"But, Miranda, are you up to it?"

"Of course I am, and anyway it will give me something to do. I am a good driver."

"Oh, Miranda, bless you!" said Maria, as both she and Cecilia gave Miranda a hug and a kiss.

Chapter Two

It was now Monday afternoon and Miranda returned from Sigma and parked the car at El Estancia. She decided, having seen Meralda in a fragile state, that she herself had fortunate good health and, buoyed up, made a brave decision to go down to the cove to feed the seagulls. She put on her red bathing one-piece and a fluffy towel around her neck, and went down the twenty-nine steps with a basket of bread on her arm.

In Seagull Cove, the gulls were waiting to be fed, so Miranda went to the same rock that Maria had previously taken her to and, to her surprise, on top of the flattish rock, was a painting, held down by a stone, and it was entitled, 'Lady in Red'.

It was a picture of Miranda in her red dress where she had sat with Maria at the weekend.

"Look birds, somebody admires me!"

Miranda threw the bread down, leaving the gulls to their feed and ran into the warm Mediterranean. She was a good swimmer. The water invigorated her, so she swam a good way out.

Robert, through his binoculars watched her. He gathered up his easel and paints and went and sat on 'Miranda's Rock', where she threw pieces of bread for the seagulls.

Miranda headed back to the beach. Seeing a lone figure feeding the gulls where she had left her white fluffy towel and basket of bread, she stroked strongly out of curiosity.

"You? You're the painter?" she asked, coming out of the water.

"Yes. Let me dry your back, the breeze is strong today."

"Who are you?"

"My name's Robert Darling, I'm a painter and I now live in Spain. This is the nearest cove to my little house."

"Were you here at the weekend when I came down to the beach with Maria?"

"Was she wearing a blue dress?"

"Yes."

"Then I am guilty. I was painting the seagulls nesting on the low cliffs, when you two appeared. I hope you don't mind me painting you?"

"No, no, not at all."

"Are you hungry?"

"Ravishingly so, but I haven't any money."

"Just your ravishing beauty is payment enough."

"Do you always pick girls up?"

"No never. I'm just a painter, and you happened along, so I painted you. I shall pay for lunch at a friend's small fish taverna."

"But I'm not dressed?"

"You don't need to, it's a beach-front taverna. There will be others there in bathing suits. Wrap yourself around with your towel."

"No. I will let the sun dry me. Which way is it?"

"Just around the headland of Seagull Cove, but when we get there you must wear my shirt."

"Why?"

"You are, may I say, a little naive. You are absolutely stunning. Your figure is perfect, every man will be after you. So cover up."

"O.K. Pass me your shirt."

"God, that makes you desirable."

Miranda burst into a big smile.

"Are you trying to seduce me?"

"No, the other way round. I am seduced by your beauty. What's your name?"

"Oh sorry, Miranda."

"Well, Miranda, pleased to meet you, and pleased to buy you a drink."

"Hello, John, how's things?"

"Busy. Always busy when the sun shines."

"Today I have brought a guest. John, meet Miranda."

"Hi, Miranda!"

"You lucky devil, Robert. How did you catch this one?"

"By accident. I was sketching in Seagull Cove, and two young ladies appeared."

"Two?"

"Yes," said Miranda, "the other one you saw in a blue dress was Maria, my maid."

"You have a maid. Are you rich?"

"Nothing like that. My father sent me to El Estancia, his holiday villa, which is looked after by Maria. My husband was killed recently and I have been grieving, but Maria showed me Seagull Cove and I have just bumped into Robert."

"Sorry, Miranda, I am too nosey. Now eat and drink. The fish is 'on the house', but Robert can pay for the wine."

John cooked small locally caught fish on a barbecue. He had several customers. His wife was both hostess and waitress and barmaid.

Miranda looked at John at work, he looked so carefree. He had a tight mop of curly hair which was shot through with attractive natural ringlets. He had a small, neat, sun-bleached moustache and trimmed sideburns. His eyes were deep set, large and almond. His cheekbones were high and he had a Roman nose which gave him a look of aristocracy. His shorts were scruffy: chopped off jeans, out of which sprung well-muscled legs. He wore Jesus sandals and no shirt to hide his tanned and weather-beaten torso.

Miranda, whispered to Robert. "He looks like a beach bum."

Robert laughed. "Linda likes him like that. He usually wears less!"

"Good gracious! Less?"

"Yes. They adore each other. When there are no customers about and it is warm they spend their time, I am reliably informed by John, making love."

"Is that how he keeps so fit?"

"I suppose, partly. No. He swims and surfs a lot. He hires out surf boards. Have you ever tried?"

"Here you are you two, a jug of sangria."

"Thanks, Linda. I'll pay you later."

"No chance, Robert. I have just made that specially for you, that will be 600 peseta."

"Have you sold any of my paintings, Linda?"

"Just one this week."

"Which one?"

"One of Seagull Cove, for 2,000 peseta."

"Then you have made 500 peseta as your 'display fee', so the sangria is paid for."

"Not quite, Mr Painter. You owe me a 100 peseta."

"O.K. Take it out of my 1,500 commission."

"Miranda, have nothing to do with this painter, he is a nice man, but poor."

"I get by, Linda."

"You should get a proper job, not paint all day long."

"It's what I am good at."

"Take no notice of our friendly squabble, Miranda, eat the fish while it is warm," said John.

"Actually, John, I think Robert is a good painter."

"That he is. Linda is always ribbing him because he spends his life on the beach or on rocks painting whatever he sees. When he's not painting he goes swimming, and, on Wednesdays, he goes to the market in St Lucia."

For the first time in over a month Miranda felt relaxed. It was the company of happy smiling people and the laughter of the other tourists. Plus something else. She felt a sense of release, a letting go. She was drifting, her mind set free, enjoying the moment, for the sake of the moment. Or was it the sangria and the fish and the crusty bread? She hadn't eaten properly for over a month. Although her ample thirty-six 'D' breasts still swelled and tugged at the fabric of her bathing costume her little tummy had completely disappeared and now she had an hourglass figure, something she had dreamed about. Her waist was ridiculously small, which only accentuated the curves of her very sexy hips and the neat two handfuls of rounded bottom.

"Robert, are you really poor?"

"I get by, my painting pays the way. On Wednesdays I am rich. I live simply. I can afford another jug of sangria. Would you like some more?"

"I'd love some. Robert I'm starving hungry, do you think I can have some more?"

"I'll have a word with Linda."

"Poor girl, been grieving for a month! Don't worry, Robert, I'll do her a complete meal with full salad, I'll take it out of your commission."

"All right. I'm attracted to Miranda, I don't mind."

"Be careful, Robert, if she is only recently widowed she will be vulnerable."

"Don't worry, I'm not going to seduce her. I genuinely like her."

"Don't go falling in love."

"Here, Miranda, my treat. Prepared by Linda."

"Can you afford it?"

"Well, have no cash, but I told Linda to keep the commission from my painting."

"But that was 1,500 peseta. That's six pounds. I'll pay you back later."

"Tell you what, would you like to come on the bus with me on Wednesday to St Lucia, it's market day? I need help to carry all my paintings."

"I have a better idea."

"What's that?"

"I'll take you myself."

"That's O.K. I can afford the bus fare."

"No you don't understand, I'll take you by car."

"You have a car?"

"It's not mine, it's a hire car, arranged by my father. You walk up the beach Wednesday morning to Seagull Cove and go up the beach until you come to some stone steps. Go up twenty-nine steps, cross the balcony and knock on the door. You will be at my father's villa, El Estancia. I will be waiting for you. What time will you come?"

"Six o'clock!"

"That's early?"

"We will have to drive to my house and collect all my paintings and then drive up into the hills to St Lucia. We have to be early to acquire a stall and set up my picture gallery."

"All right, I'll get up early. I'll be ready at six o'clock, Wednesday."

After the meal Miranda felt good, full of her old self. John got out his guitar and sat on the beach. He and his regulars started singing. Now, as it turned out, Robert had a fine voice. Miranda was impressed and sat down on the sand next to him and joined in.

After a while the sun became low in the sky and Miranda, in only a red one-piece swimsuit, felt cold.

"I'll see you back home, Miranda. Anyway I need my T-shirt back."

"Bye, John, Linda!"

They walked back along the beach to Seagull Cove and up the shore to the bottom of the twenty-nine steps.

"Thank you, Robert, I can manage now."

She took off his T-shirt, raising her arms above her head. His eyes involuntarily bulged as her breasts swelled inside the tight fitting fabric. The considerable nipples stood erect due to the cooling evening breeze. He placed his hands gently on her shoulders and looked in her eyes.

"I think you are beautiful."

There was an unspoken electricity between them. The hairs on his forearms tingled. Miranda sensed it. She flushed red and was having palpitations. Robert kissed her affectionately on the forehead.

"Good night, Miranda. I'll be here six o'clock, Wednesday."

Robert went down the beach and Miranda stood at the top of the twenty-nine steps willing him to turn round. Before he disappeared from view, he turned and waved and Miranda, waved with her fluffy white towel. Then she went indoors.

Once inside she realised she was cold. She stripped off her swimming suit and went into the bathroom and stood under a hot shower to revive herself, shampooing her hair into the bargain.

Miranda didn't know exactly what it was, but she felt alive. For the first time in over a month she opened the refrigerator and treated herself to a bottle of sparkling wine. She curled up on the sofa in front of a warm fire and read a Mills and Boon.

It was dark outside now so she put the light on. Then on an impulse she reached for the phone and called Amos her father.

"Hello, Amos, here?"

"Daddy, it's Miranda!"

"Hello, darling, it's so good to hear from you. You haven't phoned us in over a month, it's always been us calling you to check up on you. Is Maria looking after you?"

"Maria's had to go to Sigma, to nurse her mother, Meralda, who has been taken ill."

"Can you cope on your own?"

"Yes, this is why I am ringing you. You won't guess, I met a painter on the beach."

"A painter?"

"Yes a professional artist. Maria took me down to Seagull Cove and, without me knowing, Robert painted me. He's really quite good. He sells his work from a beachfront taverna, run by a nice couple called John and Linda. On Wednesday we are going to market at St Lucia to sell Robert's paintings."

"That's good. That's why I sent you to Spain, to forget the tragedy of the accident and find a new life. You are so young, you have your whole life ahead of you. Would you like to tell your mother the good news?"

"No, I'll treasure it for now, in case I wake up from a dream. It's Maria I should thank for my good fortune. She got me out of the villa and onto the beach and into the sea. Together we let Edward's photograph go in the sea and the tide carried it out. I let go, daddy."

"Don't get too involved with this Robert, Miranda. That is not to say you shouldn't have a holiday romance. You are young and so beautiful. Your heart has been broken, now it needs time for healing."

"Thank you, daddy, and good night. I love you."

"I love you too, baby, good night."

"Who was on the phone, Amos?"

"That, my wife, was our daughter, she seems happy. She's met a painter called Robert."

"That's good news, but I would have liked a word."

"You can ring her tomorrow. Anyway, as usual, you were watching damned television."

On Tuesday evening Miranda was excited and she set her alarm for six o'clock in the morning. She felt like a little girl again, waiting for Father Christmas to call so she went to bed early and, for the first time in over a month, instead of crying herself to sleep, slept a happy dream about an artist called Robert she met on a beach.

At five-thirty, with the rising of the sun, Robert woke to the early morning rays, washed and dressed and set off on foot along the beach to El Estancia. He reached the steps at six o'clock and climbed up to Miranda's balcony. To his surprise she was waiting for him, dressed in a white jumper and jeans.

"Good morning, Robert. I have just percolated some coffee, would you like some?"

"Yes please, Miranda. I didn't think you would be ready. It's cold on the beach this time of the morning, I'd love a hot coffee."

"Come in then and sit down on a stool."

"Your father has good taste, this is a nice villa. It puts my simple home to shame."

"You told me, as an artist, you lived simply, so I think your home is a reflection of yourself."

"Very true. You summed me up quickly. It is true I believe in nature and the quality of a man's heart."

"Shall we go?"

"Of course, I am keen to get to market."

Outside Miranda had a bright red sports car parked with the hood down.

"Will your paintings fit in the back?"

"Yes. Definitely."

"I'll drive, you direct."

In less than ten minutes they were parked in a narrow road with terraces on both sides.

"Mine's the one with the green door. Please come in and give me a hand."

Between them they carried out several oil paintings and a few sketches. Miranda noticed they were all signed Robert Darling. Then Robert brought out a large canvas sheet.

"What is that for?"

"It is the sun roof for our stall at the St Lucia market, to keep the sun off and to display my paintings on."

When they arrived at St Lucia, the market place was a hive of activity with traders unloading vans and putting the canvas tarpaulins on over the metal stall frames.

"Come on, give me a hand. You take this side and I'll take the other."

"Got a new assistant today, Roberto!? She's too beautiful for you!" laughed Sam who had the stall opposite selling leather goods.

"And a good morning to you too, Sam."

"If you want to, you can help me display my canvases now," invited Robert.

"Sure, I'll copy you clipping the frames to the small holes in the back of the canvas. It can't be that hard."

Even before eight o'clock their stall, with its canvas top, made a nice little room or gallery, as Robert called it.

"Breakfast?"

"Keep an eye out, Sammy, we're going for breakfast now!"

"Sure, Roberto, no problem!"

At the back of the market a food wagon was steaming with boiling water and the smell of cooking sausages and onions.

"Hot-dog, Miranda?"

"Yes please, they smell delicious. And a cup of coffee. And let me pay."

"Good morning, Jimmy."

"Hello, Robert, who's the beautiful lady?"

"Just a friend who likes my paintings."

"Hey, young lady, you have good taste."

"You keep your eyes to yourself, my husband, I know you. Can't be trusted with a pretty girl," said Donna.

"It's all right, Jimmy, Robert will look after me, won't you."

"Meet my lucky mascot, Miranda. She gave me a lift today to bring in all my paintings, which is far better than carrying them on the bus."

"Have a good day, Robert, and you, miss."

"Bye, Jimmy!"

"Now we have another job to do, which is a bit subjective, but if I don't put any prices on the canvases the tourists are frightened off."

"Surely they must be worth twenty pounds each?"

"But that's 5,000 pesetas, that can be a frightening price."

"Why not start at 2,500 pesetas, that's just a tenner, and then charge more for the full-size canvases."

"How much should I charge for the largest?"

"It's difficult to say, because the value is in the eye of the beholder. Let's say twenty-five pounds, that's 6,250 pesetas."

So they were priced from ten pounds to twenty-five pounds.

At nine o'clock some of the local Spanish and Spanish tourists, who lived in Madrid, came to the market because they were holidaying in St Lucia village.

Robert explained that a lot of city people from central Spain, especially from the built-up mass that made up Madrid, came to the South to escape city life and enjoy the Mediterranean Sea, sunshine and sand.

"Isn't Madrid a warm sunny place?"

"It's inland, Miranda. In the winter it can be freezing and in the summer it can be 35-40 Centigrade, with no winds and therefore stifling. Madrid doesn't have the sea breezes of the south coast."

"Is it a big city then?"

"Yes, Miranda, two million people live there and it is a focal point for Spain's railways and roads. And now a huge satellite airport and, like many cities, has a thriving university with thousands of students."

"Sounds like a crowded place, I don't think I would like it."

"Nor would I, which is why I choose to live on the coast and paint. Today I will make quite a lot of money, but in December and January when it is the low-season, very few tourists visit the coast, let alone St Lucia."

"How do you survive in the winter then?"

"In the cold months I paint indoors in my front room, which doubles as my studio. I do mostly portraits in the winter. Normally head and shoulders, but some gentlemen ask for a full nude portrait, usually of their mistress. For a full nude pose on a large canvas, I charge at least 12,000 peseta, about fifty English pounds."

"Would you sell portraits on the market?"

"Definitely not, it would be an insult to the sitter. And anyway, such portraits are a personal matter, and I have my good reputation to think of. However, I have done Spanish ladies."

"Spanish ladies?"

"Yes, senoritas in full traditional Spanish costume. These are especially for the tourists. My models receive one third of the sale price, which is good, because I cannot afford to pay out cash in the winter time."

A Spanish gentleman dressed in Spanish leathers, accompanied by his handsome wife, who was dripping with genuine gold jewellery, came into his stall and selected two of Robert's canvases.

"Senor, you are Robert Darling, the artist?"

"Yes senor, I will write you a note of authenticity. See this is my signature."

"Bravo! I will take the two largest. The price of 12,500 pesetas is most reasonable. I have just had a villa built on the outskirts of Madrid, and seascapes of the Mediterranean are just what it needs."

"Shall I wrap them, Senor?"

"No, they will fit in the boot of the car. My wife carries the money."

"Here, young painter, Robert Darling, 13,000 peseta."

"Sorry I don't have any change, Senora."

"I wasn't asking for any. Buy your senorita a spot of lunch, she looks too thin."

"Thank you, Senora."

And then they were gone, heading back to their car.

"How much is 13,000 peseta, Robert?"

"Well, fifty pounds is 12,500 peseta, so another 500 peseta makes it fifty two pounds. Very good for the first sale."

The locals who had come to the stalls at nine o'clock or earlier for their fruit and vegetables had now gone, and it was too early for the foreign tourists, so Robert went to the fruit stall and bought them some oranges and bananas.

"Here you are, Miranda, a reward for you for giving me a lift this morning."

"But you don't have to."

"That's not the point. I want to because I think you deserve it."

"Why do I deserve it?"

"Let's just say a part of me is attracted to you and I really like you. Be honest, we are just strangers really."

"Thanks for the fruit. Friends?"

"Yes. Two nice people together enjoying the Spanish way of life."

"Do you like wine?"

"Wine? Why?"

"There's a wine trader on the market and I think he's cheap. He's called Domingo, and you can taste his wine before you buy."

"Be back in a minute."

"Hey! Where are you going?"

Five minutes later Miranda was back with two opened bottles of wine, and some paper cups.

"Two bottles?"

"Not for us."

"Whom for then?"

"Customers of course. When they come to view we offer them a cup of wine. Sort of social-tasting to get them in the mood."

"But that will cut into the profits, Miranda."

"No it won't, I paid. My treat to the business."

"You are quite a remarkable girl. I'm glad you came along, you brighten up my day. In fact my whole world."

At ten o'clock, the first real tourists arrived.

"Would you like a drop of wine while you look around?" Miranda asked a group of young men who were in high spirits, dressed in just shorts and trainers.

They all got chatting exchanging holiday stories and buzzing around Miranda like bees around a honey-pot, which attracted more passing tourists, which, in turn, made Robert's stall busy. Miranda offered red wine all round and slipped off to Domingo's wine stall to buy two more bottles of wine.

Miranda came back. "Anybody else like to come in my stall for free drink of wine?" asked Miranda with an earth-shattering smile, a twinkle of her eyes and a toss of her hair.

Two bald headed men with their wives came into the stall and spent 5,000 pesetas each. A total of forty pounds. And so, with wine flowing, and Miranda charming the birds out of the trees, by five o'clock they had sold out.

"I've enjoyed myself, Robert, very much. The people are fun."

"That's because of the wine and your incredible charm, young lady. I could kiss you."

"Go on then."

"Go on then what?"

"Kiss me, silly. I won't break."

"You sure?"

"Yes, I feel happy today."

Some tourists standing by were listening to the happy couple.

"Go on, mate, kiss her before I do!"

Miranda laughed wickedly, and Robert laughed with her. He kissed her fully on the lips, sparks flashed between them.

The onlookers cheered before moving off, but Robert and Miranda didn't notice, they only had eyes for each other.

"In the village of St Lucia is a small discreet restaurant called La Gracia, with traditional Spanish furnishings and furniture. It is shaded, cool, and you eat by candlelight. I would like to take you there."

"Is it expensive?"

"For you it is priceless!"

"You say the nicest things to a girl."

"I accept, I'm starving, and I think a bit tipsy."

"Good. Come on, give me a hand to fold the canvas and we'll put it in the boot of the car."

La Gracia was a five minute walk up the back streets, which opened out into the old town's central square. Well not actually a square, but a cobbled area where the locals sat out on benches under the shade of ancient trees. There was a fountain set in the middle of a small planted garden and, set in stone was a drinking fountain.

"Come on, Miranda, try some mountain spring water."

She did. Washing her face and hands first.

"That's refreshing, nice and cool!"

Some of the villagers knew Robert from his painting of the little square.

"Hello, Roberto, who is the beautiful senorita?"

"My girlfriend… er, my assistant for the day. She brings me luck."

"Slip of the tongue, Robert. I prefer girlfriend."

"You mean, you will be my girlfriend?"

"Seems to me we are well suited."

"But it's only our first day together. It's too soon for you. You were only widowed a month ago. Let's just be friends."

"Don't you fancy me?"

"Of course I do. I fancy the pants off you, but that doesn't mean I should rush in. I could hurt you emotionally."

"Then that's all right then. I stayed in El Estancia and cried myself to sleep for a month solid. I don't feel like crying any more, only laughing."

"Come here."

Robert held her to him and they flowed together as one. Two minds melted together. The hairs on Robert's arms and his scalp tingled with pleasure. Where his hair rubbed against Miranda's tresses, small electric sparks flew, which shook and intensified the hugging couple, so that they became welded together.

Robert whispered into her hair close to her ear, "It feels so right."

"Mmm. Wonderful. Don't ever let me go."

They separated and looked into each other's eyes, Robert's, almond, and Miranda's, fiery emerald green. They arrived at La

Gracia, but Robert didn't remember walking there. He simply arrived when Suzanna greeted him.

"Welcome, Roberto. You haven't been in recently."

"No Suzanna, I've had nobody special to bring. I have been busy painting. This is Miranda, my new girl."

"Welcome, Miranda, you are very beautiful if a little pale. The sun will put that right. Are you here on holiday?"

"Sort of. My father sent me to recuperate."

"Oh dear, I am sorry to hear you have been ill."

"Miranda has been through a tragedy, Suzanna, but she is recovering now. We would like a quiet table in a corner, if you please."

"Always such as a romantic, Roberto. Follow me please."

"Suzanna, a bottle of sparkling wine, on ice."

"Sure, Senor Roberto," smiled Suzanna.

"Do you know Suzanna, very well?"

"Yes, she sometimes poses for me. Look on the walls here and you will see portraits of her."

"Why on these walls?"

"Because it gives Robert Darling a chance to show off his work."

"How much do you charge?"

"For the portraits, 5,000 pesetas, normally."

"And how much does Suzanna get as her fee?"

"Thirty percent, that's 1,500 pesetas, about six pounds. It's not a lot, but the money is welcomed by La Gracia'a owners."

"Who are the owners?"

"Suzanna's parents, Miriam and Zak."

Suzanna lit their candle and its flame reflected in Miranda's sparkling eyes. They sat opposite one another and played footsie under the table, which developed into 'legsie' as Miranda kicked off her shoes and rubbed her bare feet up and down Robert's thighs. He grabbed a foot and reaching under the table ran his hand up her leg. She became excited at his touch and slid down almost off her seat so that she could, under cover of the tablecloth, offer her thighs to him.

Suzanna came across with the sparkling wine in an ice bucket. Miranda sat up in her chair and waited for Suzanna to pour.

"To us," said Robert.

And they drank.

"Are you ready to order, Roberto?"

"Give us a moment," said Robert.

"Do you think she noticed?"

"I don't care if she did, I think I love you."

"Oh, Robert, you're such a romantic. It's just lust."

"No it's not. You excite me, I feel for you. It's not just sex, it's a chemical reaction. Everything feels so right and natural with you. Look how your wonderful company made me feel today. I have never sold out before. For me, you're magic."

"Oh God, have you really fallen for me?"

"Yes, in a big way. I want to spend all the summer with you, the rest of the year I don't know about yet."

"I don't know how long I am supposed to be staying at El Estancia, it's my father's villa."

"I hope he throws you out, then you can come and live with me. I'll make you spend a whole twelve months in my bed."

"God, you are rude. Do you always express yourself so freely?"

"Only when I am sure of something. You make me feel alive. I want you to be my girl. I know I am taking a risk. You may wake up from this dream next week or the week after, and decide to ditch me."

"Robert, it takes two to tango. I am entering this relationship with my eyes wide open."

"And the way you were carrying on just now, your legs as well."

"Would you like to come back to my father's villa tonight. Your place is so small, and I have a king sized bed which needs a man in it."

"If that's an invitation, I accept, but during the day I must paint. I paint to make a living. I have many sketches in my studio that need to be turned into saleable paintings, and many canvases unfinished. I also need to buy new canvases. A blank canvas costs about 1,250 pesetas."

"I have money, I don't mind buying the new canvases for you."

"But why should you?"

"Because I want to help, and I need a reason to tell my father why he should keep me at the villa El Estancia. I get an allowance you know all the time I stay."

Chapter Three

"Papa, I want to stay in Spain. I have fallen in love with my painter. Can I stay please?"

"Of course you can if you're sure."

"Today, daddy I went with Robert to market and with my help we sold all of his paintings. He said I was lucky for him, like a mascot. Oh, daddy, we are getting on like a house on fire."

Amos's wife took hold of the telephone.

"Hello, Miranda. What's this talk of love? You mustn't jump out of the frying pan into the fire. It's too soon. Please don't rush into anything, you will only end up getting hurt."

"I know what I am doing, mother. It's my life. I have met a painter and I am going to stay for the summer."

"You mean live in sin! I don't approve of that."

"Oh, don't be so old fashioned, mother. I'm definitely not going to rush into marriage again, so don't even think about organising me. And don't worry I shan't get pregnant, not unless it is deliberate."

"What do you mean deliberate? How am I going to see my own grandchild?"

"Well, daddy has the villa, you will have to fly out."

"You know I am petrified of flying."

"Mummy, people fly everyday, it's the safest form of transport."

"All right, dear. Do you want to speak to your father again?"

"No mummy. And don't worry, Robert will look after me. Goodbye."

"Well, Miranda, what did your father say?"

"Weren't you eavesdropping?"

"Of course not. A conversation with your parents is private, which is why I went into the kitchen."

"Oh, Robert, you are so considerate, which is why I am attracted to you."

"By the way, I can cook. What have you got to eat?"

"Plenty in the refrigerator and in the wine rack."

"Good idea, bottle of wine. Where do you keep the wine?"

"In the cellar, darling, it keeps cool down there."

"Be back in a minute, you get the tea things ready."

Robert went down the steps to the ground floor and then down a second flight of steps into a red-brick-built, vaulted cellar.

"My God, does he have a whole vineyard?"

The far wall was stacked with bottles; there must have been about two hundred in individual racks. Some had been there a while because they were coated with a layer of dust, while others looked shiny and brand new. He selected a new looking bottle which, from the filtered light coming through the small round cellar window, appeared to be red.

The light came on.

"What are you doing down here, you've been ages. I've prepared a salad."

"Reading some of these labels. You know this cellar is stocked with Spanish, French and Italian wine. Is your father a connoisseur?"

"Yes, I believe he is. He considers himself an expert on wine, art and antiques."

"What does he do for a living?"

"He's an architect. He designs up-market buildings, including this villa. Hence the reason why it's built into the cliff face on three levels."

"Is he rich then?"

"Yes, he is now. He's still a practising architect but he does mostly consultancy contracts now."

"Turn the light off and come here."

Miranda did. Robert approved of the sundress she had changed into to cool down. Her silhouette showed, by the subdued light coming in from the cellar window, what an attractive feminine figure she had. He went to her and without saying a word, put the bottle of wine down and drew her to him. He smelt her hair, which smelt fresh and soapy, then he kissed her neck, her ears, her nose, her eyes and then very tenderly her lips. He reached down, while Miranda pressed her body to his, melting in his arms, and took of the hemline of her short dress and pulled it up: her tummy was exposed; up, her breasts were exposed, sitting ripe in a tiny brassiere. She helped him and pulled it over her head.

"God you're beautiful," whispered Robert.

Miranda's breath was coming in small strangulated gasps as her wantonness built up. There was electricity in the air. She unhooked her brassiere and allowed it to slide down her arms. Then she held out her turgid breasts with the big raspberry nipples for Robert.

"Suck me."

He sucked greedily on one nipple and then the other. Miranda gasped at the absolute pleasure. He lowered himself and kissed her tummy, her hips, and then he removed her panties. He opened her folds to her secret place and licked her clitoris with his tongue. Miranda flooded and her knees shook. He fingered her until she called out.

"I love you, Miranda," he said standing up again, while he kissed her on the lips, pressed her back to him with his left hand so that he could feel her firm breasts pushing into his chest, and masturbated her with his right hand.

"Oh God, I'm coming again, take me, now!"

Robert yanked his trousers and underpants down and kicked them off. He grabbed her firmly by her hips and pushed her head down.

"Hold onto the wine rack!"

She bent forward as she was told and held on.

He entered her from the rear, sliding his throbbing erection up into her waiting wet vagina.

"Yes, that's it, go on fuck me, fuck me good!"

Her dirty talk, in her heightened state of arousal, was a turn on for Robert. He thrust into her for all he was worth.

Miranda called out loud and long as wave after wave of orgasms coursed through her tingling body.

She excited Robert. He reached between her thighs from behind and massaged her labia and clitoris, with both hands while he thrust into her.

"Yes! Yes, yes! That's it. Fuck me right out!"

He could wait no longer, he called out, bellowing like a bull and snorting like an animal. Then he went limp and slid out, laughing at himself.

"God, that was wonderful, what an animal I am," he said, standing her up and gathering her to him. "My knees are shaking."

"I'm not surprised, you're a terrific lover. I've never come so much before. I mean all in one go. I'm so aroused."

Robert smiled into her face, watching her eyes as he rubbed his spilt seeds into her clitoris. He shook, she trembled. He rubbed. Her eyes went very wide, then they became slitted as she concentrated on the electricity building up in her body. He mouth contorted and she started coming: quietly at first, then gradually getting louder until she screamed out at full volume. Then she went white and panted heavily for breath. She sagged against him going quite limp.

"Oh God, you've fucked me, take me to bed."

He picked up her slim figure and carried her like a first prize, with proud manliness up the two flights of stairs to the bedroom. He couldn't believe his luck, carrying this beautiful, loving, naked young lady inn his arms. He laid her gently down on the mattress, pulled his T-shirt off and curled up with her under the duvet. He felt at peace, and decided at that moment before he went to sleep, to paint Miranda, naked. She was a painter's asset, a natural beauty and he wasn't going to let her go. He slept a sleep of deep satisfaction.

Two hours later he awoke feeling extraordinarily fresh and alive. Then he remembered where he was. He opened his eyes and surveyed the room. It had unfamiliar solid wood Spanish furniture. He rolled over and saw a wondrous sight. Could it be true that this voluptuous woman was really his girlfriend? No more than that, his lover.

He slid the duvet down and feasted his eyes on her hourglass figure with the protruding full breasts. She had no tummy at all, in fact she had a waspish waist. Impossibly small, yet she was real. Miranda sensed that somebody was watching her. She opened her eyes and smiled at the vision above her.

"Are you my guardian angel, my handsome man? Why are you looking at me?"

"Just admiring the woman I love. I think I am very lucky."

"Kiss me."

He did, from her nose down to her toes, not missing a single inch on the way down.

"Take me."

He placed himself gently above her beauty and Miranda put him in. Robert squatted on the flats of his feet and stroked his full length into her. Miranda accommodated him by thrusting her hips up and pushing up with her pelvic bone.

"No! Don't touch me. Put your arms above your head. You must surrender yourself to me absolutely," chided Robert.

"Oh God, I'm coming again."

"Good girl. Now as you come keep your eyes open. I want to watch you in orgasm."

The emerald green eyes stared up at Robert with full intensity, the eyebrows knitted, her lips contorted and she took great gulps of air.

"Now let yourself go, that's it. Go on, scream, again, again. Let it all out, hold nothing back."

She reached up and clung to his muscled shoulders, and jerked her body in time with Robert's thrusting.

"Yes, yes, yes!" she shouted. That's it, go on do it to me!"

Fascinated by her shaking proud firm tits, he lay down on top of her and feverishly thrashed himself against her flesh while he tried to suck on her engorged nipples. They climaxed together. The earth shook. An earthquake roared through the building. When it subsided, they were clung one to the other, panting and trembling with a mixture of pleasure and emotional and physical exhaustion.

"God, this could go on for a lifetime," said Robert.

"I know I was only married for four weeks, but our love making was nothing like this. You are such an expert lover, Robert."

"It's you, the way you affect me. I can't help myself. I love you very much. You excite me."

"I'm starving," said Miranda.

"What is there to eat?"

"Let's shower together and then we can eat."

"Fine by me."

They soaped each other, laughing and joking, and then amour came over Robert and on an impulse of an unannounced signal he grabbed her and seduced her. She let him, she wanted him to. She never knew she could come so much. He gripped her sexy bottom, and with the water cascading down his head and his back he licked her out. She trembled, called out and fell to her knees. They entwined and kissed and Robert put his fingers in her vagina.

"Yes please! Make me come again. Oh God, I don't think I can stop coming!"

And she didn't.

Robert washed his face and hands and stepped out of the shower.

"You pig! You can't just leave me!"

"Oh yes, I can. Watch me."

36

He went to the bedroom, dressed, and then went down to the kitchen. The table was laid out with salad from over two hours ago. He looked in the refrigerator and found a cooked chicken. He tore the legs off and bit a chunk out of one, as he remembered the wine. The cellar was cool and the bottle of red was still where he left it before they made love for the first time. He smiled to himself and bounded back up the stairs. In the kitchen was Miranda biting on a chicken leg. Her wet hair was wound around with a large bath towel. She was topless and just wearing a very short skirt.

"Well, you don't leave much to the imagination do you? Cover yourself up, you're taking advantage of me."

"Serves you right for leaving me in the shower like that."

"Oh come on. We have to eat sometime."

He went up to her and they fed each other, most provocatively.

"Keep still!"

He squeezed salad cream onto her naked tits and eating salad, took licks at the nipples and bites at the lettuce.

"Suck them lovingly."

He did, both of them.

"Oh God, I'm coming again. I'm dribbling in my clean knickers."

"Let me feel."

He put his hand up her thigh-length skirt and hooked his fingers into the leg of the knicker elastic. Yes, she was wet all right. Being rude, he brought her back to orgasm through the flimsy fabric of her knickers, by rubbing it into her vulvas and clitoris. She gave him a love bite on the neck as her woman's weakness engulfed her, and she clung to him for physical support. He lifted her bodily onto the large farmhouse table and yanked her knickers down all in one movement. He shoved her skirt up around her waist, spread her thighs and put his new erection into her.

"You're driving me crazy, you vixen!"

He fully entered her and gripped her thighs powerfully in his urgency to gain maximum penetration. He was amazed that he could actually come again. His erection was so hard that it actually hurt from being so massively engorged with pulsating blood pressure. In his excitement he banged her small bottom up and down on the farmhouse table. Miranda's head was thrashing from side to side, she was doing hip thrusts for all she was worth and she started screaming.

"Yes! Yes that's it, fuck me out. Right out. Keep going, here it comes!"

She stopped thrashing with her head and looked up at Robert and exploded internally.

"Agh! You're pulling my cock off!"

Miranda, contracted violently, something else she had never experienced before, and enjoyed, this time, making Robert scream out. She let go and Robert slid to the floor, totally exhausted. He lay there struggling to get his breath.

Miranda, pleased with herself, went to the bathroom to see to her feminine hygiene and put a T-shirt on. She opened the wine and poured two glasses.

After about five minutes Robert recovered and sat at the table.

"Go wash your hands dear, before you eat."

He did.

When he came back Miranda was deliberately teasing him because she knew she was safe, because he, in turn, was spent. She stood against the worktop cutting up the chicken. She had raised her skirt up, halfway up her buttocks to let him know she had no knickers on.

"You vixen!"

"Do you like it darling?" she asked pulling the front of her short pleated skirt up to fully show him her hairy vagina.

"I've had enough. I'm starving."

"Yes, dear, you must eat to keep your strength up to keep satisfying me," laughed Miranda.

"God, haven't you had enough yet. Surely you can't come any more?"

"I read in a magazine once, that a woman can come endlessly provided her man can perform."

"Oh can she now, you prick teaser."

He picked her up and pushed her flat down on the big farmhouse table and all in one movement picked up the cucumber and thrust it up between her legs. She was taken by surprise and didn't have time to resist. The cucumber slid up, even though it was considerably wider than Robert's cock, to her cervix. She opened her thighs wide to accommodate the beautiful experience. She sat up on her elbows fascinated that she could take such a huge thing and enjoy it.

"Lick me as well. Keep me wet. God it's so big. I'm coming again!"

And his love called out, loudly, very loudly. Then she subsided.

Robert took the cucumber to the sink. Washed it, peeled it, and chopped it up for their tea.

"Now go and put some knickers on and a long skirt."

"I don't have along skirt."

"Then put trousers on, or a sundress. We can't go on like this."

They ate between them, a whole chicken, a whole lettuce, tomatoes and almost a whole cucumber.

Then they sat cuddled together on the sofa, listening to love ballads and drinking wine. It was late and they consumed two bottles of red. Exhausted they went to bed and slept heavily.

They awoke at about eight o'clock with the sun's rays shining in through the gap in the curtains. They didn't make love but cuddled together, comforting one another, for about an hour, while Robert kissed her all over, except her private parts.

"Do you know something Robert, I am sore from too much sex. You must be a sex maniac."

"You, you vixen, drive me wild. It takes two to tango. I know a young lady who enjoyed a cucumber."

"It's your fault, you get me so high. You never leave me alone."

"That's because you are like a forbidden fruit that must be plucked."

He knelt up in front of her. Took one look at her perfect tits and immediately got a huge erection.

"See what I mean," she said. And she licked him and started wanking him.

"No, not like that," he said, and pushed her down onto the pillows.

"Be gentle with me, I'm sore."

She directed him in.

He thrust slowly and gently. She clung to him.

"I want you to, every day."

"Every morning and every night?"

"Yes please," she murmured before surrendering herself to him. Doing his will, her will, in her.

The alarm clock went off.

"What time is it?"

"Ten o'clock darling. You fell asleep again."

"That's because you wear me out."

"You know, you enjoy it."

"Why did you set the alarm for ten o'clock?"

"Because that's my getting up time."

"It's a bit late isn't it?"

"Not when you've got nothing to wake up to."

"You've got me."

"Before you, I was depressed. I spent a month crying myself to sleep and staying in bed until at least ten o'clock."

"Well that will have to change. I get up at eight o'clock, go for a short swim in the sea and a quick run on the beach. When I am not painting I go surfing. Would you like to go for a swim now?"

"Sure. Good idea. But what are you going to swim in?"

"These shorts will do. I'll take off my underpants so that I have them to change back into."

"O.K. Give me a couple of minutes while I change."

"You look drop-dead gorgeous in that red one-piece."

"Especially for you darling."

They ran down the twenty-nine steps of El Estancia, and raced across the beach into Seagull Cove and dived into the sea. As it turned out, Miranda was quite a powerful swimmer. He put it down to her two beautiful buoyancy tanks and her well-muscled thighs.

As for Robert, he had grown up by the sea and was therefore a natural water baby.

They swam out together, far from the warm sands until the water turned an inky green-black and the temperature dropped considerably.

"Far enough, let's go back," said Robert.

After another five minutes they were back into a blue water which was definitely warmer.

"Race you to the cove!" called out Miranda.

"You're on!" replied Robert.

He did front crawl and pulled away from Miranda's breast stroke. Not to be outdone, she flipped onto her back, looked directly up into the sky and did a steady back crawl, skimming across the surface of the water. She passed Robert, who had slacked off now.

"Come on slow coach!" teased Miranda.

"Two can play at that!"

He also did back crawl and stretched his chest muscles reaching and stroking far ahead of himself to increase his speed. He caught up with Miranda and passed her.

"Now who's a slow coach?!"

That did it. Miranda increased the speed of her leg kicks and her arms to match. She was like a whirling wind churning up the water into a white froth as she passed Robert, and neared the beach.

"Oh know you don't!" said Robert. He increased his speed as a last flurry of activity and not seeing where he was going beached himself on top of Miranda.

"I won!" said Miranda. "Get off me, you great lump!"

"Sorry!" He grabbed her and kissed her with the shoreline surf breaking over them.

"I love you, my woman!"

"I should damned well hope so the way you have been manhandling me."

"I mean it, I love you. Can we get dry now?"

"Sure. Race you back to the villa."

Miranda set off with Robert trailing behind. Suddenly he felt tired and he knew why. The woman had sapped his strength.

"The vixen," he said to the sky.

He walked up the steps into the door just as Miranda threw her bathing costume on the floor. She put her head back and was drying her hair. She didn't see him approach. He sneaked behind her and bit her bottom quite hard.

"Ow! You fool. What was that for?"

"Because I love your body, and am too knackered to do anything else."

"I should jolly well think so. Hurry up and get dressed and I'll treat you to a fish lunch at John's place on the beach."

"O.K. But immediately after I have to go to the bank to deposit all my money from the sale of the paintings and buy new canvases. Can you sketch?"

"A little, why?"

"Because if you could we can then work together. You sketching and me painting."

"Hello, John, what have got for two starving lovers?"

"How about a Durex?"

"John, really," said his wife. "That's a personal thing. They might not want to use contraceptives."

"Actually, about sex, I am quite broad minded," said Miranda. "I'm on the pill."

"God, how stupid of me. I hadn't even thought about you getting pregnant," said a horrified Robert. "Please forgive me."

"It's all right darling you are no different to other men. The woman has to look out for herself. I forgive you."

"What would you two love birds like to eat?" asked John.

"The full works, including drinks, coffee and ice-cream."

"Can you pay?"

"For today, even from now on, I am a rich man. We went to St Lucia and sold all the paintings we took with us."

"Congratulations! About time you got lucky."

"It wasn't so much luck, it was Miranda's infectious charm. Her wily woman's assets and her beautiful persuasive flowing language and smile."

"Robert is right John, his paintings are excellent; it just needs the attention of customers in the right mood. After all, 5,000 pesetas is not a lot for a signed oil painting."

"You're absolutely right, young lady, twenty pounds is a small price to pay for a masterpiece. But many tourists are afraid to part with their cash in case they are getting ripped off for worthless souvenirs."

"What would you like to drink?"

"A beer and a bottle of sparkling water."

"What about for Miranda?"

"I'll just have the water please."

"Coming right up. And to eat?"

"Calamari, chips and a full salad with fresh crusty bread."

"You have quite an appetite today, Robert."

"He's getting old, can't keep up!" laughed, Miranda.

"I am just thirty-seven, in my prime."

"Oh I didn't realise that. I thought you were about thirty. Sure you're not too old for me?" teased Miranda.

"I think I have the measure of you sexpot."

The food came and Robert wolfed it down.

"Man, you're hungry. What have you been up to?"

"Entertaining. That's all I am saying."

John's wife, Samantha, kicked him.

"Ow! What's that for?" asked John.

"For not minding your own business."

Back in the kitchen Samantha had a word with her thick husband.

"How can you be so insensitive? Can't you see they are in love?"

"What, Robert, the artist?"

"Yes our Robert."

"But I just thought he had holiday romances."

"Not this time. They are in love. Can you blame him. She's a good looker and obviously loving."

"I don't believe it, it's just lust. It won't last."

"That's where you are wrong, John. She also sketches and admires his paintings."

"Then we'll just have to wait and see."

"Coffee. You two?"

"Yes please," said Miranda. "And ice-cream."

"You sure. A slim thing like you?"

"I need to put some weight back on, I've been fasting but now I'm cured because I have Robert."

"Robert," said John, "I do hope you are taking this girl seriously. She is very vulnerable having only recently been widowed. Don't toy with her affections."

"I'm not insensitive, as you should well know. Quite the opposite in fact, as attested to by my genuine artistic nature."

"You two, don't talk about Miranda, as if she wasn't here!" scolded, Samantha.

"Thanks for sticking up for me, Samantha," said Miranda, but Robert genuinely cares for me, which is why I am strongly attracted to him."

"There you see, John, even Miranda supports me and I've only known her a few days. I never expected this to happen. You read about it in books, fictitious holiday romances, but you never expect it of yourself."

"I still say it's early days. Could be all off next week."

"Ow!" Samantha kicked John hard under the table.

"Be quiet, else I shall become annoyed. Go and fetch some more drinks. Go on, make yourself useful."

"Sorry about that, you two love-birds. John is a good man but he always speaks his mind."

"In a way," said Miranda, "I admire John. After all he only has my best interests at heart. I think he's looking out for me."

"Yes, Miranda, John is a good friend. But that's what I do, look out for you," said an admiring Robert.

"What time is it, John?"

"About one-thirty."

"Blimey! Where did the morning go?"

Miranda, smiled at Samantha, and she smiled back with sparkly-eyed-knowing-smile because she was pleased for Miranda. And she knew that Robert was a genuinely nice person who had a kind word to say about others.

Robert paid for the meal and they left.

"Right, back to my father's villa," said Miranda.

At El Estancia, Miranda's bright red car was waiting in the sunshine.

"No need to go in, I have the car key. Let's go to your place."

At 'The Impressionist', Robert opened the door and took Miranda into his studio-cum front room. It was a south-facing room with good light for painting. Miranda, noticed.

"This is very good. I didn't know you did pencil portraits of nudes. Who is she?"

"A girlfriend."

"What was her name?"

"Rose. I met her on her holidays. We got on like a house on fire, but to sketch her nude I had to pay her. Then when she came to the last day of her holiday she came to see me with her new boyfriend."

"Her new boyfriend?"

"Yes, she came to thank me for a good time and said it had been fun for her, but now she had to go home."

"The man Bruce, he was called, said, 'no hard feelings old man, you were beaten by a younger man'."

"Perhaps you expected too much, Robert. Rose just wanted a bit of fun, and you wanted a relationship."

"I was hurt and embarrassed. And I haven't had a girlfriend until I met you."

"How long has that been?"

"Twelve long, lonely, celibate months."

"Oh poor you! Then you met me," smiled Miranda, and reached up and kissed him."

"I'm glad I waited for the right girl because with you I feel comfortable, as if I fit into your shoes."

"I feel the same way. And, you can paint me nude anytime because I love you and I love your painting."

"Thank you darling but not today. Sit at the table and sketch that vase of flowers. Pay particular attention to the effect of the sunlight and the shade. Can you do that?"

"Yes I can. I can sketch but I am not so sure if I can paint."

"Painting is a different skill, so don't try."

Miranda sketched away. The best part was the effect of the sunlight on the round vase. She cleverly didn't shade the brightest area, but instead, used the white paper to highlight pure light.

"Very good. Now I want you to sketch this hard-boiled egg and this stone. Pay particular attention to the fact that they are both spheres, there being no edges to outline the subject."

Now, Miranda was bright. She left the surface of the white eggshell facing the sunlight as pure white and only lightly shaded the rest of the egg, drawing a feint outline for the surface in shadow.

"Good, good. I see you have had drawing lessons. The reason you must be able to sketch an egg is because no naked human body has distinct edges, rather, the face, eye sockets, nose, cheek bones, lips and jaw line are all round. The face portrait does have certain character lines which can be captured, but the rest, the pinky-white flesh has no edges. It can only be drawn in terms of degrees of reflected light or areas of shadow."

"I'll do my best, master."

"Then here is a stone egg. If you look at it carefully you will see that it's not actually white, but a bit pitted with imperfections, which gives it a mottled look and very slight colour. The pitted areas will appear dark so you will be able to 'spot' with your pencil point. The rest is the absence of shade or colour. Have a go. If you can do it then you can sketch a face, because they are both round."

"All right, Maestro."

"Good, you know your place."

"I meant what I said, Robert, I will help you with your painting business. You just have to guide me."

Soon Miranda had finished sketching the egg and started to copy a portrait of a woman from one of Robert's paintings.

"What do you say, lunch on the beach at John's?"

"It's a late lunch."

"You want to eat?"

"O.K. Robert. But this time let me pay," insisted Miranda.

"All right my love."

"And I'll drive us down, it's a lot quicker."

After their late lunch, Miranda spent the rest of the afternoon sketching the Roman bust that Robert had set her as a test piece.

"Very good. Now let me see if I can teach you to paint."

"What do you want me to do?"

"Work in watercolours. That means having plenty of water on your palette and adding to it only a little paint to create a pale water-paint colour. First I want you to sketch this dried rose in a small vase, and then when you have the outline, I want you to add colour to the paper where there is colour in the rose petals, and the absence of colour by leaving the paper white. Do you understand?"

"Yes. Preparing the contrasts, the light and dark areas."

"Exactly!"

"If you can do it, I will let you colour my sketches on the canvases. Then we can be a two-man production team."

"How much will I get paid?"

"That depends on Wednesdays at St Lucia's market. But going by your charm, we should sell a good few. I will offer you twenty-five percent. What do you say to that?"

"Seems fair, but I have to tell you that my father, Amos, will pay for me while I am at his villa, so I don't really need the money."

"Then you will do it out of love?"

"Maybe, don't push your luck."

"O.K. Let's work."

The next day they worked hard in Robert's studio-cum-gallery.

"If we keep this up we will have enough paintings for next Wednesday's market."

"I told you, my lover, I could do it."

"Come here give us a kiss."

"God, are you never satisfied, Robert, you took me three times last night."

"I'm sorry, you are so feminine, and so sexy, you turn me on all the time."

"But you woke me up twice last night, just to have your evil way with me!"

"I didn't hear you complaining."

"Just because I have fallen in love with you, doesn't mean you can take advantage of me."

"Come on get your tits out and put that brush down."

She painted his face with the brush.

"Right, that's it!"

Robert chased her around the studio, grabbed her and yanked her top up over her head.

She grabbed a water pot and threw it over his head, soaking him.

He took all his wet clothes off, shirt and trousers, and, his erection in his underpants was massive.

"Have you got something for me, you're hiding?" teased, Miranda. "What the hell," and she unpinged her brassiere.

He grabbed for her pert tits and sunk his head to get a good suck on the nipples. She responded by yanking on his shaft through the cotton material. She pulled away from his embrace and ducked down, and all in one motion, pulled his pants down and sucked on his engorged penis. She licked him and double-handled him. He pulled her hands off, reached up under her little skirt and whipped her panties down. He lay down on the floor, amongst the easels, in full view of the front window, and lowered her onto him. He quickly thrust up into her waiting wetness. And she on the flats of her feet accommodated him to his full length of penetration.

"Oh my God, what if someone looks!?"

Robert was concentrating too hard to bother about anybody looking in. She was facing the window. He was lifting her up and down by her full bosoms. She was getting excited. She closed her eyes and the room became a blur as her world, at that moment, consisted only of extremely urgent satisfaction. Two bodies locked together. Two hearts as one. Two minds sharing one emotion. Then the room spun, the floor moved, and Miranda and Robert, exploded together.

She lay on top of, Robert, panting, and cuddled into him. His body was muscled, warm, reassuring. She felt safe. She listened to his heart thudding.

"I love you."

"Thank you, darling. I've never known anything like it."

"Don't ever let me go. You know, I think I might become a Spanish painter."

"With my guidance, Miranda, you will do well. We are as one. Let's move just in case somebody does walk up the path to the house. But I am sure nobody has seen us."

Together they went to the tiny bathroom and washed away the musk of sex.

In the morning, Robert said they needed time apart, as they were literally on top of one another.

"I'm going to Seagull Cove today, darling, and I shall be walking just as I've done dozens of times before. You go home and ring your father, Amos, and tell him you are all right."

"Yes, I need some fresh air we have been cooped up in here, working hard, too long. I'll see you tea-time because I need to do some washing, and check if Maria has come back, and, I could do with a swim."

"Hello, Miss Miranda, shall I do the cleaning?"

"You're back then, Maria! How is your mother?"

"Meralda sent me back home to El Estancia; she said I could do no good fussing over her, and Senor Amos is paying me anyway to keep house. So she said, 'it's best you are busy, earning a living', so here I am."

"Yes you may clean, but I don't think you will find much to clean. I have a new boyfriend now and I have been painting at his place."

"A new man in your life. That is good. A woman should have a man, like my Marco. A man makes a family, children to the family. You have come out of your grieving or are you 'putting the dirt under the carpet'. You must be honest with yourself."

"I loved Edward very much, but it was such a short marriage that we didn't really even have time to establish a permanent husband-wife relationship. No. I know my own mind now. I have met Robert, a painter, and I have fallen for him."

"How old is this young man?" asked Maria.

"He's not a stupid lovelorn young boy off the beach, if that is what you are thinking. He's a professional painter, he's thirty-seven."

"Ah, at last, a real man. Yes, an older man is good. Just like my Marco."

"How old is your Marco?"

"Thirty-two. And the good news is I am pregnant!"

"Wonderful, congratulations! What does Marco, think?"

"Oh he's so proud, bursting with joy. He wants a son."

"Did you tell him it could be a boy or a girl?"

"Yes, but he has made up his mind it will be a boy. You know what men are. He secretly wants a son."

"Men! Well you look after my father's house because today I am going to do my own washing. It is time for me to join the real world. The first thing I am going to do is strip the bed. Clean sheets, a new start to the day, and to my life."

"O.K., Miss Miranda. Together we house clean. I shake the carpets out and put them over the balcony, you hang the washing out."

After Miranda had done her domestics she had a shower and sat on her clean bed with a towel wound around her wet hair. Being warm, even in the shade in Spain, in the summer, she sat there in the mood and assumed the yoga position, in the nude. After a few minutes of relaxation she reached for her mobile phone and called her father.

"Amos, yes?"

"Hello, father, how are you?"

"No need to worry about me, you sound chippa. What's happened?"

"Nothing, papa, so don't worry. I am just happy. Everything is good with Robert. I have spent the last few days painting in his studio. We have paintings ready for next Wednesday's market at St Lucia. So you see I am working. Is it all right if I don't come back home?"

"Darling daughter, it's your life, I cannot decide for you. You must do whatever makes you happy. The only thing is, your mother and I would like to come out to the villa in July. How's that with you."

"That's wonderful, papa, you can meet Robert."

"Isn't that a bit too soon, Miranda?"

"I don't know about you, father, but mother will be chomping at the bit. I know that for certain."

"How can you be so certain?"

"Because I am a woman!"

"Ask a stupid question."

"Give my love to mother."

And she rang off.

The sea was beautifully calm, there was a clear sky and her father's private beach was deserted. She decided it was time for a swim; so she insisted Maria join her in a swim.

"Me? But I'm a servant, a housemaid?"

"My father said you were to keep an eye on me, so come along."

"But Miss Miranda, that was when you were grieving for your husband!"

"I insist you come and swim with me."

"All right, I will. Just give me a minute to change."

Maria came out on the back front steps in her one-piece canary yellow swimsuit. She had a good figure. Miranda waited in her bright red bikini, which didn't leave much to the imagination.

They went into the water side-by-side, laughing and splashing one another, like two carefree children.

Up in the rocks concealed on a ledge was, Robert. He was sketching the rock formations of the cliff and the feeding birds. They were bringing back to their fledglings small sand eels. By keeping still and being patient, Robert had got close to the nest of a breeding pair of birds. Their beaks were crammed full on each return from the sea, with at least half a dozen of the eels. The young, without teeth, simply opened their beaks and swallowed the eels down the gullet, whole.

When he stopped for a break he surveyed the horizon with a painter's eye. In the blanket of shimmering azure were two splashes of silver where the sea's surface was ruffled. He squinted against the sun's glare and the silvered areas were blotched, one with yellow and the other with red. 'Ah swimmers', he thought. He watched as the two smudged blobs of colour made their way to the shoreline. Closer now, it was obvious they were two swimmers. He surveyed the two people, who were women, through his bird watchers binoculars.

"Miranda! Must be? And a friend?" he said to nobody in particular.

He went back to sketching, concentrating on the shape of the young in the nest. It was not easy because the parent birds, in attendance, kept getting in his line of view. But one eye rotated towards the beach because he was distracted by the bright colours of canary yellow and flaming red. He took up his binoculars again, now that the two figures had walked up the long sandy beach and were towelling themselves dry.

"Definitely! It is them!"

He finished the outline of the sketch he was working on and made notes for colour, which he would add later, and put away his drawing things.

Up at El Estancia Maria and Miranda were changing into their day clothes. Miranda put on her sleeveless, summer, red dress that Robert particularly liked her in, and tied her hair back in a ponytail. Maria, being more practical, and married, put on her black cotton slacks and a cream blouse.

"Now, Maria, as I am over the death of Edward and I have a new love in my life, we will do things together. How about for lunch we take the midday bus up into the mountains to Sigma, like the local people, and when we get there we will have a bottle of local red wine?"

"O.K. But we will have to be quick or we will miss the bus."

Both laughing they walked up the hill away from Amos's villa and waited in the road with other Spanish locals.

"Ah Maria! You are going to visit your mother?" asked an old lady.

"Miranda, let me introduce, Senora Gonzalez. She is a friend of my mother, Meralda, from the village of Sigma."

"Pleased to meet you, Senora," said Miranda.

"Senora Gonzalez, this is Miranda, the English young lady who tragically lost her husband. No, we are not going specifically to meet Meralda, but we are having a Senora's day out just to enjoy ourselves."

"Miranda is so young to be a widow. But there is somebody in her life, I can see it in her eyes."

"Yes, Senora Gonzalez, I have met a painter, his name is Robert."

"Ah, I thought so, a man in your life. He makes you happy?"

"Yes, thank you, Senora."

"Stop all this Senora Gonzalez; my name is Rosa, a good Spanish name. I live in Sigma, and am a neighbour of Maria's mother. My husband, Pedro, owns the taverna."

"You have a taverna?"

"Yes, Miranda, it is where all the villagers eat on a weekend, but today it will not be too full. Mostly just tourists passing through," explained Maria.

"How long have you been married, Rosa, may I ask, to Pedro. Because you are obviously proud of him?"

"I was married young at just eighteen years. Now I am sixty-two. That's forty-four years of happy married life."

"Your Pedro, must be something special."

"He gave me two boys, Sancho and Dominique. They run taverna now, but Pedro, who is sixty-five now, still works hard and likes to be in charge of the cooking."

"It's good to have your health. I've been ill, but I feel better now."

Everybody got on the bus which was a bit of an old bone-shaker, and they set off up the hill in a cloud of black smoke as the driver pushed on the accelerator and jerked through the gears.

Rosa sat on a seat across the aisle from Miranda and Maria, and put her basket of shopping on the empty seat next to her.

"Pedro puts his robust health down to hard work and two glasses of red wine a day. You, young lady should try it."

"Senora Rosa, in England, the doctor told me that one glass of red wine a day is good for the blood and gives you that extra vitality."

"Your English doctor speaks the truth."

The bus rounded a hairpin bend which led to a relatively straight piece of road. On both sides were white-painted cottages under red tile roofs. At the end of the straight stretch was the village centre, and a turning bay to one side for the bus. Everybody got off including the driver. He went into Taverna Sigma as if he owned the place and used the washroom. Then he sat at a table in the shade and drank strong bitter Spanish coffee.

The village centre was obviously a meeting place. It was cobbled and had four mature trees, under which were placed tables and chairs, and set back from the road against Taverna Sigma's walls were several more tables in the sun, set for meals. The central feature to the village was a powerful fountain, from which came a tap for drinking water. At the tap were two old ladies filling buckets to take back to their cottages.

"All right if I have a drink?" asked Miranda.

"Of course," said Maria. "Come with me."

They went to the tap and Rosa went indoors to Taverna Sigma.

"That's kind of soft and bubbly."

Maria laughed. "That's because it is mountain spring water. It's natural."

The old men sat under the trees on the wooden chairs smiled at Miranda, as an act of charity and understanding and because she was beautiful. And old men still with their marbles kept a twinkle in their eye remembering when they were young.

In the Taverna Sigma, Rosa, was greeted with a kiss on each cheek from Pedro, and then she bossed the boys about.

"Sancho, Dominique, don't just sit there lazy good for nothings, we have a guest."

"Mama, who is it? A tourist off the bus?"

"A young lady from El Estancia and she is not a tourist."

"From El Estancia. The big villa on the coast? Must be a rich lady!"

"Now mind your manners, and your hands, and no bottom pinching."

"Ah mama, you take all the fun out of things."

"If you touch her, I will tell your wives!" laughed Rosa.

"O.K. Mama, we will behave."

"Miranda, I would like you to meet Senora Rosa's sons, Sancho and Dominique," said Maria.

"Welcome, welcome!" said the two, and took turns kissing her on both cheeks.

"O.K. that will do," said Rosa. Open some wine for our guest."

"Would you like wine, Maria, or do you want first to go and visit your mother?"

"My mother can manage without me. I'm here as Miranda's guest. We have come especially to Taverna Sigma for our lunch."

"Bravo! Bravo!" called out Pedro. "I go to prepare lunch."

"Sancho, Dominique, I can manage, go serve our other guests."

"Yes, mama."

"You must forgive my boys, they are weak where young beautiful women are concerned. Dominique is the worst, he has a wandering eye. But he doesn't ask a lady out because his wife will stab him while he is asleep in his bed."

"Oh dear, I hope I haven't caused any trouble."

"No Miranda. Men will be men, but us older and wiser women must keep them in line. Good men never grow up, inside they are still boys. My Pedro, at sixty-five, is still a boy in his head."

"Your husband, Senora Rosa, is a man full of mischief, that much I can tell by his dancing eyes. It's good that he, after forty-four years, still loves you."

"Yes, I am happy because I have so many friends in the village, and I make friends with the tourists who pass by here."

"Do tourists ever come back?"

"Come with me into the lounge. Now what do you see?"

"A bar with many bottles behind?"

"Take another look, what apart from the bottles, do you see?"

"Postcards, dozens of postcards, all pinned to the walls and the bar front."

"Now you see! Read if you want to."

Miranda did, one or two. "Oh I see, all customers on holiday here, and they send cards from all over Europe and the United Kingdom."

"And I get sometimes, letters from guests who have stayed at Taverna Sigma."

"You have rooms as well?"

"Just two guest rooms. We charge for room and breakfast. Of course they can stay for lunch or dinner if they want to, my sons see to them. But mostly people who stay here have a car and therefore have lunch somewhere else and come back here for dinner in the evening."

"Sounds very romantic."

"Yes, outside under the trees, the customers can eat by oil lantern or by the glow of the fairy lights strung overhead. Let's go back into the dining room."

Sancho and Dominique were busy serving at the tables. Pedro shouted through the serving hatch from the kitchen when the next order was ready.

Maria sat at a corner table with two glasses of red wine ready.

"There you are, Miranda? I thought Senora Rosa had recruited you to the staff," she laughed.

"You will excuse me now, Miranda, I have to organise the boys," said Rosa.

Much to Miranda's surprise and delight, Rosa could play the piano, and Sancho and Dominique started singing.

The diners were buoyed up by the whole eating experience and cheered both Rosa and her boys, and in appreciation of the entertainment, when Rosa stopped, applauded loudly.

Whilst Miranda was drinking Sancho came across with a steaming pasta dish, and two bowls for Maria and Miranda to eat from.

"Eat. Enjoy!" said Sancho. "Fresh from the kitchen by Pedro's hand."

"I'll pay," said Miranda, "it's the least I can do for you, Maria, for nursing me for a whole month. Without you I don't know how I could have coped."

"Miranda, it is not your fault. It is natural to grieve for a much loved one. But now you have met Robert, so now you are ready to face the world again."

"I mean it, Maria, I was so depressed. I often thought about suicide. You know, killing myself, but I was a coward and felt sorry for myself. I cried myself to sleep every night for a whole month until somehow, with your help, I went down to the beach. Then I realised there was a whole world outside my room. The sky, the sun, the sea and the beach with a wind blowing through my hair. In all that time I don't remember eating anything."

"You were ill, Miranda, and I was dreadfully worried about you, you were so despondent, I found it very hard to reach you. I had to coax you every day to eat a bowl of soup by spoon-feeding you. You may not know it at the time but you were starving yourself, just wasting away."

"But not now, this last week or so I have been ravenous. Robert had made sure I've had plenty to eat, and as a result I feel stronger, more alive and full of hope for the future. He says I am blossoming, especially my breasts, which have always been good, but now they are fuller, more womanly, as he calls it."

"Stop talking and eat up your pasta. Here, have another glass of wine and put some more meat on those bones."

"Do you think I am too thin?"

"Yes, definitely, you have lost so much weight. You are not slim but plain skinny. Your rib bones and your spine stick out. You must put on some more weight."

"I shall, but I shall not put on too much weight because Robert is a good lover. In fact he can be exhausting."

"Ooh La La! He's so good?"

"Yes, Maria, but it's our secret. Sometimes he wakes me in the middle of the night while I am still asleep and makes love to me."

"But what about at other times?"

"Oh he's regular. Every morning and every night!"

"How lucky you are?! My husband is an evening man. If I try to be amorous in the morning, he always says, 'Not now, I want to have the strength for work'."

"What does he do?"

"He works for builders, wherever there is a new buildings or alterations. Or, sometimes, owners putting up extensions or an extra floor. Usually it's because of more children in the family. He is a skilled bricklayer, and therefore an honest labourer's job."

"I bet he has a fit muscular body, you lucky lady."

"Yes, he has very strong hands, big shoulders and a trim body."

"Perhaps I envy you," laughed Miranda.

"What's your Robert, like?"

"Tall and slim, with long artistic fingers. He's a talented painter."

"Is that why you have fallen for him?"

"Yes, because he, like me, is sensitive, loving, affectionate and considerate. I also paint; I learnt the basics at High School when I was a teenager. So you see, we both have a shared interest and a shared talent, though there is a difference: Robert paints by instinct, whereas my talent was produced by the encouragement of a teacher. Even now I am learning under Robert's guidance. Only yesterday I was working in his studio, adding colour to some of his sketches. My skill is more in the drawing than in the painting."

"I think, maybe, you have made a good match. But forget about Robert for a day and eat up. Build up your health, you still look a little fragile."

"Don't worry about me, I have never felt better."

"In your face it is true, because you are happy, you are emotionally buoyant, but physically, you need building up."

"I think if I eat too much of Senora Rosa's pasta meals I shall become fat."

Sancho came to the table.

"Why the pretty senorita not drinking up the wine. The best of Taverna Sigma?"

"My fault, Sancho, I keep her talking because I ask too many questions," said Maria.

Pedro came out.

"How do you like my cooking, Senorita Miranda?"

"Fine, Pedro, it's just that I am not a big eater. I have to watch my figure."

"Women! A Spanish man likes some meat on his wife, not all skin and bones."

"Pedro, Miranda is English. She is naturally very slim, not like your Rosa, with a full figure."

"My Rosa, is just right for me. At our age we still make love!"

"Please, Pedro, you are embarrassing our guest, Miranda."

"It's all right, Maria; it's a wonderful thing that Pedro still confesses his love for his wife," said Miranda with an understanding smile.

"Now!" said Pedro. "We dance!"

"Rosa, the piano!"

"Yes, Pedro."

Sancho and Dominique clapped their hands to set up the beat. Pedro stamped his heels on the boards of the verandah.

"Come, young English lady," beckoned Pedro from the verandah.

Miranda, seduced by the food and wine, and enticed by Pedro and his family, left her chair and went across to Pedro.

"Hold my hand. Now stamp your feet. Like this. One two, one two two!"

Miranda got the beat and followed Pedro's lead. Others, seated outside, also took up the beat by clapping.

Maria smiled at Miranda to encourage her, and feeling reassured, Miranda threw herself into the dancing.

Now Sancho danced beside Pedro and Miranda and Dominique burst into a Spanish song, none of which made any sense to Miranda as it was all in the Spanish language.

Pedro stopped, bowed to Miranda and the onlookers applauded with gusto.

"You dance like an angel, Senorita Miranda."

"Well, thank you sir."

"That's enough, Pedro, get back in the kitchen."

"Take no notice of him, Miranda, he can't resist a pretty young lady."

"Will you excuse us, Senora Rosa. Thank you for the meal, we are going to visit my mother now."

"Oh, I haven't paid?" said Miranda.

"Let me pay for mine," insisted Maria.

"No, no! I said it was my treat for looking after me. So I will pay."

"The meal is on the house, senorita. But you may pay for the red wine," smiled Rosa.

"How much do I owe you?"

"As you are a friend of Maria's, say 500 pesetas."

"Gracious, Senora Rosa!"

"Come on Miranda, you will like my mother."

"Maria!? What a surprise! I didn't expect you 'til next week. And who's this with you?"

"This is my friend, Miranda, from El Estancia. She's the daughter of Senor Amos, who owns the villa."

"Your employer. A good man, he sends payment every month."

"Welcome, Miranda. You like tea, English tea?"

"Well, actually, Maria and I have just had lunch at Taverna Sigma."

"Ah! Pedro and Rosa. Such nice people. Then have a cake, I have just baked."

"All right, Senora Meralda, very kind of you."

"Now tell me, Maria, what brings you?"

"It was Miranda's idea. A day out in the mountains. She is thanking me for looking after her while she has been ill."

"Yes, Miranda, I am sorry to hear about your loss. There are too many widows in the world."

"I have, with Maria's help, recovered now. I have met a new man. He's called Robert and he's a professional painter."

"So you see, mama, Miranda is happy now."

"I am so pleased for you. It is good to see young ones in love. He's not an old man, is he?"

"No, no. Older than me, but thirty-seven is a mature age."

"An older man is usually more considerate, thinks more of his wife than just football."

"Oh he's not bothered about football, only art. You know, sketching and art."

"Have I ever seen any of his paintings? Does he come to Sigma on market days?"

"He does go to market, but to St Lucia on the Wednesday market."

"That's the other side of the mountain."

"Oh, mother it's not a million miles away. All you have to do is take the bus from Sigma down to Atalia's Bus Station and then up the eastern side of the mountain to the village of St Lucia."

"Why doesn't he come to Sigma?"

"Because it is only a small village with, as you know, only locals. Robert needs tourists to buy his paintings. They cost about 5,000 pesetas each."

"So much? Local people cannot afford that. They have their shopping to pay for."

"Senora Meralda, you must understand tourists have spending money with them, and that's why Robert goes to St Lucia. It is a bigger place with many restaurants to attract more people."

"Why can't they come to Taverna Sigma?"

"Oh, mama, some do come. You couldn't cope if a coach load arrived. Anyway it would intrude on the peace of the village."

"Senora Meralda, would you like me to take you to St Lucia on Wednesday and see Robert's paintings? I have a car," said Miranda.

"You would come here?"

"No, but I could collect you from Atalia Bus Station if you caught the early bus down, you know, the 'workers bus', and then I would drive you all up to St Lucia."

"You have room for me in the car as well as your painter boyfriend?"

"Yes, you and Maria can sit in the back and hold the canvases, it will be cramped, but there will be more room on the homeward journey because we will have sold many paintings by the end of the market day."

"What about the open back where you put my shopping basket?" asked Maria.

"Yes, of course, the boot, I hadn't thought about using that. Yes, I can clear it out and put several canvases in, that should free-up some room in the back of the car."

"O.K. Senorita Miranda, I will come with you on Wednesday to St Lucia's market."

"Now, mama, we will have cake and a cup of tea."

After tea Meralda took Maria and Miranda, to meet the village folk. She knew everybody by their first names and so Miranda was introduced around to all the old men who sat at the tables, some with Spanish coffee and a bottle of water, others with worry beads and a cigarette. One table was busy with a game of cards. Miranda stopped to have a look, but she couldn't understand the game because the cards had unusual symbols and were in Spanish. The ladies dressed in traditional black, sat around in two's and three's under the shade of the village centre trees, doing lace work.

"What are they making, Senora Meralda?" asked Miranda.

"I can make those, they are antimacassars for the arms and backs of lounge chairs."

"What do they do?"

"They protect the upholstery from dirty men's hair and hands."

"Oh? I thought they were for decoration?"

"Yes, Senorita Miranda, they are for making the house look pretty, but men don't wash their hair often enough, and without the protection of an antimacassar they would make greasy marks on the back of my beautiful furniture and spoil it."

"So I suppose, you sell them to the few visitors who come to Sigma Village?"

"Yes. But I also make doilies, small decorative mats to protect surfaces, and napkins for meal times. The best sellers are my napkins because they can be used as place settings on a dining table."

"Yes my mother has linen place settings."

"Yes, linen is all right but a bit plain. Macramé is a lot more attractive because you can make different patterns."

"Take no notice of mother, she thinks her macramé is the best in the village. She spends winter evenings whiling away the hours, making lace."

"And in the summer, I grow plants to produce many blossoms in pots."

"Oh mother, you don't do it just for the fun of it, you sell them to passers-by."

"And why not. I need a little money. I have to buy pots. Anyway it decorates the house."

"Mother, your house looks beautiful, everybody knows that. I'm surprised you don't charge tourists two hundred pesetas a time when they take photographs of the house."

"Maria, I have thought about that."

"Well, what have you done about it?"

"A photographer is going to produce postcards of my beautiful house and when they sell I get a small payment."

"Mother! You never miss a chance to make money!"

"I think your mother is wise, Maria, if her house makes a memorable tourist photograph then she is entitled to some kind of payment."

"I see your friend has good business sense," smiled Meralda.

"Well, I am good with people. Last Wednesday, at St Lucia, I helped Robert sell his paintings. I invited customers into his stall, which he had set up as a picture gallery, by offering a free glass of wine. The Spanish locals and some on holiday, and other tourists stopped to have a look, and while we chatted they became relaxed and browsed. By Robert's good painting and my beauty we were able to encourage many to buy. By the end of the day, would you believe it, we actually sold out!"

"Amazing!" said Maria.

"Se!" said Meralda. "Not just a pretty woman, but a clever head. Bravo! Why isn't my daughter like you?"

"Senora Meralda, we are all different."

"Yes, mama. I am happy being a wife and doing a little cleaning job."

"Where are my grandchildren? You want me to die without grandchildren?"

"Mother, I wasn't going to tell you yet, until I was sure my pregnancy was going well, but I am pregnant."

"You're going to have my grandchild, wonderful!"

"What does Marco think about you getting pregnant?"

"He's bursting with joy, he wants a son!"

"Oh good! I will buy you the best baby's cradle as a present, Maria."

"But Mama, you shouldn't spend your money on me. Marco is a very proud man, he will probably want to buy the baby's things."

"Nonsense! It is my grandchild. I will buy whatever I like. And I'll knit some baby clothes in white in the softest wool, then it won't matter if it's a boy or a girl."

"Mother, shouldn't you wait until the baby is born?"

"What do you mean?"

"Well, pregnancies don't always go to full term. You know there can be problems. Remember I am only three months' pregnant; it is only early days yet."

"Believe me, Maria, you have my blood and I carried you to full term. So don't worry, you will be fine."

"Nice to meet you, Senora Meralda, but I think I should be getting back, I want to surprise Robert."

"Forgive me, I am an old lady, I talk too much. Come again, Miranda, and thank you for bringing my daughter, Maria."

"Goodbye, mama."

"Well, Maria, what do you think of our day?" asked Miranda, as she drove back to Atalia on the coast.

"I have enjoyed our day. Travelling by car is far nicer than by bus and I enjoyed my lunch at Taverna Sigma. Thank you very much."

"Nothing less than what you deserve, Maria. If I decide to marry Robert you will be my first wedding guest."

"To say that, Miranda, you must be very sure of yourself because it is so soon after Edward's death."

"My father, Amos, said, that my happiness is up to me, it's my life. So I intend to keep Robert. I intend to stay in Spain and paint."

"Have you told Robert of your decision yet?"

"No. Meeting Rosa and Pedro and others at St Lucia Market made me realise I like the culture of Spain."

"What do you mean, Miranda?"

"The nature of the people is more friendly and relaxed. I feel I belong here."

"Are you sure? It could just be the sun and falling in-love. What about the winter when it's quieter and not so many tourists about?"

"I think I would enjoy the mild climate of winter and the peace and quiet."

"On the coast in the winter the sea can become rough."

"Oh, I think I would enjoy the crashing sounds of the waves on the shore and the empty beaches."

"Well, the Costa Del Sol is never actually empty, because British tourists do come in the winter, though, of course, not so many as in the summer. Personally, Miranda, I don't like the high season of July and August because everywhere is crowded. Not just the beaches but the town cafés as well. Of course the Spanish business people like it because of the money, but the employees who work long hours for their wages in the summer season are glad when the hotels close for the winter period, because they can go home for a well earned rest. They take home money to their parents."

"So there is still a winter market at St Lucia?"

"Of course. The locals need a market, and the tourists who come in the winter usually hire a car because it is too cool to just sit on the beach, so, therefore, they venture in land, which means they visit the villages more, and of course need something to spend their holiday money on."

"Am I right then? People with cars are more likely to buy pictures than those who come by bus?"

"Yes. Because they have more convenient transport, and tourists who can afford to rent cars are obviously better off, and therefore have more spending power."

"I expect the holidaymakers in the low season are more mature, and probably a lot are pensioners or near retirement age?"

"Yes, you are right, Miranda."

"And that means, the winter visitors are more likely to buy pictures for their houses because older clients have probably retired to detached houses with grounds, and such houses will have larger rooms crying out for good quality pictures."

"What are you thinking, Miranda?"

"Hotels. There are hotels all along the coast. The vast majority of tourists stay in hotels. Why not display Robert's paintings in hotels?"

"I think I follow your reasoning, Miranda. There are plenty of potential customers already in the hotels."

"Exactly! Robert can double the asking price of his paintings. He would get a far more realistic price, which would reflect accurately his artistic skills."

"But would the hotels allow his paintings in?"

"I would say, for a twenty-five percent commission, they would welcome his paintings."

"Now I can see why you want to stay in Spain, Miranda," laughed Maria.

"I'll drop you off and go and put my idea to Robert. I shall surprise him because I know he is working."

There was a knock on 'The Impressionist's' door. Robert laid aside his brush and cursed, as he was putting the finishing touches to a portrait. In particular the colour of the irises and the reflection of light off the blackness of the pupils. It involved using a single hair brush to add such delicate detail and it required a very steady hand.

"Yes? Who is it?" asked a slightly annoyed Robert as he approached the door and flung it open by the handle.

"It's me, darling!" called out Miranda.

"Miranda?! What are you doing here? I thought we were having a day apart."

"Well, we have. I've been to the village of Sigma with Maria, my maid. But the day is over now, so here I am. Are you annoyed?"

"Not with you, but with being interrupted. I am doing a portrait."

"Well, am I welcome? Can I come in?"

"I suppose so. It's just that I didn't expect you. It's a bit inconvenient."

"Have you got somebody else inside?"

"No, it's not that. It's just that you can't come in at the moment."

That did it. Jealousy rose up in, Miranda, and she burst in.

"O.K. who's in here?"

"Nobody else!" protested, Robert.

"Oh Robert! That's beautiful! I'm sorry, I thought you had another woman in here. Forgive me?"

"It was supposed to be a surprise, a gift for you. I have been working on your portrait day and night. What do you mean, another woman?"

"I thought somebody else was posing for you."

"You mean you were jealous of another woman?"

"Well, yes."

"How dare you! What if I had another woman in my house. I am a painter, that's what I do for a living. If I decide that a lady should pose for me, that's my business!"

"I'm sorry! Robert!"

"I should damned well think so. Whatever happened to fidelity and trust?"

Robert, felt compromised and was angry.

"Explain yourself?"

"I only over reacted because I love you. I can't help being jealous."

"Of what, your own portrait?"

"Guess I made a fool of myself. Can I have a kiss?"

She put her arms around Robert's neck and pushed her breasts into his manly chest.

"Please?"

"I forgive you. But God help me if there had been another woman."

"I would have clawed her eyes out. You are my man and nobody else's."

"You don't need reassurance; I have just painted the portrait of the woman I love."

"Me?"

"Yes, you. What did you want anyway?"

"Just to see you, tell you I love you. I was with Maria today, and met her mother, Meralda, but a part of me missed you."

"We agreed to have some days apart."

"Actually, Robert, it was you who suggested we have some days apart, not me."

"I have to work."

"Can I stop the night?"

She kissed him and fondled him through his baggy cotton trousers. He got an erection immediately.

"Make love to me. I need you. Please!" she insisted.

Miranda took her sundress off and stood in front of him in her tiny lace bra and panties which left absolutely nothing to the imagination.

"Come here." He kissed her and led her by the hand to his small, cluttered bedroom, kicking the door shut with his foot.

"It was precisely because of this that I suggested a few days apart."

"I don't want to be apart from you. I love you."

"I can't live with you, and I can't live without you," said Robert. "Don't you understand? You intoxicate me. You get under my skin. I don't just love you. I am in-love with you. We are as one."

"Don't talk, make love to me," said Miranda, taking her brassiere off.

That did it. Miranda had such perfect tits that Robert couldn't resist them. He cupped their fullness gently and sucked on the nipples, the effect of which, tugged physiologically on Miranda's crutch. She dribbled in her panties at her sudden arousal. She kicked them off and sat on Robert's lap.

"Make me come! I want it now, urgently!" she whispered into the crown of his hair as he bent to minister to her breasts.

"Lie down."

He placed himself between her legs. He gripped her knees and folded her legs up so that her thighs were spread widely and her vulva's were fully exposed. He bent to his duties and licked her, and when she squirmed on her pert little bottom, he changed tactics and pulled on her clitoris gently with his teeth. The slight pain combined with the sexy arousal made, Miranda, high.

"Yes that's it! Go on! I'm coming!"

He let go of her open legs and placed his left hand under her bottom to hold her up a bit, and with his right hand put two fingers fully into her vagina.

Miranda, excited, and offering herself to him, raised her bottom off the bed, helping him to administer to her more thoroughly with his experienced hand work. She reached overhead and gripped with both hands the wrought iron bed head as her whole body convulsed from the electrified hair on the crown of her head to the tips of the toes on her feet. She was fully ignited with pulsating power. Her whole body shook: her standing up tits swayed from side to side, her body vibrated making her buttocks contract and, out of control, the heels of her feet drummed on the bed. And so it was, she climaxed. The bed head was bent on its fixings as Miranda's orgasmic strength increased, with increasing explosions of contractions from her inner sanctum, and then she let it out, taking in great gulps of air, between intensive screams of release.

Then exhausted, she went limp and reached up to Robert. He sat up and cradled her in his arms like a babe. Then Miranda cried. She wept on his shoulder.

"Shh baby! I love you. I didn't hurt you, did I?"

"No, no. It was wonderful," she murmured between sobs. "I love you so much."

"Is that why you surrender yourself so much?"

"Yes, completely. To show you how much I love you."

"Thank you. With my mind and my body I honour you also."

"Will you marry me, Robert?"

"Oh darling, I'd love to, but it's too soon. What on earth will your father say?"

"Daddy loves me. He says to do whatever makes me happy."

"But your mother would never forgive me. She would say I was ruining your life and taking advantage of you while you are vulnerable."

"I know my own mind. I loved Edward very much. He was my first true love, at least I thought he was. But I was not in-love with Edward. What we have is chemical, it's something special. I've never felt like this before."

"No. I won't marry you, at least not yet. It's too soon. It would be wrong of me. You must have more time to be sure of your decision. You may come to your senses and decide it was just a holiday romance."

"I'm not in a dream, Robert. I'm clearheaded. Being apart from you made me realise that."

"I still say it's too soon. And anyway even if it's not, we first have to live together. You know, to see if we can stand each other day and night. Living in each other's company for twenty-four hours can be stressful. That's the first test. We must have a common interest because a relationship must be able to stand up on just friendship. You cannot spend a lifetime based just on sex. There is a saying about marriage: 'marriage is like a hot bath, when it cools it's not so hot'. Then you have to decide if you really want to be married or just in a relationship. They are both the same, except the marriage has a Marriage Certificate."

"We are in a relationship, aren't we, Robert?"

"Of course, darling. And we love each other very much. The only difference is we don't have a signed piece of paper, that is, a Marriage Certificate."

"But a Marriage Certificate means we are legally married. It is a public declaration in front of witnesses that you belong to me."

"You make me sound like a piece of property, Miranda," said Robert.

"I don't mean to. I just don't want to lose you."

"Are you feeling insecure?"

"Not when I am with you."

"I think you are. You are afraid of getting hurt, and that's because you are still vulnerable. I think it takes at least a year to adjust to losing someone you loved and was the centre of your world.

Miranda cried openly on Robert's shoulders.

"That's it, let it all out."

She cried for a long time.

"Thank you, Robert. Yes, I think you are right. I am full of hurts."

"What you said about relationships. May I move in with you and test our relationship. I mean I will work, I will paint alongside you."

"Well, all right, but only because you have El Estancia as a bolt hole if anything goes wrong and we need time apart."

"Oh thank you, Robert."

"Don't get over excited. I'm only allowing this because as you have your own place, you are not totally dependent on me, which you would be if we were married, and with marriage comes children. You had better give your marriage proposal some more thought."

"I have no desire for children, which is why I am on the contraceptive pill."

"But if we were married you might change your mind, and that means intentionally skipping the pill."

"I wouldn't do that."

"Maybe. Women who are married and in a happy relationship get to depend on their partner and, therefore, lose by way of security, their independence. This means they feel so safe that they, without telling their partners, because they feel broody, stop taking the pill to get pregnant."

"That can't be such a bad thing if they love each other, surely!?"

"Babies put a strain on the marriage. They get in the way of the marital relationship. When a mother has a baby, provided she feels all right, she dotes on the baby giving it her full attention. The husband gets pushed out. If this is allowed to continue while the baby becomes a toddler, the husband gets rejected, and as a consequence he feels unloved. In this situation the husband feels cheated, used, and will look elsewhere for a new soul mate."

"I wouldn't deliberately get myself pregnant. I am not that selfish. Anyway, I am too young, I am only twenty-three. I want to see some of the world before I marry. A lot of women these days have their children a lot later."

"When I marry, Miranda, it will not be to raise a family, it will be to have a relationship, an affectionate and sexual relationship, for my natural life. I and my partner will grow old together, gracefully, and in the autumn of my years there will still be a loving bond between my partner and myself."

"You have thought about this, haven't you?"

"Yes, over the years I have had girlfriends and they have all been selfish. They think about their own pleasure and sexuality, using men for their own needs. Then when they decide the conquest has become boring they move onto another man to have fresh fun with."

"I'm not a user, Robert."

"Are you sure? At the moment you are experimenting with your sexuality because, as you said, I am your first true lover. True we love one another, but it may be just the chemical reaction of sex. What about when the bath water cools, does the baby get thrown out with the bath water?"

"I don't know? I haven't known you long enough to tell."

"Exactly! At least you are being realistic now. When we have been together for six months and summer has turned into the cool of winter, ask me again to marry you, that's if we are still together and you still love me."

"Stop it Robert! You're frightening me."

"What are you frightened of?"

"Being left on my own."

"Then don't be, you're a nice person and beautiful with it. You can have your choice of men."

"But I don't want a choice, I am happy with you."

"Perhaps I happened along at a convenient time and you needed a crutch to hold you up."

"I hadn't thought about it like that."

"Then it's time you did. I don't want to marry you only to find out six months later that you decide you have made a mistake. Because when I give myself I give completely, my heart, soul and mind. It would damage me terribly, and I'm not prepared to risk that."

"Then what am I to do?"

"Just be yourself and be honest about your own feelings over the coming weeks. I know I love you, I think you are special, you light up my life, but I am not sure you know your own mind. You may just be infatuated with the love of an older man, or simply feel protected."

So, Miranda moved into The Impressionist and in July her parents, Amos and Annette, arrived at El Estancia for their holiday.

"Well, Miranda, where is he?"

"Don't say it like that! He's not a he, he's called Robert, Robert Darling, and I love him."

"Oh calm down Annette, you have been fretting ever since we stepped on the plane."

"I don't like flying and there wasn't a car to meet us."

"Why should there be a car, we are not royalty."

"Oh mummy, put your case down and come and give me a hug."

"Sorry, darling. It's your father he gets me all hot and bothered."

"Stop complaining woman. You will meet Robert when Miranda is ready."

"Where is he dear?"

"At his own house, working."

"That can't be bad, Annette, the lad has his own house and works. That's two out of three in my book."

"Daddy, what's the third one then?"

"Emotional stability. If a man truly loves a woman he will be affectionate, considerate, and have an eye for no other woman."

"Daddy, we have been together nearly two months now and we still feel the same about each other. Would you like to meet Robert?"

"All in good time. How have you settled in? I must say I've never seen you in such radiant health. You are positively glowing and your eyes are full of life. You have quite a sparkle."

"The sparkle is because of Robert. He worships me."

"Let your mother and I unpack and have a shower and then we could invite your boyfriend round for dinner this evening."

"No, father, I have a better idea. I'll collect Robert and then drive us all up to the village of Sigma."

"Why there, darling?"

"Because friends of Maria's, Rosa and Pedro, very friendly people, own a nice taverna called Taverna Sigma. It is up in the mountain so you will like it. It's away from the oppressive atmosphere of the summer-beach."

"A beer and a cooling breeze, our Miranda, is just what the doctor ordered," said Amos.

"Hello love, have your parents arrived safely."

"They are dying to meet you, well mother really. They are outside in the car."

"Hell! I'm in a scruffy T-shirt and jeans, that won't make a very good impression."

"Mother might sniff and turn her nose up, but she's privately a snob. Papa is wiser. He will be looking out for your character not at your clothes."

"O.K. I will come out. Let's get it over with."

"Mum, dad, this is Robert. He's a painter."

"Hello, Robert, looks like we are interrupting your work?" said Amos.

"Oh, sorry about the brush, I forget, it's an extension of my right hand. To be honest I wasn't expecting anybody."

"It was our daughter's idea to dig you out."

"Would you like to see my studio while I change my shirt?"

"If we are not intruding on your privacy."

"I have nothing to hide. And you must be mother?"

"Mother? Well, yes I am Miranda's mother. You are a big lad, aren't you?"

"I suppose so. Would you like to come in or wait by the car? I'll only be a minute."

"I'll just pop in, Robert."

Robert went into the kitchen to rummage through the laundry basket in an effort to find a clean T-shirt.

"Oh my God!" said Annette. "She's nude! Amos, this cannot be allowed, it's our daughter!?"

"Ah! If I had known you were coming I could have covered it up. Well at least she's wearing a G-string."

"Makes no difference, it's as good as nude. Come on Miranda, we are leaving. You cannot stay with this painter person!"

"Mother, I am not a little girl any more. This is Robert's house and I am proud to pose for him."

"Papa, am I not beautiful?"

"Miranda, I am seeing you for the first time."

"Yes. Robert you are a lucky man. I can see you are broadminded."

"Amos, may I call you that? I love Miranda very much and am proud of her. We work together, two dedicated painters. We are as one."

"Don't agree with the boy, Amos. It's pornographic!" .

"Miranda's mum, it is a full length portrait and very lifelike. When I have put the finishing touches to it, I will hang it in my bedroom."

"Mother, it is art. And beauty is in the eye of the beholder," said Miranda.

"I think you are beautiful, Miranda, and I am glad you are proud of yourself," said Amos.

"I agree. Miranda deserves to be carved in marble!"

"Men! Always the same. Nothing on their minds but sex!"

"Annette, are you jealous? After all, Miranda, gets her looks from you."

"Pah! I still cut a good figure."

"Prude! If I was a naked young man I bet you would have a look," laughed Amos, which broke the atmosphere.

"I'll just cover it up," said Robert.

"Good idea, Robert. I'll sit with you in the back seat of the car, it will give mother and daughter time to gossip."

On the way up the winding mountain road, Miranda was suddenly confronted by the bus as it skidded well across the centre-line on a notorious hairpin bend.

"Look out!" shouted Annette, her mother. Miranda braked and swerved all at the same time, but the front of the bus slewed across the road and the bumper struck Miranda's car and it was pushed off the road. It easily went through the flimsy crash barrier and careered on down the steep mountainside like a hell-slide. The car bounced from rock outcrop to rock outcrop with the sickening sound of crunching metal.

The only reason they weren't thrown out of the battered car was because they all had seat belts on. Then the car dropped into nothingness.

"Oh, my God!" screamed Miranda, "we are all going to die!"

Annette, too terrified to scream, said a silent prayer.

There was a sudden jolt and a huge plume of water washed over the car. Then the battered car came momentarily back to the surface of the lake.

Clear thinking, Amos, took charge.

"Release your seat belts! Now swim for it before this thing sinks for good!"

With the windows smashed the water rushed in and swamped the car.

"Forget the doors, they won't open because of the force of the water. Swim straight out of the windows!" commanded Amos.

Miranda was a good swimmer and was the first out. She was quickly followed by Robert and Amos. The water swirled around Annette's head as the car began to sink. She held her breath.

"Robert, where's mother!?"

Robert followed the car down, holding his breath. The car was dragging Annette down. He grabbed hold of her and yanked her out of the open door and pointed up.

Annette's lungs were burning. She could see the surface. She would never make it.

Robert, seeing the panic in Annette's eyes as she breathed out, put his lips to hers and gave her half of his breath. They climbed to the light, which didn't seem to come soon enough. His ears were bursting. Annette's brain was buzzing as was her ears, when together at the very last second they burst through the surface, taking in a great gulp of air.

"Oh my God, I thought I was going to die." Oh thank you, Robert, you saved my life!"

"You two all right?" asked a worried Amos.

"Amos, Robert gave me his breath. The car was dragging me down. He got me out!"

"Then you're a hero, Robert."

"Come on let's stick together and make for the rocks," said Amos, taking charge again.

It was only a short distance to the rocky beach, but there was no way they could climb up beyond the beach because they were hemmed in by almost vertical rock faces, so they sat on the rocks of the beach and wrung their sodden clothes out while they collected their thoughts.

"If we can't climb up, Amos, then somebody will have to come down," said Robert.

"Well where did we fall from?" asked Amos.

"From up above, but we cannot see the road because of the overhang of rock."

They strained, in silence, for any sound. Now Miranda, who had acute hearing, heard somebody calling.

"We're down her. Help! Help us!"

"Who are you calling to, Miranda?"

"Somebody is shouting: 'Wait. Help is coming'!"

"I can't hear anything?"

"But I can!" insisted Miranda. "Do they have mountain rescue in Spain?"

"Yes," said Robert. "They have climbers and helicopter rescue."

"Then the best thing we can do while we have the warm sunshine is dry all our clothes on the rocks."

"I'm not taking my clothes off!" said Annette.

"Don't be a fool, woman, it will be cold tonight. In wet clothes you will be taken ill, so get undressed now!"

"All right you don't have to shout at me."

"It is for your own good."

"We should also drink," said Robert. "We are in the full glare of the sun with no shelter."

"I agree, Robert, dehydration is the last thing we want."

"Well, to stop us from overheating couldn't we just swim. After all we are all in our underwear?" said Miranda.

"I don't fancy going back in that icy water," said Annette. "Once is enough!"

"You don't have to swim, dear, just paddle on the edge. Thank our lucky stars that we were all strapped in."

"I wonder what shall I tell the car hire company, father?"

"I don't care if I have to pay for a new car. The important thing is that my wife and daughter are safe."

"You call this safe?"

"Annette, we are all very lucky to escape with light cuts and bruises. Somebody will probably come first thing in the morning."

"In the morning? I'm not waiting down here all night!"

"O.K., dear, where are you going to go?"

"I don't know," and she started to sob.

"Come here, Annette, it's probably shock. I think at some time during the night we will all suffer from shock. It's only natural."

"I suppose the bus driver will drive down to Atalia and get word to the mountain rescue team, and then they will contact a helicopter, and at first light come looking for us."

"You're probably right, Robert, but where can a helicopter set down here. It's too rocky and the cliffs are too near the shore. The rotor blades will strike the rock."

"They could hover over the water while they lowered a harness and hauled us up, one at a time," suggested Robert.

"Sensible thinking, Robert."

"I'm not going back in that water!" shouted Annette.

"Pull yourself together. You are not hurt, you have a good figure, are fit, and a good swimmer. Do you want to stay behind?"

"Of course not!"

"Dear, you will feel better when your dress has dried and you are dressed again."

Just before the sun went down, and the survivors enjoyed its last warmth, they all dressed.

During the afternoon Robert collected old pieces of driftwood, which had been a long time ago washed up on the rocky beach. Now, with the dark descending, Robert borrowed Amos's cigarette lighter which, with luck, was in his trouser pocket, and being a gas lighter in its own sealed plastic unit, was unaffected by the lake water.

It took a few tentative attempts, but eventually the wood caught and a small fire blazed inside Robert's makeshift rock fire.

During the night, though it was not pitch black, it provided a central focus which cheered the four figures crouched under the stars.

"There won't be any wild animals, will there?" worried Annette.

"If there are any, dear, they will have more sense than to come down here. It's a dead end. The only predator is likely to be a shark and since this is fresh water there's not even a chance of that, so go to sleep."

"How can I go to sleep?"

"Just sit with your back against mine."

"Damn! I wish I had a cigarette."

"I agree with you there," said Amos.

"Mine are in my handbag at the bottom of the lake."

"Think yourself lucky it's only your handbag at the bottom of the lake."

"Go to sleep, Annette. Miranda will keep me company while I keep the fire alight," offered Robert.

"It's nice to have a strong dependable man about in a crisis. Thank you, Robert, I will have a little sleep. I am tired."

"What are you looking at?" asked Robert.

"The stars, darling. There are so many of them. They are beautiful in their own way. The only star I know, is that one over there, the Pole Star."

"Yes, as far as I know the Pole Star points the way north. At least in the northern hemisphere, because ships navigate by the Pole Star."

"You are clever, Robert."

"No, not really. All I know is that it is in the constellation Ursa Minor and that it lies very close to the north Celestial Pole so that it seems to remain motionless in the sky with all the other stars revolving around it."

"Do you think the helicopter will find us in the morning?"

"Of course, love. All they have to do is look below the road, at the bottom of the sheer drop, and that's the lake."

The night cooled down and a wind got up. Each of the four was glad of the heat of the fire, which Robert was feeding with driftwood.

"I missed my meal last night," said Robert. "My stomach's grumbling."

"Let's sing," said Miranda.

"What for?" complained her mother. "I'm cold!"

"Stop grumbling, Annette. It's only for one night. Think yourself lucky you have me and Robert's fire to keep off the cold."

"I'll start," said Robert, "and you can join in when you feel like it."

"I'm with you, Robert," said Amos.

After the singing they took turns at short naps until the pre-dawn glow cut across the lake. Slowly the disc of the sun lifted above the horizon which cheered the small group.

"Now, Annette, brace yourself to swim in the lake because that's the only way the rescue helicopter can get near us."

"What get soaked again!?"

"Once in the helicopter you will probably be wrapped in a warm blanket."

"Quiet! Quiet you two!"

"Don't tell me to be quiet, Miranda!"

"For once in your life, shut up, mother!"

"Well, really!"

"Annette, be quiet. What can you hear, Miranda?"

"A helicopter! The sound is bouncing off the cliff face."

"I can't hear anything?" said Robert.

"Climb up on the rocks and wave your shirts!"

"I haven't got a shirt?" complained Annette.

"Oh for goodness sake!" said Amos, and promptly ripped the bottom of Annette's dress off. "Now you have a flag!"

"Yes! I can hear it now!" exclaimed Robert.

A whirling blade from high overhead came into view. Then it was a helicopter. Then it blew a strong wind down and manoeuvred away from the cliff face and the rocks. At the door stood a winch man who signalled for them to swim out and take hold of the harness.

"Annette, you go first. Then you, Miranda, followed by Amos, and I will come last," offered Robert.

"O.K. We'll swim out one at a time, so that we spend the least time possible in the water," suggested, Amos.

"Good idea," said Robert.

The winch man lowered the harness until it floated in the water. Annette put her legs through the harness and before she knew it she was being winched to safety.

They followed in quick succession until all four were safely in the rescue helicopter. Then the pilot went vertical climbing up from the lake to where the barrier was broken on the road above.

"That's where," called out the winch man, over the noise of the helicopter's rotor, "you plunged off the side of the road. It is a miracle you weren't all killed!"

"I think the car took the full impact and the fact that we were all wearing seat belts saved our lives. If any one of us had been thrown out we would have been killed for sure."

An ambulance at Atalia was waiting for them and they were whisked off to Atalia Hospital, where they were wrapped in warm blankets and given hot soup. The incident from the night before had reached the news media and at the hospital a reporter appeared.

"John Menzies from the Spanish Gazette. I just want to take your photographs. You had an amazing escape plunging down five hundred feet to Lake Endorado. Is anybody hurt?"

"No, young man. Just bruised and hungry. We're not heroes or anything, just bloody lucky. God must have been watching over us. We were meant to survive."

"Can I take your names for my story?"

"Sure, I'm Robert Darling, a local artist and this is my girlfriend, Miranda, and her parents, Annette and Amos."

"How did the accident happen?"

"We were hit by the bus coming down from the village of Sigma. Is the bus driver all right?"

"Well, he's not hurt, the bus came down safely, but he's in shock. He's sedated in this hospital. Would you like to see him?"

"Yes, put the poor man out of his agony, he probably thinks he's killed us all."

"Juan, you have visitors," said John Menzies.

"Who said you could come in here? This man has suffered a trauma and is not to be disturbed," said a protective nurse.

"But Juan has nothing to blame himself for."

"What do you mean?" asked the custodial police officer.

"Officer, we were in the car that went over the side of the cliff. We were saved because the car landed on water and we swam to safety."

"You survived? All the way down to Lake Endorado?"

"Yes. So tell Juan, the bus driver, not to punish himself."

"You're all safe, no broken bones. That's amazing!" said the nurse.

"Senor Juan, sit up please. I have good news for you. These are the people who were in the red car that went over the cliff. Therefore, sir, there will be no charges against you, unless these people want to prosecute?" explained the officer.

"No, no, officer. It was an accident on a notorious bend on the side of the mountain."

"You're not hurt? I'm not going to prison? God bless you, senor! It's a miracle!"

"My name is Robert and this beautiful lady is Miranda. And these are her parents, Annette and Amos."

"But you are in blankets. You are hurt?"

"No, only our clothes are wet. The rescue helicopter picked us up from Lake Endorado. So Juan, please don't worry."

"I have been driving up and down that mountain road for ten years and never had an accident. I have asked the bus company many times for a mirror to be fitted on that dangerous bend. Now I will insist before there is another accident."

"I think, Juan, you should talk to this reporter, he is from the Spanish Gazette. You can tell your side of the story and, hopefully, get that dangerous bend improved."

While the crying-with-relief-bus-driver Juan was telling his story to John Menzies, Robert escorted Miranda and her parents to Reception to get their clothes back and prepare to go back home.

"Now," said Amos, "you have gone up in my estimation, young Robert. You saved my wife's life and that heroic act, I think, is enough for me to give my blessing to your relationship with my daughter, Miranda."

"Well, man to man, thank you, Amos," and they shook hands on an unsaid understanding that Robert could be trusted to look out for Miranda's welfare.

"One piece of luck, Miranda, I am the same as Robert and keep my wallet in my trouser pocket. So the next thing is to hire a car with the plastic."

"Yes, lucky that," said Robert. "You can always buy a new jacket."

"I don't think we shall go to the same hire company, yet, let's get back home first."

"Hertz, Rent-a-Car, that will do nicely," said Robert.

From his wallet, which was dry now, Amos removed his driver's licence identity card which, being plastic, was unaffected by the lake water.

"With air conditioning please," said Amos.

"Ye, senor, here are the keys. Is everything all right, the senora's dress is torn."

"We had a small accident. We are going home now to change."

"Have a nice day."

Back at El Estancia, there was a slight problem. Neither of them had keys. Miranda and Annette's handbags were at the bottom of the lake with Amos's jacket.

"What type of lock is it, Amos?"

"The best. A seven lever mortise lock and the door is solid wood with security hinges."

"Wait a minute," said Miranda, "Maria the maid may be in."

They rang the bell. They listened and could hear it reverberating inside the villa."

"There's only one thing for it. There isn't a back door so I'll have to smash a window."

"We'll wait here," said Miranda, "until you let us in."

Amos opened the shutters on a back window and peered in. There was no sign of Maria. He picked up a large terracotta planter and threw it at the window with considerable force. The glass splintered with a terrible stressed cracking sound.

Maria, in the garden behind the trees, was hanging out the washing. She jumped with fright and ran from the garden to see what had happened.

"What are you doing…? Senor Amos!"

"Sorry to frighten you, Maria, we are locked out. We have lost our keys."

"I have a set of keys."

"Why is the front door locked if you are at home?"

"Because, when I am out the back here in the garden, I don't know if anybody is calling at the villa, so I lock the door to make sure. I am responsible for your house. I am not just the maid but also the housekeeper."

"Very commendable. Could we have the keys please?"

"But how have you lost all the sets of the keys?"

"Come inside, Maria, and I will explain."

"I have to finish hanging the washing out."

"Here we are girls!"

"You have the keys?"

"Yes dear, Maria is in the garden hanging out the washing. We have her set."

"Why doesn't she hang the washing up on the line on the first floor verandah?"

"I've asked her that before. She says the villa faces south, so the verandah is in the shade, while the garden gets the sun."

"Lucky Maria was in the garden or I would have had another crack at that toughened glass, and shards could have flown all across the room," said Amos.

Maria came in carrying an empty laundry basket.

"Senor Amos, what have you done?"

"Don't worry, Maria, I will call a glazier," said Robert.

"And Senora Annette, your dress is almost torn in half?!"

"Come with me, Maria, and I will explain. Run me a warm bath."

In the bath Annette relaxed, enjoying the cleansing bath foam.

"Please sit on the bathroom chair, Maria, and I will tell you what happened."

"That's terrible, and after all that you sat on the lakeshore and waited for rescue? You were very brave."

"No, Maria, I was frightened, and glad that I was strapped in a back seat of the car so I couldn't see the terrible plunge to our deaths."

"Senor Robert was very brave."

"He was more than brave, he was a her. He dived down to save my life. Soaking in the bath it seems like a dream."

There was a knock at the door and Miranda brought a cup of coffee in.

"Thank you, Miranda, I'll have it in the dressing room. Would you like my scented bath water while it's still warm?"

"Yes, I will. See you in a few minutes."

In the lounge Maria found Amos and Robert, having whisky.

"Senor Robert!" And Maria gave him a kiss.

"What's that for?"

"For being such a good man to Senora Annette and looking after Miranda. You save people's lives."

"I'm a scruffy hero. I need to shave," said Robert.

"I'll join you."

In the luxury marbled bathroom the air was steamy and hung with the scent of roses. The ladies were dressing and could be heard talking excitably.

Using the double washbasins Amos and Robert shaved side by side.

"I reckon," smiled Robert, through soapsuds, "this is the second close shave I've had."

"I don't know about you, Robert, but I think a juicy steak is in order for lunch, washed down with a smooth bottle of red wine."

"I agree," said Robert.

"Let's go to St Lucia. I know a nice quality restaurant there."

"La Gracia Restaurant?"

"You know it?"

"Of course. You forget I live in Italia and go to St Lucia's Wednesday market every week with my paintings."

"Girls, we are going out for lunch."

"Oh good! Can Maria come?"

"What about the damaged window?"

"The glazier can't come till tomorrow. Robert has arranged for him to come in the morning, so don't worry."

"And you, Annette, don't your worry about the window either, we have our lives to celebrate," said a reassuring Amos.

"Yes, bubbly, would be nice!" laughed Miranda.

"Then bubbly it is, daughter," smiled Amos.

"Where are we going, darling?" asked Miranda.

"To St Lucia."

"To that nice restaurant, where we went before?"

"Yes, La Gracia Restaurant."

"Hello, Robert, what brings you here, it's not Wednesday?"

"Hi Suzanna. Miranda's father, Amos, is treating us."

"Celebration?"

"Sort of. Just glad to be alive!"

"Suzanna, champagne please, on ice!"

"Champagne! Welcome Senor Amos, Senora Annette. You are celebrating?" asked Zak, the restaurant owner.

"Yes. Yesterday we had a bad accident in the car. The car is a total wreck and at the bottom of Lake Endorado, but we all survived. Thank God!"

"A miracle! Miriam! Senor Amos is here, he is celebrating."

"Hello, Senor Amos, so pleased to see you. Your daughter, Miranda, comes here with Roberto the painter."

"Yes, so she tells me. A large jug of sangria please, Zak!"

"Meralda? Meralda! Come and join us. You remember me?" asked Miranda.

"Who is the old lady?" asked Amos.

"You don't remember, father? It is Maria's mother."

"Oh of course! We haven't met but I send payment every month for her daughter's services as my maid at El Estancia."

"Senora Meralda, I am Senor Amos from El Estancia. I am visiting my daughter, Miranda. We have come across from England, please come and join us."

"I don't want to be any trouble."

"Nonsense! You are Maria's mother, so I would like you to join us as my guest. I insist."

"Come on Meralda, come and join us," encouraged Miranda, taking Meralda by the arm.

"It is nice to meet you at last," said Amos, rising, and kissed the kindly lady on both cheeks.

"Zak! Another champagne glass please!"

"What are you celebrating, Senor Amos?"

"Dear lady, just being alive. A relief from a close shave."

"What is this close shave?"

"It means in English, a lucky escape from a terrible accident. The four of us survived so we are happy."

"Mother, please sit down, Amos is my employer he's honouring you by offering you champagne. I also want you to join us. I am a guest the same as you."

"In that case, Maria, I will."

"Champagne, Zak, for Senora Meralda!"

"Dear, there are six of us. I think another bottle is required," pointed out Annette.

"Another bottle please Zak."

"Miriam! Another bottle of champagne on ice for Senor Amos's party."

Zak's wife came out with a large jug of sangria.

"Shall I pour, Senor Amos?"

"No, Miriam, you go see to your other customers, I'll pour."

"I'll bring the champagne in ten minutes. It needs to stand in the ice bucket, Senor Amos."

"Thank you, Miriam, you go tend to you kitchen now. Zak can look after all of us."

"O.K. Senor Amos."

"Now Zak, we would like to order lunch. I want a steak with chips and salad.

"How would you like your steak cooking, Senor Amos?"

"Just rare and bloody."

"Yuk!" said Miranda. "How can you eat it uncooked, daddy?"

"Easy. That's how I like it."

"So do I," supported Robert.

"And for the ladies?"

"Oh, I'll have a chicken sandwich with a side salad," said Annette, "I have to watch my figure."

"Make that two, please, Zak, because I do not want any chips, they are not good for a slim figure," explained Miranda.

"I have to eat for two now," said Maria, "so I'll have chicken and chips with plum tomatoes."

"You have to eat for two? Maria, you are expecting a child. You're pregnant?" asked Amos.

"Yes, Senor Amos. You won't dismiss me from my job will you?"

"Good God no! You can be the keeper of my villa and bring along your baby if you want to, after it's born."

"Thank you, Senor Amos."

"No need to thank me, you're a valuable worker."

"I am?"

"Of course, you are honest and reliable. I cannot just pop across from England to check on my villa, so I rely on you. Congratulations on your forthcoming event."

"Zak, more champagne for my maid, Maria!"

"Senor Amos, are you trying to get me drunk?"

"No, no. I am just trying to include you in the family celebrations, so that you know you are appreciated."

"If you don't mind I'll just have a glass of sangria."

"Very wise, Maria," said Miranda. "We don't want the baby being drunk, do we?"

"What will you call your baby?" asked Annette.

"If it's a girl, I would like to call her Miranda, but if it's a boy I will let Marco choose because he dearly wants a son. He'll probably name him after a footballer."

Meralda spoke up. "What about Zak for a boy's name?"

"I don't know, mother."

"I am the boy's grandmother, so what do I know?"

"Mother, it may be a girl. And my pregnancy is only in the early stages, anyway."

"I agree, Meralda, us mothers should have a say. I wish my daughter, Miranda, would have a child. I would like to enjoy my grandchild before I am too old."

"Mother you are expecting too much. One minute you say don't marry again too quickly, the next you say where is my grandchild."

"That was before I met Robert."

"You mean you approve of him?"

"Just because I don't say so, doesn't mean I don't approve. And, anyway, your father has taken to Robert, like a duck to water."

"Everybody back to El Estancia!" called out Amos. "And Zak, two bottles of your best red wine!"

On the private beach at Seagull Cove, the foursome, plus Maria, were invited to wine, sand and sun by Amos. They were all changed into their swimming costumes, Miranda in her very sexy red bikini and Maria in her canary yellow one-piece. The surprise in the party was Annette, having a figure similar to Miranda's in her polka dot bikini. The men donned Bermuda shorts in two-tone blue.

"Put the towels, Robert, by the base of the rocks, then we can sit on the sand and rest back against the rocks."

"Maria, pass me the beach bag. I'll open the wine while it's cool," said Robert.

They assembled around the opened bottle and Robert poured in to the plastic cups except Maria, who only drank modestly.

The day was warm, Amos and Annette sat side by side holding hands. Feeling happy under the warming Spanish sun, they supported each other until they, in turn, dropped off to sleep on their respective towels.

Being younger, Robert and Miranda, fared better from the previous night's sleep deprivation, and therefore, paddled out into the refreshing waters of the Mediterranean. They frolicked in the warm shallows splashing one another like two playful children, before wading further out to swim.

Maria, contented, took the bread out of her beach bag and went down to the waterline, where seagulls stood on rocks, while watching the sea for tasty tit-bits to swim by. She threw pieces of broken bread up into the sky at her usual feeding place. Being used to the 'bird lady' the gulls quickly gathered, wheeling back and forth across Maria's bit of sky, catching the offered bread in midair. She returned to the rocks where Annette and Amos were sleeping, and sunbathed. It wasn't often Maria was invited to Senor Amos's private beach so she made the best of it. The second bottle of wine stood opened in the sand, and she thought it would be a waste to leave it to spoil in the sun, so she drank it, what was left of it, straight from the bottle.

Amos and Annette slept on under the warming sun. Robert and Miranda came out of the sea both invigorated and the spark of romance rekindled after the trauma of the last twenty-four hours.

"Come here, I love you! I love your body," said Robert.

"I know that look! Not on the beach!" laughed Miranda, and ran along the shoreline towards the cove.

Robert chased after her, and she ventured further than she had before, coming to a sea cove. She laughed and ran in.

"Did you know this place existed?"

"Of course. I walk here sometimes. It's perfectly safe; the sea is only shallow in here and is warmed on the sand. Further more it is private. All you can see from here is the open sea, unless someone arrives by boat."

She kissed him meaningfully and he removed her bikini top and wrapped his muscular flesh around her smooth soft yielding body. She stood there and let him seduce her. She felt safe, always, in his embrace. He removed her bikini bottoms and kicked his Bermuda shorts off, throwing them both onto the sand. She felt his urgent erection pressing against her soft flesh.

She instinctively reached down and encircled his engorged length with her small hand. He brought her quickly to orgasm, so that she lubricated copiously.

He picked her slight form up in his strong arms and she wrapped her spread thighs around his waist and guided him in. He took her Indian style, cupping her buttocks as he thrust into her waiting flesh, her breasts pushing into his chest. He bent his head, lifted her up higher and sucked greedily on her swollen and erect nipples. Then they kissed as he did his will, her will, in her.

Exhausted but happy Robert and Miranda laid down on the sand and cuddled up together and slept in the safety of the sea-cave.

Outside in Seagull Cove Amos and Annette were sound asleep lying on their towels.

Maria was happy and relaxed because she was partly inebriated, not being used to alcohol. With a smile on her face she was using the plastic drinking cups to make sand castles. Then she took one of the cups and went down to the shoreline to collect shells washed up by the light tide. Once her cup was full she walked back up the wide stretch of the beach, back to where the base of the cliff was.

Amos and Annette, having enjoyed a much needed nap, awoke.

"What have you got there, Maria?"

"Oh, you are awake now, Senor Amos?"

"Yes, I feel much better now."

"Seashells, I have collected from the shore."

"Good. It's good to be child-like again; it makes you remember the simple things in life. The world today is one big rush of technology."

"I don't know what you mean, Senor Amos?"

"Business, Maria. The world spins on the axle of business. You come from the mountain village of Sigma, which is visited by happy tourists, so you miss the stress. You will soon become a mother and dedicate your time and probably your whole life to raising a family. But remember you must continue to work for me part-time, because that will give you an interest outside your family."

"Oh I see. It is true, I only know the village of Sigma, which is enough for me, because I am happy as I am now."

"Yes, you are right, Maria; if more people could be content with less, we would have a happier world and there would be more peace."

"Perhaps, Senor Amos, more people could live in the country and enjoy a slower rate of life?"

"If it were so it would be true but, unfortunately, the opposite is happening. All across the world, as far as China and Indonesia, the population is migrating from the country into the cities."

"Why is that, Senor Amos?"

"Because the lure of the city is work, and work means wealth. In the rural parts of China, especially in the north, there is a great deal of poverty."

"What is poverty, Senor Amos?"

"It is the life of very poor, where a man may have ten children and he can't afford to feed them all. There is a shortage of food, lack of clean water to drink and no proper housing, which often means sending out children only ten years of age to find work to feed themselves. The gap between rich city dwellers and the rural poor is ever widening as the peasants who work the land are leaving their shanty homes in the hillsides and move towards the cities."

"Why does man give his wife ten children if he can't afford to feed them?"

"Many reasons: boredom; nothing to do but copulate; ignorance; poverty. He can't afford contraception or knows no better, so he just keeps breeding."

"Then they need education and financial support. Education to learn to raise themselves above their subsistence level of existence."

"Correct, Maria, who is going to educate them?"

"The church? They have missionaries don't they?"

"True, Christians from the United Kingdom do go to India and China to some of the poorest regions. They teach about a moral life, having a spirit to believe in themselves, and in particular, an education in contraception, especially for the younger girls so that they do not get trapped into having an unwanted pregnancy or a family too soon."

"I'm glad I live in Spain," said Maria.

"Yes, I agree. Western Europe is more civilised than the Middle East or the Far East."

"And I am so glad that Amos is a successful professional. I suppose I live a privileged life being the wife of a Consultant Architect," said Annette, hugging onto Amos.

"Where are Robert and my daughter?" asked Amos.

"They went for a swim as far as I know," said Maria.

"Come on, Annette, let's go down to the waterline and see if we can find them."

"Well, they are not swimming, so they must be on the beach?" said Annette.

"Yes, you're right. Look! Two pairs of footprints, one large and heavy and the other light and small."

"Let's follow them," said Annette.

"They lead right into the cove, and then disappear at the waterline here?"

"Perhaps they ventured into this sea cave, though I don't see why, there's no sunshine in here?"

"Come on, let's have a look. I was young once and would investigate caves just to see what's in them."

Annette called, "Robert! Miranda!" but only the echo came back.

Then sharp-eyed, Amos, saw their forms in the shadowy interior. They lay together in each other's arms, asleep and naked.

"I don't like it in here," said Annette, "it's dark in this cave."

"All right, dear, I'll meet you outside."

Amos picked up their swimming costumes and placed them, gently, strategically, on their exposed private areas so as not to embarrass them when they woke up. Then he strode the half dozen yards to the shallow water inside the cave and scooped up a double handful. He dumped the water on their faces and they awoke.

"What the… is going on!?" demanded, Robert.

"It wasn't me?" said an awoken, Miranda.

"As long as you are safe, I'll go back to the beach now."

"Daddy? Daddy!" And she scrambled for her bikini which luckily lay against her.

"What are you doing in here?"

"Not as much as you, as it turns out," laughed, Amos. "Your mother was worried about you because you were last seen swimming out to sea by Maria."

They were dressed by now.

"Don't worry, Miranda, your mother never saw you because she was wearing her designer sunglasses. And anyway it's quite dark in here so I didn't see much either."

"Thank you, Amos," said Robert.

"What are you thanking, father, for?"

"Because he threw our costumes across to us, sent your mother away and kept his distance."

"What about the water that woke us up?"

"He probably threw that on us at a distance and, anyway, what are you ashamed of, you pose for me nude, don't you?"

"Well, yes, but that's for your eyes only!"

"Your father has seen your full length nude portrait so there is nothing to hide. And it could have been embarrassing."

"What do you mean?"

"What if your parents had come in while we were making love?"

Even in the shadowy interior with the half-light from the shallow water reflecting off the cavern roof, Robert could see Miranda flush red with embarrassment.

"I need to go into the sea to wash myself, your seeds are leaking out of me."

Thankfully Amos had disappeared from view, so Miranda felt more confident now, and relieved ran into the Mediterranean Sea and frolicked in the sun.

"Well, have you found them?" asked Annette.

"They weren't lost. They were having private time together in the back of the cavern."

"Men! All they think about is sex!"

"Tomorrow," said Robert, "is Wednesday, market day in the village of St Lucia, so Miranda and I will leave you now and return to my place."

"Goodbye for now, Miranda, see you in a few days," said Amos.

"Maria, while, Senor Amos and I are at El Estancia for the next two weeks, you may have a holiday. Where is it you come from again?"

"The village of Sigma, Senora Annette."

"You go home, we will be all right."

"Senor Amos, will I still have my cleaning job?"

"Of course, Maria, don't worry. I will still pay you to retain your maid's service."

"Thank you, Senor Amos, then I shall go home to my husband, Marco."

Back at 'The Impressionist', Robert and Miranda came back to reality with a bump, and Robert became businesslike.

"Come on, Miranda, help me wrap some of these canvasses ready for the morning's market."

"What about if we load the car this evening so we could have more time in the morning. You know, get up later?"

"Sleepy head! I know for you it's an early start, but we can't risk being broken into, and I can't afford the risk."

"You have crime in this street?"

"Oil paintings loaded in the back of a car, wrapped up as parcels, could be thought of as something else more valuable. In the mind of a thief they represent money. Maybe drug money."

"Yes, I know drugs are a problem, and I'm not that naïve that I don't know criminals deal in drugs. But I didn't know it was a problem in Spain."

"With tourism comes money and that attracts dealers out to make a quick buck."

"O.K. so I promise to get up early, but we can at least wrap the canvasses ready for loading?" asked Miranda.

"Sure that's what I suggested, except yours, that's not for sale. It goes in my bedroom in pride of place, above the bed."

"You're a rude bugger."

"Oh no I'm not. When I have you in bed I can look at two of you for double pleasure."

"Isn't one of me enough?"

"As the saying goes, 'a bird in the hand is worth two in the bush', don't you agree?"

"I couldn't possibly comment, I am not a man."

"Am I glad of that," he said, reaching out to fondle her.

"Get your hands off, you've had your share for today."

"Yes, and I enjoyed it. It was rather rude and exciting in that cave."

"What if somebody had come in?" asked Miranda.

"They almost did, your father."

"Well, at least he kept his distance when he discovered us and left quickly."

"Not too soon as far as I am concerned. Being caught by your parents while you are in the nude is not funny."

"Oh come off it, it's not as if we were doing anything. And he did throw our costumes over us when he discovered us."

"Fat lot of good my bikini bottoms are for covering anything up."

"Then wear a more decent costume."

"Why should I, I have a sexy body and like to show it off."

"Perhaps, because I don't want other men ogling you?"

"You get jealous?"

"Yes! But only because I love you and you are my girl. I mean you are not just a casual girlfriend, we are in a relationship. You are my partner now."

"I'm glad to hear it. Just one thing though, you are never to take me for granted."

"Sex kitten, how can I? You are so beautiful and very loving. I will always worship you."

"Always is a long time?"

"Then I hope we are together for a long time. How long have your parents been married?"

"I'm not exactly sure, but I think mummy said something about being married twenty-five years this summer."

"Perhaps that's why they have come out to El Estancia this particular year, you know, to celebrate their Silver Wedding Anniversary."

Early in the morning Robert and Miranda arrive at the village of St Lucia, as do the other traders. Miranda is in the routine now of putting the canvas roof on and unpacking and displaying the canvasses. Miranda had brought along from El Estancia a pot-plant display table onto which she could place her paper cups and two bottles of wine taken from Amos's cellar.

"Did you pinch that wine, Miranda?"

"No, of course not. I explained to daddy how I got the customers to buy and he said I had a good business head, so he said I could take two bottles with his blessing."

"I think, because he loves you, you can wrap him around your little finger."

"It works doesn't it?"

"Yes, Miranda, darling, and I love you for it."

As usual, it was quiet on the market in Robert's stall until ten o'clock, though the locals were out in force as usual before it got busy. They had first pick of the fruit and vegetables.

About ten thirty an earlier, light rain shower moved away, the sun burst forth with more gusto, and the prospect of a bright sunny summer day cheered traders and tourists alike.

Miranda went into her 'wine-routine' and with her gorgeous looks it wasn't long before she made her first sale.

One sale attracted another and after a few successes a gentleman wearing a heavy gold chain and a very smart designer jacket approached Robert.

"You are Robert Darling?"

"Yes, Senor, I am the artist, Robert Darling."

"To satisfy my curiosity, please sign your name in my notebook."

"Of course, Senor."

"Please, Robert Darling, call me plain, Teddy, I am English. Yes, the signature is yours. What would you say to displaying your work in London?"

"Back home in England?"

"It's the only London I know, Robert."

But I have left England behind and come to work in the sun. Why should I move back to London?"

"Two reasons: first, your work is too good for this backwater, and second, I can make you rich."

"I'm listening."

"I have a gallery in Central London. The artists who display in my gallery sell their works for tens and hundreds of thousands if the right buyer comes along. Put simply, rich collectors come to my gallery looking to spot new talented artists."

"And what's in it for you? You aren't going to display my works for nothing."

"Very shrewd. For money that's why. You get a very good price, enjoy a little fame, and I take twenty percent."

"Suppose I stay in Atalia and send you the paintings?"

"That's no good. It is a condition of displaying in The Arch that you are available for promotions. That means living in London."

"What do you mean, be available for promotions?"

"Publicity, the press. My new discoveries, of which you are one, will be featured in the London papers – The Times and The Guardian at the very least. Art critics will be invited to view your work. Don't worry, if you are selected to display in The Arch you will be looked upon favourably."

"Sounds too good to be true, but then there's the expense of living in London. I can't afford a house at London prices, and then there's the dreary weather."

"Accommodation I can help with. With other artists you will have a flat in The Block, with every possible convenience, at a nominal rent. Rent will not be a problem once you have sold one or two of your paintings. The weather I can do nothing about. But you could rent out your present house in Spain, and go back periodically for a holiday to enjoy the weather?"

"How long have I got to think about it?"

"When do you pack up your stall?"

"About four thirty to five o'clock."

"Good. This is my telephone number. It is a car phone, so I will get your call when you ring me at five o'clock with your decision."

Chapter Four

Amos, at El Estancia, backed Teddy's idea of Robert going to London to make a name for himself. He took care of the renting of The Impressionist and arranged, through a small fee, for Maria his maid to service Robert's house.

At Heathrow Airport Robert and Miranda were met by a chauffeur holding a sign which read, 'Robert Darling and Miranda', in the arrivals hall.

"I am Robert Darling and this is my partner, Miranda."

"I am Max, your driver. I am instructed by Mr Rosenburgh to ask for identification."

"Here, Max, our passports."

"Very beautiful photograph, Miss Miranda. The car is outside."

Max was obviously a minder as well. He was about two hundred and forty pounds and not an inch of fat. Robert was unsure of his age, but he reckoned the black man was in his thirties.

"Max, who is Mr Rosenburgh?"

"You met him in Spain. Teddy Rosenburgh. Mr Rosenburgh is my employer, a big shot in the fine art world. He knows anybody who is worth knowing. Sit back and relax, enjoy a drink from the cocktail cabinet if you like. The traffic is hell in Central London, but I know a few cut-throughs – just follow the taxis."

Max was right, the traffic in London was heavy but Robert and Miranda took Max's advice and sat back and relaxed. The flight from Spain had been delayed two hours because of a work-to-rule by Spanish Air Traffic Controllers, so they helped themselves to a drink, sank back into the luxurious white hide seats and listened to the classical music.

The glass screen to the cab was up but they could see Max gesticulating to drivers who got in his way and he frequently sounded his horn.

"Remind me never to get on the wrong side of Max. He's a mountain of a man. I wouldn't want to run into his car."

The car glided to a halt and Max opened the door.

"Here you are, Mr Darling, sir. Would you like a hand with your cases?"

"I'll manage," said Robert.

"That would be very nice, Max," said Miranda.

They entered a glass and chrome foyer. The security man waved him through and handed him a key.

"Welcome, Mr Darling, sir."

"How comes, Max, the doorman knows my name?"

"Because you were expected. Mr Rosenburgh is very thorough in his dealings. Pat at the desk is more than a doorman, he's in charge of security. This is your flat, number fourteen, on the top floor. Once you have unpacked you will need to go out a get a portrait photograph."

"What's that for, Max?"

"Your identity card. Every artist in The Block carries one. You will be in The Arch, and everybody who enters there must show his identity card. Goodbye for now."

"Will we see you again, Max?"

"Sure will. When you have your first exhibition, you will be called for and I'll chauffeur you to The Arch."

"O.K. Thanks. Am I supposed to tip you?"

"Wait until you have made some money, Mr Darling."

The 'flat' as it turned out was a penthouse. With the blinds raised there was a glass-eyed view of the city. There was a lounge, a neat kitchen, a bedroom with nothing much in it except a substantial double bed, above which there were mirror tiles. The most impressive room, facing south, with all glass windows, was the studio. It contained easels, mounted canvasses of various sizes and a whole selection of brushes and paints.

"Our Teddy Rosenburgh has been busy buying. I think he means business."

"Robert, we must start work immediately. Unpack your case of folios and let's see what drawings you've got. Teddy said he very much admires beautiful women. How about me, head and bust?"

"But you will be seen in public?"

"Yes. I could be come famous. Just think, I could be hanging on the wall of some millionaire's mansion."

"But what if you get into the papers, I mean big time, for example, The Times or The Guardian?"

"Then maybe I could become a model. You know, go to fashion shows and wear the latest designer clothes for famous fashion houses."

"Do you know anything about being a model?"

"No. But your portrait of me doesn't lie. The camera catches the truth. All I have to do is pose, just like when I sell paintings on St Lucia's market."

"I have to say, Miranda, your confidence has grown tenfold since I met you."

"You met me at a bad time. I was grieving over Edward."

"He would have been so proud of you. All right, I'll paint you again and hang you in The Arch."

After a month of working in The Block Robert Darling, assisted by Miranda, was ready to exhibit his works.

Teddy Rosenburgh informed his clients of the forthcoming exhibition and invited them by ticket only. The Times carried a short article accompanied by a recent photograph of Robert Darling.

Max called for them in the limousine and he personally transferred all the canvasses from Flat Fourteen to the stretched limousine. At The Arch Max hung all the canvasses on the prepared chains and hook, then he photographed every one of Robert's paintings and handed the camera to Teddy Rosenburgh.

"Now, Robert, relax, have a coffee. In about thirty minutes the gallery will open and The Press will arrive first. Max will be on the door to let the rich and famous in by ticket only.

When the photographers take your picture I want you to put your arm protectively around your girlfriend Miranda, because beauty always attracts the wealthy."

"Do I have to do anything?"

"No, just be yourself, and follow my introductions. The portrait of Miranda, head and bust, is bound to be a hit. I will invite the highest offer. Don't be surprised if it goes for half a million or more."

"Pounds Sterling?"

"Of course, Robert, you have a rare talent, otherwise I would never have had you invited to exhibit at The Arch."

The Press arrived.

"This way, Miss Miranda. Now pout. Look directly at the camera. Now a full length shot. Thank you, you're a natural on camera."

The clients arrived and they, to a man, were bowled over by Miranda's beauty.

"How much for Miranda's portrait, gentlemen?"

"You have no price on it, or even a price guide?" queried Sir Arthur Bolton.

"Make me a bid, Arthur."

"Two hundred thousand?"

"Four hundred thousand," said Sir Clive Jenkins.

"Half a million!" declared the Duke of Rochester.

"Seven hundred and fifty thousand!" said Lord Beacon, aloud.

"Sold to Lord Beacon, for seven hundred and fifty thousand!" accepted Teddy Rosenburgh.

"Are they talking pounds?" asked Miranda, of Robert, in a whisper.

"Yes, darling, I've just earned eighty percent of seven hundred and fifty thousand. Which is six hundred thousand pounds!"

"Young lady have you ever thought of a career as a glamour model?" asked Sir Arthur Bolton.

"Not really, well not seriously."

"Well, with your looks and a body to kill for, I recommend you do. That dress you are wearing shows every gorgeous contour of your body. If you didn't have this very talented painter I would marry you."

"Thank you for the compliment but I am only twenty-three years old, you are well into middle age."

"She's got you there, Arthur."

"Then you, Clive, at fifty, have no chance either, and I don't blame her, she's too beautiful for you, you letch."

"I always admire a thing of beauty, whether it be a work of art, a ceramic, a jewel, a fine painting or a gorgeous body," said Sir Arthur Bolton, with a smile.

The following morning Robert was featured in the newspapers and there was a prominent photograph of Miranda's portrait. The papers asked, 'Who is this mysterious Miranda, is she the new Madonna?'

"Well, you have fame already, Robert."

"The papers are talking about you too, Miranda, as the new beauty," said Robert. "Do you realise, on that one portrait of you, we are rich?"

"We?"

"Of course, what's mine is yours."

"I love you, Robert, even when you are rich you are willing to share with me."

The doorbell rang.

"I'll get it!" said Miranda.

"Miss Miranda."

"Max?"

"I have a gentleman and a lady to see you. Here is a note of introduction from Teddy Rosenburgh, so they have been checked out."

A light flashed in her face, capturing her in a natural pose, encapsulating her beauty.

"Please read the note," said a very well dressed lady in her thirties. "My name's Pauline, this is my card. I am the Chief Editor of Vogue Magazine."

"Clarence, put the camera away a minute, we haven't been invited in yet."

"Sorry, Pauline, but she's as beautiful as her portrait."

"Max is right. You have been vetted. Come in."

"Robert, this is the Chief Editor of Vogue Magazine."

"Vogue? What do they want?"

"Your wife, Robert, is truly beautiful. Forgive me, may I introduce myself. Clarence, here is my features photographer. I am here to do a photographic shoot."

"Brian, bring the equipment in."

"Hello, Robert, I am Pauline, pleased to meet you. May I sit down? I would like to do a feature on you and Miranda. Could you tell me how you met and a little about your painting? Don't let Clarence my photographer bother you, his assistant Brian will set up the lighting equipment."

"You're a natural," said Clarence. "Thank you very much. We would like to put you on the front cover of Vogue."

"That's my decision, Clarence," said Pauline.

"Well, dear, is she a beauty, the face to launch a thousand ships?"

"Yes. Definitely yes! I would like you to sign this contract, Miranda."

"My girl signs nothing until I have read it," said a protective Robert.

"Good, I am glad to hear it. Here, I brought a spare copy along for you to read."

"A hundred thousand pounds to go on the front cover with the rights to further photographic shoots with fashion houses to be featured in Vogue over following weeks?"

"What's the catch?" asked Robert.

"To be frank," said the Chief Editor, "time. It will take up quite a lot of Miranda's time, including weekends at fashion shows and fund raising events."

"Can I do it, Robert?"

"You can do whatever you like, Miranda, provided it doesn't impinge on our relationship too much."

"In that case, Pauline, I'll sign."

"When we have published the next edition of Vogue and have distributed the copies you will be paid. Do you want to give me your bank details now or would you like the office to deal with that?"

"We have a joint account, the money will go into that."

"Very well. How old fashioned of you. Brian, you can pack up now, we have all we need."

"Thank you for your time," said Clarence, addressing Robert.

"Thank God they have gone. That Clarence gives me the creeps," said Robert. "I think he is effeminate."

"You mean a homosexual?"

"Probably, I didn't like the way he kept looking at me, like some love-sick puppy. His handshake was wet and pathetic."

When the next issue of Vogue hit the shelves several product representatives phoned into the office and Pauline, the Chief Editor, at Vogue was bombarded with offers for Miranda, their new Cover Girl.

"Hello, Miranda, this is Pauline, at Vogue. Could you come into the office today, I want to put some ideas to you."

"What sort of ideas?"

"How would you like to become a fashion model and endorse beauty products for famous names?"

"I'll have to talk it through."

"Yes, you will. I'll send a car for you at eleven o'clock. Can you be ready?"

"O.K. What do I wear?"

"Relax, darling, this is not a photographic shoot but a business meeting. If it makes you feel better bring along Robert, your painter."

"All right, I'll be ready for eleven."

"Good girl, see you later."

"How are you today, Miranda?"

"Very surprised that other companies should be interested in me. I'm nobody. I know I have a good body, but that's all."

"Correction, Miranda. You were a nobody out of the ordinary yesterday, but today you have been launched onto the beauty stage of life. How does that make you feel?"

"Awestruck, I think."

"At least you are honest and that adds to your charm and beauty. Now you will need my protection from the promoters of brand names."

"What do you mean, protection?"

"Darling, it's a jungle out there. Every big name will be after you to promote their beauty products. Don't go with any of them to your home address or you will be pestered to death and have no private life."

"What about Max, Teddy Rosenburgh's chauffeur, can't he keep them out?" asked Robert.

"He can if that is your wish. The security man at The Block, will not let anybody in unless you tell him to."

"I know Max well. He chauffeurs for me if I ask him, but to be polite, I have to ask Teddy first."

"How comes you know Max?" asked Robert.

"My job, as Editor-in-Chief of Vogue, makes it my business to know anybody who is famous, and Teddy Rosenburgh and his man Max, come with the territory."

"So how do I go about selecting a company to represent?"

"Miranda, I will negotiate on your behalf, then you will get a fair deal."

Estée Lauder, are one of the most famous names in the beauty business with their face creams as are Chanel with expensive perfumes. They have both made approaches to me today, and I have said you are contracted to me. So would you like me to draw up a contract for you?"

"No thank you!" exclaimed Robert.

"Robert!?" gasped, Miranda.

"Darling, I love you, and therefore I am determined to protect your interests. Vogue are only out to make money out of you. If you are in Vogue promoting the Estée Lauder products, or anybody else's come to that, Vogue will be making money off your back. It is much better if I act as your agent."

"To be fair, Robert, I spotted Miranda," said Pauline.

"No you didn't. I painted Miranda in a full length naked pose in my studio in Spain. Then the Press pounced on Miranda's natural beauty at The Arch, when Miranda and I were exhibiting our paintings, thanks to Teddy Rosenburgh."

"Well, Miranda is still contracted to Vogue to pose for photographic shoots."

"Sure, Pauline, I'll be glad to pose for Clarence your senior photographer."

"Good. But think on other 'doors' I can open for you."

"Goodbye, Pauline," said Robert.

Outside in the street Robert phoned Teddy Rosenburgh.

"Teddy, this is Robert Darling, may I have the services of Max to introduce Miranda to Estée Lauder etc."

"Sure, but it's unusual for the model to make a direct approach. It's normal practice to make appointments via a manager or an agent."

"I've told Pauline, at Vogue, that I shall be Miranda's agent."

"You're a brave boy. How did you get away from her so quickly?"

"I just don't like her, I walked out."

"Bravo! She may cut you off from Vogue."

"No problem. First of all I have a contract for Miranda to be paid for the front cover of Vogue, and after that I don't need her, Miranda is a natural beauty."

"Where are you?"

"Outside the Head Office of Vogue."

"Stay where you are. I'll send Max round with the limousine."

"Thanks, Teddy, see you later."

"Good luck, not that I think you need it."

"Hi Max!"

"Where to, Miss Miranda?"

"The London office of Estée Lauder."

"With your face on the front cover of Vogue I would say, Miss Miranda, the world is your oyster."

"Have you an appointment, Miss? The Editor doesn't see anybody without an appointment."

"I know your just doing your job, but this is me on the front cover of Vogue."

"Oh, you're the new face! May I have your autograph?"

"Sorry Miss Miranda, I'll ring the Editor's Office straight away."

"Who?"

"Miss Miranda, the beautiful lady on the front cover of Vogue. She's here now in the foyer. Shall I send her up?"

"No, I'll send Jackie down, the Assistant Editor, to collect her. Is she with her agent?"

"Excuse me sir, are you Miss Miranda's agent?"

"That's right. Tell your Editor I am her manager."

"May I have your name please?"

"What do you want to know my name for?"

"For security clearance, sir. Lots of people off the streets want to get into Vogue."

"The name's Robert."

"Thank you, sir."

"Miss Swanson, Miranda is with her Manager, Robert."

"Thank you for the names, keep them talking. My Assistant Editor will be straight down."

"The Editor will see you now; the Assistant Editor, Jackie, is on her way down to collect you."

"Thank you," said Robert.

"I'm quite excited," said Miranda.

"Let me do the talking when it comes to money."

"What do I say?"

"Just be yourself and exude loads of naivety and charm. The dress you are wearing really shows off your figure. I bet you could easily get a job as a super model for a famous designer, naming your own price."

"Hello, Miranda and Robert? My name's Jackie. I am the Publicity Manager. Miss Swanson is looking forward to meeting you."

They ascended several floors in a nicely carpeted lift, which was silent. The doors opened and they stepped out into a carpeted corridor.

"This way, please," said Jackie.

The door read, 'Marketing Director'. It was opened by a young lady.

"Please come in. Thank you for coming," said a lady in immaculate make-up. "Tea or coffee?"

"Tea will be fine."

Daphne, who was Miss Swanson's Personal Assistant, smiled on, Robert and Miranda. "Sugar?"

"No thanks, just milk," replied Robert.

"Nice to meet you. I am Felicity Swanson, Marketing Director for Estée Lauder. It's unusual for a client to approach me directly. We usually pursue the client but as you are the Cover Girl for Vogue I was intrigued. If I may say so, your photograph does you justice, you are a natural beauty."

"That's why we are here," said Robert. "Miranda will make a great ambassador for Estée Lauder beauty products."

"I can see why you are her manager. You don't believe in a middle man, am I right?"

"Exactly so!"

"Yes, we can promote you as the face of Estée Lauder but it will have to be a new product. Your photograph will have to be on the new package, and then there's the point-of-sale display material to promote distribution. That requires full size posters of you on advertising hoarding. You will become a public face. Are you prepared to go public?"

"Well I'm already the Cover Girl for Vogue. Isn't that public?"

"It is and it isn't. With Estée Lauder we will feature you in different ladies magazines, in famous stores and on television."

Felicity pushed the button on her intercom. "Jackie, would you come in please."

"Miranda, Robert, this is Jackie, who is our Publicity Manager."

"We met in the lift."

"Jackie this is the new face of Estée Lauder. How would you like to promote her?"

"That's great, Miranda, you will have a busy but famous life. My job is to get you as much publicity as possible. That can mean Estée Lauder face creams, a hair makeover and a shopping trip for a completely new wardrobe. We will represent you from head to toe. Once you are launched many fashion houses will be after you to model their clothes. Are you sure you are ready to become public property?"

"I'll look after her," said Robert.

"Felicity, our Research and Development Department have put forward a new product. It's a scented moisturiser. I've only just received this sample. Do you think Miranda here is the right person to promote it?"

"If she is, it's good timing. I could market a new product with a new face, but first of all it has to have a name."

"May I make a suggestion?" asked Miranda.

"By all means, Miranda. It's a good thing if you can identify with the product from the outset."

"I think something natural and naïve would be appropriate. Like, 'Virgin's Blush'."

"Virgin's Blush? The desire for young skin? Yes, I can see it, Virgin's Blush! What do you think, Jackie?"

"It's unusual, it makes you think of bridal times. The first time to become a woman. 'Don't be the bridesmaid, be the bride with Virgin's Blush'. How's that for publicity?"

"Yes," said Felicity, "I like it. It conjures up the picture of a radiant bride. Every woman wants to be more beautiful, the radiant one."

"You want to call it, 'Radiant One'?"

"No, Jackie, I like Virgin's Blush. I am going to make the unusual step of taking Miranda through the General Office, if Miranda's agreeable?"

"What do you want me to do?"

"Just go through the General Office with Jackie, and she will introduce you as the new face of Estée Lauder's Virgin's Blush. Smile, be yourself, I want their reaction to your desirable perfect looks."

"O.K. Jackie, go for it!"

"Now, Robert, while Miranda is out of the way, shall we talk business?"

"That's why I am here."

"It will have to be an 'unfolding contract', which is to say, payment will depend on how the new product, Virgin's Blush, performs. I have to budget for promotions, packaging, displays and broad-spread advertising. This is good for you and Miranda, because the more I call on your time the more Miranda will be involved and consequently paid."

"How much will she be paid?"

"I can't tell you that at the moment. I have to draw up a multi-million pound marketing package, which will be distributed worldwide."

"Instead of a fee, how about a commission based on sales?"

"We don't normally do that at Estée Lauder, we usually offer a fixed contract."

"Out of the question. In the beauty world Miranda is the best discovery since sliced bread. It's a commission or nothing."

"It's possible, but how much are we talking?"

"One percent of sales!"

"I don't know, one pound in a hundred sounds very greedy. I'll have to have a Board Meeting of all the Directors to agree to that."

"Ask your Accounts Director whether one percent is greedy?"

"I'll ask. Give me a minute."

"Kevin, could you come into my office for a minute."

"What's up?"

"A contract deal with a client."

"I'll come straight across."

"Kevin, this is Robert. He's the Manager for the new face of Vogue, Miranda."

"The girl I saw in the General Office?"

"That's the one."

"Hello, Robert, how can I help?"

"Your Marketing Director here says it's unusual for Estée Lauder to offer a client a percentage of sales in place of a fixed fee contract."

"That's true. How much are you asking?"

"One percent of sales, and no fees."

"Well, let me think. What product is Miranda, going to endorse?"

"A scented moisturiser which should sell for about £19.99p."

"Which one is it?"

"Miranda has just chosen her own name for it. 'Virgin's Blush'. What do you think?"

"Catchy. Twenty pound price tag, that's twenty pence per sale. I think the Board could agree to that. And no other charges?"

"No other charges," said Robert.

"Draw up a contract, Felicity. You have my support."

"You sure, Kevin?"

"Sure, draw it up and be sure to sleep on it."

"O.K. Robert, in theory we agree to your request. We will be in touch. Nice to meet you. Give us a few days."

"Well, Jackie, how did you get on?"

"Brilliant, Felicity. Virgin's Blush is a hit with the girls."

"You look positively radiant, Miranda. If you can have this much effect on the girls just walking through the office, how much more will the public react with my marketing package?"

"I think Virgin's Blush is a hit!" exclaimed Jackie.

"They like the name then?" asked Miranda.

"Love it!"

"Looks like we are a winner then," said Robert.

"Max, back to The Block, Miranda and I have something to celebrate."

"May I ask what, Robert, sir?"

"Sure, our first scoop. I have just negotiated a one percent deal with Estée Lauder's new face cream, Virgin's Blush. Miranda, named it herself."

"If I may say so, sir, that is not much of anything?"

"It is for me, Max. I get one percent of gross sales of Virgin's Blush anywhere in the world. That's twenty pence on a twenty pound price tag for the cream."

"It means I get promoted all over the world, Robert. I'll become famous: papers, magazines, posters, hoardings, television and radio will advertise Virgin's Blush with my photograph on."

"Congratulations to the pair of you! Ready to go?" asked Max.

"Drive on chauffeur."

"O.K. sit back and relax."

At The Block Robert tipped Max a tenner.

"Thank you, sir. If you want me again just telephone Mr Rosenburgh. Have a nice day!"

"Can we afford ten pounds for a tip, that's two thousand, five hundred peseta?"

"I've been paid six hundred thousand pounds for my portrait of you, so we are not short of funds."

"You've been paid?"

"I didn't want you getting over excited. Yes, I have been paid and opened an account in our joint names. Which reminds me, you will have to go into the National Westminster to confirm your signature so that you can draw money. I also have a debit cash card with a one thousand pounds a day withdrawal allowance."

"We don't need so much. I definitely don't need anything because my father is still sending me an allowance."

"Haven't you told Amos yet?"

"Not yet, in case it all falls through. At the moment it's a dream. And, anyway, I don't get paid by Vogue until the distribution figures are known. It may be a bit of a damp squib?"

"Nonsense! Ye of little faith. You are a success. Don't you realise, if Estée Lauder give me a contract for one percent of sales of Virgin's Blush I'll have screwed them and you'll become rich and famous."

From Flat Fourteen Robert buzzed the intercom.

"Sam, send up a bottle of champagne from the nearest convenience store. Tell the delivery boy there's a fiver in it for him."

"Sure thing, Mr Robert."

Sam phoned the store and in three minutes a delivery boy appeared in front of Sam's security screen.

"Where to, Mr Sam?" asked the lad.

"Mr Robert, Flat Fourteen."

The doorbell rang and Robert looked through the security spy-hole and saw a young man with a bottle in his hand.

"How much do I owe you?"

"Twenty pounds, please, sir," said the teenager, who looked a doubtful eighteen delivering alcohol.

"Here a twenty and a fiver for your trouble."

"Thank you, sir," and he disappeared into the lift, clutching his pocket money.

"Take your clothes off, I want to sketch you."

"You rude bugger! Couldn't I have some champagne first?"

"That's a good idea. I'll sketch you as the 'Champagne Lady'."

Miranda drank a glass of champagne straight down and Robert closed the blinds to the city. He put on some mood music and drank with her. Then he caressed her all over urgently and Miranda became excited as she thought he was going to make love to her, but instead he undressed her and put a second glass of champagne in her hand.

"Drink up my beauty and radiate that glow of yours when you get excited."

"Ah ha! No touching! Just lean against the mantle and let the champagne dissolve you."

"What about my high-heeled shoes, I've still got them on?"

"Leave them on it's very sexy, it accentuates your lovely legs, right up to your button bottom and your fanny."

"You're enjoying this, aren't you?"

"I didn't say I wasn't."

"At least Vogue are only interested in my face."

"I'm glad about that because what I have got here will only make them jealous."

"You're just rude."

"No darling. Here, another glass of champagne. I'm an artist. Robert Darling of The Arch."

"Don't get big-headed, lover."

"Well, I am a lover and painting you in the nude excites me. Gives me a thrill. I look forward to manhandling you later, just the way you like it. Can I have your permission to hang your full length portrait in The Arch?"

"Now that Vogue and Estée Lauder are going to make me famous, I don't see why not. How much will it fetch?"

"Well, if Teddy Rosenburgh sees it, I should think over a million. But, to be honest, I don't really know."

"Could you disguise my private parts with a flower, I think it would make the portrait more artistic and less suggestive."

"A bright red rose placed strategically on your fanny may well look artistic, but your swollen nipples I will paint as a 'woman's passion'. How does that sound?"

"Hurry up with the sketching, the champagne is going to my head."

"Good. I want to capture your curvaceous form: your hips, lovely slim waist, and long, long exciting legs from your bottom to your shoes."

"How much longer?"

"Just a minute, I have to think about the red rose, the exact positioning of it."

Robert went close up to Miranda and kissed the outside of her fanny.

"No, don't move. Keep hold of your champagne glass and one hand on the mantle."

He lifted one of his larger paint brushes from his easel and inserted the tip between Miranda's labia and made brush strokes, gently, up and down so just the bristles did the work, highly arousing her clitoris. Miranda was relaxed, so she enjoyed the tingling sensation which gradually crawled inside her crutch. Then he stopped. He transferred the brush hairs to her erect nipples and tantalised Miranda until she started to squirm.

"You bastard. You are taking advantage of me," she said in short excited breaths.

"I love you, and worship you. I enjoy playing with you. Vogue may have your face, but I have your body, the real thing, not just a photograph."

Robert had another glass of champagne and, both now in the nude, toasted one another.

"Body of Estée Lauder, I am going to make love to you," and he carried her to the huge double bed.

The following morning the phone rang. Now the only people who had Robert's and Miranda's telephone number were Teddy Rosenburgh, Vogue and Estée Lauder and, of course, Amos, Miranda's father.

"Get that love, I'm cooking!" called out Robert.

"Hello, Miranda."

"Good morning, Miranda. Felicity here, from Estée Lauder. Is Robert there?"

"He's cooking."

"Well, I can tell you, you're his partner and my future client, I hope. I have slept on Robert's proposal of one percent of gross sales and, after discussing it with my colleagues, I agree."

"I'll tell him."

"Tell him, what?" asked Robert.

"It's Estée Lauder, darling; they have agreed to your proposed contract."

"Give me the phone."

"Hello, yes, who's calling?"

"Robert Darling, this is Felicity Swanson, Marketing Director for Estée Lauder. May I send Max round, say in an hour, to fetch you to my office?"

"Fetch me for what?"

"Oh come on, Robert, you must be dying to sign. You wanted one percent and you've got it."

"O.K. I'll be there about eleven o'clock!"

"Yippee!" shouted, Robert, and he swung Miranda around the room.

"You're the new model for Estée Lauder! We are going to be rich!"

"How clever of you, Robert. I never thought they would agree to that. You're not just a lover, a business man as well, with an eye for beauty, who can paint a bit," laughed Miranda.

"Paint a bit! Bloody cheek! Come here!"

"Calm down you are burning the breakfast!"

"Oh damn! Never mind, won't be the first time I've eaten shrivelled bacon."

The intercom buzzed.

"Yes? Robert Darling."

"Mr Darling, sir, Sam here. Max has arrived."

"Thanks, Sam, send him up."

"Good morning, Max, coffee?"

"Well, Mr Robert, sir, Miss Swanson is waiting for me."

"To hell with her, she can wait. Sit down, Max, relax. You said to me to tip you when I can afford it. Well, Max, meet the face of Vogue, the body of Estée Lauder and the portrait artist of The Arch."

"I'm not sure I follow, sir, completely?"

"Max, I'm due to come into mountains of money, so you may be my chauffeur as well."

"Congratulations, Mr Robert, sir. I do have to say Miss Miranda is a beauty."

"Would you like to know a secret, Max?"

"Is it good, Mr Robert, sir?"

"Brilliant. Come with me into the studio. What do you think?"

"Marvellous! That's a marvellous drawing and so lifelike. I like the rose, sir, it makes it an attractive portrait without sexual implications."

"Yes. Yes, we thought that. I'm going to call it 'Virgin's Blush'. You're the first person to see it."

"Then, Mr Robert, sir, I consider it a privilege."

"In that case I'm going to have made some prints from it, and I'll sign them, and then sell them in The Arch. Say a limited quantity, of just one hundred, signed copies. And you, Max, can have the first one as a gift."

"I'll look forward to that, sir."

"Are you ready, sir? I don't like to be late because I chauffeur for Miss Swanson as well as Mr Rosenburgh."

"Don't worry, Max, from now on I'll pay you as well. Miranda and I are about to become famous."

"May I ask how, sir?"

"Miranda's photograph is going to be beamed to the four corners of the entire world. My portrait of Miranda is going to hang in the gallery of The Arch and I shall invite the press and television reporters to view it, but allow no photographs whatsoever. I shall sell the prints, all ninety-nine of them, to the highest bidder."

"An auction, Mr Robert, sir?"

"Yes an auction, but I shall only allow one print a day to be sold, say, at two o'clock each day. The newspapers or television can reproduce the prints as much as they like but they will not be the original signed prints, because I will see to it that they are on canvas instead of cheap paper copies."

"Very shrewd, sir, Mr Robert, if I may say so."

"Are you married, Max?"

"Yes sir, I have a beautiful little wife. She works in a nice ladies clothes shop."

"When I am paid for my Virgin's Blush prints of Miranda's portrait I will invite you and your wife, Max, out to dinner."

"I'll remember that, sir. But I don't drink and drive."

"Rightly so, Max. I will pay for a taxi right to your door."

"Thank you, Mr Robert, sir. I'll hold you to that."

"Now that you have signed, Robert, Miranda is my property for photo shoots and promotions. The first thing that is going to happen is that you will go to a studio here in Knightsbridge with Clarence," pointed out Felicity Swanson.

112

"O.K. Miranda, you are on your own now, apart from Suzy here, who will do your hair and makeup. Let's see how you perform in front of the camera."

"What do you want me to do?"

"Just follow my directions."

"Do I leave my jacket on?"

"Sure, for a start. I'm going to take a lot of head and shoulder shots. Keep the jacket on for the sophisticated look. Think happy thoughts. I want you relaxed now, looking normal. No, don't smile; I want to catch your look of natural beauty. How can I describe it? Your teenage innocence, the look of the virgin's blush."

"Hey! Watch what you are saying, that's my copyright, 'Virgin's Blush'. My product name."

"Sorry. Just trying to draw a word-picture."

"O.K. Take the pearl necklace and the earrings off now, I want a plain look. I don't want any jewellery detracting from the simplicity of your perfect skin."

"Can you see my ears with my long hair?"

"Good point, Miranda."

"Suzy, put Miranda's hair up. I want to photograph the creamy texture of her slim neckline."

"Right, take your jacket off now and undo two buttons of your blouse, I want to see a hint of cleavage. What are you 34\36 D?"

"36D."

"Good you have a full bust. Every woman will be jealous of your curvature by the time I'm finished."

"Now I want some shots of your bare shoulders. Do you have a bra on?"

"Of course I do!"

"Take your blouse off, please."

"I don't think so!"

"Don't be shy, I see women all the time, it's my job. Glamour is part and parcel of beauty. Suzy will be in the room all the time, if it is me you are worried about."

"Suzy, is this normal?"

"It is for beauty shots because in television advertising a woman's beauty includes her shoulders, especially in summer shots, when models wear dresses with shoe string straps."

"All right. Suzy, you stay where you are."

"Wonderful! Wonderful! I think, Miranda, you could get contracts for creamy face soaps and designer brassieres. You have beautiful shape and perfect skin. Take my word for it the camera doesn't lie."

Estée Lauder held nothing back. In Piccadilly the launch of Estée Lauder's 'Virgin's Blush' was up in lights. Miranda was displayed life size on London Buses and on posters on dozens of bus shelters.

The Central Line and The Circle of London Underground had adverts on the walls for Virgin's Blush, which you could read when you rode the escalators.

Chapter Five

Miranda was excited by all the activity and pleased to go to Grand Canaria the following week to do a fashion shoot.

"Miranda, meet Richard Jackson, clothes designer to the rich and famous. And these are his wardrobe ladies," introduced Clarence, the photographer.

"So you are 'Virgin's Blush' the new promotion name, Felicity Swanson at Estée Lauder told me about."

"Yes, I am Miranda. But why am I flown to the Canaries to do a photo-shoot. Won't London do?"

"Miranda, let me worry about the whys. You just be beautiful."

"I am not an idiot!"

"Sorry. O.K. I'll explain. The weather in London can be overcast regularly and that's not good for professional photographic work. Here on Grand Canaria I have good light from morning to evening, which gives me better exposures, which means the shots of you are a hundred percent. You do want to look truly beautiful, don't you?"

"Of course."

"Then we will be photographing against the reflection of the sun's light off the sea's surface, and the glares off the white sands. Also we will be going up into the mountains to give your shots a touch of raw nature. The beautiful woman contrasted to the elements. On the beach I will also, this evening, take some sunset shots. Now do you understand?"

"Yes, thank you, Mr Jackson."

"Relax, don't be so formal. Drop the mister and call me plain Richard, or Dick if you like. You are the important person in this set-up. You are central to my work. Now come across to my mobile wardrobe."

"This big van is a wardrobe?"

"Wait 'til you see inside."

"Wow! Dozens of designer dresses."

"O.K. ladies, over to you. You've seen the light on her face and the cut of her hair, what styles do you think?"

"I think, Dick," said Mary, "because Miranda had jet black hair, she will contrast well with a bright red."

"Yes, Mary, I'd like to try that, but one of the summer dresses with a shoe string strap because she has creamy shoulders and a porcelain neck."

"Yes, Dick, I like red. It's my favourite colour," said Miranda.

"I can understand that, Miranda, you are truly beautiful. And you have a very shapely, full bust. So many models who have beautiful figures have lacking busts."

"Yes, I am proud of my figure. Robert loves it."

"Who's Robert, your husband?"

"No, we are not married."

"Perhaps I should throw my hat in the ring?"

"No, Dick, Robert is my partner and we are very much in love. He is an artist you know. He exhibits in The Arch in Knightsbridge."

"Now, The Arch, I have heard of. That belongs to the multi-millionaire, Teddy Rosenburgh."

"That's right, Robert is going to hang a full size portrait of me in The Arch."

"I hope you will be wearing one of my creations?"

"Oh no, Dick! It's to be a full length nude portrait."

"Lucky for the artist," laughed Richard.

"Don't even think about it. I'm not even going to bare my breasts. I'm here to show my face and model whichever of your creations you so choose."

"You've been told," said Mary, in the back of the wardrobe van."

"Well, I'll just be outside while you change, with Clarence," said Richard.

"Don't worry about, Richard, Miranda, he's into men," said Mary.

"You mean he's a homosexual?"

"Yes he is, so you're safe, which is more than can be said for Clarence, the poofter."

The girls had a good laugh.

Mary released Miranda's shoulder-length, shiny hair so that it would be caught by the breeze coming off the land.

"Not enough breeze, Clarence, hold on!"

"Mary fetch the fan from the van and plug it into the generator."

"Ready, Miranda? Ready Clarence? How's that?"

"That's O.K. looks natural."

"Miranda, turn your face to right profile to catch the wind of the fan."

"Right profile?"

"Turn your head so that your right cheek is facing the camera."

"O.K. Sorry."

"Don't worry. You'll soon get the hang of it. Now look down a bit. Right, think happy thoughts. Think about your boyfriend in bed with you."

Miranda did, she blushed slightly and her pupils dilated."

"That's it, beautiful. That's the 'Virgin's Blush' I am after," congratulated, Clarence.

"What do you think, Richard?"

"Have you captured my creation, that is, 'Fire Red'?"

"Yes I have, but do you want a full-length shot?"

"Not with 'Fire Red', but with another creation of mine."

"Which is that?" asked Mary the Wardrobe Mistress."

"The green silk, Chinese number."

"O.K. Richard."

"Miranda, come on, time to change."

"This is beautiful!" exclaimed Miranda.

"Yes, figure hugging and full-length. You will do the bodice justice. Let me put your hair up because this is a round, high neck number."

Miranda stepped out of the van.

"Wow! A supermodel. A film star!" exclaimed Richard Jackson.

"Mary, some emerald earrings."

"O.K. Dick, give me a minute."

"Clarence, I want full-length shots, plenty of flat tummy and slimline curvaceous hips and pert bottom."

"Mary, switch the generator off and unplug the fan until I say."

"Miranda, to finish this session of the shoot off I want you to wear a mini-dress in peacock blue with a flared skirt. I want to see your legs, Miranda."

"Clarence, I want a Marilyn Monroe shot."

"Mary, fetch both fans and place them on the ground, horizontally, to make a maximum up-draft."

"O.K. switch on."

"Ready when you are?" said Richard.

"O.K. Miranda, pout!"

"Like this?"

117

"That's it! Look into the camera!"

"Wow! Beautiful legs!" said a very pleased Richard.

"No! Don't hold the skirt down! Let the fans do their work," said an excited Clarence.

"Sexy panties," whispered Richard into Clarence's ear.

"Even I like those," smiled Clarence.

"O.K.!" shouted Richard, "as they say in the movies, 'that's a wrap'!"

"You have perfect legs, Miranda. Ever thought of modelling the latest fashions in stockings, or even lingerie?" asked Mary, who herself had done some leg's modelling.

"It's all new to me. One week I am in Atalia, Spain, and the next I am in London, living at The Block with Richard. The next month my portrait is hanging in The Arch in Knightsbridge, and sells for seven hundred and fifty thousand pounds. Now Robert and I are rich. The next thing I am photographed in the London papers and from there on I am snapped up by Vogue Magazine and Estée Lauder. Now I am on the beach of Grand Canaria."

"Having met you and seen you in front of the camera I think the world is your oyster, Miranda," appraised Mary, who had been around cameras and beautiful women, with Richard, for years.

The following day, unbelievably thought Miranda, started at six o'clock in the morning.

"Why so early, Richard?" asked Miranda.

"Because we have to get up into the mountains and catch the early morning light. I want to photograph you before the tourists get up: just you and nature without any interferences from people or traffic."

"Oh I see," said Miranda.

"Today is not about faces, hair or skin tone, but about the whole of you. Your figure silhouetted against the sky or contrasted against the rocks of the mountainside. Of course, every shot in one of my creations. Today is a fashion day."

"Where will I be displayed?"

"Once I have finished, I will have Pauline, the Chief Editor of Vogue, eating out of my hand."

"I thought we already had an agreement with Pauline for the 'Cover Girl' of Vogue?"

"That's a deal you made with Robert, your manager, just for your face. But, you must realise, Vogue is not only a glamour magazine but also a high fashion magazine. Ladies who are famous, or stars or celebrities, always want creative dresses because they want to appear on camera making headlines in the papers. They want the 'wow factor'. Not just beautiful but exciting, modelling the latest creation. A film star will pay a thousand pounds for a dress, especially if it's made by a famous dress designer, and even more if it's a one-off."

Back in London Miranda returned to The Block in Knightsbridge with Robert.

Richard Jackson, armed with a portfolio of Amanda's photographs, in which she looked absolutely gorgeous, went gloating to the Chief Editor of Vogue, Pauline.

"Wonderful, Richard, all for me?"

"At a price."

"There's always a price, how much?"

"Shall we say, Pauline, a commission on the photographs depending on the sale of my creative designer dresses, as displayed in each photograph."

"That's a bit back to front. Surely, you should pay me a commission from the sale of your dresses promoted in Vogue."

"I disagree. I am providing the promotional photographs of Miranda, and I pay my staff to make the dresses."

"How about, Richard, an open-ended contract? After all, you want your name to be more famous, and I want to increase the sales of Vogue and all its commercial spin-offs."

"All right, you pay me, according to the increased sales of Vogue and the business it promotes from readers and commercial investors in Vogue."

Vogue was released and Clarence, the photographer had been busy. He wanted fame for himself. He released the look of 'Virgin's Blush' to Independent Television, and the following morning, Thames Television had the headlines, 'The New Face in the Beauty World – Miranda, a gorgeous twenty-three year old with a prominent 36 D bust, and an hour glass figure is being promoted by Vogue Magazine and Estée Lauder. She lives with her partner, Robert, 37, a professional painter. He is exhibiting his work in The

Arch, the famous gallery of Teddy Rosenburgh. A couple for London to keep their eye on.'

At The Arch Robert was mingling with the general public and listening to comments. Many of the other artist's paintings were being admired but not selling particularly well.

"Hello, Max, what are you doing here?"

"Acting as security officer, Mr Robert, when I am not chauffeuring."

"I thought you were only the doorman when Mr Rosenburgh had a private exhibition for his friends by ticket only?"

"Since Mr Rosenburgh, has recruited more artists to The Block, to exhibit their works in The Arch, there has been more public interest. There are no other galleries in London where you can view and buy, unless you want to go to an auction house and bid for a painting."

"I guess you have a point there, Max. I imagine bidding at an auction against others can be expensive."

Miranda hid amongst the members of the public while Robert, having become known as Robert Darling the artist, signed autograph books or signed leaflets.

"And this is Miranda, my girlfriend and soul mate."

"Miranda? Miranda, I have heard that name today? Of course! Thames Television. You were on the news this morning. You are the new discovery. Are you a model?"

"I suppose so, but I have only just started. I have just come back from Gran Canaria where I did a fashion shoot for a famous designer."

"What was his name?"

"Richard Jackson."

"Oh, the man who makes dresses for the rich and famous. I've seen some of his creations in Vogue."

"Then what's your name?"

"Daphne."

"Well, Daphne, you are about to see some more of Richard Jackson's creations in Vogue because I have been modelling them."

"Can I have your autograph beside Robert Darlings', in my autograph book?"

"I don't see why not. You, Daphne, can be my first fan. I've signed it, 'Miranda the face of Vogue' how's that?"

"Fine, thank you."

"I don't know, Robert, if I want to be famous. I mean, if people recognise you all the time then you have no privacy."

"Miranda, darling, if people recognise you while you are on the street take it as a compliment. Just smile, and if anyone wants your autograph give it willingly and think of that person as a casual friend."

"You mean their heroine?"

"That's right, you are becoming a celebrity. Young women and impressionable teenagers will look upon you as a role model."

"A role model?"

"Yes an example of fashion and beauty, among ordinary every day working people and the more envious rich and famous. Every beauty-aware woman wants to look like a princess and be adored like a goddess."

"Is that what I am?"

"Yes, my darling, the face and body of today, to be looked upon as very desirable by both men and women."

"Men and women?"

"Of course, women will be jealous of your natural outstanding beauty and gorgeous dress sense, and men will fall in love with you and want your sexy body in bed with them."

"Will I be a sort of pin-up for men?"

"Yes, probably. How does that make you feel?"

"Kind of special, Robert. A little while ago I was a grieving widow, but since I met you my life has been turned upside down. I like myself a lot more and feel more comfortable with the world. I think I have got over my initial shyness because I am confident in front of a camera now."

"Great. You have blossomed. You like people now and being with people, which means you exude natural beauty, Miranda."

"Thanks to your loving of me, Robert, I have come out of my shell, and am starting to feel like a film star."

"I'm glad you are happy, Miranda. You are not exactly a film star because you are not appearing in a film, but with all the increasing advertising on television and in the papers, you certainly are on your way to becoming a celebrity."

"I have one fan," laughed Miranda.

To get away from the public Robert and Miranda decided to dine out that evening. They hailed a taxi outside The Block.

"Where to, guv'nor?"

"A good quality Chinese restaurant where we can dine by lantern light."

"Right you are, guv'nor."

The taxi turned off down a side street and, in what seemed less than five minutes, pulled up outside a Chinese restaurant, which had several large red lanterns hanging out the front.

"There you are, guv'nor. The Red Lantern."

"Thanks cabby. Here a tenner."

As they stepped inside the door they were greeted by a beautifully dressed Chinese girl who placed an orchid in each of their right hands.

"Follow me, please," and she sprinkled flower petals on the carpet where they trod.

"Good evening sir, madam," said a young man dressed formally wearing a black bow tie.

The flower girl sprinkled their table with scented rose petals.

"May I take madam's jacket, before you are seated?"

"Yes please," said Miranda.

"You are, if I may say so, madam, a stunningly beautiful lady," smiled the young man with the bow tie.

"Please, just call me, Miranda, and this is my partner, Robert."

"Pleased to meet you, Mr Robert, sir. I am the owner of The Red Lantern, Yan Chong, but my regulars know me simply as Mr Yan."

"Yan, you are very young to be the owner."

"I worked very hard for many years as a manager of another Chinese restaurant and saved all my wages so that one day I would own my own restaurant. Also, I have youthful looks, which makes me look a lot younger than I am. But yes, I am young to own The Red Lantern. The Chinese community lent me some start-up capital as did the bank. The difference between the Chinese community and the bank is that the Chinese community do not charge interest. We help each other. Soon it will be my time, once I have re-paid my debt capital, to help others who feel ready to start their own venture."

Another customer arrived, a big rugged man with weather beaten features and on his arm a blonde young lady.

"Good evening, Mr Jake, your usual table?"

"Yes please, Yan, and a bottle of Chinese wine."

"Right away, Mr Jake."

The Chinese girl did her flower routine.

"Good evening, fellah, haven't seen you in here before?" said Jake to Robert.

"No, er..."

"Jake's the name."

"No, Jake, we are new in London."

"What brought you here?"

"Pictures, I am an artist."

"Have I heard of you?"

"Doubt it, I am new to The Arch. Teddy Rosenburgh's place."

"Teddy Rosenburgh. What's your name?"

"Robert Darling."

"Ah, Darling! Now I know, you painted Miranda, the new face of Vogue, nude, in The Arch."

"Now Robert was facing Jake, but because Robert and Miranda were at a table for two, Miranda, had her back to Jake."

"Who's the lucky lady with you?"

"You ask too many questions. My girlfriend."

Jake had a nose for stories, so he came forward, and before Robert could do anything, Jake had raised his camera and took a shot of Miranda, who was doing her best to be inconspicuous.

Robert jumped up, offended, and punched Jake powerfully on the jaw. He reeled back but didn't go down. He put his camera on the table and Miranda snatched it up and dragged the film out, exposing it to the light.

"Hey! What do you think you're doing!? I'm Jake Higgind, Picture Reporter for The News of The World. There were some valuable shots on that film."

He snatched up the camera and, angry, slapped Miranda around the face.

"That's private property, keep your fucking hands off!"

That did it, Robert saw red. Jake had struck the woman Robert loved. Robert went blind to all around him. All he could see was Jake, the offensive face that had to be punched-in. His ears buzzed and his rational brain fogged. He became pure hatred. Before Jake could turn on Robert, he snatched the camera, threw it on the floor and stamped on it repeatedly.

"Hey! My camera...!"

Was the furthest he got. Although Jake was considerably bigger than Robert he wasn't afraid. Jake had insulted Miranda without cause and he was a bloody reporter invading their privacy.

Robert kneed him in the groin with all his strength. Jake groaned and doubled over and Robert made good of the advantage. He flat-handed Jake's exposed jaw, crashing his teeth together. The jarring effect made Jake hold his jaw, and he felt his jaw and teeth with both hands. While he was defenceless Robert karate-punched him hard, twice in the windpipe. Jake, out manoeuvred and gagging for air, was defenceless, so Robert poked him in the eye with his index finger. The jab made Jake stand up straight and, in the next instant, Robert punched with all his strength into Jake's solar plexus. He went down coughing. Robert grabbed Jake's beard and shouted, "That's for striking Miranda!"

Immediately the big man, only superficially hurt, came to his senses. "Miranda? The face of Vogue! Let me up, you fool!" said an angry Jake. He produced a miniature camera from his jacket pocket.

"Come on, Miranda, pose for me!"

As he held up the camera Miranda, annoyed, leapt forward and bit his wrist.

"Ow! You bitch!"

In that instant Miranda, grabbed the miniature camera and threw it across the room.

"Right, that's it!"

Jake never lost an opportunity. He pushed the nearest table over and made for his miniature camera on the floor, but not before Robert got in his way. Jake bodily lifted Robert and threw him across the next table. The table smashed and collapsed, spraying its contents across the floor.

Jake was thinking of nothing but the story. All his life he had been single-minded and no artist was going to stop him. He bent down to pick up the camera, but he never got that far, because Robert smashed a chair over his head. The chair shattered and Jake, enraged, grabbed the nearest table and hurled it at Robert.

In the meantime Yan Chong, the owner, had telephoned the police. In the reception area other customers who had come in for a Chinese meal, cowered out of the way while the two men fought.

"You ladies come with me," said the Chinese girl. And she led them to safety in the ladies rest room.

The fight continued. Both Jake and Robert by now had bloody noses, but Jake appeared to be worst off because he was bleeding copiously from his scalp, where Robert, had broken a chair over his head.

The police arrived. Two burly sergeants, experienced officers, who had in their time been in many fights, and brooked no nonsense.

Mack blew his whistle to get their attention.

"O.K. show's over. What's the fight about gentlemen?"

"That bastard hit my girlfriend!" shouted Robert, making ready to throw another fist.

Mack shoved roughly, his baton under Robert's chin making him gag.

"That's enough fellah! You're under arrest for affray!"

"Who's going to pay for all this?" cut in Mr Yan.

"Mr Yan, if you will come down to the police station and make a statement we can sort this out."

"I'm not going to any bloody police station!" shouted Jake. "This idiot smashed my camera and exposed my pictures. I want compensation!"

"Who are you, sir?"

"Jake Higgins, Picture Reporter to The News of The World."

"Well, Jake Higgins, you are also under arrest for affray."

"Go to hell!" shouted big Jake.

Billy had been on the force for thirty years and stood for no nonsense. He side-swiped Jake on the side of his neck with his baton. The fight went out of Jake. Billy cuffed him.

"O.K you two, outside!"

"Officer," asked Mr Yan, "can I make a statement in the morning?"

"Sure, Mr Yan. We will leave you now. Looks like you have some clearing up to do."

"It's gone quiet now," said the Chinese girl to Miranda and Yvette, Jake's girlfriend. "Let's go out into the restaurant."

"Mr Yan, where is Robert?"

"I'm sorry to tell you the police took him away with Mr Jake in the police van."

"Oh dear. How much do I owe you for the damage?"

"That will be sorted out, I hope, in the court tomorrow."

"What will happen to Robert?"

125

"I heard the officers say they would keep the two men in the cells overnight and bail them to appear in Knightsbridge Magistrates' Court at a later date."

"All rise! Mr Justice Calverley, presiding."
The Clerk of The Court read out the charge.
"Would the defendants state their names for the record."
"Robert Darling of The Block."
"Jake Higgins, Picture Reporter for The News of The World."
"May I remind you, Mr Higgins, while you are in my court, you are not here as a reporter but as a criminal, so you do yourself no favours by your arrogance."
"Sorry, Your Honour."
"Your Honour, my client, Yan Chong, owner of The Red Lantern, asks for compensation for the damage done by the two men in the dock."
"Very well, Mr Waverley."
"Your Honour," said Mr Charlton, Defence Counsel, "my clients are very sorry for the damage they caused and are willing to pay compensation to put the matter right with Mr Chong, the plaintiff."
"Your Honour, may I speak for myself?" asked Robert Darling.
"Is that all right with you, Mr Charlton?"
"Yes, Your Honour."
"Officer, escort Mr Darling from the Dock to the witness box."
"Well, Mr Darling, the Court is waiting. Get on with it."
"Your Honour, the reason I struck Jake Higgins is because he slapped my girlfriend around the face."
"Why did Mr Higgins slap your girlfriend, Mr Darling?"
"Because she opened his camera and pulled the film out."
"So there was provocation on the part of Mr Higgins?"
"No, Your Honour, there was not. My girlfriend, Miranda, and I were sitting at our table in The Red Lantern enjoying each other's company when this reporter comes in and disturbs our privacy and starts taking photographs. At the effrontery of Jake Higgins, Miss Miranda grabbed his camera and threw it on the floor. She was furious that he wouldn't leave her alone. He was in the wrong, but it was he who struck Miss Miranda around the face.

Because of the unprovoked assault on my girlfriend, I punched Mr Higgins on the jaw and that's how the fight started. I am sorry for my action, but I am old-fashioned and was defending the honour of the lady I love, and I hope will be my bride."

"I understand your actions, Robert Darling, but why was Mr Higgins taking photographs of Miss Miranda?"

"Because he's a nosey reporter and thinks that the News of The World is more important than a person's privacy."

"Mr Waverley, as Prosecution Counsel, are you prepared to accept Mr Darling's account of what happened?"

"I am, Your Honour."

"Very well, Mr Waverley. This is an open and shut case. The plaintiff, Mr Yong, wants compensation for £2,000, which you, Mr Darling, and you, Mr Higgins, will pay a £1,000 each, payable at the Court in seven days. However, Mr Jake Higgins, for Common Assault, causing actual bruising, you will remain in custody for seven days."

"What about my camera!?"

"Officer, take him down."

Outside the Magistrates' Court, to their complete surprise, is a horde of photographers.

"Miss Miranda, this way please!"

Instinctively Miranda looks across and a camera flashed in her face.

Robert puts his arm around her protectively and says, "Smile, put your beauty charm on."

"Miss Miranda," asks a lady reporter, "what do you think of Justice Calverley's sentence?"

"My honour has received justice. Jake Higgins was out of order striking me."

"Do you intend to sue him for actual bodily harm?"

"Miss Miranda, has given her answer, there will be no more questions answered," said Defence Counsel, Mr Charlton. "Get in the taxi."

"Cabbie, we want to go to The Block, the home of artists whom paint for Teddy Rosenburgh's gallery, The Arch. But I don't want to be followed by the press so, if we have a tail, please lose them."

"For, Miss Miranda, sir, it will be a pleasure. Hold onto your hats."

The Cabbie drove into the West End, around the Elephant and Castle and Piccadilly then doubled back to Knightsbridge.

The following morning The Times carried the following story: 'Miranda gets a slap in the face as News of The World Cameraman, Jake Higgins, takes liberties and gets seven days behind bars for common assault.'

"Well, Miranda, at least we were photographed together. You look beautiful. You took my advice and smiled."

'Miss Miranda, the "Face of Vogue", seemed unfazed as she emerged from Knightsbridge Magistrates' Court. In fact, it is easy to see why she is rapidly becoming a celebrity. She is seen on posters, hoardings and in fashion magazines, modelling for Estée Lauder. The photographs do her justice, as she truly is a beauty, with a body to kill for. It's a privilege to get near to her in the flesh, so to speak.'

"All the publicity, Miranda, means you are not only becoming famous, but infamous. You are becoming 'Virgin's Blush', a real person, not just a face on a jar of beauty cream."

"Answer the phone, Robert."

"Hello, Robert Darling."

"Good morning, Robert, you and Miranda got a good press. This is Pauline, Chief Editor of Vogue. May I speak to Miranda?"

"Sure. Miranda! Pauline at Vogue."

"Hello, Pauline, you want me?"

"How do you fancy a free holiday in the Caribbean?"

"The West Indies?"

"Fancy a holiday in the West Indies, Robert?"

"Maybe. They are wrongly named anyway. Columbus called the islands between Central America and the Caribbean Sea, the West Indies, when he discovered them, because he believed he had reached the Indies off south-eastern Asia. What's the catch?"

"Hello, Pauline, Robert's asking what's the catch?"

"No catch, darling. Shall I send Max round?"

"She wants to send Max round."

"Give me the phone."

"Pauline, this is Robert. I don't believe there is such a thing as a free lunch. What's cooking?"

"A photo-shoot in Jamaica on silver sands under a glorious sky with an inviting ocean. Come on, Robert, wake up, this is an opportunity for Miranda to earn a lot of money."

"What does she have to do?"

"Model tropical clothing for a famous designer who has approached Vogue, to use my model for Vogue, that's Miranda."

"How do I know she won't be exploited?"

"I'll give you a contract. Let Max collect you and as her manager you can do business with Vogue."

"Hello, Max, won't be a minute."

"I'll wait in the limousine, Mr Robert, sir."

"Thanks for coming. Robert, Miranda, I would like you to meet Jacques Ferineaux from Paris. He has a new designer collection which he would like you to launch, Miranda."

"Where do I come in?" asked Robert.

"Well, Jacques, has seen your photograph and thinks, with your good looks, you could model as well."

"What, dresses?"

"No, young man. I would photograph Miranda first, and then you both as a couple."

"What do I have to wear?"

"Let Jacques show you," said Pauline.

"Come see for yourself." In a small adjoining room Jacques Ferineaux had a rail of samples. "These are my creations."

"Do I detect a wedding theme?" asked, Robert.

"Yes, with some of the outfits. It is becoming increasingly popular to get married on the beach, especially in the West Indies, where a holiday is combined with a wedding."

"What do you think, Miranda?"

"You will make an ideal couple in Vogue," said Pauline.

"You will get loads of publicity, Robert, which can only be good for an emerging portrait artist. Soon you will be famous."

"I hadn't thought, Miranda, of us as being a couple. But I suppose we are, now that we both live at The Block."

"I know, darling, that we have separate careers now. I am a model and you are an artist, but why shouldn't the public see us as a couple?"

"Jacques, may I try on some of the designs for men?"

"Of course, if it will make you feel more relaxed about my proposition as promoting my collection as admirably suited to couples."

"What do you think, Pauline?" asked Robert.

"It's rather dapper, tones you down from the casual artist, towards the gentleman's role model."

"You serious, Pauline?"

"Absolutely! Well? Do you agree to go to Jamaica, all expenses paid, for two weeks, and become a male herald for Vogue as the ideal ladies' partner?"

"Come on, Robert, I think it's a great idea. It means we can have a holiday together instead of being separated."

"If we are models all day long for Jacques how much time do we get to ourselves?"

"Most evenings, though there is a scheduled fashion show for just one evening, which it will be compulsory to attend."

"A fashion show? I thought the sales would come via Vogue?"

"Indeed they will, but on Jamaica there will be a lot of rich and famous American tourists from the United States. The Americans are big on evening wear. They like to stand out in a crowd, so you will be modelling my evening wear collection as well," explained Jacques Ferineaux.

Chapter Six

The plane touched down after a nine-hour flight and it was early evening, just after teatime.

As they emerged from arrivals a Jamaican held a board up which read, 'Jacques Ferineaux'.

"Hello, I am Jacques Ferineaux. There are four in our party and a lot of luggage, can you manage us all?"

"Yes, sir, the car is outside. My name's Sammy."

"O.K. Sammy, lead on."

"Wow! A sixties classic. I like the chrome bumpers and the rear fins. Reminds me a bit of Ford's Zephyr and Zodiacs you see at Classic Car Shows back in England," said Robert.

Robert couldn't tell what model it was originally, but the body had been patched and repaired and now painted in contrasting canary yellow and bright grass green.

"I'm glad you admire her," said Sammy. "She's my baby. I scavenge in the breakers yard for spares to keep her going. The engine I have in is a rebuild from an old one. She has new bearings, pistons and camshaft."

"You are technically minded then, Sammy?"

"No man, necessity is the mother of invention. My father taught me that when I was a boy."

"Ah! Here's our luggage."

Jacques tipped the porter two dollars, and the young man was happy with that.

"Lot of luggage, sir. I'll put all the suit carriers on the luggage rack on the roof. The cases can go in the large boot."

Clarence the photographer and Jacques the designer sat on the front bench seat with Sammy while Robert and Miranda sunk into the off-white hide seats. It had chrome window trims, a chrome cased speedometer which didn't work, and a chrome ring horn, Robert observed.

When the taxi set off it was low-slung to the ground and while the big tyres did their best to ride the bumps it was obvious that the suspension had long gone past its best. While it still worked, it rocked from side to side like a slow motion roller coaster. Sammy drove the old girl with the respect she deserved.

"Here we are, Mr Jacques, your hotel."

"Thanks, Sammy, ten dollars O.K.?"

"Sure, man. What time do you want me in the morning?"

"Be outside the hotel at nine o'clock, but first give me a hand with the luggage."

"No need, Mr Jacques, this young man is your porter."

"How you doing, Mr Sammy?"

"Fine, young Hickory. This nice rich man will give you a tip."

"Hello, sir, welcome. Your name please?"

"Robert Darling."

"Don't call me darling, sir, people will think I am a homosexual, and that I'm not."

"Sorry. You misunderstand me, my name is Robert Darling, as in a capital 'D' for Darling."

"Oh I see. My apologies, sir. You must understand I get to meet all sorts in this job."

"Yes, you probably do, and to confirm my manhood this is my beautiful Miranda."

"Yes, a booking for a party of four. The lead name is Jacques Ferineaux. Is he here?"

"Jacques is just coming with the luggage, he's a designer and he won't let his creations out of his sight."

"Here we are, Mr Robert Darling, room 221. Second floor with sea view."

"Hickory, take Mr Darling to room 221."

"Follow me please, sir."

They went up in the lift to the second floor.

"Thanks, Hickory, here's a five."

"Thank you, sir!" The five dollars brought a big smile to young Hickory's face.

"I don't know about you, Miranda, but I'm not going to unpack now. After a long flight I am going for a refreshing swim in that inviting shimmering sea."

"Race you to get changed!" laughed, Miranda. She was naked in seconds, all that delicious flesh. She posed for just two seconds in front of Robert. It had the right effect. With his trousers off and his underpants his testosterone kicked in and his penis distended.

"Don't even think about it, it is too late for that."

Miranda spun away from Robert and quickly put her red one-piece swimsuit on.

"O.K I'm ready! Come on slow coach!"

He put his swimming trunks on, but it didn't hide his erection.

"Serves you right, you randy bugger!" laughed, Miranda, as she pushed past him.

"See you later, Jacques, we are off for a swim."

"Hey! What about my designer collection?"

"Clarence can help you with it. Might put a few muscles on him."

The sea was refreshing and the sun still comfortably warm.

"Jacques Ferineaux?"

"That's me."

"Mr Robert Darling has taken his room keys. You must sign the Hotel Register, please, as you are the lead name, before I give you your keys. And your passport, please, which will be kept in the hotel safe for the duration of your stay at The Flamingo."

"I could do with a drink," said Miranda, "but I haven't any money on me."

"No problem. Reception said that with these wristbands on we can get a drink at the Beach Bar, and it is simply charged to our room. It's a good idea, it means we don't have to worry about carrying money on the beach."

"Hello there. Are you new arrivals?"

"How do you know?"

"Two reasons: first, I am good at faces, and a body like your wife's I would not miss, and second, you are only a little suntanned. After two weeks on Jamaica's beaches you will be well tanned."

"Yes, we are new."

"Welcome, welcome. My name's Jim. What's your poison?"

"A cool beer please for me and, for Miranda, a pina colada, with crushed ice."

"Coming right up. What's your name?"

"Robert. I'm here to model clothing for a fashion-shoot."

"Are you somebody famous?"

"No. Just the partner of a beautiful lady. She's the new face of Vogue."

"Vogue magazine, now that I have heard of. Miranda's a lucky lady, I would say."

"You've unloaded then?" asked Robert, of Jacques.

"Yes, but no thanks to you. We also would like a refreshing swim. You could have helped us."

"No man, let the hotel staff do that."

"Hickory's only a boy. I'm not trusting my creations to a boy."

"What about Clarence? Couldn't he help you?"

"He did. He's a gentleman."

"What's your beef then. You're all men together. And Clarence's costume is a disgrace."

"I am a man, that's how I like them."

"You had better watch out for the men!" laughed, Robert.

"Come on Jacques, ignore him."

Jim said, as soon as Clarence and Jacques were out of earshot, "Poofters, I take it?"

"Absolutely so. Very effeminate."

"Well, believe it or not, there are plenty of homosexuals on the beach. There are nightclubs near the beach front for both gay men and lesbian women. The lesbians are the worst. They don't mind making a spectacle of themselves in the nightclubs. They get each other's tits out and suck on the nipples."

"I hope we don't go into one by mistake," said a concerned, Miranda.

"No worries, young lady, they have huge pink, illuminated, flashing signs outside, saying, 'Gay Bar'."

"Hey man. Look after your lady on this holiday, some of these lesbian women are predatory. They see a beautiful woman and try to latch on."

"No problem there, Jim, Miranda only has eyes for me."

"Good luck to you, have a happy holiday."

"Come on slowcoach, hurry up and dress, I'm starving!"

"It's all right for you, just a shirt and a pair of shorts and you're ready. I have to dress my hair."

"I can't help being naturally handsome. My hair has always been wavy and neatly compacted. If I wash it, it comes out just the same."

"Lucky you! You could brush my hair."

"What rub that conditioning crème in?"

"Yes, do that thoroughly. Use both hands, working from the roots to the ends. Then brush it thoroughly to make it shine."

"O.K my lover. For you, I will."

"Stop it, don't kiss my neck, that gets me going."

"Because I'm so hungry I'll let you off, but another time I'll have you naked."

"You rude bugger, just brush my hair."

Once finished, he lifted her by the shoulders and spun her round to him and gave her a passionate kiss.

"What's that for?"

"Because I love you."

"Soppy sod! Come on let's get to the restaurant."

"Coo-ee! Over here!"

"Oh God, the poofters. Do we have to sit with them?" complained Robert.

"Robert, they've seen us now and, anyway, they are our meal ticket for this holiday."

"O.K., Miranda, put on a huge smile. After all we are models, so let's be professional."

"No wonder Vogue wants you, Miranda, you are truly beautiful," said Jacques. "Come sit next to me."

"That's fine with me, Robert, I prefer men anyway."

"Not me you don't, I'm a strictly one woman man. So, Clarence, don't make any moves on me."

"Oh dear. And you, Robert, so good looking."

"Sorry, Clarence, Miranda's the one for me."

"To tell the truth," said Jacques, "I am, if I so wish, a bisexual."

"Does that mean, Jacques, you have had a girlfriend?" asked a miffed, Clarence.

"Of course, old boy. You must remember, I am a fashion designer, and work with beautiful women all the time. Young beautiful models, like to be flattered by a successful designer. Sometimes it's just a drink or a night out at a nightclub for the fun of it. However, other times, there's chemistry. On such rare occasions, like any healthy male, I fall in love, and a relationship results."

"You could have told me this before. Now I feel compromised," said a sulky, Clarence.

"Clarence, we are both professionals. We are on Jamaica to do our own thing, so you keep to photography and I'll keep to design and promotion of my creations."

They all enjoyed their evening meal and retired to the verandah for drinks. A steel band started up and the troupe of professional dancers invited members of the audience to dance with them.

"Come on, sir, you look like a lithe dancer. You are tall and slim," and she slipped a pink garland around Clarence's neck and led him onto the dance floor.

"Come on, darling, we can do that," encouraged Miranda.

"I don't want to make a fool of myself," said Robert.

"With your permission, Robert," offered Jacques, "I would love to dance with Miranda."

"Go ahead, Jacques, at least your sexual orientation can be normal if you so wish."

So Jacques danced with Miranda and the other Jamaican entertainers.

Miranda showed the dance troupe that she was as fit as them by bending over backwards and going under the limbo bar, which was set at about two feet high, to the beat of the drums.

"Bravo! Bravo!" shouted Robert, as he stood up to applaud.

"Come on, sir, let the people see you do the limbo dance," said the pretty troupe leader.

"What under that? But at over six feet tall, I have no chance!"

"Come on we will go together, hold my hand."

With a young lady in a grass-like skirt, and Robert in his brightly coloured Hawaiian shirt, they went together under the limbo bar. Robert couldn't get that low and fell flat on his back. The Jamaican dancer raised the bar up.

"Now, sir, try again."

And he did and went under the bar with his back bent over backwards, to rapturous applause from the audience on the Flamingo's verandah.

Robert and Miranda, for their willing participation, were rewarded with a bottle of champagne.

"Now ladies, the steel band will slow down the tempo so that you can encourage your men folk to take to the dance floor, and while our men play rhythmically on the steel drums, we will mingle with you on the dance floor to show you some of our dance moves. Please join in, you will enjoy yourselves."

In the morning Sammy arrived in a battered blue van rescued from a bygone era.

"Good morning, Sammy. Have you brought a van with headroom as agreed?"

"Yes, Mr Jacques. It is outside."

"Good, help me transfer all these designs to the rails in the van."

"What the hell is this?"

"A van, sir. It's in good running order. I borrowed it from a friend. She's mechanically sound. Just needs a lick of paint."

"Looks like something out of the scrapyard. Well, can't stand here gaping, let's get loaded up and be off."

"Give us a hand, Clarence!"

"No man, I'm a photographer, I have my equipment to carry."

"Bloody wimp!" shouted out Robert. "Come on, Sammy, I'll give you a hand."

"Have you a reliable generator on board, Sammy?"

"Yes, Mr Jacques, a nearly new one. I've rented it for a week."

"O.K. Everybody on board," instructed Jacques Ferinaeux.

They piled into the front but the bench seat was for only three people.

"Move over, let me in," whined Clarence.

"Sorry chum," said Robert, "no room at the inn, try the back."

"Come on Jacques, you're my friend, let me ride up front."

"I am not your friend. On this trip you're just a business colleague sharing the modelling profession. You'll have to sit in the back."

"That's not fair!"

"Look, Clarence, all your photographic equipment is in the back of the van, somebody should look after it and, as it is yours, you're the obvious choice."

Sammy drove for a while up into the mountains and then down a steep valley track, at the head of which was a lake and a magnificent waterfall cascading down.

"Now that's what I call a view!" sounded an excited Jacques. "Well done, Sammy, that will make a perfect background. Wait till I tell Clarence."

"Here we are," said Sammy. "As per your instructions man, a beautiful location, isolated, with no interruptions from tourists."

"Somebody let me out!" shouted Clarence from the back when the van had stopped.

Sammy released the side door and Clarence stepped down.

"Well, what do you think, man?" gestured, Sammy.

"Great, Sammy! Magnificent waterfall cascading off these rocks. Can you walk behind it?"

"Sure can, that's one of the reasons I brought here, man."

"Be great for my cine camera. I can make a sixty second movie for television."

"Nice to see you enthusiastic," said Jacques.

"Yes, friend, I'm going to take some fantastic shots. The light reflecting off the little lake and the waterfall will give a brilliant shimmering effect. No need for artificial light here."

"Sammy, drive a little closer, it will be nearer for Miranda and Robert once they have changed in the van."

"O.K.," said Jacques, "you two in the van. Let's model my tropical wear first."

"Where do you want them, Clarence?"

"Standing on the rocks in front of the waterfall."

"We're ready, Clarence."

"Good. Face one another and smile. That's it, good side profile. Now face the camera but reach across the rocks so that your fingertips just touch. Good, good, good display of the fabrics. Now walk round behind the waterfall until I stay stop. Keep going, a bit more, hold it. Now stand there where there is a natural break in the cascade. Yes, that's good, stand cheek to cheek. Got it on the cine. Right that will do for the first outfit, go see Jacques to choose the next creation."

"It's a warm day, how about a swim suit?"

"Swimwear, Clarence, where do you want your models?"

"In the water at the foot of the waterfall."

"Clarence, let me test the depth of the water first!" shouted Robert, over the sound of the rushing water.

Robert, barefoot, carefully stepped off the rocks into the pool at the foot of the waterfall and swam out. He couldn't touch the bottom and the undertow was dangerous. He quickly swam back to the edge of the pool.

"Too dangerous, Clarence. Too deep, too much current!"

"All right. Go back to where you were before on the rocks in front of the waterfall. Robert, hold Miranda's hand for confidence and security, because I want her to lean back until her hair, at the back of her head, only just cuts into the cascade, so that I can still see her face while the water cascades down her hair and not her body. O.K. let's try."

Clarence signalled and Robert instructed Miranda. The sheer shock of the cold water made Miranda's eyes fly open and her mouth agape: Clarence, captured the natural reaction.

Clarence signalled and Robert pulled Miranda out of the cascade.

"Now, Robert and Miranda, you have the idea. This time it won't be such a shock. Think smile this time as you partly immerse your head in the cascade. Robert, you look at the lady of your life and laugh lovingly. Invigorated by the water, Miranda, you look back at Robert, and smile widely. I want one of your best beauty smiles, as if you were posing as Cover Girl for Vogue."

Clarence got some beautiful shots.

"Now, come out of the waterfall and kiss very gently, keeping your arms at your sides because I want to be able to photograph your swimming costumes."

They took a break. Sammy heated up lake water and put it on the single Calor Gas ring, ready to make the tea.

To warm up, from the chilling effect of the waterfall, Robert and Miranda selected a large flat rock and soaked up the sun. Robert brushed Miranda's wet hair out to help it dry.

"You did just great," congratulated Jacques. "The next stop is a beautiful isolated beach. Sammy will drive us there."

Sammy changed direction and headed south towards the coast. As they crested a rise the reflection of the sun's rays off the glassy sea was obvious for all to see.

"Beautiful view," said Miranda.

"How do we get down there?" asked Jacques.

"Don't worry, man, there's a track a bit grown over now but it leads down to Smugglers' Cove."

"How exciting! Smugglers!" laughed, Miranda.

"Well, there used to be, and there may still be, but the Coastguard patrols the beaches now. One thing for certain, nobody is going to risk being caught by the Coastguard in broad daylight."

"Is it still used then?" asked Robert.

"I can't say, you know it's illegal smuggling goods in, but it's the nature of the Jamaican natives to do a bit of trade. We all have to make a living. It's not like in England where the Welfare State looks after the poor. Here you have to look out for yourself, man."

"Sorry, Sammy, I won't ask any more questions."

The van suddenly trundled down steeply as the track gave way to a rocky uneven surface. Clarence appeared at the rear cab window.

"What the hell are you trying to do to me?!" shouted Clarence, through the glass.

"Sorry, man, sit tight, it won't be long now!" shouted back, Sammy.

The track levelled out and took a turn and suddenly they were on the beach.

"What a lovely cove. Like a picture postcard, lovely silver sands and a few gently swaying palm trees and nobody to spoil it," admired Miranda.

"And if you look round, caves to hide in," pointed out, Sammy.

"Oh yes!" said a surprised, Robert.

"Jacques, as it's such a lovely day with a slight breeze, is it O.K. if Robert and I go swimming?"

"Sure. But, Robert, but don't let her go near any rocks, we don't want any blemishes on that beautiful body. The camera picks out every detail."

"Fancy a swim, Clarence, to cool off before we do another shoot?"

"I haven't a swimming costume?"

"Hell, man, there's nobody here to see you," said Sammy. "Well, I'm going in, in my shorts."

"All right, Jacques, I'll swim in my shorts."

Jacques took off his cotton trousers, threw them into the back of the van and ran bare-arsed naked down the sands and plunged into the sea.

"Nice bottom," said Clarence, and ran after Jacques.

"Well, you're not getting a look at my backside!" laughed Sammy, as he rushed past Clarence, heading for the water.

Sammy was a good swimmer and stroked strongly chasing after Jacques who was heading out to sea.

Miranda and Robert swam to the right of the cove, staying in the bath-warm sandy shallows, where an almost horizontal palm tree leant out over the crystal sea providing shade from its fronds. They frolicked like children, taking private time to rekindle their romance.

"You know, Robert, these last few weeks our lives have changed. When we were in Spain I was at my father's villa, El Estancia, and you were working from The Impressionist."

"I know, darling, but we were inseparable. We wrapped around each other in one house or the other. Our life was simple, we painted, we went to the Wednesday market at St Lucia, and the rest of the time we made love."

"Robert, I miss our intimacy. One minute we are in London: you at The Block, painting to display in The Arch, me being chased by Vogue or Estée Lauder for photographic shoots. It isn't the same any more."

"Miranda, my love, this is only our first day. You know, on this contract, it's all day work, so we have two weeks of evenings all to ourselves in The Flamingo."

"I hope so, I need you. My life is meaningless without you. Give me a cuddle."

They stood waist deep in the crystal water.

"Come here." Miranda wrapped her thighs around Robert's waist and he hugged her and pressed her firm young breasts into his manly chest.

"I love you. Your mind, your body, your soul. You are the best thing that has ever happened to me."

"Do you mean it, it's not just the ideal location and the fact that we are on a working holiday?"

"I loved you intensely when we were in Spain, didn't I?"

"Yes you did."

"Well, my sexpot, doesn't that tell you something?"

"Yes," she smiled, "it means you really love me."

He kissed her: her nose, forehead, cheeks, neck, nibbled her ears, tweaked her bottom and finally he kissed her on the lips.

"Come on, we had better swim back otherwise Jacques will wonder where we are."

The men were on the beach, drying-off under a Caribbean sun, and smoking. Robert knew that smell from one of the bars in Spain. It was marijuana. Robert thought it most likely that it was supplied by Sammy. At least marijuana is not as strong as the resin hashish from the flowers of the Cannabis plant.

"Hello you two lovers, you have come back then?" smiled, Sammy.

"Ready for work, Clarence?"

"Good," replied Jacques. "I see you wore your swimming cap, Miranda, to keep your hair dry."

"I tried."

"Come into the van and I will brush it out for you. I must have my model looking glamorous."

"It's O.K., Jacques, Miranda prefers me to do that," cut in Robert.

"This cove, Clarence, has a natural beauty, I want you to capture on camera. My models can have a backdrop of palm trees or a gentle shimmering sea to show off my evening collection."

"Come on you two, time to change. This evening gown should look a million dollars on you, Miranda. And this outfit, maestro, is for you, complete with the crocodile shoes."

"Right, Robert, Miranda, I want the first shots on the silver sand. I'm going to use the sun's natural reflection to produce a bright natural background, which will produce a fine contrast to your two figures."

"In evening wear, I have to say, Robert and Miranda look like a natural couple. I did a wise thing asking you, Robert, to be a model," said a self-congratulatory, Jacques.

"Well, to tell the truth, Jacques, I took it as an opportunity to be alone with Miranda."

"If I was in your shoes, I would have done the same thing," said Jacques.

"Really?"

"Sure. You are younger than me, and Miranda is a real catch. I think you are a really lucky man."

"Thanks, Jacques. She's a treasure. I met her when she was at a low, her husband had just died, and I came along at just the right time."

"I say, good luck to the pair of you."

Miranda was in the back of the van with Clarence putting her evening gown on. He, to her surprise, put her hair up with pins. Then showed it to her in the mirror.

"What do you think?"

"Clarence it looks great! I didn't know you were so talented."

"Just one more thing, Miss Miranda. Pearl earrings and a pearl necklace. How's that?"

"I think the word is, sophisticated, Clarence."

"Yes but a bit of a connived look."

"I agree, Miranda, you are at your most adorable, when you convey your natural naivety, not as worldly-wise."

"I think I would look my best as a blushing bride."

"But, Miranda, this is modelling. It's a glitzy world of business, not the least, profit."

Robert was waiting outside.

"Bingo! That's just the ticket, Miranda, a jackpot winner!"

"Glad you approve," smiled, Miranda, radiantly.

"I'd bet on you, Miranda, odds-on. Now, can we make a start please?"

"Sure, I'm ready."

"Robert?"

"Waiting to be commanded, Jacques, our leader."

"Come on Clarence, I'll help you with your equipment," offered, Robert.

"Thank you, I appreciate that. I'm not so young or as strong as you, Robert."

On the beach, Clarence was pleased the way the photo-shoot went, which pleased Jacques.

Sammy, being just the driver, took no part in the shoot so he smoked marijuana under the warming sun and totally relaxed.

"Now some shots at the top of the beach with the palm trees," said Jacques.

Clarence came into his own: composition, according to Clarence the photographer, was everything. And to that end he had Robert and Miranda peeping out from between tree trunks and, wrapped around tree trunks, which showed off the evening wear from different perspectives.

After the day's shoot Sammy drove the van back to The Flamingo.

"Same time tomorrow, Sammy."

"Sure, Mr Ferineaux. Should I help Mr Clarence with his photographic equipment back into the hotel?"

"Yes, please, Sammy," said Clarence.

Together, with Robert's help, Jacques Ferineaux wheeled the dress rail of designer clothes back into the hotel lobby for safekeeping.

"Want a hand, sir, Mr Jacques?" asked Hickory.

"Yes, Hickory, I want a secure room overnight for my collection."

"Follow me."

Hickory led Jacques down a corridor behind reception to a locked door.

"Wait here a minute while I go to the Duty Manager, to fetch the key."

"What is this room, Hickory?"

"The overnight security room. Nobody can get in here without the Duty Manager's permission."

"O.K., Hickory, here's a five, look after my designs; it's my living."

"Sammy!"

"Yes, Mr Jacques?"

"Before you go, make sure the van is locked up tonight and nobody steals it. Here's a ten, I'm relying on you."

In the evening Robert and Miranda decide to go into town. Running along the top of the beach is a promenade fronted with souvenir shops and open-air restaurants. Every small business has its own music with speakers competing for space and sound. The overall effect, with many brightly strung lights from unit to unit, is a carnival atmosphere.

"Hey beautiful lady, hair braiding only five dollars," offered a street hawker.

"No thanks, man, my girl's happy the way she is."

"Come on, man, only five dollars, good deal."

"Sorry buddy, not interested. Now stop bothering us."

"Lady, lady, portrait painting. You're a stunner. For you ten dollars."

"Young man," said Robert, "you should pay Miranda ten dollars for the privilege of sketching her beauty."

"What's with you, man, you gotta be joking, me pay?"

"I'm serious man," said an adamant Robert.

"Hey! On your way. Have a nice day!"

And so they strolled along amongst the music and the coloured lights, being offered as they went, dodgy cameras, watches and fake designer sunglasses, until they came to a restaurant which read, 'English Owner'. Their attention was caught by two large, glass fish tanks.

The sign said, 'Choose your own, fresh caught'.

"What are they, Robert?"

"Lobsters, darling, very tasty to eat."

"They look frightening, with those ugly heads and big claws."

"Have you eaten crab before?"

"Well, yes."

"Did you enjoy it?"

"Yes, I did actually, my father said it was a treat."

"There you go then. A lobster is a bit like a crab, except tastier. Shall we give it a try?"

"Hello, sir, are you coming in?" asked Mike.

"Possibly. How much is a lobster whole?"

"Ten dollars. What's your name?"

"Robert."

"Pleased to meet you. I'm Mike. Is this your beautiful wife?"

"Yes this is Miranda. O.K., tonight we'll have lobster and a bottle of white wine."

Robert and Miranda were waiting for their meal when a drumming noise could be heard. It appeared to be coming from the long stretch of beach, but it was hard to tell with the sand being dark. Then it got as lot louder until a steel band eased its way along the promenade and played outside Mike's restaurant.

The musicians were young men and a number of youths: both boys and girls, and they wore bright psychedelic clothing. The leader was a tall young man with arms full of flowers.

"Happy people, you like to dance?" asked the leader.

He held out a hat which contained several one dollar bills.

"Something for the hat?"

He placed a garland of flowers around Miranda's neck.

"There we go. Thank you, sir. Have a nice day!"

And he moved onto the next restaurant with his steel band trailing behind.

"Have a nice day? Obvious American influence here," said Robert.

"I don't know about that, I just think they want the benefit of the United States dollar. Let's face it, they are a bit backward with transport. Some of their cars are post-wartime."

"They probably don't manufacture any cars on Jamaica."

"I think it's unlikely, though they have some half reasonable buses, I've noticed," said Miranda.

"I bet they are imported from South America, probably Colombia or Venezuela."

"Could be from the much larger island of Cuba, because it's not so far across the Florida Strait to Florida from Havana," suggested Miranda.

"More likely the coachwork is formed on Cuba because the island has vast deposits of iron ore held in reserve by American companies. And then the engines are probably made by Ford and imported from Florida."

"You're too technical for me, Robert."

"Sorry, don't mean to be, I'm just full of useless information."

"Here you are, Mr Robert. Just what the doctor ordered."

"How do we get into it? I've never had a whole lobster before."

"With these," said Mike. "Crackers, a bit like nut crackers we use at Christmas. Let me demonstrate." And he cracked a claw open.

"Oh, I see. You use your fingers."

"That's right, darling. And sprinkle a little black pepper on it enhances the flavour of the white meat."

"Enjoy your meal," said Mike, and he poured the wine.

Once Miranda started cracking she couldn't stop. She made good use of the finger bowl with bits of lemon floating in it and the generous sized napkin.

They both tucked into the tasty lobster accompanied by fresh crusty bread and salad.

A short while later the steel band made a return pass along the promenade, and this time the musicians were singing. They stopped on the beachfront and half the musicians became dancers. The young ladies in the band invited several of the diners, who had finished their meal and were now enjoying after-dinner drinks, to come and dance on the sand.

Miranda wiped her face and hands on her napkin and stood up.

"Come on, Robert, let's dance."

Miranda went with the Jamaican girl and danced in front of the drummers, as did a few of the other couples.

The Jamaican girls thumped the sand with their feet in time to the steel rhythm and shuffled forward. Miranda mimicked the girls and was justly rewarded by the clapping of the on-lookers, the captured passers-by.

Robert crossed the promenade and went onto the sand in front of Miranda.

"Yeh man," said the leader, "get with the beat, let yourself go. Get those feet jumping and a thumping!"

"O.K. You're on!" said Robert, and he kicked his sandals off.

Robert found the cool, soft, silky sand refreshing.

"Hi Miranda! If you can do it so can I."

He went behind Miranda, and put his arms around her waist and bent his knees outward and joined in the thumping beat.

The other musicians cheered them on, and after five minutes quite an audience had built up as tourists stopped to listen to the steel band and watch the cavorting couple in the middle.

The band leader encouraged clapping to the rhythmic beat and the audience joined in.

When the band stopped Miranda and Robert fell down on the sand exhausted and there was general applause. They strolled back across to Mike's restaurant.

"You two were great!" congratulated, Mike.

"Two long beers, please, Mike."

"You want with ice?"

"Sure, good idea."

"Please sit at your table. I have a surprise for you. Fresh strawberries and cream or fresh bananas with vanilla ice cream?"

"Neither. We'll have strawberries with ice cream because that's the coolest choice."

"O.K., ice cream with strawberries it is."

And so the two weeks passed: daytime was for photo-shoots; evenings were for pleasure.

Chapter Seven

Back in London Jacques Ferineaux had done himself proud. The next issue of Vogue was, in the main, about Jacques's creations, with page after page of glossy glamour photographs of Robert and Miranda.

There was such a rush from clothing manufacturers, all begging for the copyright to produce Jacques's designs, that Jacques launched his own clothes label, simply 'J. Ferineaux', at a fashion show.

He contracted a manufacturer in Leicester because labour costs were a lot lower than in the London area. Jacques went personally to supervise the on-site copyright designer, and inspected the finished products after the first two weeks' production. It was just a small batch of two of his creations, but he found fault with Quality Control and immediately suspended production until the garments were re-worked to his total satisfaction.

The manufacturer said his workers had to be paid, whether or not the first order was sold, to secure their commitment to produce Jacques's garments to his high standards in the forthcoming weeks.

"All right, Ranjit Singh, as I have made the alterations, without giving you notice, I'll pay your workers for the first two weeks. But if you screw up on the new alterations you lose the contract and the right to use my label, 'J. Ferineaux'. Is that fair?"

"You must remember we are working with new materials, my machinists and seamstresses need time to adapt to the patterns and colours. I suggest you stay at a hotel in Leicester this week so that you can see the prototypes of each of your creations as they come off the production line. After all, you are my customer and you have chosen me and my experience to be your supplier."

"I agree, but at the end of the day we are making quality not quantity. The prices are to be kept artificially high and the supply deliberately in short stock. You will, initially, only produce a hundred of each of my creations."

"You are a crafty businessman, Jacques."

"Yes, we will see which of my designs has the greatest demand. I will choose which shops are privileged enough to stock the 'J. Ferineaux' label."

With the sudden rise in Jacques Ferineaux's fame came the rise in celebrity status of Robert and Miranda.

At The Hilton in London the Chief Editor of Vogue, Pauline, held a photo-shoot for the world's press – not just local newspapers or weekly magazines but the glossy monthlies, the national papers, and, in particular, The Sunday Times and The News Of The World.

Jake Higgins, the Picture Reporter for The News Of The World, who had had a close shave with Miranda in The Red Lantern, was also present. He approached Robert, and Robert immediately went on the offensive. He stared, his neck muscles tensed and he clenched his fists ready to strike to defend his beautiful Miranda. But Jake Higgins smiled and offered the hand of friendship.

Jake shrugged his shoulders, all twenty stone of muscle and sinew.

"Am I forgiven? I've come to apologise for the rumpus in The Red Lantern restaurant. Sorry, I'm a bit like a bloodhound, I follow the scent going for the story and sometimes get overexcited. Come on, I spent seven days in the police cells because of my stupidity. I got the worst deal."

"O.K.," said Robert. "No fists?"

"I promise," said Jake, "to behave myself."

They shook hands.

"A shot, Miranda, with Jacques?"

"All right," agreed Miranda.

"Hello, Miranda, may I introduce myself. I'm Veronica Lawnswood, Literary Editor for The Sunday Times Supplement."

"Yes, I've read some of your reviews, I believe? You review films, theatre, books and, recently, the lives of famous people in fashion. Am I right?"

"Yes, that's me. Though I don't do it all by myself. I have staff to assist me. May I ask how you became a model?"

"This is Robert, my partner. I think he can explain better than me."

"Hello, Robert, Veronica Lawnswood. Can we try and find a corner away from photographers?"

"Sure, out the back. A bit about Miranda, what will you call it?"

"How about, 'Miranda's Story'. I don't do fashion or glamour photography that's the remit of the Fashion Editor."

"Well, the beginning is sad. I met Miranda this summer in Spain, really by accident. She was staying at her father's villa, El Estancia, on the coast of Atalia, and I sort of bumped into her. The fact of the matter is she was on her own grieving over the death of her new husband, Edward."

"Her new husband?"

"Yes, she had only been married four weeks when Edward was killed in a road accident."

"I'm sorry to hear that, but go on."

"Well, I live a few minutes from Seagull Cove, that is a cove at the beachfront of El Estancia, and the place where I paint."

"Of course, you're Robert Darling, Teddy Rosenburgh's new artist at The Arch. And you painted and displayed Miranda nude?"

"That's right. I didn't know I was that famous."

"Carry on. You were painting at Seagull Cove."

"Yes, I was up in the rocks painting the nesting gulls and my eye was caught by something bright red on the beachfront. Well, for my work I carry binoculars and seeing the lady in red on the beach I was inspired to paint Miranda, sitting on the beachfront rocks. After she had gone I left my painting on the rock where she had been sitting, weighted down by a flat stone.

"The next day she was on the beach again, this time, as it turned out, with her maid, Maria, and she picked up the picture. I came down from the rocks where I was painting and introduced myself. I took Miranda to lunch on the beachfront at John's Restaurant. It turned out she had stayed inside her father's villa for a month solid, grieving over the loss of her husband, Edward, and had hardly eaten. Well, she came down to the beach and I asked her if she was hungry, and she admitted, for the first time in a month, she was famished. I took her to lunch, nothing special, just local fish with crusty bread and a bit of salad.

"John pointed out I had no money and, therefore, how was I going to pay? But Linda, John's wife, said they had sold one of my paintings hanging in the restaurant, and therefore the pesetas I had made from that would pay for the meal.

"Then, from there on, Miranda trusted me and we saw each other regularly. We went together to St Lucia's Wednesday Market and, with the help of Miranda's bubbly personality and beautiful looks, we sold all my paintings. At the market I was discovered by Teddy Rosenburgh, who brought me to England, to paint in The

Block and display in The Arch. Miranda and I were photographed in the London papers, and since Miranda's beauty has been captured she has been contracted by Vogue and Estée Lauder. She even has a beauty product named after her called 'Virgin's Blush'.

"Once Miranda became Cover Girl for Vogue fashion designers came after her. We have just returned from Jamaica, doing a fashion-shoot for Jacques Ferineaux. He is launching a new range of designer clothing for the 'J.Ferineaux' label, which means I had to model the clothes as well as Miranda."

"That's what I am after, Robert, the story of the 'inside-girl'. How does your relationship work?"

"Very well, thank you. We work together at sketching and painting, and are both romantics. Miranda is a very generous, open, loving young lady, and that, I think, wraps it up."

"Thank you, Robert. It is the person I write about, the 'human interest', not the surface glitz. I review the person behind the story. Do you think Miranda would like to write a book about her life, something like: 'From Death To Fame'?"

"I don't think so, she's so young, still only twenty-three."

The world's press published the photographs of Jacques Ferineaux's fashion show at the London Hilton, and soon Robert and Miranda became international celebrities.

In Paris, France, the exclusive fashion houses wanted a bite of the cake, and manufacturers were clambering over one another to be the first to produce and stock the 'J. Ferineaux' label.

The Sunday Times was flown across the Atlantic carrying Veronica Lawnswood's story of the 'Real Miranda', and hinted at a book on Miranda's rise to fame.

The News Of The World was read in New York. Jake Higgins plastered page after page with pictures of Robert and Miranda, modelling Jacques Ferineaux's creations with titbits written in between.

The next step was that Miranda and Robert were interviewed live by Thames Television. Robert Darling the artist became every young woman's heart-throb until he announced to the media that he was getting married, and this was even a bigger surprise to Miranda.

"What's this, Robert? 'Artist, Robert Darling to marry', in The Guardian?"

"Sorry, darling, I was asked and it just sort of popped out."

"You might have asked me first! I presume it is me you are marrying?"

"Of course, darling, I love you very much. I wanted it to be a surprise."

"It's a surprise all right. You haven't proposed?"

"That's because I wanted to make the cottage ready first."

"What cottage?"

"Our marital home where you can raise our children."

"You've bought a cottage without telling me?"

"It's my wedding present to you. I was going to propose as soon as the decorators had finished."

"Haven't you forgotten something?"

"What's that my love?"

"Our engagement. It's normal and traditional to get engaged first."

"Well, I haven't forgotten. Come here."

He got down on one knee and flipped open a ring box with a huge diamond inside.

"Miranda, will you marry me?"

"Of course I will. When did you buy it?"

"Secret. Never mind. Try it on. Do you like it?"

"Yes! Yes, and I will marry you. I didn't want to push you, that's why I didn't mention marriage, because you said to wait."

"You're part of me now, Miranda, I couldn't live without you."

"Do you, Robert, want children?"

"Yes, very much. Perhaps they will be artistic also."

"Or all girls, and take after me and be beautiful!" laughed Miranda with happiness and relief.

"I don't mind if we have boys or girls as long as we have healthy children."

"Good, let's start now!"

"Start what now?"

"Having children!" and Miranda dropped her dress to the floor and bared all.

"But it's day-time and I'm reading the paper?"

"Never mind that." She took her brassiere off and sat on his lap. "You never bothered before we were famous, whether it was day or night, you just desired me," said Miranda, rubbing her beautiful begging-to-be-kissed tits in his face.

"You vixen!" He took her there and then on the lounge carpet, and because they were not on a springy mattress Robert gained extra penetration, which drove Miranda wild with excitement.

Afterwards they cuddled up in their double bed, contented, and Robert thought about their new cottage.

"You do like the name Rose Cottage, don't you?"

"Sounds perfect, how did you know what I wanted?"

"I remembered one day when we were out for a drive south of London, and you said, 'Look my ideal home, Rose Cottage', don't you remember?"

"Yes I do. But I was only fantasizing, Robert."

"That may be so, but the fantasy is a reality now. The Block has served its purpose. I don't have to live in it. Teddy Rosenburgh has got what he wanted but I can, from now on, travel into The Block and paint. Of course I will keep exhibiting my works in The Arch and Teddy will get his commission, so everybody will be happy."

"Especially if we are to have our own home. Thank you, darling. Fancy, me with a husband and children and Rose Cottage. Can I go and see it?"

"Of course, my darling. You took the very words out of my mouth."

"It's just perfect! What a romantic you are, Robert Darling!"

"Yes, unusual isn't it. A small arbour to lead into the front door. Makes a change from a traditional porch. I chose the bamboo trelliswork myself and the roses."

"Can we go in?"

"Of course, I have a set of keys."

"Mr Darling, sir, I thought I heard voices," said Jack, who was there with his son, both decorators. "Would you like to see the finished job?"

"Yes please!" said an excited Miranda."

"Son, put the kettle on while I show Mr and Mrs Darling around the cottage."

"Lead on, Jack, but it's Miss Miranda and Robert Darling, we aren't married yet."

"Ah well, Mr Robert, it's none of my business, I'm just the decorator."

"Look, Jack, we have just got engaged!" said an excited, Miranda, waving her diamond solitaire in Jack's face. "I have to tell someone or I'll burst!"

"Then congratulations, Miss. Looks an expensive ring. And, as I understand it, this thatched cottage is a wedding gift to you from Mr Robert here. Do you like it? I have carried out Mr Darling's instructions to the letter?"

"You've done grand, Jack. The rooms, as instructed, are all light and airy."

"I've tried to make it bright and spacious, sir, and in here I've used the picture wallpaper you chose."

"A nursery! But I'm not pregnant yet?"

"I can soon put that right!" laughed Robert.

"Oh, Robert! I love you!"

"If you'll both excuse me, I think it's time for that cup of tea," said Jack.

"Good idea, Jack, let's celebrate."

They all went into the kitchen.

"Good gracious, Robert! All new units, and in Antique Oak! It's beautiful! How did you choose?"

"Jack advised me as to what was the most suitable in a period thatched cottage."

"Thank you, Jack, you have done a wonderful job. I like the built-in cooker and, dishwasher with matching front panels. But what about the washing machine and a tumble dryer?"

"That you will have to ask your new husband."

"Well, Robert?"

"I thought, as I have chosen the decorating, the rest: furniture; curtains and carpets; light fittings and electrical appliances should be the woman's choice?"

"Very sensible, I agree. A housewife should be allowed to make a house a home."

"Mr Darling, sir, about payment?"

"I know you have spent a lot on the kitchen with units and appliances, let alone the rest of the cottage, which is why I have brought my chequebook with me."

"I appreciate that, sir. Could we discuss the matter in private?"

"Of course, your van do?"

"If you don't mind, Mr Robert, and here's the keys."

"Thank you, Jack. Could you recommend a reliable removal van?"

"Mr Robert, if I may say so, you would be wise buying all new furniture and letting the various retail stores supply all the transport, then you wont have all the hassle of moving house, or the expense of a removal wagon and two men to pay for."

"Hadn't thought of that. Thanks, Jack, good idea. Goodbye and thank you."

"Here you are, sweetheart, the key to the door."

"Let's go shopping, Robert."

"Where do you want to go first?"

"Mothercare!"

"Mothercare? That's a bit previous. We need carpets and curtains first. Let's get some suppliers round."

"Where do we start?"

"I've had the telephone installed so let your fingers do the walking, sweetheart."

"Yellow Pages?"

"Exactly! If the traders want the business let them do the legwork and bring their samples to us."

"Yes, I like pattern books," said Miranda.

"First of all let's go buy a washing machine and a tumble dryer."

"What about furniture?"

"Darling, when I said let's go shopping I meant for everything."

"Oh goody! But furniture I think you buy to order?"

"I'll invite a carpet company to call tomorrow, then we can stay in while our new washing machine and tumble dryer are delivered."

"We haven't bought them yet?"

"But we are about to. Come on, let's go get in the car."

"Where shall we buy?"

"Somewhere like Comet or Currys. It depends on who gives the best service. If they have the showroom models in their warehouses ready for delivery then we'll buy."

"That was easy at Comet. Can we go to Mothercare, next?"

"If that's what you want."

"I would like a wool carpet the baby can crawl on and feel comfortable and warm. Also a child's chest of drawers for the baby clothes and a half-space wardrobe, and a crib fashioned out of bamboo. And, oh, one of those baby intercom things."

"Good idea. I don't think it is a good idea to have the baby's crib in the same room as our bed. We would never get any sleep and he would always cry for attention."

"Who's to say it will be a he?"

"Figure of speech dear. All right, baby boy or girl."

"In Mothercare Miranda bought first size baby nappies and various baby products: a carrycot and several sets of baby clothes, and blankets for the crib.

"What do you want a potty for, it's not born yet?"

"Just being practical for when he can sit up. Anyway, I have to conceive first. Shall I come off the contraceptive pill this month, or do you want to wait until we are married, Mr Darling, darling?"

"Well, we have had fashion shows and photo-shoots. Now it's time for us and a family."

They next went to Customer Services.

"Can we have help with delivering all this lot to our estate car in the multi-storey?"

"Yes sir, I'll get two assistants to help you with your purchases."

"Should I have bought a pram?" asked Miranda when they were back in the car.

"Darling, we haven't got a baby yet and, anyway, it will have to be delivered. Do people still use prams? I thought it was more baby slings and fold-up pushchairs, seeing as children are transported by car these days."

"Let's go order some furniture then," suggested Miranda.

"Where to? Furniture Village or maybe John Peters?"

"I don't know, Furniture Village?"

"They are all huge modern showrooms usually sited on a Retail Park. There's bound to be one off the M25."

"Yes sir, may I help you with your search, this being an expansive showroom. This your first visit to our store?"

"Yes, you can help us. I wish to furnish a whole house and would like a complete delivery."

"The delivery would be six to eight weeks as our quality furniture is bought in to order."

"That's O.K. we're not in a particular hurry, but we would like all our furniture delivered together."

"In that case, as your orders arrive we will store your furniture for you, but we have to put a limit of three months as we are always pressed for space in our warehouses."

"Fair enough but we would like one delivery when it is all ready."

"Are you prepared to pay for a driver and a mate for half a day?"

"How much will that cost?"

"I will have to O.K. it with our manager but, bearing in mind delivery for single items is £35.00 or more, I would say a fee of £100.00 would be very fair."

"I agree. If we have a settee, a rocking chair, desk with chair, dining table and chairs, bedroom furniture and a double bed, plus occasional furniture, then a £100.00 is probably a good deal."

"O.K. would you like me to help you out by showing you around our extensive showrooms?"

"Yes please. When you arrive in one of these huge places it can be overwhelming, so I am pleased if a friendly salesman comes and talks to me to break the atmosphere so to speak."

"Well, to be honest, some people don't like to be helped, they just like to wander around. The problem is, on a Retail Park, there are several furniture stores, and having already been in one or two it can be confusing and, over time, stressful. So we invite our customers to relax. Have a sit down and a cup of coffee, and give them time to explain what's in their mind when it comes to choices, because many customers have a good idea of what they want, even before they come into the store because they have discussed it at home. I find that my customers don't suddenly make a decision to buy furniture, they have been thinking about it over a period of weeks, because either they are moving house and want new furniture, or their settee or bed is worn out and they are looking for a replacement."

"You seem very knowledgeable for a salesman?"

"That's because I am a Sales Consultant. It's my job to learn product knowledge from suppliers and sales representatives. Where possible I go to the manufacturers' factories so that I have knowledge of what I am selling, which means you consult me on product knowledge.

"For example, customers like to know what settee covers are made of and how to clean them and, with mattresses, what's inside them: the spring count for support and the upholstery for comfort. The best mattresses are hand finished using a long needle and thread for edge stitching, and placed in a compressing machine when strong tufts are added, which holds the upholstery in place, which means the mattress is more durable and therefore retains its shape for comfort and support."

""Right, this is a list of the furniture we require," said Robert.

"A salesman's dream."

Some ten weeks later, on a prearranged date, a large furniture wagon from The Furniture Store arrived at Rose Cottage.

By that time the cottage had all its light fittings installed, every carpet fitted, curtains hanging and pictures displayed, most of which were chosen by Miranda. All that was required was for the dining room, the lounge and the bedrooms to be furnished, including the spare room and the nursery, which was rather bare being furnished with a sole crib.

The kitchen appliances had been delivered weeks ago, but the general furniture had had to be ordered from the various manufacturers.

Before the delivery men had time to knock on the front door Miranda, swung it open and said with a big smile, "You have my furniture then?!"

"Good morning, Miss. We have a delivery for Mr Robert Darling, Rose Cottage."

"Yes, you have the right place. I am soon to be Mrs Robert Darling. Robert is my fiancé," she said waving her engagement ring.

"What would you like in first?"

Robert took charge. "Let's start at the top and work down. How about the wardrobe and the double bed first?"

"Fine with us, sir, you're the customer."

"Bert, untie the double wardrobe, it's going up first."

As fast as the men carefully brought furniture in Miranda unwrapped it like an excited child, and between them, Robert and Miranda, assembled the double bed, putting the castors on, clamping the two halves of the base together and screwing the headboard on.

The sheets of corrugated cardboard, webbing straps and protective plastic corners from all the packaging were removed and piled in the front garden.

It took between them two hours to unload and place all the furniture in the rooms exactly where directed by Miranda.

"Thank you, gentlemen. Now that we have a table and chairs to sit on, please come into the kitchen and enjoy a cup of tea. Now, here's a fiver each for your trouble. I would like you to take away all the packaging in the house and in the garden. Is that O.K. with you?"

"That's fine, Mr Darling. Soon as we have had our tea."

"Relax, there's no hurry. I know modern furniture made of high-density fibreboard can be very heavy, and a good quality double mattress can be excruciatingly heavy, so take your time."

"At least we are not double-handling. Many customers want their old three-piece suite and double bed removed. Well, they have to be disposed of."

"What about recycling? I mean a good suite will have a strong frame. With seasoned wood being expensive nowadays, wouldn't an upholstery company be interested?"

"Possibly. That's not up to us. That's up to the Warehouse Manager. But I see your point; a company that does re-upholstery may be interested, but I'd imagine that the labour cost of stripping down and reupholstering would make the new suite expensive."

"As long as you clear up after you, that's all I am bothered about," smiled Miranda.

"Right, thanks for the tea. We'll be off now, Miss, Mr Darling."

"Right, Mr Darling, we need a baby in the nursery."

"What right now?"

"Come on, we have a beautiful, pocketed sprung bed. I've made it, now is the time to christen it!"

"Are you sure about this?"

"Yes, about four weeks ago I stopped taking the contraceptive pill. I should be fertile by now. Come on, I want a baby."

"You never told me?"

"Well we haven't discussed a wedding date yet."

"I guess if you are planning on a baby it had better be sooner rather than later. Then we had better go and see the Reverend Thompson in Lower Dale."

"We hardly know him, we only met him last Sunday. Do you think he will marry us in St. Winifred's?"

"Let's go ask him."

"You mean surprise him?"

"Why not, he lives in the vicarage, just down the lane," suggested Robert.

"What about the baby?"

"Wedding first!"

"O.K. The vicarage, it is."

"Yes. We didn't get time to be acquainted last week. I can certainly marry you. You will have to attend three weeks in a row for the banns to be read. I will need your full names."

"Robert Darling and Mrs Miranda Saunders."

"You've been married before. I'm afraid the Church of England is rather old fashioned on re-marrying divorced ladies."

"No, no, vicar, I am not divorced. My husband was killed in a road accident. I am a widow."

"Dear God, I am so sorry to hear that. And you so young. Please forgive me. I shall be pleased to marry you. For church formalities I will have to see the Marriage Certificate and a copy of the Death Certificate. I'm sure you understand."

"How soon can you marry us?"

"My, you're in a hurry. Are you in the family way?"

"No, not yet, vicar, but we have just moved into Rose Cottage and are planning to start a family straight away."

"Ah! The old brigadier's place. Pity none of his children wanted the cottage, so the estate was shared out between them. I'm glad it has gone to a young couple. Lower Dale is mostly inhabited by elderly people looking for somewhere quiet to retire. It will be a refreshing change to hear some children's voices in the village. On the banns I need to state what your occupations are?"

"I'm an artist," said Robert. "And Miranda is a model. Perhaps you've seen her photograph in Vogue."

"Can't say as I have. Vogue is a fashion magazine isn't it?"

"Yes that's right."

"My reading matter is more Church Reporter and the bishop's letters. No call for it, you see, in the village shop. I don't think Mrs Burns would stock anything more exciting than Family Circle or Woman's Weekly. You know, traditional women's magazines. I don't think the Women's Institute would approve of a glossy magazine like Vogue."

"Are the women here very conservative?"

"Yes, Miranda, with a capital 'C'. All tweeds and brogues. In fact, at a distance, you can't always tell the women from the men," laughed Reverend Thompson.

"I hope they will like children around the village."

"Of course they will. Your forthcoming family will have loads of grandparents."

"That's a relief."

"So, shall we say three Saturday's from this weekend for the wedding date?"

"Yes, please."

"Good. And welcome to the village. Now, if you will excuse me, I have to visit one of my parishioners who is in need of some company."

"Goodbye, vicar."

"Come on, Robert, now that we are members of the village of Lower Dale let's go and introduce ourselves."

"Where to, Miranda?"

"The vicar mentioned Mrs Burns at the Village Shop, so let's start there."

"Do we want shopping?"

"Men! You have no idea. The tea making things we used today I brought from The Block in London. We have nothing to eat. In case it hasn't sunk in, we moved in today. From tonight we are living at Rose Cottage, not just fixing it up with curtains and things as we did before. We live there now."

"But what about my work?"

"You said you would commute."

"Maybe. I could live and work at The Block from Monday to Friday and come home at weekends."

"Let's not decide that now because the simple solution would be to keep on The Block, paying Teddy Rosenburgh his rent, and live at Rose Cottage as and when it suits us. Don't forget we are a partnership. I work as well."

"O.K., as I know nothing about the kitchen situation let's go fill up the refrigerator at Mrs Burns'."

"Hello, Mrs Burns?"

"Yes, who wants to know?"

"We've come to introduce ourselves, we're the new owners of Rose Cottage."

"Yes, word has it that there has been various tradesmen's vans coming and going from Rose Cottage. I guessed somebody had bought it."

"Well, that's us. Robert and Miranda. And you can come to our wedding at St Winifred's if you like."

"Not married then. I don't approve of young people co-habiting."

"We are quite respectable. We have more than one bedroom. The wedding is three weeks from this Saturday."

"In that case, welcome to Lower Dale and congratulations. Now, what can I get you?"

"A bit of everything, I think. We have to stock the kitchen up."

"Are you paying cash?"

"As good as. I have plenty of money in the bank, so I use my debit card."

"Well, that's all right by me, because I don't take credit cards. I can't afford the merchant's commission, not at my prices. The big supermarkets put the squeeze on me."

"Don't worry my card is good, you can check it in your machine if you like."

"You seem like an honest young man, so I believe you."

"And, before I forget, I would like to order a copy of Vogue as a regular order."

"Vogue you say. Well, I can get it but there will be a pound handling charge. The post van drops off my magazine orders weekly."

"That's O.K., Mrs Burns, we don't mind the extra charge, do we, Robert?"

"Absolutely not. We are not on a fixed income like a pension, so money is no problem."

"Glad to hear it. It's about time some working people, beside myself that is, brought some new money into the village."

"We'll take one of almost everything, Mrs Burns."

"Even firelighters?"

"Firelighters? No, we have got gas central heating."

"Lucky you. Not everybody in the village has the luxury of mains gas. Many have Calor Gas and only use the cylinders in the cold winter months. Mind you, those that have it, suffer damp from the condensation."

"What about coal fires, Mrs Burns?"

"Well, some burn coal but have you seen the price of coal lately? Dearer than gold dust."

"Don't they have an Aga or a Rayburn?"

"Yes, many do. And on them you can burn almost anything. But there again, the price of logs has gone up."

"Surely there's plenty of trees around Lower Dale."

"Of course there is, but the woods, for the most part, are privately owned and managed. There's signs on most of the copses around here saying, 'Trespassers will be Prosecuted'.

"And the landed gentry, here about, employ wardens who patrol the woods protecting trees and game birds alike."

"I say, old chap, are you buying the whole shop, because if you are I'll come back another day."

"Don't be such an old fool, Percy. Meet Robert and Miranda, new residents of Rose Cottage."

"Ah, the brigadier's old place. Just popped in for my usual, Mrs Burns."

"We'll be a while, go on get your order in."

"Name's Percy Lennox, retired of the army years ago, Captain Lennox."

"Old Holborn for your pipe and a paper is it, Percy?"

"Yes, and I'll have a quarter of jelly babies."

"As a welcome gift, Percy, you can put the jelly babies on my bill."

"Awfully good of you, Robert. I'm not mean, you know, just that my service pension isn't worth very much nowadays."

"Mrs Burns, make that two quarters of jelly babies. I haven't had any for ages."

"Since, Mr Robert, your bill is over a hundred pounds, I'll treat you to the jelly babies."

"Thank you, Mrs Burns, and good day to you, Captain Percy."

"What other shops are there, Mrs Burns?"

163

"At the other end of the village, opposite the Black Bull on The Green, you'll find a butcher and a small bakery-cum-cake shop."

"Yes, I noticed the Black Bull when we were house hunting. What's it like?"

"All right, I suppose, if you're disposed to drinking. Don't touch the stuff myself, except for a small brandy for medicinal purposes."

"I think that's enough, Robert. If you pay I'll start taking it out to the car," said Miranda.

"How much, Mrs Burns?"

"One hundred and nine pounds, and forty-six pence, please."

"Thank you and goodbye."

"Robert, I'm starving. Let's get to the baker."

"Hello, sir, haven't seen you in here before. Are you visiting?"

"We are new neighbours. Just moved into Rose Cottage."

"Yes, I heard there were new people in. The tradesmen tell me you see. They drop in here for elevenses. You know, a crusty sandwich and a pork pie."

"You do sandwiches?"

"Yes, sir, fresh baked bread. Though we don't do pork pies. You can buy them next door in the butcher's."

"A ham sandwich, Miranda?"

"Yes, please! And a bloomer and a tinned loaf fit for sandwiches."

"Coming right up."

"And," said Robert, "a couple of custard slices. I used to love them as a kid."

"You, Robert, are still a big kid."

They sat in their estate car and munched their crusty sandwiches.

"Meat," said Robert. "That's what a man needs."

"Hello sir, miss. What can I get you?"

"Please just call me Robert. We have an empty freezer, as we have just moved in."

"Will that be Rose Cottage, Mr Robert?"

"That's us. This is my fiancée, Miranda. We will be getting married in St Winifred's Church three Saturday's from this weekend so, if you like, you are invited to the wedding."

"Yes, we will be there," spoke up Mary, the butcher's wife. "I like a wedding, thank you."

"Now what will it be, Mr Robert?"

"Two one pound bags of best beef mince, two one pound bags of best stewing steak, some steak and a couple of joints, and a couple of chickens for freezing."

"What about bacon and fresh eggs?"

"We've bought eggs at the Village Shop, but bacon I'll have two one pound's of smoked back bacon, and two one pound strings of Cumberland sausages."

"Now the joints, what would you like?"

"Something small, suitable for two people."

"I have a large joint of topside of beef, which I could cut in half for you to make two smaller joints."

"How much is the joint?"

"Ten pounds fifty pence, sir."

"O.K., cut it in half."

"There you go, Mr Robert. Now what steaks do you want?"

"Do you have rib-eye?"

"Yes, in the cooler. I'll just fetch it. Now what size of steaks do you want?"

"Half a pound each. Let's say six."

"I would like a leg of lamb, Robert," said Miranda.

"And a leg of lamb please."

"Would you like the bone cut off and the joint halved to give you two half-legs of lamb?"

"Good idea, there will only be two of us eating."

"I have some loin of pork if you would like some."

"No thanks, but a couple of choice pork chump chops would be very nice."

"There's your order then. Thanks for your business, do come again."

"Just a minute, how about a couple of individual pork pies for our lunch."

"Not for me, Robert, I have to watch my figure. Too much fat in a pork pie, and they add all that gelatine."

"Right, just one pork pie."

"Here, as a valued customer, have it on the house."

Three weeks from Saturday, on the twenty-fifth of August, the bells of St Winifred's were ringing out, thanks to real campanologists. The sun was blazing and there was a light breeze which ruffled the leaves of the trees in the churchyard.

Of all people Max was the best man, and he was proud to be chosen. Max greeted Pauline from Vogue; Felicity Swanson from Estée Lauder; Teddy Rosenburgh from The Arch; Jake Higgins from The News of The World, complete with cameras. Jake was busy snapping everybody as they arrived: the traders of Lower Dale, Mrs Burns from the Village Shop; Sam Smith from the Black Bull; the butcher and the baker and their wives and, Captain Percy Lennox, retired.

Robert waited with baited breath for Miranda's parents, Amos and Annette, to arrive from Atalia in Spain.

A black London taxi pulled up outside of the church and Amos and Annette piled out followed by Maria, Miranda's maid and John and Linda from the beachfront restaurant next to Seagull Cove.

"Welcome, welcome!" boomed Max. "And who are you lucky people?"

"Let me introduce Amos and Annette, Miranda's parents from Spain, and this is Maria the maid. We offer special thanks to Maria because, if it wasn't for her, Miranda and I would never have met," explained, Robert.

"I've come as a bridesmaid to surprise, Miranda," smiled Maria.

"Hello, John and Linda, thanks for coming."

"Max, these are my friends from Spain. They helped me sell my first paintings when I had no money."

"This is Max, my chauffeur when I am in London."

The Reverend Thompson kept looking at his watch.

"Don't worry, Reverend," said Max, "I'll have them all seated before the bride arrives. This is Amos, the bride's father, he has flown in from Spain to give his daughter away."

"At last, the bride's father is here. Thank God for that. Usher can you ask the guests to be seated please."

"Sure thing, Rev," said Max, with a big smile.

"You had better go to the front of the church now, Robert. You're not supposed to see the bride in her wedding dress until she walks down the aisle."

"Go on, Robert, I'll bring Miranda down the aisle on my arm as soon as the car arrives."

The wedding car drew up, a white Rolls-Royce convertible with the top down.

"See you in a minute, dear," said Amos to Annette.

"You look absolutely stunning, Miranda."

"Oh, father, thank you for coming, are you going to give me away?"

"Of course, darling. It will be my utmost pleasure."

"Hello, Miranda!"

"Maria! Oh what a surprise! I didn't know you were coming?"

"It was Robert's idea. His way of saying thank you, because you brought us together."

"Only by accident."

"Well, I'm overjoyed that you are here."

"I've come to be your bridesmaid."

"Oh bless you. You can carry my train, just like in the old fashioned weddings."

"Come on, Miranda, the vicar is getting fidgety. Put your veil down. Take my arm."

"Oh dear, dad, I've gone all nervous."

"All you have to do is smile, be radiant. For you that's natural, just be yourself."

The usher signalled the organist. The Reverend Thompson rushed to the altar and awaited the bridal procession.

The organist struck up 'Here Comes The Bride', and the congregation all turned to look at Miranda. There were many wide smiles, even old Captain Percy gave her a smile. Mrs Burns may have been only the village shopkeeper but she was moved and wept into her handkerchief, remembering many, many years ago when she was a bride.

Miranda carried a bouquet of freesias and lily-of-the-valley, which gave off a beautiful sweet scent as she passed all the happy faces.

She came to stand beside Robert, who dared to steal glance at her. She put out her hand, gripping Robert's, and said with simplicity, "I love you."

"You're beautiful my bride," and Robert's face lit-up with supreme joy.

"Ah hum!" coughed Reverend Thompson. "Face the front, please," he whispered to the glowing couple.

"We are gathered here in the sight of God…"

"You are now husband and wife. You may kiss the bride."

Robert lifted Miranda's veil as if it was made of gold leaf and, in that moment, just before their joining, Miranda gave her 'Virgin's Blush'.

The cameraman, Jake Higgins, was quick; he took the picture with the look, immediately after her veil was lifted.

"Go on then, Robert, kiss her, she's your wife now," encouraged Jake.

Jake, again at a discreet distance in the wings, took another beautiful photograph, and with his expensive camera, zoomed in for a close up.

"Thank you, you two, I'm going to put your wedding on the front page of The News of The World. You make a perfect couple."

After signing the Register of Marriage it was time to walk back down the aisle.

While the Reverend Thompson didn't allow confetti in the church he just smiled because it was thrown in the church porch, the well-wishers pent up with adoration had to have a joyous relief.

"Congratulations! What a beautiful couple!" shouted the usually reserved Mrs Burns. "I have a present for you."

"That's very kind of you," said Robert, almost overcome by so many well-wishers.

Amos stepped in, "I'll take care of that son-in-law."

"Thanks, dad."

"Let me give my married daughter a kiss."

"You're so beautiful, Miranda," cried her mother, Annette, with relief and pride, "and so young to be married for the second time."

"Oh, mother, give me a hug. Before you know it you'll be a grandmother."

"A grandmother? You mean?"

"Yes! I'm excited, but I haven't told Robert yet. I haven't had a check-up yet at the doctor, but I've missed my period, so keep it to yourself."

"Oh that's wonderful news! Did you plan it?"

"Oh yes, mother, Robert wants children."

"You've got yourself a bonny bride there, young Robert. Congratulations! I'll see you at the Black Bull for the reception. I best nip off and unlock," explained the landlord, Sam Smith.

The Reverend Thompson spoke to some of his regular parishioners from Lower Dale.

"Should have more weddings, Your Reverence, it brings the village to life," said Captain Percy.

"Well, to be honest, Percy, I would also like to see some young new residents in Lower Dale. But you know how it is in our sleepy village; it's a retirement village where professionals and successful business men come to get away from the hustle and bustle of London."

"I understand, Your Reverence. Young people starting out in life simply can't afford the high prices of the property here. I should know, my home is worth about £450,000 at today's prices, but when I bought it, it was only £40,000, and at that time it was considered expensive. Will you be coming to the reception, vicar?"

"Yes, I will, as Robert Darling has invited me, but I shall go home to the vicarage first and change out of my 'dog-collar outfit' into a lounge suit, so I can relax. You know me Percy, I may be a vicar but I enjoy a pint the same as any man. In my circle of acquaintances, I get far too many well-meaning ladies, offering me cups of tea. I wonder sometimes, without the teapot would the Church-of-England survive in the rural countryside."

"Get away with you, vicar. See you a bit later at the Black Bull."

"You can count on it."

"Verger, just one thing, before we shut up shop, get the Vac out, please, and hoover this confetti up before the wind blows it all along the path and across the graveyard."

"Straight away, vicar."

"And, Bernard."

"Vicar?"

"Do come to the Black Bull where I, personally, will buy you a pint of best bitter. And don't say no, because I know you drink."

"Only in moderation, vicar."

"Bernard, I've known for years, your weakness for a drink, but I've always turned a blind eye."

"I won't lose my job, vicar, will I?"

"No, no, Bernard, a reliable verger who does God's work for almost nothing is hard to find. You just carry on, nobody is perfect, and that includes me, Bernard."

"Thank you, vicar, I'll just clean up, lock the door and hand the key in to Mrs Bernstein at the Vicarage."

"Very well, Bernard, see you at the Black Bull, later."

"Right you are, vicar."

Not everybody in the village of Lower Dale was invited to Mr and Mrs Darling's wedding, but all the residents knew about it. When the vintage white Rolls-Royce slowly travelled the length of the village past the shops in Main Street, from St Winifred's to the Black Bull, the roadsides, both left and right were lined with well-wishers, waving, cheering and offering flowers.

Miranda and Robert stood up in the back of the Rolls and called out to everybody, "Please join us at the Black Bull! Everybody welcome!"

The word passed from mouth to mouth and, surely but slowly, the residents of Lower Dale followed the wedding car to the Black Bull. As it was a sunny day Sam Smith the landlord and his wife Brenda, had set out extra tables and chairs on The Green, as requested by Robert.

The ladies of the Church Circle, wanting to be involved with the wedding, volunteered to be waitresses. They brought out dishes of nibbles and trays of sparkling wine, which Robert had organised through, Sam Smith.

Many of the locals gathered around the wedding car to take photographs of the happy couple, who were, from their superior standpoint, toasting those gathered, until Jake insisted they come down from the car.

"You are supposed to receive your guests at the entrance to the reception hall," said Amos.

"Just enjoy yourselves," said Robert.

"Time to thank your guests for coming," whispered Max in Robert's ear.

Behind the lounge bar in the Black Bull was the reception room, which was set up for tables for the bride and groom and relations. The centrepiece was a three-tier wedding cake.

Just inside the door was a trestle table, which soon became piled up with guests' gifts.

From somewhere Sam Smith had rustled up a D.J. and he was playing some background music while everybody arrived, before the dancing kicked off.

As Best Man, Max read the cards of greeting. "This is a good one," said Max, "it reads, 'Congratulations! A little something enclosed to help you on your way'. Ladies and gentlemen, a cheque enclosed for a thousand pounds from Miranda's parents, Amos and Annette. Thank you parents."

There were also monetary gifts from Pauline of Vogue Magazine and Felicity Swanson of Estée Lauder.

The butcher gave a tray of prime joints of meat and the baker provided the wedding cake. All in all, it was a good turn out for the residents of Lower Dale. They all had a chance to renew old acquaintances over a drink or two, and all agreed it brought the sleepy village of Lower Dale to life.

Robert and Miranda were almost overwhelmed by the generosity of people whom they had yet to meet. Each brought a small present and, most, a card of congratulations.

After the speeches the D.J. asked Robert and Miranda to take to the floor and, as requested, he played 'Great Balls of Fire.' Now nobody new knew that the newly married couple danced rock'n'roll. Robert put on a good display. He threw Miranda one way and then the other. When the music stopped there was stunned silence followed by rapturous applause.

"All right, everybody on the floor, let's see who can do The Twist," called out the D.J. over the microphone.

It seemed everybody, whether they were somebody or not, were determined to join in the festivities at the Black Bull reception. The tills were constantly clocking up sales. The lounge bar was full to overflowing. The reception room was packed with drinkers and dancers alike, and the general congregation overflowed outside onto The Green, where guests were seated at trestle tables and tables, enjoying all sorts of food paid for by Robert and Miranda. The Green had a party atmosphere.

"The last time we had a village gathering like this, vicar, was at the Queen's Golden Wedding Anniversary," laughed, a happy, slightly tipsy, Captain Percy Lennox.

"I agree, Percy, then the gathering was based around St Winifred's and the Village Hall," replied Reverend Thompson.

"Church Hall, Your Reverence."

"Percy, don't call me that, I am neither a bishop nor the Pope. My correct title is Reverend. And yes, strictly speaking it is the Church Hall, but it is for the common use of the villagers of Lower Dale, in particular the Ladies Circle and the Women's Institute, and therefore it belongs to the people I like to call it the Village Hall."

"As you wish, vicar, but the key is held at the Vicarage, which places it under church guardianship."

"Don't be pompous, Percy. Whatever you call the hall it is run by the ladies of Lower Dale, and that makes them happy, which in turn gives me an easy time."

"If you say so, vicar, I'm having another pint. I don't normally have more than one pint, but today I am entering into the spirit of things."

"Good day to you, Percy, I must circulate."

"Verger, you look a bit unsteady on your feet. How many have you had?"

"This is my second one, Reverend."

"I only paid for one pint for you. Where did you get the money from? I thought you were penniless."

"This good gentleman bought me a drink, vicar."

"Ah, Amos! The bride's father. Thank you for looking after my verger, he likes his drink, though you wouldn't know it."

"I'll look after him, vicar. Mustn't let poverty come between a man and an honest pint. What will you have?"

"Well, as everybody else is drinking and I'm off-duty, I'll have another pint of bitter, if that's all right with you, Amos?"

"I insist."

"Sam, a pint for the vicar, and one in the pot for the threadbare verger, here."

"Verger, don't you come to the Vicarage drunk, and why didn't you change?"

"That confetti took some cleaning up, by which time I was thirsty, so I came straight to the Black Bull."

"Oh very well. But remember tomorrow is Sunday, I don't want a verger looking miserable for the Sunday Service because you have a hangover."

"As my wife and I are staying at Rose Cottage tonight, vicar, we shall be pleased to come to your Sunday Service," offered Amos.

"Where are the happy couple going for their honeymoon?"

"Oh, Miranda says they have been abroad a lot just recently on photo-shoot contracts, and Robert has got behind with his painting, so they are not having a honeymoon because, Miranda, says, their entire life is one long honeymoon," explained, Amos.

"Such a romantic couple. They are both professionals so they know what they are doing."

"Hello, vicar, collared my husband have you?" asked Annette.

"Your husband was just saying that our newlyweds are not having a honeymoon."

"That's right, Robert has commitments to work at The Block and exhibit in The Arch. He has already told me that when Miranda, has their baby he will work in London, Monday to Friday, and come home for the weekends to Rose Cottage."

"I see," said Reverend Thompson. "A modern marriage. Well you cannot fault, Robert, on his loyalty to his work."

"I suspect," said Annette, "that as soon as Miranda's baby becomes a toddler she will have him photographed as well. It stands to reason, whether she has a boy or a girl, if it follows after Robert's and Miranda's looks, he or she will be handsome or beautiful, respectively."

"I, for one, will welcome children into the village because, as we are with an aged population, the death rate is greater than the birth rate, and that needs reversing," pointed out the vicar.

Chapter Eight

It was time for the birth of the baby. The little blighter had been kicking Miranda's insides for the last week like a football. They decided, as there was no hospital near Lower Dale, that the baby would be delivered in London. To that end Robert took Miranda, along with the crib and necessary baby things, to their apartment in The Block. Then it happened.

"Oh my God, my waters have broken!"

"Don't worry I have Max on standby."

"Hi, Max, we need a chauffeur straight away please, Miranda's having the baby."

"Be there in five minutes, Robert. I am the quickest taxi in London."

"Thanks, Max."

"Here I am, Mr Robert, sir."

"Right put Miranda in the car."

Max swept Miranda up in his considerable arms, like a china doll.

"There you go, pet, be at the hospital in no time."

"Right, Max, sod the speed limits, let's get to Queen Elizabeth Hospital."

Robert phoned ahead and news spread through the private wing that they had a celebrity coming in.

At admissions a nurse and a doctor were waiting for Miranda with a bed-trolley.

"Welcome, Mr and Mrs Darling, everything will be fine now."

"I'm coming to the delivery room as well," said Robert.

"That's good, sir," said the doctor, "we encourage the husband to be present at the birth."

Max waited outside in the corridor. When his own son had been born, he fretted just as much.

Not that much later, for a firstborn, Miranda safely gave birth to a yelling boy.

"There we are, Mr Darling, a healthy baby boy," said the doctor, showing him to Robert.

"Hello baby!" exclaimed Robert, "what a clever mummy."

"Doctor, ask Max to come in."

"Max?"

"Big black fellow outside. Friend and chauffeur."

"Come in, Max. It's a boy. What do you think?"

"A cracker, Robert, he has your eyes. What are you going to call him?"

"Well, that's why I brought you in, I would like to call him Max, after you, if you don't mind."

"Well, that's very nice of you, but I don't know if I deserve the accolade?"

"Sure you do, Max."

"What do you say, Miranda?"

"That's fine, darling, may I sleep now."

"Sure, you are exhausted."

"Max it is. Max, say hello to Baby Max!"

"Hello Baby Max."

"I'll go now, Robert, if that's all right with you."

"Sure, Max, and thanks."

They stayed a few weeks at The Block until baby Max got into his sleep routine and Miranda got some much needed rest.

Robert worked hard, Monday to Friday at The Block. Now that baby Max was settled and Miranda was 'baby-happy', Robert felt inspired to paint new models. From the nearby Art College there was no end of student sitters who volunteered to be models for the famous Robert Darling. Robert paid thirty pounds for a sitting, which was normally two to three hours. He had offers of nude young ladies, but Robert insisted they kept their knickers on and, to reinforce his situation and so as not to be compromised, he had a large photograph of Miranda on the wall of his studio, next to which was a black and white photograph of his son, Max.

Robert, as ever, was busy at The Block when the intercom buzzed.

"Cover yourself up a minute, young lady, I have a visitor.

Robert had a look at his recently installed monitor and, as clear as life, Teddy Rosenburgh was on the screen.

"Come on up, Mr Rosenburgh."

"Sorry to disturb you. I was passing so I dropped in to ask how you were fixed for a new exhibition."

"Lydia, this is Teddy Rosenburgh who owns The Arch."

"How do you do, sir, excuse my state of undress. I know of your reputation. I hope, one day, when I have finished Art College, to display in a galley and be famous like Mr Darling, here."

"It depends on your talent, Lydia."

"When is the exhibition, Mr Rosenburgh?" asked Robert.

"Four weeks' time."

"And what are the subjects?"

"Nude portraits of men and women, and mother and baby. Would you be interested?"

"How about a portrait of Miranda and baby Max? I could call it, 'Miranda with child'."

"You would do that?"

"If you think it was commercially viable."

"My dear, Robert, it would sell for a fortune."

"Then you are giving me a commission?"

"Definitely. Mother and child it is."

"Excuse me, Miss Lydia, I will be going now, my apologies for interrupting your sitting."

"Goodbye, Mr Rosenburgh."

"I'll tell you what, Lydia, you bring one of your best paintings to my studio and I'll show it to Teddy Rosenburgh. Can't say fairer than that, can I?"

"The only portrait I've done, Robert, is of myself. Will that be acceptable?"

"Right, that's all for today, Lydia. Bring your own portrait along to the next sitting."

"Goodbye, Mr Robert, sir."

"Goodbye, Lydia."

At the weekend, Robert, Miranda and baby Max, moved back into Rose Cottage at Lower Dale. Max was now four weeks old, and the exhibition of portraits in The Arch was just two weeks away.

Fortunately, baby Max was into a sleep routine now, waking only once during the night to be fed. Miranda's nursing breasts were bursting with milk and made a good subject for Robert to paint.

He had started on 'Miranda with Child' a week ago, and was now ready to prepare the oil on canvas for Teddy Rosenburgh's exhibition.

"O.K., Miranda, settle yourself down. Put Max to the right breast so that I can have continuity of the last sitting."

Motherhood seemed to suit Miranda, for she blossomed. She had a new look in her eyes, one of adoration of her own flesh and blood. She clearly doted on baby Max.

"I've been thinking, Robert. Are you sure you want our baby son christened Max, because it's confusing with our friend and chauffeur, Max?"

"We could call baby Max, Max Junior, if you like?" suggested, Robert.

"That's all right by me, because we can't keep calling Max baby Max, especially when he's no longer a baby."

"All right, let's go and see Reverend Thompson tomorrow and organise a christening."

"Who shall we have as God Parents, you know, bringing Max Junior up in the way of the church?"

"I'd say Captain Percy and Mrs Burns?" offered, Robert.

"Mrs Burns and Percy?"

"Yes, because they have both lost loved ones, and are, in my experience of them, in need of someone to love."

"What do you mean?"

"They are both lonely, and clearly love children, so they have time on their hands, and a space in their hearts to devote themselves to another."

"I think you have the makings of a counsellor, Robert. You are clearly a thinking, feeling person. You are very sensitive and accept everyone."

"I try my best, my darling."

"You do more than that. You bring happiness to others and you practice being impartial. The normal reaction of a person to someone they don't know is to be judgemental. Like when an over strict parent automatically chastises a child without giving the child the benefit of the doubt."

"That's because I believe children should be cherished not punished. A child is an adult in the making and, in turn, a parent in the making. So as parents we need to be role models. Children should be shown love so that they become proud of their parents and respect them out of love as they grow up."

"There's hidden depths to you, Miranda, when you speak from the heart," praised, Robert.

"I think, deep down, we are very much alike."

177

He put down his brush and went across to Mother and Child, and gave each a kiss on the forehead.

"What's that for?"

"Because I love you the way you are."

"You mean naked with swollen breasts?"

"Well, yes, actually. The sight of you tugs on my loins."

"Keep your mind on the painting, on the portrait on the canvas and not on me. Remember, I am just art."

"Yes, darling, you are art, living art."

"I know that look. The doctor said six weeks before we can have intercourse."

"It seems for ever. I can't help wanting you, I love you intensely."

"I know you want children, but I'm not a sausage machine. I have to go back on the contraceptive pill first."

"How long will that take?"

"Four weeks before I am properly protected."

"Four weeks! Why so long?"

"Because, darling, my body is in receptive mode having just been pregnant. The pill makes my hormones adjust to a contraceptive level."

"Damn! Another four weeks?"

"I'll tell you what, you can have me next week, if you're really careful."

"If I'm careful?"

"Yes. You can use a condom."

"I hate the damned things."

"It's that or nothing."

"Oh all right."

"You're like a sulky little kid, Robert."

"Sorry. It's just that it hurts not to have you."

"You'll have to stop now, Robert. Max is making my breast sore, I'll have to move him."

"O.K., darling, that's enough for today anyway."

"I'll just wind Max, and put him to sleep."

There was a knock at St Winifred's Vicarage door.

"Come in! Be with you in a couple of minutes."

Robert and Miranda knocked again.

"Oh damn!"

The vicar put his pen down and went to the door.

"Yes... Oh, it's you Miranda. And you've brought the baby. Sorry, I was composing a sermon. Do come in."

Miranda wheeled her sheepskin-lined buggy in.

"We've come about the christening, vicar."

"The christening?"

"Baby Max, here."

"Oh, I see. Have you registered the birth?"

"Yes, we've seen the Registrar of Births and Deaths."

"Good. What name have you given your son?"

"Max. Well, Max Junior actually."

"Are you sure about that? I don't quite follow why you are calling him Junior, when your Christian name is Robert?"

"That's easy to explain, Reverend Thompson. Our chauffeur in London is called Max, and we have named our baby after him but so as not to get the two Max's confused, we wish to christen our baby, Max Junior."

"Ah! Now I understand. And when were you proposing to christen Max Junior?"

"We thought as soon as possible."

"How about a week Saturday? Is that too soon for you?"

"That's fine, Reverend."

"You will need, as it is the tradition of the Church of England, two Godparents. Have you thought about that?"

"Yes vicar," said Robert. "I am going to ask Mrs Burns from the Village Shop and Captain Percy."

"Excellent choice. I'm sure Mrs Burns will spoil Max Junior rotten. And, Captain Percy Lennox finds time weighs heavy on his hands, so he can devote plenty of time to help you bring up the baby."

"Right, Mr and Mrs Darling, I will pencil you in my Church Diary. Good day to you."

"Thank you, vicar, and goodbye."

During the week Mrs Burns' Village Shop was quite quiet.

The shop doorbell rang, and the sprightly Mrs Burns came to the counter.

"Oh hello, Robert and Miranda. My favourite customers, what can I do for you?"

"Well, actually we have a request."

"A request?"

"Yes. Would you like to be Max's Godparent at his christening?"

"A Godparent me? It would be an honour! When is the christening?"

"A week this Saturday."

"Oh dear, Saturday is my busiest day."

"Well, if it's inconvenient…"

"No, no. My assistant can manage. It's only a small shop. I shall be there even if it costs me a bit of lost trade."

"I'll tell you what, what if I put twenty pounds in the till as a donation to 'shop funds'."

"That would be appreciated, Robert. Can I have a cuddle of the baby?"

"He's had a feed and he's sleepy now, so I don't see why not," said Miranda.

"Hello baby. What's your name?"

"Max Junior," replied, Miranda.

"Oh, he's opened his eyes. What a nice smile. He looks just like his daddy. Even got your blue eyes, Robert."

"I think he has the look of both of us," said Miranda.

"It will be nice to have children in the shop again. You know, my boys were in the army and were killed on active service. After all these years I still miss them. I think without the business I would go quite mad. Can I come and visit on my day off. That's a Wednesday?"

"Of course, you are very welcome to visit Rose Cottage," said Miranda, "but on most weekdays Robert will be working away in London, so I will be on my own."

"Then I'll come and keep you company, perhaps take Max Junior for a walk, which will give you some time to do some home baking. Have you done any home baking yet?"

"Not yet, Mrs Burns. I've been too tired feeding Max, but just now he is into a sleeping/feeding routine. So I would say I'm ready for home baking any time now."

"Then it's a date, I'll come this Wednesday."

"While I'm here, I'll have a fresh loaf and two pints of milk."

"My bread's always fresh."

"Of course it is, Mrs Burns, but mine goes stale before I use it, so I put it out for the birds. From now on I am going to give Max a little bread sopped well in milk. He's a hungry baby now, so I am introducing him to a baby spoon. I want to get him sleeping right through the night."

"That will come with time, Miranda. Max certainly seems a bouncing healthy baby. Bye, Max, see you, Wednesday."

"Well, that went well. Mrs Burns is keen to be a Godparent. We just have to ask Captain Percy now. Where will he be?"

"Oh, I know that. Sam Smith told me that the old ones go to the Village Hall during the week and play cribbage and indoor bowls."

"Hello, Percy, can we have a word with you?"

"Er, umph. In a minute, it's my end next."

Percy rolled the four woods and it seemed he was quite an expert bowler, for all his bowls surrounded the jack.

"Well done, Percy," said Sam Smith from the Black Bull.

"That's five ends to three, in our favour. I reckon we are a winning team, Percy."

The other team shook hands with Percy and Sam.

"Time for tea, Sam."

"Now then, you young ones, what did you want a word about?"

"The christening of our baby Max, here. We would like you to be a Godparent at Max's christening at St Winifred's Church, a week from this Saturday."

"A Saturday, you say. That suits me fine. Saturday is my day off from any Village Hall activities. On Saturdays I treat myself to a pint at the Black Bull."

"We will be having a reception for Max at the Black Bull, so you can have as many pints as you like, Percy."

"That's very civil of you, Robert. I'd be very proud to be a Godparent and bring young Max up as a soldier. You know your soldier, he honours his uniform and regiment and respects his fellow men."

"No tea for me, please, Percy, I've been trapped indoors with Max now for over a month. I can't face any more tea, either here or at The Block in London. I need something stronger. Would you like to go to the Black Bull for a pint?"

"That depends on Sam here, he's the landlord."

"Well, I would have unlocked at five o'clock anyway, what's fifteen minutes between friends."

"Can't turn custom away, it's just that with lunchtimes being twelve to two-thirty, I don't get away until three, and that gives me two hours' break from three to five. Come on, let's walk back through the village."

"Thanks, Sam. Come on, Percy, I'll buy you a pint."

"I've not seen you out before with the baby, Miranda?" queried, Sam Smith.

"No you haven't. This is his first real day out. He's just met Mrs Burns and he smiled for her. He's really contented."

"That's because he has loving parents," said Percy.

"You know, when my boy was young we used to dip his dummy in cider, it always put him to sleep, he loved it."

"Well Max is not having any cider. He'll get no beer until he is eighteen."

"That's a long time, Miranda."

"Just wait here," said Sam, "while I go round the back and unlock."

Five minutes later, the bolts were drawn back on the front door."

"Good boy, Bouncer, outside for your toilet!"

"Is he a guard dog, Sam?"

"Sure is. I don't feed him at night. He has a free run of the premises. God help anybody if they break in. The stairway is also open at night so he can come and go at any time. The only door that is closed is our bedroom door, he knows he's not allowed in there."

"On the house, to wet the baby's head," said Sam. "A pint each."

"I think you should let me pay," replied Robert.

"If you argue, I'll be offended," countered Sam.

"O.K., Sam, a pint each it is."

"Cheers, Percy!"

"Very sporting of you, Mr Robert, Miss Miranda."

"Not a Miss any more, Percy. A Mrs Darling. A mother and baby."

"Well, here's to you, Mrs Darling, and the baby."

"Cheers, Percy!" saluted, Robert, tipping his pint of bitter up.

"What will you have, Miranda?"

"A large Bacardi with Diet Coke."

The week of the nude portrait exhibition came. Both Robert and Miranda were at The Arch, and Robert's 'Mother and Child' received a lot of attention.

"This is for sale, isn't it, Robert?" asked Teddy Rosenburgh.

"Sure, I said it was. How much do you think it will sell for?"

"I have no idea, but somewhere between half a million and a million, less of course my twenty percent, as agreed."

"So much?"

"Well, Robert, you are an acknowledged artist now and Miranda's face, since her launch on Vogue as Cover Girl, has made her famous, not to mention her whole body in an intimate role of feeding Max Junior."

"Have you had any offers so far?"

"The Duke of Gloucester has intimated that he would like it to hang in his stately home, Chestnut Towers."

"Can he afford it?"

"Oh yes! He opens his home and grounds to the public all year round now, except at Christmas when he has a family get together. He makes a mint, so half a million to him is quite affordable."

"Hello, Miranda, may I photograph you?"

"Who are you?"

"May I introduce myself. Virginia Waters from the Sunday Times Supplement. Teddy Rosenburgh says as I am from a respectable paper I may photograph 'Mother with Child'."

"In that case, Virginia, you may photograph me."

"May I photograph you with your baby in your arms?"

"Sure. Pass Max Junior to me, Robert."

"There you go, little fellah, back to your mother."

At the entrance there was a kerfuffle and raised voices.

"Miranda! Help me!"

Miranda, with baby in arms, went immediately to the main door where Max was preventing a woman from getting in.

"What's the problem, Max?"

"This woman wants to see you, but it's strictly viewing by ticket only. She is not an invited guest."

"Oh, I see. Who is she from?"

"She says she's the editor of 'Mothers Today', a publication of Mothercare."

"Hello, I'm Miranda. What can I do for you?"

"My name's Rosemary. I would very much like to do an advertising feature about you."

"What sort of feature?"

"Well a promotion for Mothercare products, with a feature on the 'mother behind the model'."

"Let her in, Max, I think she means well."

"If you say so, Miss Miranda, it's yours and Robert's exhibition."

"How would you like to be Patron of Mothers Today?"

"Patron? I don't know."

"Well, I know you shopped at Mothercare in Knightsbridge. Our readers would love to hear about your story, from meeting Robert to becoming a mother. I've seen your photographs of husband and wife: the ideal couple in the News of The World. Now it's time for mother and baby."

"O.K., you may photograph me now, and after the exhibition you can have an hour of my time at The Block."

"The Block?"

"Yes, our London residence and Robert's studio. Max, who is acting as our doorman at the moment, is also our chauffeur and he will bring you to The Block."

"Thank you, Miranda. May I photograph your husband holding the baby?"

"Sure. Robert's a proud father."

"What's his name, Robert?"

"Max Junior."

"Is that after Max the chauffeur?"

"Yes it is."

"Max is very defensive of you."

"Yes, he's a gentle giant. He befriended us when we were new to London and The Block, so we are grateful to him."

The Duke of Gloucester came across the exhibition hall and made a beeline for Robert.

"May I introduce myself, young man? I admire your artist's skill, how would you like a royal commission?"

"A royal commission, Your Grace?"

"Edward, please."

"Excuse me, Rosemary, you talk to Miranda a moment."

"Now, Edward, what have you got in mind?"

"A double portrait of myself and the Duchess."

"Well, Your Grace, I could do that."

"How much would you charge?"

"Somewhere around fifty thousand pounds. The preliminary work would be around a number of sittings to produce pencil drawings of exact proportions of yourself and the Duchess, followed by outline painting of your chosen clothing. Then a number of sittings to add detail and colour to your outfits. Finally, I would finish off with the facial details and your hair."

"For such a lot of work, a double portrait by a fine artist as yourself, Robert Darling, sounds about right."

"Your Grace, I could do the work for half the price, but it would not reflect my genius as a portrait artist."

"I agree. Each piece you produce is unique."

"Exactly, Your Grace."

"Fifty thousand it is. When do you want to start?"

"No hurry. Ask your wife, the Duchess, when she would prefer. The work will take three to four weeks. A double portrait is a lot of work involving very many sittings."

"I will convey your intentions, Master Robert, to my wife."

"Thank you, Edward, and good day to you."

"What have you been doing?" asked, Miranda.

"His Grace, the Duke of Gloucester, has offered me a commission to do a double portrait of himself and his wife."

"And how much is that going to cost him, darling?"

"We have agreed on a fee of fifty thousand pounds."

"Phew!" said Rosemary. "I'm obviously in the wrong business."

"Genius, Rosemary, doesn't come cheap," smiled Miranda.

The Sunday Times Supplement published the nude photograph of Miranda and Max Junior, titled 'Mother with Child'. It was rumoured at The Arch that a friend of Teddy Rosenburgh's bought the unique portrait for a cool million pounds.

Mother's Today, the magazine of chain-store Motherecare, wrote an article: 'Mother behind the Model.'

Readers of Miranda's story, from the death of Edward Saunders, 25, her first husband, to the present day and the birth of Max Junior, were enthralled. They wrote in saying how they admired and envied Miranda. Miranda became a household name with Mothercare shoppers, and received further fame by going on television and promoting Mothercare's baby products.

Thus the next four years Miranda dedicated her time to bringing Max Junior up. For some unknown reason, during all that time, Miranda never conceived again, though both she and Robert longed for a brother for Max.

However, during those four years other professional couples moved into Lower Dale, replacing aged residents, who sadly passed on into God's realm. The result was Max Junior had six other infants to play with. Miranda, when Max Junior was an active toddler of two years, started, with the support of the Reverend Thompson, a children's playgroup. They grew up together, and Miranda, throughout the village, became known as the Nursery Teacher, which she willingly took on.

On Max Junior's fourth birthday, Miranda invited all the children to Rose Cottage for a birthday party. Max's favourite playmate was David Braun, a bright, sandy-haired, blue-eyed, young man. David spoke excellent English, and to hear them together an observer would think it was two educated teenagers.

"Max Junior had taken to a pencil ever since his father, Robert, had shown him, at the age of two how to sketch. Now, David and Max didn't draw matchstick men, flowers or animals, but buildings. They drew intricate designs taking care to put in details of windows, gutters, fascias, etcetera. They had an eye for detail, so while Robert worked away at The Block, Miranda encouraged the two boys to design on Drawing Paper with a ruler, set square, pair of compasses and a protractor, in the Village Hall nursery classes.

Now David's father, Humphrey, was a qualified architect who worked away in London, and he suggested the two boys, even at such a young age, should use their God-given talents and move towards becoming architects as well.

To that end, Robert and Humphrey got together and discussed the boys' future.

"There's no school in Lower Dale," said Humphrey, "so they will have to go to the nearest town."

"There's an infant and junior school in Maples End, but it won't stretch the boys, it's just a basic country school," said Robert.

"I think they should go to a special school for gifted children," said Humphrey.

"I agree," concurred, Robert.

"But I won't see my baby if he goes away," said an upset, Miranda.

"Darling, Max Junior is exceptionally bright, a local village school would hold him back. We must let him learn at his own speed. Look how advanced he is for a four-year-old in arithmetic. He thinks for himself."

"I know, Robert, but I don't want to lose him."

"A child, who is to become an architect by his natural talents, needs to be keenly numerate, as both Max and David are, so I say we pick a school for gifted children," repeated, Humphrey.

"They are too young to be come boarders."

"In that case, Miranda, would you be prepared to take the two of them to André Laceys in the car, every morning and collect them at four o'clock?"

"Yes, I would be willing, as long as they can come home at night."

"Good, Miranda, because I've made preliminary enquiries of the Head Teacher, Peter Davidson."

"What, without consulting me, Robert?"

"I knew you would be upset, so I didn't tell you."

"But, André Laceys is twenty miles away, in mid-Surrey."

"I know, darling, but that's the nearest school to Lower Dale for gifted children."

"Boys, come here a minute, leave your Meccano, you'll have plenty of time later to design a skyscraper. I want to ask you something."

"Yes, papa?" asked Max Junior.

"How would you like to go to a big school, where there are older boys, from whom you could learn, and lots of really clever teachers who could help you with building design and mathematics?"

"Would they be cleverer than the old people in the Village Hall?" asked, David.

"Much brighter," replied, Humphrey.

"Shall we go, Max?"

"Yes, it will be an adventure, won't it father?"

"That's right, Max. You'll have the chance to learn mathematics, science, architecture and engineering," smiled Robert.

"Yippee!" said the boys together. "When can we go, father?"

"As soon as I ring the Headmaster, Peter Davidson, and confirm we want to book two very clever young boys in, to start as soon as possible."

"Are you sure, Miranda, you don't mind doing all the driving," asked Humphrey, "because my wife, June, could take turns."

"I'll be fine. I know June is a homemaker and doesn't like driving very much but, tell you what, June can drive sometimes when I feel the need for a day off."

"You're very quiet, June?" asked Humphrey.

"I'm upset at David being taken away at such a young age. But, yes, Miranda, I don't mind driving some days and you will have to show me the way to André Laceys."

"I think, tomorrow, the six of us should make a visit to André Laceys and let the boys familiarise themselves with the grounds, while we adults look at the classroom facilities and meet the teachers."

"We want to meet the teachers, don't we, David?"

"Yes, of course, Max."

"Good idea," the parents agreed, and the boys were really excited.

Robert telephoned Peter Davidson and arranged for them all to visit the following day.

"Pleased to meet you, Mr and Mrs Darling and Max Junior, and Mr and Mrs Braun and David," welcomed the headmaster.

"This is Mr Tomkins, the Master who is in charge of four to seven year olds."

"Boys," said Mr Tomkins, "please come with me."

"Where are we going, sir?" asked Max Junior.

"To meet some of your future classmates."

"Oh, all right."

"This, Max, David, is a day school, which means that we don't generally take boarders. That's those who don't stay Monday to Friday and go home at the weekend, but rather daytime only. However, the Senior School, from eleven to sixteen, does take boarders if the pupils so choose."

"Mr Tomkins," asked Max, "how many boys are in the school?"

"About a hundred and twenty. We are a school of exceptional quality not quantity. Do you understand?"

"Oh yes, sir," said David Braun, "you take boys who are gifted."

"Exactly, young David. Now I am going to show you into some of the classes under my jurisdiction. First, Mr Thomas's class. Mathematics and arithmetic."

They went inside.

The blackboard was covered in calculations. They were formulae.

"Oh, today's algebra, I see," said Max Junior, "they're doing quadratic equations."

"You're very observant, Max."

"I can do them as well, can't I, Max?" supported, David.

"Yes, Mr Tomkins, we have our own calculation book, don't we, Max?"

"Of course, sir. Can we see the science class next?"

"This way boys."

"Mr Perkins, Science Master, I have two new boys for you."

"What's their names, Mr Tomkins?"

"Max Junior Darling and David Braun."

"Welcome, boys, come and sit at the front. Have your parents signed you up to André Laceys yet?"

"No, sir, this is just a visiting day," said Max.

"Well, that's all right, just pay attention and see if you can understand what's being taught."

"Simpkins, you are seven now, one of the oldest in my class, come out to the front and explain to the new boys Boyle's Law."

"Right away, sir."

"No, no," said Max, "that's joules, you're expressing the equation in calories. You must allow for the Latent Heat of Cooling for one degree of centigrade."

"Come out to the front, young Max, and explain Boyle's Law to the class."

"That's right, Max," said David, "it's the energy used to raise the temperature of water at 15 degrees C, by one degree. 15 degrees C is the scientific standard temperature used by the National Physics Laboratory at Teddington, London."

"Oh, now I understand," said a very polite, Peter Simpkins.

"Thank you, Max, you may sit down now."

"Mr Perkins, when we have learnt all the formulae do we get to do experiments?" asked Max.

"Yes, Max, but that's not until year two or three, when you are a six to seven years old. Experiments can be dangerous."

"Will we be able to do experiments with electricity, you know, bulbs and switches?" asked David Braun.

"How do you know, David, about electricity at only four years of age?"

"My father, Humphrey, is an architect; he has to know about electricity when he designs shopping centres, for lighting, security, doors, lifts, escalators and alarms etcetera."

"O.K., you two boys, you go back to the Headmaster, and tell him Mr Perkins thinks you will be suitable for André Laceys."

"All right, Mr Perkins. See you later, Peter Simpkins."

"Thanks, Max, for helping me."

"Oh, that's O.K. I think I'll like this science class."

"Bye, Mr Perkins."

"Father, father, David and I went into a science class, it was brill."

"And, Mr Headmaster, Mr Perkins, says we'll be fine in his science class," chirped up, David.

"Well you two are happy," said a relieved Miranda.

"Right, Mr Davidson, where do we sign-up for the term for Max and David?"

"You're quite sure?"

"Absolutely!" pronounced Humphrey Braun. "My David is an architect in the making. I think he will read for his degree by the time he is eighteen."

"What will you design, Max?"

"I haven't decided. Maybe jet planes or rockets to outer space. Perhaps an anti-gravity spaceship."

"Now you're exaggerating, Max, even Einstein couldn't produce a law for anti-gravity. It is one of man's great quests to produce perpetual motion," said Humphrey.

"Max can do anything," said young David.

The headmaster said, "Go with my secretary, boys, time for tea and cake."

"If you would be so kind, Mrs Pickles."

"Come along, boys, the headmaster wants to talk finance with your parents."

"Oh, money. My dad's a famous portrait artist and my mother is a supermodel, we have pots of money," said a chirpy Max Junior.

"And my dad has designed a fantastic house for my mother to live in," said a very proud David.

"Well, I've a small two bedroomed cottage with a thatched roof and I am very happy."

"Oh, Mrs Pickles, you must be a grandma then?"

"Well, actually I am, I have three grandchildren."

"Can we play with them?"

"I'm afraid they go to an ordinary State School, they're not special like you two, I think you would find them very boring."

"That's O.K. But could you be my grandma? I don't think I have a grandma?" said a very serious, David.

"I think every young man has a grandma."

"No Mrs Pickles, I have a mother and a father but not an elderly kindly, grandmother like you."

"That's very kind of you, David. O.K, while you are at André Laceys, I'll be your grandma."

"Oh goody. Can I kiss you then?"

"Dear child, of course you can."

"I have a grandpa and a grandma," said Max.

"Oh, and what are their names?"

"Grandpa is Amos, and he's a Consultant Architect and grandma is Annette, and she's beautiful for an old lady."

Mrs Pickles split her side at the boys' antics. She knew André Laceys would have their hands full with these two. Especially, at fifty she was definitely not old, it was that the boys were infants and only just infants at that. 'Really, discussing mathematics and science at only four-and-a-half-years-old! Whatever next?' she thought.

"Hello boys, had a good time?"

"Yes, thank you, father," answered, Max Junior.

"Father," said David, "an elderly lady gave us tea and a cake," smiled the satisfied boy.

"Oh, that's probably Mrs Pickles, the headmaster's secretary," said Miranda.

"Yes," said Peter Davidson, "I sent the boys off while we discussed fees."

"What did you learn, David?"

"Science mostly. Max explained to a class of older boys Boyle's Law."

"Did you, son?"

"Yes, father. I had to because they forgot about the law of the Latent Heat of Cooling."

"And you put them right?"

"He sure did, Mr Darling," said an admiring, David.

"I think our boys, Robert, are going to get along together famously at André Laceys," said a reassuring, Humphrey Braun.

"I don't know about you, Humphrey, but I didn't learn the basics of science until I went to Junior School at seven-and-a-half. Our two must have photographic brains because they both read at a phenomenal rate, devouring all manner of books since the age of two. The question is, when they are about eleven-years-old, will we be able to keep up?" wondered, Robert.

"I doubt it, and I have had a University education and further professional training to get to be a Consultant Architect?"

Both men laughed at the prodigious gap that threatened to loom between themselves and their offspring as they advanced in an academic life until they became, in their own rights, professionals.

Being four-and-a-half at André Laceys made you a new boy. The first thing you did was mix with the five to six year olds as a group. And free time in the grounds, which were extensive, was to test one another out. To that end, a fight broke out between David Braun and Rodger, a bigger and older boy. Now David was one of the youngest but he was no coward.

Rodger accused David of cheating at marbles, and young David was a little man of honour.

"Don't call me a chea, you bully!" yelled David, as they rolled over and over on the grass.

Rodger was on top now and punched David, giving him a bloody nose.

Max went across to see what the fight was about.

"It's Rodger the Bully, he always picks on new boys," said Percy, a boy Max had befriended.

Poor David was getting pummelled by the bigger boy. Max Junior was enraged, he pulled Rodger up by his hair.

"Ahh! I'll get you!"

"Come on then, bully!"

Rodger jumped up.

"Oh, it's you, the clever science kid. Want a bloody nose do you?"

Rodger flew at Max Junior.

Max dodged to one side and bully-boy went flying. The other boys gathered around at the excitement.

"Go on Max Junior, give him what he deserves!" shouted out an encouraging Percy.

Now, Max Junior was well-built and taller than average for a four-and-a-half-year-old, but still not as big as the older Rodger. Robert, as his son was mad on sport, especially on watching tag-wrestling and kick-boxing on television, had taught him the rudiments of kick-boxing. Max had practised in the garden at Rose Garden with David as his partner.

"You're dead, Darling! Stand still and fight like a man!"

"Come here, coward," Max stood his ground.

Rodger came forward, fists raised. He swung at Max, but Max kicked out as Robert, his father, had taught him. The kick struck Rodger on the inside of his thigh, which made him hesitate. In that moment Max came forward and smacked his opponent one-two on the jaw, jarring his teeth.

"Had enough, bully-boy?"

"I've got friends in the school, I'll have you!"

"I'm not going anywhere."

"Let it be a lesson to you. David is my friend, so next time I won't let you off so easily."

"I'll have my marbles back now," said David.

"You cheated, you little runt!"

Max struck out, full stretch with his left foot, which connected powerfully with Rodger's guts. Winded he went down.

David jumped on top of him and punched him on the nose.

"Give me my marbles, bully!"

"Blast you, here they are! I'll get you another day, squirt."

So Max's and David's school life was initiated. It was a threesome: Max, David and Percy. Now Percy was a rather rotund jovial lad of five-and-a-half. He had little piggy eyes but a wide welcoming smile. He liked everybody to be his friend. After the fight with the First Year's bully, Rodger, Percy looked up to Max Junior and they became close friends. Percy could not only look out for himself, but he defended the smaller weaker boys in the school. Max admired that quality in Percy. Percy also gave out sweets to younger boys and, of course, his chosen friends.

"Here, David, have a gobstopper."

"Thanks, Percy, you are really a kind boy."

"Hey, don't embarrass me. Anyway, that Rodger bothers you again, you tell me."

"Shake hands, Percy. You're the same as me, ready to protect the smaller boys. My dad taught me that," said Max Junior.

"What does your dad do, Max?"

"He's a painter."

"Like a painter and decorator?"

"No, no. A portrait artist. He does oil paintings and exhibits them in a gallery called The Arch, in Knightsbridge, London."

"Gosh! He must be rich, Knightsbridge is a posh district?"

"Well, we don't actually live in Knightsbridge. It's where my father works. We live in the countryside in Surrey in a village called, Lower Dale."

"Is it a big house, Max?"

"No, Percy. A small cottage with a large garden. It's called Rose Cottage."

"Sounds really nice, Max."

"It is, Percy. I also live in Lower Dale," said David.

Mr Tomkins, the Year Master, came striding across the grassy grounds.

"Young Darling, I want a word with you."

"Yes, sir," said Max.

"Have you been fighting Rodger Bottomsworth?"

"If that's his name, yes, sir."

"Then come with me."

"And you, David Braun, have you been fighting?"

"Yes, sir."

"You had better come along as well."

"Mr Tomkins, sir, Rodger started the fight. He's a bully. He picked on my little friend here, David, and I defended him."

"That's not what Rodger Bottomsworth said."

"Then, sir, he's lying."

"You are new boys," said the huge figure of the Headmaster, Peter Davidson. "Is it true you have been fighting?"

"Yes, sir," they both answered together.

"At least you are truthful."

"Now, Mr Tomkins, tell me the story please."

"Ah, now I understand," said Peter Davidson.

"Mr Tomkins, bring Rodger, in."

"You come crawling to me because your father is a School Governor, but this time, Rodger Bottomsworth, your lies will not protect you."

"Punishment duty, Mr Tomkins!"

"Yes, headmaster."

"You two boys may go, but no more fighting. Is that clear?"

"Yes, Mr Davidson, sir."

"Bend over the desk, Rodgers."

"Mr Tomkins, six of the best with the plimsole."

Max and David listened through the door at Rodger Bottomsworth's baby wailing.

"He only got the slipper," said Max. "I'm glad I hit him. How's your nose, David?"

"Oh, it's nothing, but thanks for sticking up for me."

"That's what friends are for," smiled Max Junior.

Chapter Nine

Three years later, Max Junior and David were both seven-and-a-half and progressed from Infant School to Junior School, and were still friends with the affable Percy. Now, as it turned out, Percy, being a year older, and very likeable, had ingratiated himself with many other sporty pupils and, as a result, had been made, at the tender age of eight-and-a-half, Junior School Cricket Captain.

Percy was bright, but not as gifted as Max and David so, in return for homework coaching, Percy taught his two favourite chums how to become good cricketers.

Mr Tomkins, with the passing of time, had also moved up to Junior School, and was now Year Master for seven-and-a-half to ten-and-a-half year olds. The trio of chums really liked Mr Tomkins because he was a kind master, who praised results for effort in academic studies and sport. Indeed it was Mr Tomkins, who organised Max Junior's first inter-school cricket match.

The rival private school to André Laceys was St Mark's Roman Catholic School, who had thrashed André Laceys Senior Team last summer, so Mr Tomkins was very keen indeed for Percy's Cricket Junior Eleven to win.

"It's a matter of pride," said Mr Tomkins. "I don't believe it's just about taking part, we need to lift the trophy."

On the day of the Junior School cricket match, Percy's eleven players and two standby boys boarded the coach for St Mark's Roman Catholic School.

Max, David and Percy sat at the back of the coach and encouraged the players to sing one of their school favourites, which was a great morale booster. Even Mr Tomkins, a Welshman, encouraged singing.

"Sing up lads, it's good for the soul!"

"Hooray for Mr Tomkins!" shouted out the boys.

St Mark's was a small school, controlled by the Catholic Church, but let no boy be put off by size because they were well ordered. The driveway, lawns, shrubs and borders were immaculate. Obviously no shortage of funds. The school house appeared to be an ancient mansion adorned with cherubs and festooned with hanging baskets.

"Now, lads, what have we come for?" asked Mr Tomkins in a loud voice.

"To win, sir!" chimed Percy's team.

"Good, lads, remember that!"

It was an ideal cricket day, sunny, but with a light protective haze and a gentle crosswind. The pitch was in superb condition, the grass as green as green. St Mark's obviously had a first class groundsman.

André Laceys turned out in their whites while St Mark's turned out in their school colours, maroon and white, with matching school caps.

"They look like a bunch of clowns," said Percy.

"Don't judge them yet," said Max Junior, "they may be damned good."

"David, you're our best bowler, so I am putting you in first. Take it easy, take your time, if you can get one or two wickets that will be enough. We know they are supposed to be good, but you, David, are fast. I don't know if they can stand up to a fast bowler," explained Percy.

David bowled; the pitch was slow because of the lush fresh grass, so David tried a bouncer, which was more effective off the springy ground.

Percy had a quick word in David's ear.

"Try a googly, the ball's bouncing well."

David loped a ball in, which appeared to move to the off-side, then, as the batsman raised his bat, it twisted in at the last split second, so that it curved to leg-side and crashed into the stumps.

"Out!" shouted, Mr Tomkins and Percy at the same time.

The umpire raised his hand, signalling out.

"Well done, David," said Max Junior.

"Over," called the umpire.

"Not bad, David, one down after only six balls," encouraged, Percy.

After over after over the bowlers changed ends until the whole innings was out at ten for one hundred and fifteen.

"Right lads, were in," said Percy.

St Mark's School was weak at bowling. Percy opened the batting scoring a health thirty-five; the entire innings was not necessary as André Laceys declared at nine for one hundred and thirty-seven.

"Three cheers for St Mark's!" called out Mr Tomkins.

Putting aside their maroon team colours, St Mark's were just a bunch of lads enjoying cricket the same as André Laceys, so in the Cricket Pavilion a camaraderie was established between the two opposing teams, which meant all inter-school differences were forgotten about, and the boys enjoyed the mutual satisfaction of home made lemonade, sandwiches and sponge cakes.

Mrs Timmins, the cook from St Mark's, made sure everybody had plenty to eat and, boys being boys, they had a very healthy appetite.

'An inter-school cricket match on a summer Saturday, sure as hell beat weekday academic lessons,' thought Mr Tomkins.

The headmaster of St Marks, a formidable, ferocious sort, dressed all in black, prowled among the boys as if he knew every one.

"Well played, lads."

"Thank you, sir. We'll get them next year headmaster."

"See that you do, boys. I don't like losing, it's not good for the school's reputation."

"Come now, sir," said Peter Davidson, "inter-school competition is a healthy thing."

"Not if I lose, Peter."

"Well, like it or not, you will have to present my boys with the cup."

"I will, I will."

"Percy, call the team together," instructed Mr Tomkins.

"Can we have a team photograph, sir?"

"Of course, Percy, I came prepared."

"Thank you, Mr Tomkins, sir."

The thirteen boys of André Laceys' Junior School Cricket Team lined up for their photograph. Percy stood dead centre of chums, Max Junior and David Braun, with the remaining ten spread on the wings.

"Say cheese!" called out their master, Mr Tomkins.

"O.K. time to go."

The coach, with the team on board, plus the headmaster, Peter Davidson and their Year Master, Mr Tomkins, headed back to André Laceys.

"How about a song, lads?" asked Mr Tomkins.

The headmaster stood up. "A victory song, lads!" he encouraged.

"We Are The Champions…" sang the lads, aided and abetted by both Peter Davidson and Mr Tomkins.

Back at Rose Cottage Max Junior was full of himself.

"You're very full of yourself, Max?" asked Miranda.

"Do I have to ask who won the Junior School cricket match?"

"No, mother, we did."

"So where's the cup?"

"Oh, Percy, our Team Captain, took it back to André Laceys. Mr Tomkins says it's a school's trophy."

"Well, at least you won, and you not eight yet. Wait until your father gets home tonight, he will be pleased."

Max Junior sat at the window waiting for his father to arrive home from working in The Block. Normally he would be playing with his pal David after school, but tonight was different.

Robert came home.

"Hello, darling, give us a kiss. I've missed you this week. However, I have got a lot of work done for Teddy Rosenburgh."

"That's good, dear, I've been busy with the pre-school children and Max has some news for you."

"Come here, soldier, give your father a hug. So what's your news?"

"André Laceys, we won the cricket match."

"The cricket match?"

"Oh father, I told you, have you forgotten?"

"Oh, now I remember, you were playing another school, is that right?"

"That's right. We played St Mark's Roman Catholic School. Load of stuck-ups if you ask me. They think because their team is in colours they are better than us. Well, I'll tell you one thing, when I'm in Senior School my team will give their Senior Cricket Team Eleven a jolly good thrashing."

"That's the ticket, son, be a winner!"

"Robert, how many times have I told you, don't encourage Max to just be a winner. It's important to be a team player."

"You don't mean the rubbish spouted by physical education masters, 'that it's the taking part', do you? Surely not!?"

"Look, if Max can't win at everything he will see himself as a loser."

"Oh no, mother, I will not. I'm good and I know I'm good. David and I help each other. And, what's more, the school bully, Rodger, daren't pick on David while I am around, because I'll give him a thrashing."

"Oh, Max, not fighting, surely?" said Miranda, aghast.

"Mother, I only fight if there is a reason. For example, if somebody picks on my pal David or says something untrue about father."

"Good for you, son. That's my boy."

"Robert, really, you're incorrigible!" laughed Miranda.

"Tell me, son, what do the boys say about me?"

"Well, father, that Rodger, because you are an artist, says painting is not real work and, therefore, you are not much of a man."

"Cheeky boy!"

"Never mind, father, I defended your honour and gave him a bloody nose and made him kiss my shoes."

"Should a boy of seven-and-a-half, at a school for gifted children, be doing that, Robert?"

"Miranda, much as I love you, you have to let the boys fight their own battles as they grow up."

"But what if Max Junior gets hurt?"

"Oh, mother, Percy our cricket captain, who is a whole year older than me, is my friend, as are all the members of the Junior School Cricket Team."

"You sure nobody will give you a bloody nose?"

"Sure, mother, us junior boys stick together. We are a gang. If there is a fight, and a Senior Boy is attacking a Junior Boy, we pull the senior down and give him a kick in the nuts and a bloody nose."

"You sound like a hooligan!"

"Don't be melodramatic, mother, we are only vigilantes at break-time in the playground or on the green at lunchtime."

"Robert, Max is taking the law into his own hands!"

"Mother, what the headmaster doesn't see can't do any harm. We're not breaking any school rules. We just maintain fairness between Junior School and Senior School. I don't like bullies."

"Touché, my son!"

"Thank you, father, we are learning French."

"You want to work in France?"

"That depends on the attitude of the French. We have Francois and Jacques from Paris at André Laceys, and they come from an aristocratic background. They are spiteful and full of arrogance. Some of the junior boys suck up to them, just because they have fabulous wealth. But, if they are an example of the French citizens, then I am glad I live in England."

"You know, Max," said Robert, "for one so young, you have an old head on young shoulders."

"I'll take that as a compliment, father."

"Are you hungry, Max Junior?"

"Starving, mother, I thought you'd never ask."

"Well, now that your father is home for the weekend and you have boasted of your news, it's time to eat."

"What is it, mother?"

"Stewed steak in rich gravy, in a hot-pot."

"Oh yummy tummy! Can I have seconds?"

"Don't be greedy. You know your father always has first pick."

"That's not fair!"

"Do you want a thick ear, son?"

"No, father, just that when I am older can I have first pick?"

"You can when you are older than your father."

"Gosh! I'll be an old man by then. Probably a grandad!"

Miranda and Robert laughed together over their priceless son.

The following day was Saturday, so Max Junior went along the lane to David Braun's house and together they went down to Dale Brook.

Captain Percy Lennox was by the bridge as agreed at nine o'clock. He had the fishing rods with him and a good tin of bloodworms.

"Good morning, Percy!" chirped the boys.

"Hello lads, have a look at these."

"Gosh, bright red and very wriggly," said Max.

"They smell!" said David, screwing up his nose.

"Where did you get them from, Percy?"

"Oh, from Farmer Sykes' dung heap."

"Phew! I bet that stinks. I've talked to Farmer Sykes when he's been mucking out his pigsties. Haven't I, Max?"

"You sure have. His sows are friendly enough though. Mr Sykes let's me stroke them; their skin is tough and the hair on their backs is very stiff like yard broom bristles."

"What sort of worms are they, Captain Percy?" asked, David.

"Bloodworms. Scientific name, Annelida. You can tell because they are red and segmented. Fish love them as bait. As a matter of fact, boys, I'll tell you a secret. If you were to fish on a trout fishery, or a fly fishing water, you would be arrested because bloodworms are strictly illegal."

"Gosh! Illegal? Why is that?"

"Because trout, officially, are supposed to be caught by a fly."

"Captain Percy, how can you catch a trout with a fly?" asked David Braun.

"It's called fly fishing because the hook to catch the trout is disguised by making it look like a fly. This is one," said Percy, taking a Mayfly from his fishing hat. The line when fly fishing floats on the water and the artificial fly on the hook looks to the hungry trout like a real fly, so they take the bait and are hooked. But, today, we are going to use these bloodworms instead of our usual chopped up garden earthworms."

"You sure these red worms will work?"

"Of course, David. The trout love them. The reason they are illegal is because the trout swallow them and the hook gets stuck in its gullet, which is not sporting if the fish has to be killed. The sport of game fishing is to catch and return to the water so that they can be caught another day."

"You mean we put them all back?" asked an incredulous Max Junior.

"That's right, son. So today when I teach you how to 'finger-fish', as soon as you feel a vibration on the line you strike, that's to make sure the hook is in the mouth of the trout. If done properly the trout should be hooked in the upper lip."

"Come on, David, let's get down to the brook. First off, boys, there's a few lessons to be learnt. Don't let your shadow fall on the water, otherwise the fish will know you are about, and, don't stamp on the riverbank because fish are very sensitive to vibration."

"But the fish are in the water, Captain Percy, how do they know we are on the bank?"

"Good question, David. The side of a fish has a lateral line which is highly sensitive to vibration. If you step on the bank heavily the vibration travels through the water and the fish feels the vibration on its lateral line and will hide away."

"Oh, now I understand. So we stay away from the water's edge?"

"Not exactly. Watch me. We stand upstream from where we fish and let the current of the stream take the worm under the banks and among the tree roots. Now you see what I am doing, I am pulling the line across my fingertips, which are sensitive to the slightest pull on the line. Now! That's got it, I've hooked one. I'll just reel him in."

"A small trout, Percy! It's beautiful. What sort is it?"

"It's a brook trout. They have this light golden sheen on their flanks and these attractive spot markings. Let me take the hook out."

"Can I let him go?" asked David.

"Sure, just lower him into the water and hold him facing up river to get the water flow into his gills. That's to make sure he gets enough oxygen before you release him."

"Like this, Percy?"

"That's it, just wriggle him a bit. As soon as he feels lively and ready to swim let him go."

"Can I have a go now, Percy?"

"Of course, Max, but we will have to move downstream a bit, because we have disturbed the bank's hiding places here."

Dale Brook ran down beside Dale Lane and then veered off under the road and turned into Thwaites Wood. Now Thwaites Wood was owned by Lord Lonsdale who lived in the Manor House, but Ben the gamekeeper knew the likeable young Max Junior and was friendly with his father, Robert, so he allowed Max, with his friend, David, to play in Thwaites Wood, on the understanding that if they came across any poachers they were to tell Ben.

"Now, here's a good spot," said Captain Percy. "Stand back behind the bush and dangle the hooked worm until it floats in the water."

They were at a point in Dale Brook where the water turned a bit muddy and the current was slack as the stream meandered through the trees, which meant the water was deeper and, at selected spots formed deeper pools.

"That's right, Max, let out a little line so that the worm floats under the tree roots."

Max tried again, getting the hang of it. The line suddenly went tight.

"Strike, Max! Drive the hook home."

Spiked, the trout fought hard.

"It's a big one, Percy! Look at the rod bend!"

"You can stand up now. Hold the rod tip out in the middle of the pool. Get the trout out into the open, otherwise he may try to wind the line around a tree root."

Max did as instructed. After a struggle the brook trout came to the surface.

"Nice fish, Max. Hold the rod up now so that it takes the strain. Slide him on his side to the edge of the pool so that I can get my net under him."

"Hey, David! Come and have a look! A big fish!"

"Not bad, Max, for your first fish, about half a pound."

Percy unhooked the trout and knocked it on the head smartly with a short iron rod.

"It's best to be cruel to be kind, Max, because otherwise it is cruel allowing the fish to suffocate slowly to death."

"Can I show my father the trout I have caught?"

"Of course, Max. Here, put it in this bag to keep the flies off."

"Can you help me, Captain Percy?" asked David.

"Come on, David, I'll show you a pool where a bigger trout lives. I've caught him before and released him to be caught another day."

"If I catch him, can I keep him?"

"Well if you do, David, he won't be there to be caught another day. The idea of trout fishing is that it's a sport. Catch and release."

"All right, if I catch him can I let him go?"

"Sure, Captain Percy has brought along his little camera so if you catch him I'll take your picture of you holding him."

"Thanks, Percy, that's a good idea, then my father will know what I've caught."

They walked into the middle of Thwaites Wood following the meandering of Dale Brook. The stream banks got higher and higher and branches hung across its watercourse.

"Right, David, past the next oak tree there is a deep pool. You need to keep your reflection from showing on the pool's surface. I'll stay here. You carefully and quietly climb down the bank to get low down and then flip your baited hook into the middle of the pool.

The water is very slack here so don't move the bait. Just keep perfectly still and wait. If the big 'un takes the bait let him move off for a couple of feet before you strike to make sure he has the worm in his mouth. Then strike quickly and hold your rod up to let the bend take the strain of the line."

David waited and waited. His knees were aching with being crouched down.

"He's not here, Percy."

"Patience, lad, wait a bit longer. He's old and wiley. He's checking to see if the worm is a trick. He should take it because it's only a sixteen hook, which is quite small for trout fishing, and the bloodworm is new on, which means it will wriggle a bit as if it is a caterpillar that has just fallen from the branch of the oak tree overhead."

David waited. He was about to give up when his nylon fishing line started to move off. Captain Percy was watching his protégé.

"Strike lad! Strike you have a bite!"

David struck and his rod bent right down to the water.

"It's a big one, Percy, what do I do?"

"Hold on, I'm coming down."

"Here lad, hold the rod up and let the trout run around in circles in the pool. The idea is to let him tire himself out without putting undue strain on the hook and pulling it out. Also, you only have very fine monofilament line, which we don't want to force or it will break."

"Like this, Percy?"

"Good lad. Just wait. In five minutes he'll come to the surface."

Eventually the hooked trout lay on its side gasping from the effort of the fight. Percy slid the net under the water and the trout made a last minute dash for freedom, leaping and splashing on the surface.

"O.K., David, the fight has gone out of him slide him across the top of the net. Got him!"

Max came down the bank to have a look.

"Gosh that's a big one!"

"Yes, about a pound and a half, which is a really good size for a brook trout. He's probably been in this pool for ten years, so we will put him back."

"What about my photograph?" asked David.

"Come on, Max, stand close to David."

"David, hold the trout out in front of you. Ready?"

Captain Percy took a photograph of two smiling young lads in a shade dappled oak wood.

Back at Rose Cottage, Robert asked his son, what he had caught.

"This, father, a brook trout. Captain Percy says it's about half a pound, which is good for a brook trout. But David caught a big one, didn't you, David?"

"Yes, Mr Darling, but Captain Percy said I was to put it back because it had lived in the pool in the woods for about ten years."

"Yes, it's true, father, it was about a pound and a half."

"Son, you are exaggerating, brook trout are usually only small," laughed Robert.

"Don't tease the boys," scorned Miranda.

"Father, Captain Percy took a photograph of us, that is David and me, holding out the trout!"

"There, Robert, what did I say," smiled Miranda.

"O.K., boys, I'll believe you when I see the photograph. Then I'll know if it's a boys' fishy story."

"Tomorrow, Mr Darling, I'll ask Captain Percy to show you on his little digital camera."

"O.K., David. Now is my wife going to cook it for you?"

"Please, Miranda," said David.

"You should call Max's mother, Mrs Darling, David."

"But her name's Miranda, Mr Darling."

"O.K., David, you may call my wife Miranda, but only in private. Is that clear?"

"You mean, when we are outside with other people, I call her Mrs Darling?"

"Exactly! David."

"Miranda, could I have a cup of tea and a biscuit?"

"Well, you could David, but as we have trout there's just enough for a fish sandwich each. Would that do?"

"Yes please."

"And me, mother."

"Right boys, go take your coats off and your muddy boots and wash up."

"Yes, father."

"Boots off in the back porch!"

The lads took their boots off and rushed upstairs to the bathroom to be first with the flannel and soap.

"And don't muddy the towels!" called out Miranda.

"It seems, darling, David and Max have found a good and trusted friend in Captain Percy."

"Well, our good Captain Percy is retired from the army, but he's only young yet."

"How old do you reckon?"

"Probably between sixty and sixty-five because he still looks fit."

"I think he gets bored," said Robert, "and the boys give him another interest in his life."

"I like living in Lower Dale, Robert, we seem to have been accepted by the locals and Reverend Thompson is glad to have a few children in St Winifred's on Sunday."

"And it gives you a teaching job, darling."

"God this trout is slimy, Robert. Yuk!"

"Give it to me, watch. Cut the head through the backbone and give the head a good pull."

"What's that?"

"It's the guts, darling. Now watch: slit the underside open, right down to the vent. Then open it out and clean it. Have you some plain flour?"

"Yes, in the cupboard."

"Well, pass it to me. Put some flour on the board and coat both sides of the fish, then put a pinch of salt inside to season. Now you put a little oil in the frying pan and cook for about ten minutes each side."

"I can cook, Robert, it's just that I've never gutted a fish before. Now I know, next time I'll be able to do it."

"O.K., I'll make the tea."

"Come on down boys, trout in five minutes!"

"Coming, father!"

"Put two plates in the warming rack, Miranda, while I butter some bread for the starving lads."

"There you are. What have you been doing?"

"David splashed me with some water so I got him back with a sopping wet flannel."

"Water fight, eh? Well, I hope you've cleaned up?"

"Yes, mother, we used the clean towel to dry the floor."

"Then I bet it's dirty again!"

"Give them a break, darling, I was a boy once. It's only natural high spirits."

"Well, don't just stand there, Max Junior, sit down and your father will pour you a cup of tea."

"Robert, the trout is ready."

"O.K., pass it to me. Now watch: you open the side of the trout by slitting it down the entire length of the lateral line and slide the fish off from both sides of the bone. Then you take hold of the backbone at the head end and carefully lift it off the flesh underneath, like this, by sliding a knife between the bone and the meat. Now you have the other half of the fish. But remove the fins, because they contain a row of small bones."

"Hungry, boys?"

"Yes, father, but there isn't very much."

"Just one sandwich each with a pinch of salt for taste because it's only a small fish."

"Pass me the warm plates, Miranda."

"There you are boys, your first trout!"

The boys gobbled the single slice of bread down with just three ounces of fish in.

"Well?" said Robert.

"Quite tasty, father, but not much of it. Was there David?"

"Maybe, Max, we should have put him back to grow a bit bigger," said David.

"Perhaps. I'm still hungry, mother."

"Old hollow legs. Would you like a bowl of cornflakes with fresh milk?"

"Yes please, mother. And David."

"Of course. Here you are then."

"Right, you two, we are going to the Village Shop to stock up. Will you be O.K. on your own for a little while?"

"Of course, mother. We aren't infants any more. We'll go to David's and see Humphrey; he's helping us build a go-cart so we can whiz down the hill."

"That's all right then, Max Junior, but you shouldn't call David's dad Humphrey, he's Mr Braun to you."

"Oh that's all right, Miranda, my dad doesn't mind," spoke up, David.

"I don't know, you boys aren't eight years old yet and yet you act so grown up."

"We are Juniors now, Mrs Darling."

"That's better, David. Then off you two go. Your father and I are going shopping."

"Can we have some sweets, we aren't allowed any at André Laceys?"

"Very sensible school rule. You know very well that too much sugar rots your teeth. I'll bring you back some cakes, how's that?"

"Thanks, mother. See you later."

"Bye, boys."

And with that, Max Junior and David raced down Dale Lane to Humphrey Braun's house. In the garden, shaded under a canopy, was a pram from which crying was erupting, and, on the driveway, Mr Braun was washing his estate car with a power washer.

"Look out, Max, my dad will soak you!"

"Father, the baby is crying!"

"Sorry, I didn't hear him, what with the noise of the compressor. Look, I'm all wet, can you fetch him indoors to your mother?"

"O.K. father."

"Come on, Max, let's take baby Johnathon into the house."

"Can you do babies?" asked Max, incredulously.

"Sure, come with me," said a confident David.

David put baby Johnathon on the kitchen table.

"Right, you hold him still while I get a nappy."

David returned with a box of wipes and a fresh nappy. He unfastened the soiled nappy, wiped Johnathon clean and dry, and put a clean one on.

"How do you know how to do that?"

"Oh, it's easy, Max, my mother showed me. Anyway, baby Johnathon is happy now because he is dry."

"Can I hold him?"

"Sure. You haven't got a brother, have you?"

"No I haven't. I asked my mother why not and she said God hasn't blessed her with any more children."

"It's nothing to do with God, Max. It's sex; my dad has explained it to me. Perhaps your parents don't do it any more."

"Do what?"

"Make love, you know, to produce babies."

"Oh yuk! That's what old people do."

"How old is Johnathon, David?"

"Almost a year, he can sit up to be fed and crawls about on the carpet like a scuttling rabbit."

"Can he walk yet?"

"No, not yet, but he pulls himself up by hanging onto the furniture and then falls down again. So he's trying."

"Let's take him for a ride in the go-cart," suggested, Max.

"He's too small, he'll probably fall out."

"What about if you push me and I steer with my feet, and Johnathon can sit on my lap. I'll hold him and keep him safe," offered, Max.

"O.K. but don't drop him or I'll be for it."

So David set off pushing Max in his go-cart, with Max steering with his feet and holding onto baby Johnathon on his lap.

"Come on David, faster!"

The go-cart went down the hill towards Dale Brook.

"Whee!" shouted Max Junior as the cart picked up speed.

Baby Johnathon shook his little arms and gurgled with happiness.

"Now it's my turn, Max," said a bit puffed David."

"O.K. you get in, and I'll push you home. I'm the strongest anyway. He's laughing. Perhaps we should take Johnathon every weekend."

June Braun came down the stairs from changing the beds and put the soiled sheets in the laundry room. Next she went out into the garden to check on Johnathon. She moved the cat net back and, to her horror, Johnathon was missing.

"Hunphrey! Humphrey, the baby has been stolen!"

She shouted at Humphrey who was oblivious to her panic. He was busy washing down the suds off his car. June pulled at his arm.

"What? What is it?"

"The baby's gone!"

"The baby's gone?" He switched off the compressor immediately.

"What do you mean the baby's gone?"

"Johnathon is not in his pram!"

"That's because I saw the boys take him indoors. Don't panic, they're probably playing with him on the lounge carpet. You know what a great helper David is."

"Oh, I hadn't thought of that."

She rushed indoors.

"David! David, are you in here?!"

June rushed upstairs to David's bedroom and flung the door open. Then she panicked and checked all the rooms.

"Humphrey! Humphrey, David's not here!"

"Calm down, David's probably taken Johnathon for a walk."

"But his pram's still in the garden."

"David could have carried Johnathon; he was here with his pal, Max Junior. You know how big Max is for an eight-year-old; he could easily be mistaken for eleven or twelve. Max could easily carry a baby."

"But they shouldn't take him without telling me," sobbed June.

"Whee! Faster, Max, come on Johnathon is liking it, he's laughing!"

June had never seen such a beautiful sight. Her son, David, laughing, with baby Johnathon on his lap also enjoying himself.

"Hello, Mrs Braun," said a very cheerful, Max, "we have taken Johnathon for a ride. He loves it!"

"I can see. But I'm very cross. You had me very worried when I found his pram empty. You must never take baby Johnathon without telling me first!"

"Sorry, Mrs Braun," said Max. "We thought it would be fun for Johnathon."

"Don't get upset, Max, but my wife is right. You may play with Johnathon, but you must ask our permission first, you understand?"

"Yes sir, sorry sir."

"Give me, Johnathon, David."

"He's not hurt, mother, I held onto him tight. Johnathon enjoyed the ride."

"I know you are protective of your baby brother, David, but he's not a teddy bear to play with. He's a little person."

"And, Mrs Braun, David changed Johnathon's nappy. He's pretty good really, I think," smiled Max.

"Did you, David, without my help?"

"Sure, it's easy when you know how."

"That was very considerate of you, David, thank you."

"I think, wife, the boys deserve a reward," said Humphrey.

"Would you boys like some ice cream with chocolate sauce?"

"Oh yummy! Yes please!" they chirped together.

Back at Rose Cottage Robert helped Miranda unload the car.

"Ah! Good timing, you two, you can help carry in some groceries."

"O.K. father. Come on David."

"What have you two been up to while we have been shopping?"

"We took baby Johnathon for a ride in David's go-cart."

"Isn't that a bit dangerous, he's only a baby?"

"No, mother. David sat in the box and steered with his feet and held baby Johnathon on his lap with both arms."

"Oh, O.K. Did you tell Mrs Braun first?"

"No actually, Mrs Darling. My mother and father told me off."

"I should think so too!"

"We said we were sorry. But Johnathon enjoyed himself because he waved his little arms and gurgled out loud. He likes going fast."

"Boys will be boys," said Robert.

"I suppose you are both hungry again?"

"Just a bit, David's mum gave us ice cream."

"Ice cream. After you were naughty? You were lucky."

"Did you get some cakes, mother, from the bakery?"

"Yes, hollow legs, doughnuts and custard slices. But you can't have both now."

"Can we have the doughnuts, please?"

"Of course. What would you prefer, David?"

"A doughnut, please, Mrs Darling. I like the raspberry jam."

"Yes, so do I," said Max Junior.

The two boys, with their sugar-coated trophies, set to work and sucked the jam out, getting a sugar-frosted face for their trouble and jam smeared mouths. Then they tore the dough to pieces and gobbled it down.

"Messy boys! Go to the sink and wash your faces off."

Instead they went to the hallway mirror to look at themselves.

"I'm Dracula," said Max.

David just laughed back at his reflection.

"And I'm Dracula's mother, now get into the cloakroom and clean yourselves up, and don't put jam and sugar all over my clean towels!" called out Miranda.

"Race you!" said David, and they both dashed for the hand basin, covering the sides and the taps with a sticky mess. They dried their faces.

"Better clean up," said David.

Max got a face flannel and David got toilet tissue to wipe down the bowl.

"And don't put sugar sticky-mess all over my clean hand basin!"

"Has your mother got radar?" asked David.

"O.K. mother!" called back, Max.

"Better use some hot water and soap," suggested, David.

"O.K."

Max soaped the washbasin with the face flannel and David dried it off with toilet tissue.

"What are you two up to in here?"

"Cleaning up, mother."

"Makes a change. Right, outside and play."

Because Rose Cottage was built when plots of land were inexpensive it had a huge garden – about half an acre, including the trees at the bottom of the garden, which formed a boundary with Farmer Brown's fields.

Robert had helped Max Junior build his tree house because Miranda insisted it had to be safe. She didn't want her son falling down breaking his leg or his neck come to that. So Max and David had a purpose built rope ladder to climb up to get into their tree house.

Once up they got out their bow and arrows, which they kept hidden in the holly bush behind the big oak tree.

"What shall we shoot today?"

"Well, Max, we can't play cowboys and Indians because there's only two of us," said David.

"What about next door's cat? It's always coming into my garden and doing its toilet amongst my mother's plants. You know my mother gets angry because she likes flowers and that pesky cat pees on the petals and that kills them."

They waited, and sure enough, Tiddles, for that was what they nicknamed next door's cat, came into Max's mum's garden and started digging in the flowerbeds.

"Now!" whispered, Max. And they both let fly their arrows.

Tiddles was in the middle of his business when David's arrow went uselessly past, and Max's struck home. They didn't have any real points on the arrows because they were just bits of branches, but Max's arrow hit Tiddles' fur enough to make him jump. The old tomcat meowed, looked up and trotted off as if nothing had happened. Then he turned back to his recent toilet and covered it over with his back feet and slouched off with his head held high, his tail erect and a self-satisfied smile, as if he owned the place.

"Bloody cheeky cat!" said Max. "Let's go tell mother."

"That Tiddles has just done number twos in your flower bed."

"Damned cat! I'll teach it!"

"What are you going to do, Miranda, smack its bum?" laughed, Robert.

"It's not funny, my geraniums are full of cat mess."

"I'll deal with it," said Robert.

"Come on, boys, let's get it once and for all."

"How will you get him, father?"

"With the hosepipe. Cats don't like getting wet."

"Yippee!" shouted Max Junior.

"Be quiet, Max, we need to creep up on him. I'll fix the hose to the tap; you two pull the pipe out into the back garden. When he comes back you tell me."

"O.K. father."

"How about a game of marbles on the lawn, David?"

The two boys were engrossed in their game when an orange blur caught the corner of Max's eye.

"He's here, David. Go tell my father. I'll creep up to the end of the hosepipe."

"Robert, the cat's in the garden again."

"Right you are, David, here goes, tap on full."

The pipe hissed and the water rushed out. The cat was alerted and looked up in its normal nonchalant manner. It was slow to escape the full pressure of the hosepipe as it tried to run away. Max gave it a good soaking. It screeched, raised its back so its fur stood on end, and hissed, and then, realising it was outmatched, bolted back to next door.

"Hooray!" shouted the boys.

Then Max's wicked side escaped and he turned the hosepipe onto David. Now David was quick witted and realised what was about to happen. He ran quickly to the bottom of the garden, out of reach of the arc of water.

Max was playing thus when his father came out to see how the boys were doing, scaring the cat away.

"Have you got him?" asked, Robert.

"No, but I've got you!" laughed Max, as he turned the water on his father.

"Ugh! You little brat, you've soaked me!"

"Quick up in the tree house!" shouted Max.

David was already heading for the rope ladder; he didn't have to be told twice. He was quickly followed up by Max Junior.

"David, quick pull the ladder up!"

Robert ran, after his initial surprise, to catch the two boys and give them a thick ear.

"Ha, ha, ha!" laughed Max and David, together. "Can't get us now."

"We'll see about that!"

Robert unwound the drum of hosepipe to its full extent and sprayed it towards the tree house. It didn't quite reach, so Robert put his thumb over the end of the pipe to create a more pressurised jet.

"Bingo! Got you now!" shouted out Robert, but the arc of water just failed to reach by about a yard.

"You can't get us, father!" they taunted.

And as Robert walked back up the lawn, distracted by the boys, he inadvertently squirted Miranda's washing on the line.

Miranda came out in the garden just at the wrong time.

"Robert! Don't play with the hosepipe, you're soaking my washing!"

"It was an accident, I was trying to get the boys!"

"Likely story. You are worse than they are!"

"Honestly! Max soaked me and then ran away into the tree house. I was trying to soak them back, but the hosepipe isn't long enough. I was coming back up the garden when they distracted me and I accidentally squirted the washing."

"Well, just stand still while I turn it off! Really you are a big kid!"

Then Miranda saw the funny side of it and burst out into howls of laughter at her dishevelled husband.

"I don't see what's so funny. I'm bloody soaked!"

That did it, Miranda became hysterical and curled up on the lawn in uncontrollable laughter. She laughed that hard it hurt and she couldn't get her breath.

Then Robert, seeing his wife thus, laughed at her laughing.

The boys were watching all the time, so they burst out laughing at Max's parents.

"Come on, David, I think its safe to come down now," smiled Max Junior.

"Sorry, father, it was just a spur of the moment thing. You aren't cross with me, are you?"

"I was for a minute, but the time has passed now. Pick your mother up."

"Give me a hand, David, I think mother is in stitches."

"Miranda stood up, tears of laughter wet her cheeks.

"Robert, go and get changed, you look like you have wet yourself."

"Are you cross with me, mother?" asked Max Junior.

"No, Max, I've not laughed so hard for a very long time. In fact, you have cheered me up."

The following day was Sunday. Max met his pal David at the church gate.

"Really, Max, you should come with us," said Miranda.

"I have a watch, mother, it's only ten to ten. Humphrey will be here with David, any minute."

"All right, Max, but you had better not be late coming in, or I'll be really cross."

"Oh mother, I will soon be eight years old. I do have my watch. I'll be in on time."

Seeing his friend waiting outside the gate, David rushed forward. "Hi Max! Look what I've got!"

"Gosh, where did you get those from?"

"Up on Barker's Wood. Do you want to go after church?"

"O.K."

"Don't dawdle, David, you're getting under our feet," said June Braun, carrying baby Johnathon in her arms.

"Bossy parents!" whispered David.

"How many conkers have you got?"

"Just four, but really big ones, my father says they are windfalls."

"Couldn't you get more?"

"No. In Barker's Wood the trees are ancient and the horse chestnut's branches are high up."

216

The organist in the church, Old Smithy, started to play some incidental music, which meant it was time to settle down and for the congregation to pay attention to the Order of Service.

"Come on Smithy has started up. We'd better go in," said Max Junior.

The front pew was always reserved for any visitors or church dignitaries of the Diocese, so there were a few hushed gasps of surprise when Max and David sat in the front row.

The vicar was pleasantly surprised that the boys, apparently unsupervised, behaved like saints.

"Would you all please stand for hymn number two hundred and twenty, All Things Bright And Beautiful."

Max and David stood up smartly, raised their chins and pushed their chests out as they were taught at André Laceys. They smiled an unspoken communication, and in tune filled the nave with a young boys' harmonious falsetto.

Inspired, the vicar, Reverend Thompson, conducted the boys and encouraged them to ascend to full volume, which in turn uplifted the body of the congregation to greater achievement – the sound filling the normally echoing vacuum of the church.

"Well done everybody, please sit down. Let us pray."

The parishioners filed out of St Winifred's to a campanologist's treat ringing out loud and clear. It seemed to wake up the normally sleepy village of Lower Dale and bring it to life.

Several people walked down Dale Lane to the Black Bull, where a pint and a traditional roast beef Sunday lunch awaited the customers.

"Your mother and I, David, are going home now, what will you do?"

"I'm taking Max to Barker's Wood to look for some more large conkers."

"Well make sure, David, you tell Mr and Mrs Darling."

"O.K. mother."

"See you again, Humphrey, June," said Robert.

"Mother, would you like to come to Barker's Wood?"

"Your father and I used to do some of our courting there before you were born, Max Junior."

"What's courting, mother?"

"Boys and girls going out together."

"Yuk! Girls are silly."

"Wait until you are fifteen, son, then perhaps you will change your mind."

"I don't think so."

"But you would like some really big conkers?"

"Yes please, father. David has some."

"Show him, David."

"Good size, but you want to soak them in vinegar and then bake them for an hour in a hot oven."

"What does that do, Mr Darling?"

"Now, to win at conkers you need a really hard one. When I was at school I had a 'fiftyer'."

"What's a 'fiftyer'?"

"A strong conker that broke fifty other boys' conkers before it broke, itself."

"Gosh, won't that be something at André Laceys?" said a surprised and crafty thinking David.

"Come on, Miranda, my lover, we're off to the woods."

"I thought you would never ask, lover."

"Behave yourself!" and Robert slapped Miranda's pert bottom.

She raced ahead. "Come on boys, I'll race you to Barker's Wood!"

Now David Braun was quite little, but he made up for that by sheer speed.

"You'll make an athlete, David!" called out Robert.

Miranda was first into the woods, so she found a hiding place behind a large trunk of a horse chestnut which was obscured by a thick, ground hugging holly bush.

Under the shaded trees, with their considerable umbrella of overhanging branches, the light was diffuse and the eyes had to take a few seconds to adjust to the low light. Miranda could see David from her place of confinement, but he couldn't see her.

"Where are you, Miranda!?" shouted out, David.

David was followed by Max and then Robert.

"Father, is mother up a tree?" asked Max.

"Maybe. She is good at climbing trees. What was she wearing, Max?"

"Her casual clothes. You know: jeans, sweatshirt and trainers."

"Hmm? Miranda, I am going to throw a large dead branch up into the horse chestnut so, if you are up there, you had better come down before you get hurt!"

No reply.

"Do you hear me?"

"Go on, father, give her a scare," said Max.

"A scare's one thing, Max, but actually hurt your mother, never."

"Mother, where are you?!" called out Max.

"Probably behind another tree," suggested David.

"O.K. boys, pick a tree each and go look behind it."

Robert moved slowly round the second tree, avoiding the prickly holly bush. As he passed, Miranda picked three red holly berries and threw them at the back of Robert's head.

Startled, he said, "O.K., Miranda, you can come out now, I know where you are!"

Thinking, 'Where the hell is she?'

Behind, and partially immersed in the holly bush, was a safe place for Miranda.

Robert walked right into Miranda, only separated by the immediate branch. She shot her arm out and grabbed him around the neck as he turned his back on her.

"Arrgh! shouted Robert with the combination of being scared and shocked.

"What the hell!?" he spun round, and to his surprise and relief, Miranda, stepped out of the holly bush.

"Had you going there! Definitely for a minute."

"You vixen! You scared me half to death!"

Miranda burst out laughing.

"Come here, give me a cuddle. Didn't that holly bush prickle you?"

"Just a bit. It's not too bad if you move the branches apart to get in. The prickly leaves all seem to face outwards as if the bush is trying to protect itself."

"O.K. boys, Miranda's found, you can come back now!" called out, Robert.

"Come on Max, David, let's find some conkers now!"

"I think they are playing your game, Miranda. Hide and seek," smiled, Robert.

"Well, let's teach them a lesson," whispered Miranda. "We'll scoop up a double handful of leaves each, creep up on them, and dump it on their heads."

"Miranda, darling, you have a wicked side to you."

Miranda and Robert circled as silently as possible, allowing for the slight crack of twigs underfoot, around the trunk of each mature tree, which could be a potential hiding place. They found not a soul.

"We're coming for you, David, Max!" called out Robert. "We know you are hiding!"

Crafty David took Max deep into the woods and, keeping at a distance, circled around, such that as Robert and Miranda penetrated anti-clockwise, the boys circled clockwise, which meant that as Robert and Miranda moved forward, ever deeper into the woods, David and Max moved outwards towards the original starting position.

"Ha, ha!" laughed David. "They have no idea, we are now behind them."

"Very clever thinking," said Max. "Should we tell them or let them carry on searching?"

"No. I have a better idea," said David. "Let's go home to my house and tell my parents we have lost Miranda and Robert in Barker's Wood."

"O.K. David."

"Hello boys. Has your mother sent you to play?" asked June Braun.

"No." said Max. "We have lost them in Barker's Wood."

"Lost them? How can you lose them?"

"Well, we were playing hide and seek, and David and I were hiding, but Robert and Miranda couldn't find us."

"Where are they now?"

"Somewhere in the woods."

"And you left them there?"

"Yes, mother, it was my idea," said David.

"I think we should go and look for them," said June.

"If I may put a word in," interrupted, Humphrey. "It could very well be that Robert and Miranda don't want to be found."

"You mean, they want to be alone?" smiled June.

"Yes, if you know what I mean," winked Humphrey.

"Oh you mean they will be doing it again," said Max.

"Doing what?" asked David.

"You know, we talked about it at André Laceys last week."

"Oh, sex? Yuk!"

"Well, my parents do it every weekend. They send me out to play, but I sneak back in and listen through my bedroom wall."

"Do you?" asked David.

"Yes, I use a glass to my ear against the wall. My mother screams a lot."

"Max Junior, really!" said a very cross June Braun. "When parents love one another it's a private matter; do you want me to tell your parents you listen through the wall?"

"Oh no, please!"

"Then promise me you won't spy on them any more."

"I promise. You won't tell will you?"

"Not as long as you promise not to be so nosey, because there's a saying, 'curiosity killed the cat'!"

"What does that mean?"

"Sticking your nose in where it's not wanted can have dire consequences. Punishment!"

"I won't do it any more. Will I, David?"

"I don't think you should."

"And, David, don't you spy on me and your father, clear?"

"Yes, mother."

"Right, out and play!"

"Come on, David, let's go to my house."

"How will we get in, the door will be locked?"

"That doesn't matter, we can climb the trees at the back of the garden and over the rear garden fence, and then climb up into the tree house."

"All right, Max Junior, that's a good idea. It means we don't have to go into Rose Cottage."

"And," said Max, "we can spy on my parents from up in the tree house. That's not naughty or nosey because we will not be in Rose Cottage and the tree house is ours."

"Did you really listen through the wall to your parents making love?"

"Yes, and it sounds rude."

"Yuk! I don't want to know. Anything to do with girls is soppy."

"What about when you are a grown man and get married?"

"Well, I don't know about that," said David. "That's in the future when you are quite old, like your father, Robert."

"I suppose so," said a serious Max Junior, from the comfort of their tree house. My mother though is a lot younger than my father and still beautiful."

"Yes she is, Max. That's probably why at the weekends, when Robert comes home, he makes love to your mother."

"I hope when I am older," said Max, "and I have to marry, my girlfriend is as beautiful as my mother."

"Well, Max, Miranda is a famous model. Even I know that."

"Only because, David, I cut out the stories from magazines and newspapers about my mother," said Max.

"I also read the magazines my mother leaves lying about the house. I think my mother is jealous of Miranda."

"How do you know that?" asked Max Junior.

"Because, when I sit and watch television, mother always says when there is an article on Miranda, 'I wish I had her looks'."

"It's because, David, my father explained it to me, companies in the health and beauty business use beautiful models to sell their products."

"You mean they make money because Miranda is beautiful?"

"Sure David, of course."

"Then I wish I was beautiful, so I could have a lot of money."

"Don't be daft, David, if a boy dresses like a woman and wears make-up he will be called gay."

"What's gay?"

"It means a man who doesn't love a woman, but instead prefers another man to love."

"You mean a man kisses another man?"

"Yes, another man."

"Yuk! Are you sure?"

"Yes. My father explained it to me. He said some men are born that way, they simply are not attracted to women."

"So they don't have children?"

"That's right, David, but father said it's not something that young boys need know about."

"Thank goodness for that because, Max, you are my best friend, but I would never marry you."

"I should jolly well hope not, because when I am a successful businessman, I will marry a beautiful woman like my mother."

Max and David stayed up in their tree house for about an hour.

Now Robert knew that Max climbed over the back fence by scaling the trees, because he had seen him do it on numerous occasions, but turned a blind eye. So now he called out from the backdoor of Rose Cottage.

"O.K., you can come down, Max, I know you are up there!"

"Come on, Max, they have found us," said David.

"Coming, father!"

"You couldn't find us, could you mother?"

"No, we gave up and guessed you had gone back home, so we left you to it."

"Why have you got pieces of straw in your hair?" asked Max.

"Oh, that's because we went into Farmer Brown's fields looking for you, and your mother tripped on a fallen branch," said Robert, defensively.

The boys, being innocent, didn't guess the real reason, they just accepted Robert's explanation.

"Mother, we are hungry again."

"I'm not surprised," replied Miranda, "it's all that running around playing hide and seek and climbing the back fence and the trees."

"You know we climb the back fence, and you don't punish us?"

"Boys will be boys!" laughed Robert. "I was a boy myself, once upon a time."

"Oh! What is there to eat?"

"How about some fish paste sandwiches?"

"I like fish paste," said David. "My mother makes father sandwiches and I always share."

"O.K. Wash your grubby hands in the cloakroom and sit at the table."

Later, Sunday evening, Robert kissed Miranda goodbye to set off on his journey back to Knightsbridge in London.

"I wish you didn't have to go, Robert."

"You know what Monday morning traffic is like in the West End. Absolute murder. It would take me ages with bumper-to-bumper traffic jams. I would arrive at The Block exhausted, and in a foul mood, definitely not good for painting. It's best, as you well know, for me to go now."

In the morning, Max Junior jumped in to the car and they went along Dale Lane to David's house.

"Go fetch him, Max."

Max Junior opened the gate and, as he did so, David came out of his house, with his school satchel on his shoulder.

"Hello, Max."

"Morning, David, see you are ready."

"Come on, David, get in. I'm running a bit later this morning," said Miranda.

"Yes, I know, mother told me to watch at the window."

"Have you done your homework, David?"

"Yes, Mrs Darling. Has Max done his?"

"Of course!" said Max. "I had to learn some stupid Latin words."

"It's not stupid if you want to become a doctor, Max, because human anatomy has Latin nomenclature."

"Mrs Darling, I'm not sure what I want to be. My father thinks I should become an accountant because I am good at mathematics. My homework was all about fractions. I don't see what that has got to do with accountancy?"

"Well, I would say fractions are all about proportions, and proportions are similar to percentages. Now, accountancy, as you know, is about finances and balancing the books, which means percentages are important. When you are an accountant you have to know about taxation, and taxation is based on income and allowance bands, which are worked out in percentages. So you see, three quarters or decimal 0.75 is the same as saying seventy-five percent."

"Oh, Mrs Darling, I know what percentages are because Max and I, from our pocket money, have started a savings club at André Laceys' School Bank."

"You didn't tell me there was a School Bank?"

"Oh yes, the headmaster, Mr Davidson, encourages the boys, starting in Junior School, to invest any spare money they have, starting at as little as fifty pence," said a pleased with himself David.

"Yes, mother, David and I invest a pound a week in the School Bank, and now we have started our own loan company."

"I beg your pardon, a loan company?"

"Yes, mother," said Max. "We lend money out between one pound and ten pounds at ten percent a week."

"Good God, ten percent a week, that's robbery!"

"No it isn't, mother. The loan is only for one week."

"And what do you call yourself, Mr Businessman?"

"Our loan company is called DAX. It is the 'D' of David in Max."

"Very shrewd, you two, why doesn't your father and I know about this?"

"I didn't think you would approve, so we kept it secret."

"Mrs Darling, my father knows. He actually approves of us being wise with our money," supported David."

"Well, it doesn't seem to have done you any harm. Is it working?"

"Oh yes, Mrs Darling, the money we make from Dax we invest in the School Bank. Fifty pence on a five pound a week loan is not much in itself but, together on other little loans, it adds up. So, you see, we are making a steady profit, albeit, only small amounts."

"I admire your guts and your tact, boys, I think I congratulate you."

"Thank you, Mrs Darling."

"Let's say no more about it. But when your father is next home for the weekend, Max Junior, I think you had better tell him of your little scheme."

"Yes, mother. But I'm glad you're pleased for us."

Max and David sat in the back seat of the car and compared conkers they had picked up on the day before.

"Have you got some string, David?"

"No, my father said it's better to use a boot lace, because boot laces are strong and do not fray and break like string. Also he has given me these."

"What are they?"

"Washers you use on nuts and bolts."

"What for?"

"Good question, Max. When you thread the conker and tie a knot, the knot, after the conker has done battle with other boys' conkers, can pull through the conker and split it. However, if you put a washer over the knot, before you thread the lace through the conker, it supports the knot so that it cannot be pulled through. Which means you have a very strong conker."

"No, David. You have forgotten. First we have to soak our conkers in vinegar to pickle them and then we bake them in a hot oven to make them hard as stone."

"What are you two talking about? You sound like a couple of conspirators."

"We are planning to blow the school up!" laughed Max Junior.

"I hope that is a joke, otherwise you will end up like Guy Fawkes who attempted to blow up the Houses of Parliament in 1605 and, in so doing, lost his head."

"We know about bonfire night on November the 5th, mother. It was just a joke. But next year, Year Two of the Junior School, we will be learning science."

"Saints preserve us!"

At André Laceys, several parents were pulling up around the large sweep of the long gravel drive and dropping their charges off. It was, in the main, wives dropping boys off at the school, the men having set off earlier to their places of business in London.

"Goodbye mother," said Max in an offhand manner and disappeared in the crowd of milling boys, all looking similar in their school uniform.

"Goodbye, Mrs Darling. Take no notice of Max, he becomes the centre of attention when he arrives at school as he has loads of chums."

"I can see that. Well, goodbye, David, see you tonight."

The day's schooling went well, even though on a Monday they have Mr Smithers for a double maths lesson.

"Come on boys, settle down, you have had all weekend to let off steam. What have you been doing this weekend?" asked Mr Smithers.

"Please sir!" called out Max, with his arm raised. I have been fishing, sir!"

"Have you, Master Darling? And what did you catch?"

"A trout, sir. Half a pound, and David Braun and I ate it for a snack."

"Not very big then. Where did you catch it, young Max?"

"In Dale Brook, sir, in the woods near where I live."

"And what about you, David Braun, did you fish as well?"

"Yes, sir. Captain Percy showed me where to fish. I fished with a worm in a deep pool, under the tree roots, and caught a big one."

"Are you fibbing, Braun, because you know what I do to liars?"

"No sir, our friend, Captain Percy, who is an elderly man retired from the army, took a photograph of Max and I holding out the trout."

"Hmm. Then I suppose I'll have to believe you."

"It is true, sir."

"Anybody else want to tell a tale before we settle down?" asked Mr Smithers.

"Conkers, sir," said a young lad with glasses.

"Stand up when you address me!"

"Yes sir, sorry sir. I collected some conkers, Mr Smithers, from the village green."

"Collected conkers, Jutson?"

"Well, there were some windfalls on the road but the cars had run them over and squashed them, so I used a stout piece of wood tied to a length of rope and threw it into the tree branches."

"Did it work, Jutson?"

"Oh yes, sir. Look!"

"Good, good. Now I know, boys, autumn is the time for conkers, I should know I was a schoolboy once, but keep them in your pockets. If any boy starts playing conkers in my mathematics lesson, or even takes them out of his pocket to brag to his friends, I will confiscate the whole lot. Is that clear?"

"Yes sir," said Jutson.

"Is that clear, Junior School?"

"Yes sir!"

"Now, which boy can tell me what Pythagoras' theorem is?"

"Please sir," said David. "I know Pythagoras was a Greek philosopher and mathematician about 500 BC."

"Very good, David. How do you know this?"

"Pythagoras is in my book, The History of Famous People, sir."

"Thank you, David, you may sit down. We have been doing fractions; well today we are going to talk about geometry. That's shapes. Copy this down from the blackboard. This is a right-angled triangle. This slanted side is called the hypotenuse, and the base line is the opposite, and the vertical line is the adjacent. Now copy this down: 'the square of the length of the hypotenuse of a right-angled triangle equals the sum of the squares of the lengths of the other two sides'.

We express this as a sum : (h)squared = (a) squared + (o) squared.

Which on a 3, 4, 5, triangle is 5squared = 3squared + 4squared. That is 25 = 9 + 16.

Now, boys, concentrate. Pythagoras named the angles in his triangle trigonometry. There are three, and for today you only need to know their names. They are known and remembered by the following nomenclature: SOH, CAH, TOA.

Think of soaking your big toe in the bath water.

This is what they mean:

- Sine = Opposite over Hypotenuse
- Co-sine = Adjacent over Hypotenuse
- Tangent = Opposite over Adjacent.

Right lads, say after me. 'Soak a toe. Spelt, Soh Cah Toa.' Have you got it?"

"Yes sir," said David. "I can now do trigonometry when I have a bath!"

"Good lad! That will do."

"Got it lads?"

"Yes, sir, Mr Smithers!" laughed the boys.

"O.K. that's enough for today. Class dismissed!"

"Hooray!" shouted the boys and they rushed out into the playground to play conkers.

Now David, the brains of the pair, was crafty.

"Let's go see cook in the kitchen, Max."

"What for?"

"Just wait and see."

"Cook, can you help us?" asked David.

"That depends, young master, on two things: first, have I got time and, second, what are you up to this time, David Braun?"

"Just conkers, Mr Pastry."

"You shouldn't call me that."

"But you make the best meat pies, all the boys know that!" insisted, Max Junior.

"O.K. I know what you want, your conkers hardened in the oven to beat all the other boys?"

"Yes, Mr Pastry. But first soaked in vinegar to pickle them so the insides set solid and don't crack when whacked by the other boys' conkers."

"Who taught you that old trick?"

"My father," said Max. "He used to play conkers when he was a boy and he had a 'fiftyer'."

"And why should I help two nuisance Junior School boys?"

"Because you're our friend," smiled Max Junior.

"And," said David, cutting in, "because we will each give you a pound."

"Aha! Bribery eh?"

"Just a business incentive," said a straight-faced David.

"All right, because you like my pies and we have become friends, I'll soak your conkers for you. Have you made holes ready for the string?"

"Not yet, could we borrow a couple of skewers?"

"We'll do it together, but be quick before chef comes in. If he knew he wouldn't allow conkers in his ovens."

"Thanks, Mr Pastry. See you tomorrow for the conkers."

"Just a minute, haven't you forgotten something?" said cook, holding out his hand.

"Ugh! O.K. two pounds."

"Pleasure doing business, boys. Never forget, business is business!"

"O.K. Shake," said Max Junior. "Bye, Mr Pastry."

"Get out, the cheeky pair of you, before I flip you with the glass cloth!"

They ran out laughing, and bumped into chef.

"Stand still! What are you two urchins doing in my kitchen? Speak up before I call the headmaster!"

"Please sir, we went to ask cook if we could have any stale pies, you know, left over from yesterday."

"It's all right, chef, I've told the boys that, unfortunately, all leftovers go to the piggery. Boys will be boys."

"Very well, but if I catch you in my kitchen again you will get a spanked backside. Is that clear?"

"Yes chef, sir. Can we go now?"

"Run along, it's playtime. You should be running around the playground not my kitchen!"

"O.K. cook, you can tell me now. What were they really up to?"

"You won't get mad if I tell you."

"Try me?"

"They were after free food to sell to their chums. You know, to make pocket money."

"Cheeky monkeys!" laughed chef. "You know, cook, I went to a private school and at playtimes I did exactly the same. At least they show initiative."

The following day, Max Junior and David Braun, at playtime, sneaked into the kitchen again to see cook.

"Are they ready, Mr Pastry?"

"Just. I pickled them overnight, and they have been baking in a hot oven since seven o'clock this morning, so if I get them out now they will be hot."

"Quick, Mr Pastry, before chef comes."

"Don't worry, chef won't be in until lunchtime. What have you got to put them in?"

"A cloth bag, one I use for marbles."

"O.K. that will do. Here, a tray of rock-hard conkers."

Two crafty, smiling, junior boys already had a knotted lace with a washer fitted over the knot.

"Thanks, Mr Pastry!"

The boys rushed out into the playground, they had just twenty minutes of playtime left.

Lovable Percy was showing off his prowess as a conker basher.

"Hello, Max. This is a 'fourer'. I've just smashed four conkers in a row," bragged, Percy.

"This is a 'noner', but I'll challenge your 'fourer'!"

"O.K., Max, as we are friends, I'll let you have first whack."

"Your conker looks a bit black and burnt, I bet its rotten," smiled Percy, full of confidence.

Whack! Crack!

"Blimey! Your conker isn't rotten! O.K. my go."

Percy had perfect aim. He brought his conker down on top of Max's with all his strength. To his utter dismay his conker split clean in half and flew off his string onto the playground in shattered pieces.

"Bloody hell!" said Percy.

"I win, Percy, I have a 'fiver'!" declared Max, to the circle of watching boys.

Now the lads with virgin conkers were crying out to play Max Junior to make their conkers a 'sixer'.

The boys crowded around, Max.

"O.K." said David, the tactician. "Line up if you want to win a 'sixer'."

Max smashed four conkers in a row. "I have a 'tenner'!" declared, Max.

"Blimey!" said Percy. "Tell you what, Max Darling, I'll give you a pound for your 'tenner'!"

"Sorry, Percy, you are a friend, but it's worth more than that!"

Timothy Pendelton came forward. Now he was the son of an airline tycoon, who gave his son plenty of pocket money.

"I'll give you five pounds for it."

"O.K. Timmy, but I keep my boot lace, you have to find your own string."

"O.K. Here's a fiver."

"Thanks, Timmy."

"Cuthbert, give me your string please."

"All right, you may as well have it because Max smashed my conker."

"I challenge anybody with my 'tenner'!" shouted out Timothy Pendleton.

He had several instant challengers who wanted to win a 'tenner'.

"I'll smash that conker!" said Beefy Biffo.

The bell rang and all the boys lined up ready to return to class.

"Right, today," said John Jackson, the Physical Exercise Master, "you will be introduced to rugby. A man's game. Right, everybody get changed into your sports strips and wait for me in the gymnasium."

"O.K. settle down. Put down the floor exercise mats."

"Can I volunteer, sir!" asked Max Junior.

"Quick thinking, Darling. Have you played before?"

"Only on the village green, sir, with David my friend and our fathers."

"Right, boys, watch. Safety is the first thing. When you lock together, you keep your head down and thrust with your shoulders."

"O.K. Percy, you come out, you're a fairly large lad."

"Ready, Max?"

"Yes sir!"

"Percy and Max, I'll challenge the pair of you. Now engage! Now push! That's it. Disengage. Good."

"Now boys in pairs, practise, until you feel you have the idea."

Mr Jackson blew his whistle.

"That's enough, outside!"

"Percy, fetch the House Colours and, Max Junior, fetch a rugby ball."

"Yes sir!"

There were over thirty boys in Max's class, so the Master split them up into two teams of fifteen. Red House versus Blue House. There were two boys for linesmen.

"Now lads, this is the rugby field for the Senior School, so this is for real. Range out across the pitch in two opposing lines. All I want you to do today, as this is your first practice, is to run forward and pass the ball backwards as you gain ground. If you cross the line with the rugby ball in your hands and touch down it's a try. Now, you can tackle as many times as you like, around the legs, waist or shoulders, but not swinging on the neck. I don't want any broken necks, your parents who pay for you to go to André Laceys, would be most unhappy."

'J.J', as he was affectionately known, blew the whistle and the boys challenged one another. Max, being one of the biggest, picked up the ball and charged forward. Percy was ready for him and tackled him, but Max, with Percy clinging on continued charging forward. Beefy Biffo launched himself at Max and Max went down.

"Good tackle, Beefy!" called out Mr Jackson.

"Right lads, scrum down! Remember what you learnt in the gymnasium earlier!"

The ball came out of the scrum and quick thinking David, picked it up and ran with it. Percy blocked David, so David glanced round and, on the run, did a quick back pass to Max Junior who barged past Percy, ran for the line and crossed it just as Beefy Biffo pounced on his back.

"Yes!" shouted a mud spattered, Max.

"Try!" called out 'J.J.'

"Well done, Max Darling! You all right?"

"Yes sir!" smiled Max. "Good fun, sir!"

"O.K. lads, line-out."

"Timothy Pendleton, make yourself useful and throw in."

"Me, sir?"

"Yes, you, you lazy good for nothing and put your back into it!"

"Yes, sir!"

Now Max was getting the measure of the game. As soon as Timmy threw the ball Max hoisted David bodily up to catch the ball. David grabbed the ball and dashed forward weaving between two of the opposition.

Beefy Biffo stood in his way. Looking round, David saw Max on his wing, so he quickly back-passed the ball to Max. Max, head down, charged forward, pushing with an outstretched hand, Beefy Biffo out of the way and ran like hell to the touch line.

"Try!" shouted out 'J.J.'

And so the Junior School were introduced to rugby.

In the showers, Max's winning team, Red House, gave the losers, Blue House, a smacking with wet towels.

"Come on, lads, that's enough, get dried and changed, or you will be late for lunch," called out Mr J. Jackson.

"Ready, sir!" called out each boy as they lined up outside the changing rooms ready for lunch.

"Everybody ready?"

"Yes, sir!"

"O.K. you may go!"

It was shepherds pie with cabbage and carrots followed by apple pie and custard.

"Yummy!" said Beefy Biffo, "my favourite. I think I'll have seconds."

"You're getting fat, Beefy," said David.

"You calling me fat, pint-pot?"

"And me," said Max. "Want to make something out of it?"

"Friends, Max, O.K. I just have a big appetite."

"Come off it, Beefy, you're plain greedy."

"Ha, ha! Better than that rabbit food they serve up as an alternative."

"Salad and fruit is healthy," said David.

"Well, if you like it so much, David, you have a double helping," laughed Beefy.

"Take no notice, David, I'm going to have a cheese salad, because my mum's told me to lay off the fatty meat," said his friend, Percy.

"Is shepherds pie fatty?"

"Sure, David, it's made from lamb, which is a bit fatty. The meat containing the fat goes straight into the pie."

"Then, for a change, I'll have a salad as well, but I'll still have a few chips," said David. "That can't be bad for you, can it?"

"David, my mum knows about nutrition, you know, things you eat. She says as long as we have plenty of physical exercise and burn off the fat there's no problem."

"Oh, O.K., Percy, I'll remember that."

"You pig, Beefy, shepherds pie and a big plate of chips!"

"Hey! I played rugby as well, so I deserve a big lunch."

"Only teasing, Beefy. If you can eat it, that's O.K."

David and Percy settled down to cheese salad and Max and Beefy tucked into firsts and seconds of shepherds pie.

"Gosh! I'm full!" declared Max.

"Wimp! Can't you manage apple pie and custard!" boasted Beefy Biffo. "More for me then!"

The end of lunchtime bell sounded and the boys lined up in the playground ready to start the afternoon classes.

Geoffrey Sellers, the geography Master, ran a tight class; he was a disciplinarian to the letter.

"This afternoon, following on from last week's lesson on capital cities of the world, we will talk about major ports of the world. Who can tell me what a port is?"

"Please sir!" said Percy, "it comes out of a bottle."

Now that was quite funny, but even the biggest boy in the class, Beefy Biffo, didn't dare laugh.

"Come out the front boy! Do you think you are funny?"

"No, sir. My mother drinks port out of a bottle."

"Does she now!" He cracked Percy hard around the head with a thick textbook, which partly dazed Percy. "Now, smarty pants boy, stand in the corner, balance the book on your head, and face the wall for the rest of the lesson!"

Percy did as he was told. His pride was knocked out of him. He was only making a joke. He felt unloved, rejected, and his shoulders slumped as he cried silently, the warm tears running down his cheeks.

Now David was a friend of Percy's, so he thought he should get Mr Sellers back in a good mood quickly.

"Please, sir!"

"Yes, Braun? And no funny remarks!"

"A port is where ships dock, sir. They transport goods around the world."

"Thank you, David Braun."

"Who can tell me what kind of ships we have?"

"Sir," said Max, standing up. "There are tankers that carry bulk goods, anything from food to coal and oil; there are fishing boats that are so huge they are called factory ships, which process the fish before it reaches the port so that, by the time it is unloaded, it can be packed directly into ice ready for delivery; and there are container ships."

"Well done, Max Darling."

"Can anybody tell me what a container port is?"

"I know, sir."

"Who said that?"

"It was Percy, sir."

"Ah! I had forgotten about you. Well then, take the book off your head and come and stand in front of the class and explain to your fellows what a container port is."

"Yes sir."

"A container port handles the forty foot containers on the back of lorries. A container port has special cranes along the dockside, where a lorry with its container can park under the crane. The crane driver lifts the container from the back of the lorry straight onto the deck of a ship waiting in port. Containers are all the same size for ease of handling and to save storage space. They can be stacked four to six high. Containers are handy and, therefore, can be used for small items like clothing, footwear, handbags, jewellery or anything small that can be neatly packed into a container."

"Excellent, Percy. Because you are being sensible now and paying attention, you may be excused punishment and go and sit next to your friend David."

"Thank you, sir."

Percy went back to his seat, and David admired him and shook his hand.

"Well done, Percy," whispered David.

"Does anybody know where the busiest container port in the world is? No?"

"It is Hong Kong. The port is open twenty-four hours a day. It is so busy that if it stopped moving containers for just one day the whole port would clog up. There is only ground space for a single day's cargo. The container cranes move up and down the dockside on tracks loading, unloading and stacking containers twenty-four hours without stopping. The men who work on the cranes work on a shift rota. The crane driver has a lot of responsibility; he is lifting heavy loads and must be inch perfect as he loads a container onto a lorry ready for delivery. The crane drivers work for four hours at a time then take a break, but the port and the cranes cannot stop working, so all the time fresh crane drivers must climb the ladders to the overhead driver's cabin to keep the port moving.

"In the days of the British Empire, when British shipping was at its height, the Port of London was possibly the busiest port in the world. But today there are major ports around the coastline of the British Isles and London has become the financial capital of the Western World."

"Now tell me, Percy, how do you know about container ports, I am intrigued?"

"My father, sir, is in the Merchant Navy. He's an officer. He works on different ships and he tells me sometimes when he comes home about the ports he has visited. The last merchantman he was on was a coal lugger, that's a tanker with her hold full of coal but on the deck are stacked several containers. His job is to supervise the unloading of the containers at a container port and the bringing up from the hold on a conveyor the coal, which is transported in rail wagons that come right down to the dockside by a rail siding. My father says they have shunting engines which push and pull the coal wagons onto the mainline, so that two powerful diesel engines can pull a train of fifty wagons of coal, weighing hundreds of tons. He says, in Europe, rail lines can go for thousands of miles on the Trans European Line."

"I thought, Percy, coal was transported by train from the Eastern Block countries to the West of Europe?"

"I don't know, sir. My father says, because labour is so cheap in South America, it is now transported to the British Isles and Western Europe, even though it is shipped right across the Atlantic Ocean."

"Well lads, we should thank, Percy, I think he has hit on economics. We are now in the twenty-first century, a time of computers and electricity and, a search for alternative energy sources, such as sea power, wind turbines, hydroelectric and solar power. Whereas a few years ago in the twentieth century, 1900 – 1985, coal mining was the main supply of fuel for our power stations, coal today is more expensive and, as Percy has pointed out, it is now imported because imported coal is cheaper."

"What other type of power, now that British coal is virtually exhausted, should we consider in this twenty-first century?"

"Please sir!" called out David.

"Yes, David Braun?"

"Nuclear power, sir!"

"Correct, David. Atomic power can be the answer, but what are its drawbacks. Can anybody tell me?"

"Sir!" Beefy put up his hand. "I think I know the answer?"

"Stand up, Beefy, and tell the class."

"Well, sir, to make nuclear power you need an atomic reactor, and the risk with plutonium is that it is radioactive for many years after its use."

"Thank you, Beefy, you may sit down."

"Class, it is important to know that nuclear waste, after the nuclear reactor rods have been used, are highly dangerous to all forms of life, not the least man. Therefore, we have to discuss in geography the economics of ores we dig out of our planet in different countries.

"Can the United Kingdom afford the cost of building nuclear power stations and nuclear processing plants? We have to ask because, throughout the world, traditional supplies of oil and coal are dwindling. What will replace oil and coal?

"There is gas under the oceans, but to get to remaining supplies rigs have to be built and floated out on the oceans that drill deeper and deeper, and the deeper the oil giants like B.P., Shell, Esso and Texaco, explore, the more expensive the supplies get. The twenty-first century is hungry for electricity. Even today, in the United States there has been a total blackout in an area nicknamed 'Silicon Valley', and Las Vegas, the gambling city of the United States, has such extremes of electricity use that the power stations that supply it constantly struggle to keep up with ever increasing demand."

"Now, let's get back to transport. Do you think nuclear fuel rods can be transported in containers and moved across oceans on ships?"

"Please, sir!"

"Yes, David Braun?"

"I think nuclear fuel rods, once they have been used, have to be buried in the ground?"

"Correct, David. They are dangerous and have to be buried deep under ground in impervious rock like granite. But first they have to be processed to a form that is less dangerous. Now, fortunately and unfortunately, Great Britain has a backbone of granite. Fortunate, because we can bury it safely, and unfortunate because France and Germany dump their nuclear waste on us. It is transported on special goods trains, as far as I know, in special wagons sealed by a lead wall a foot thick, and, when it is transported, anti-nuclear campaigners come out in force to protest, so spent nuclear fuel rods in a less dangerous processed form are moved in secret for security reasons. I don't think there is any alternative to nuclear power because the population of Britain is now sixty million, and set to rise as more countries of Eastern Europe join the European Union.

"So you see, ports and communications, especially railways, are inexorably linked to geography and economics. Economics being the cost of goods and services, and geography places and distances.

"In today's modern world the planet is said to be 'shrinking', because ports, whether in the Western World, that is the United States of America and Western Europe, or the fast developing Far East, such as South East China, Malaysia and Indonesia, are both exporting and importing right across the planet.

"Who can tell me another way to travel, which can be said to be 'shrinking' the whole world?"

"Please, sir!" called out David, with raised arm.

"Yes, David."

"Aeroplanes and space travel, sir."

"Ah! You have caught me out there, David. Well done. Space travel is not shrinking the Earth, but is attempting to travel within our solar system which is only a fraction of the galaxy of the Milky Way.

"But, jet aeroplanes, yes. Man can travel to Australia on the other side of the world within twenty-four hours, whereas ships, even high-powered diesel turbines, still take weeks to travel the globe. But nevertheless, ports play a huge role in the movement of goods between countries.

"How else can supplies be moved across oceans and overland?"

"I know, sir!" said a knowledgeable, Percy.

"Yes, Percy?"

"Pipes, sir. When you have oil exploration in the North Sea, the oil and gas is brought ashore to refineries by huge pipe lines."

"Correct, Percy. Anywhere else?"

"Yes, sir. Oil from Iraq and, more recently, oil and gas pipes from Russia because Russia still has huge reserves of untapped oil and gas underground."

"Very good, Percy, how do you know this?"

"Because, sir, I like to watch the news on the television."

"Good for you, Percy. And that brings me to another form of communication. Television is communication, and by using satellites we get television signals from all around the world."

"Why do we need satellites to communicate with, say, China?"

"Please sir!"

"Yes, David."

"Radio waves travel in straight lines, sir, and the earth's surface is curved because it is a sphere, so by going up into space a signal can be transmitted via a satellite, and bounced off the satellite, so that it is received by our televisions on the earth's surface."

"Very good, David."

"Now lads, how do we know what David has just told us is true? Well, you can easily prove to yourself that radio transmissions travel in straight lines by switching on a car radio to BBC2 and driving around, say, Snowdonia in Wales. When you drive behind Mt Snowdon you will find your radio goes off and all you can hear is static, that's because the mountain is in the way of the transmitter on the ground and the signal is blocked off."

"O.K. lads, I'll write up a few key words on the blackboard as reminders and you can make some notes as to what we have been talking about. Put a heading, Ports and Communication of The World. I'll come round and help you with any questions to complete your notes."

After twenty minutes, sufficient time to summarise the lesson, Geoffrey Sellers, the Geography Master, dismissed the class.

"Goodbye and thank you, sir."

"You're only a Junior School pupil, David Braun, but you have a quick and inquisitive mind. I think you are destined for university. Maybe a Masters in Physics or Mathematics. Off you go and enjoy your last playtime before you go home."

"Goodbye, sir."

239

"Run along with you, Max Darling."

After school the boys were keen to show off their conkers.

Master Pendleton stood outside the door of his father's Rolls-Royce, the chauffeur at the wheel sitting patiently waiting for instructions.

"Just a moment, Curuthers, here comes Max Darling."

"Hey Darling! Want a good whacking with my 'tenner'?"

"No thanks, my mother is here now. How about tomorrow?"

"O.K. Darling, you know you are going to lose."

"Who's that pompous rich boy, Max?"

"Oh that's Pendleton, his father owns an airline. He thinks he can buy people. In fact, he's so vain that I sold him a conker for five pounds."

"Five pounds for a conker!?"

"It's true, Mrs Darling," said David Braun.

"How did you manage it, Max?"

"He's greedy. Always has to have the best. Mr Pastr, the cook at the school, soaked David's and my conkers in vinegar and then baked them in the oven to make them hard. I smashed the other boys' conkers with my baked one until it became a 'tenner', so Pendleton wanted it."

"So you sold it to him for five pounds?"

"That's right, mother, didn't I, David?"

"Sure did, Max. And tomorrow we will have other winners."

"Other winners, Max?"

"Of course, mother. We put a bootlace through our conkers with a small metal washer protecting the knot in the lace, so that it doesn't pull through the body of the conker when other boys whack it with their ordinary soft conkers."

"Isn't that cheating?"

"No, mother. It just means we have better prepared conkers."

"Does that mean you will be selling more conkers for five pounds each?"

"I don't think the other boys can afford five pounds for a conker. But it cost us two pounds for Mr Pastry to pickle and bake our conkers, so we may charge a pound each for our conkers."

"Is the school cook really called Mr Pastry?"

"No mother, that's just an affectionate name for Mr Popadopalous or something like that. He's a Greek."

"Oh I see. Doesn't he mind being called Mr Pastry?"

"Not really, mother, he's our friend. Sometimes we sneak in the kitchen when chef is out and Mr Pastry slips us a meat and potato pie. He makes the best pies in the school, that's why we call him Mr Pastry."

"Well, how was your Monday?"

"All right. David was good in mathematics. We learnt about Pythagoras' Theorem today."

"Pythagoras? He was something to do with triangles, wasn't he?"

"Yes, mother. It's called trigonometry. The sides of triangles and 'soak a toe'."

"Soak a toe?" laughed Miranda.

"Yes, it's a mnemonic for SOH CAH TOA."

"What on earth does that mean?"

"Well, Mrs Darling, it's only our first lesson about Pythagoras' Theorem but it stands for Sine, Co-sine and Tangent."

"Oh yes, I remember now, it's to do with angles. I took the General Certificate Examination in Mathematics at school, but I can't remember any details now. I believe you have trigonometry tables for different angles; it was all a bit beyond me, and, anyway, you're very young to be introduced to Pythagoras' Theorem, aren't you?"

"It was just an introduction to triangles, mother."

"Let's go home."

"Can we stop off at the bakery at Lower Dale before we go home."

"Hungry again, Max Junior?"

"Yes, mother. I'd like a custard slice and an iced finger."

"What do you say?"

"Please, mother! But you don't have to pay. David and I have the five pounds from Pendleton, haven't we, David."

"Well, yes. But not exactly, because we had to pay Mr Pastry two pounds, so we actually have three pounds to spend."

"O.K. boys, I'll let you pay, but only a pound each, you have to learn to budget."

"Budget, mother?"

"Yes, learn to save something."

"Oh we do that with Dax, our school loans' service."

"Custard slice and an iced finger please, Mr Baxter."

"Hello, Max. Hungry after school. That will be one pound ten pence."

"Oh, mother says I'm only allowed to spend a pound, Mr Baxter."

"Hand over your pound then. As it's the end of the day and I want to clear the display so that nothing goes stale, I'll let you off the ten pence."

"Thank you, Mr Baxter. Can my friend, David, have the same deal?"

"Do you want the same, David?"

"No thanks, I don't like too much sugary things, I'll have an individual pork pie, please."

"Very sensible. That's ninety pence, please young man."

"Mr Baxter you can keep the ten pence, because it's the balance of Max's purchase."

"You'll make a good mathematician, young David, always ready to balance the books."

"That's what my teacher says, Mr Baxter."

"Get off with you, Mrs Darling is waiting for you outside."

"Goodbye, Mr Baxter."

"Good day to you, son."

"Well, did you have enough money, Max?"

"My custard slice and iced finger came to one pound ten pence, but Mr Baxter let me off the ten pence."

"But my pie, Mrs Darling, came to ninety pence, so I told Mr Baxter to keep the ten pence change to pay for Max's shortfall."

"That was very magnanimous of you, David. Thank you."

"That's O.K., we make money at school with our Dax loan scheme."

"One thing's for sure, David, as soon as you are grown up you will be a successful businessman."

"We already are, mother."

"I'll just stop off at your house, David, and you can tell your mother you are home, before you come to play at Rose Cottage."

"Hello, mother, here's my satchel. I'm going to Max's for tea."

"What are you eating?"

"An individual pork pie, mother, I bought it at Baxter's."

"Sure it's O.K., Miranda?"

"Yes, June. They are like two peas in a pod. Maybe they should share a double bed since, it seems, these days they are inseparable."

"Yes, mother, can we?" asked a widely smiling, Max.

"No, David, Mrs Darling is just joking."

"Oh mother, it would be fun!" laughed David.

The two mothers just burst out laughing.

"I don't know, June, these two are incorrigible!"

"They are just children in high spirits. I wish my childhood was as much fun. Being at home all day I feel left out, as though the world is passing me by."

"Why not come home with the boys, we can have a good chin-wag while they play outside in the tree house?"

"O.K., I will. Humphrey won't be home for at least an hour. As a Consultant Architect he has a huge project on at the moment designing a new shopping complex with an all glass roof, and it's taking up all his time."

In the kitchen, over coffee, June explained how she felt.

"You, Miranda, have a talent for painting and looking after and teaching the nursery school children. And Robert and Humphrey are both talented in design: Robert with phenomenal artistic ability and Humphrey with designing futuristic buildings. What have I got?"

"You have motherhood. You have Johnathon. How old is he now, eighteen months? Well, you can watch his first steps, his first teeth. I am denied any more children. Max Junior is happy enough, but he should really have a brother to play with."

"He has my David."

"Yes, and I am very grateful for that, because David is like the brother Max never had. I am envious of you, June."

"Envious of me? But you, Miranda, are the glamorous supermodel!"

"Fame and money isn't everything. I'd love to have another baby. I'm jealous of Johnathon."

"But, Miranda, you have never said before?"

"That's because I don't like to admit, not even to myself, that I have missed out on a family."

"Oh, Miranda, you could adopt a brother for Max."

"Perhaps. But it would be like buying a special present from a shop. I mean it's not getting pregnant, is it?"

"Have you thought about adopting, Miranda?"

"No, actually."

"Have you discussed how you feel with Robert?"

"No, I don't want him to think I'm being selfish."

"You're not being selfish. You're a woman; it's natural to feel broody sometimes. Here, hold baby Johnathon."

Miranda did. Then she started to cry, great wracking sobs. Tears warm and salty ran down her cheeks.

"Oh, Miranda, whatever is it?"

"Johnathon, he's so perfect. He's beautiful, he smiles back up to you and I can't have any more children," laughed and cried, Miranda, all at once.

"If it's so important to you, I think tonight, as soon as Robert makes his evening call from London, you should tell him how you feel, and then give him time to think about it. When he has had a few days to come to terms with the idea, you must push the point when he arrives home on Friday evening."

"You're right. Do you know, June, you're the first person I've told how I really feel. Can I have some more coffee, I think I need to drown my sorrows?"

"It's good to talk. What do you think friends are for? Have you got any strong drink in the house?"

"I have Bacardi on the worktop, but I don't touch it unless Robert is at home. He makes me come alive."

"Here, put Johnathon down, he will be all right he gets around by holding onto the furniture. It's excellent that Robert makes you feel alive, that means you love him very much. Here, have a Bacardi and Coke."

After another two drinks, both June and Miranda were a little merry and laughed at each other's situation.

"What's for tea, mother, I'm hungry?" asked Max.

"Oh! I had better go home," said June. "Humphrey will be home by now and wonder where I am. Doesn't time fly when you are enjoying yourself. David, are you coming home for tea?"

"I want to stay over with Max."

"What do you say?"

"Please, mother."

"That's better. Is that all right with you, Miranda?"

"Sure, June. When they are together they are better behaved. Max gets restless on his own."

"Hello, darling, good day at work?"

"All right. Where have you been?"

"Just round to Miranda's for a chat. Oh, and David is sleeping over at Max's, so we will have the place to ourselves once I've fed Johnathon."

"I'm going to relax in front of the television with a large whisky and Canada Dry."

"O.K., darling. I'll finish off the tea. I have a leg of lamb in the oven. Are you hungry?"

"Starving. I didn't have much time for lunch, it was all business today. Mondays are always hectic."

June put the vegetables on and while they were cooking fed Johnathon. She wanted to put him to bed before Humphrey ate, so that they could be alone. She went and changed into a little black, very short, slinky number and lit the candelabrum.

"Tea's ready, Humphrey!"

"Oh, candles, that's romantic. Dinner smells nice?"

"Roast lamb and mint sauce, one of your favourites."

"Sit down then."

"You smell nice."

"It's your favourite perfume, 'Virgin's Blush'. And I've changed for you."

"You look really nice, June. What's the special occasion?"

"Just telling you that I love you, and today I spoke to Miranda."

"And..."

"Well, I told her I was jealous of her fame but, it turns out, she's jealous of me."

"Jealous of you, June."

"Yes. Miranda can't have any more children, whereas I can. She says I have motherhood and I want you to know, Humphrey, how precious that is to me."

"Are you feeling broody?"

"Maybe. Could we have another child? By the time Sophia is born Johnathon will be two and a half, so I could manage another baby."

"I follow your logic, but what's this about Sophia?"

"Well, I would like a girl to dress in pretty clothes and make a fuss of and I have decided, if it is a girl, then I will call her Sophia."

"And when is this baby going to be conceived?"

"How about an early night," smiled June.

"Come here, give me a kiss, you little sexpot."

"You rude bugger! I'm supposed to be eating my tea."

"You are my wife, you agreed 'to have and to hold'…"

"But the curtains are open, what if somebody goes past."

"They can't tell you have no knickers on, all they will see is a man cuddling his wife."

"Oh God, I'm coming. You rude bugger!"

Humphrey got up and closed the curtains. Then took his wife in front of the roaring fire and pulled her dress up completely over her head, threw her bra on the floor and enfolded her nakedness.

"So you want another baby, sexpot. Get on your hands and knees on the hearth rug."

Trembling and excited, June did as she was bid. Humphrey dropped his trousers, gripped his wife's buttocks firmly and slid up inside of her. June called out with pleasure at the full penetration. Humphrey gripped her tightly and pulled her back onto him. He stroked her slowly, allowing her and his excitement to build up until she called out.

"Yes, Humphrey, yes! Go on fuck me! Do it faster. Faster!"

Humphrey complied with his wife's demands. Soon she was screaming, totally abandoning herself. Humphrey reached under her and pulled her back by her tits, against him and exploded into her.

Gasping for breath, he lay down beside her on the hearth rug until he felt relaxed.

"I love you! God I'm starving!"

"Well, you could have waited until after dinner, you rude bugger!"

"I fancied some starters. I haven't had sex-before-dinner before. Sure as hell beats a bowl of soup!"

They both went into the shower and quickly washed away the musk of sex and changed into fluffy white dressing gowns.

"Sit by the fire, Humphrey, while I re-heat our dinner. It won't be long the oven is still quite hot."

"How about a bottle of Rosé?"

"Sure, I'll bring it across."

In front of the fire Humphrey, with left hand holding his glass of wine, placed his right hand inside his wife's dressing gown and caressed her.

"I like you without underwear on, it excites me because I know you are available."

"That's the alarm on the oven. Come on, you need to eat to keep your strength up for later tonight," smiled June.

"What? Starters and Afters? What's come over you?"

"I want a baby and you're the baby making machine," laughed June. "I take my knickers off and feed you, and off you go!"

"Bloody cheeky little girl!"

"To the table, I'm putting the dinner out."

"I like a nice bit of tender meat, wife," smiled Humphrey.

"Not this sort you don't. All you are getting right now is lamb with mint sauce."

"Even lamb I can fancy."

"There you go then, get it down you, while I re-heat the gravy."

"Mmm! Delicious!!"

"I should hope so after all the trouble I've been to. Mind out, here's the red-hot gravy."

After dinner June didn't wash up as usual. Instead they lay back on the large settee, toe to toe, and drank two bottles of wine between them. Both very relaxed they played footsie until Humphrey, with a smile and a glint in his eye, reached forward with his foot and lifted up the hem of June's dressing gown exposing her pubic mound. June didn't complain. She opened her thighs and allowed Humphrey, using his big toe, to masturbate her clitoris. With feeling fine from drinking the wine, June undid her dressing gown and exposed her pert breasts, the nipples of which were engorged with blood and begging to be sucked by Humphrey.

He came to her and pulled not too gently with finger and thumb on her raspberries until her pupils dilated with increasing excitement. Humphrey picked her slight form up in his arms and cuddled her to him. Then he lowered her onto the settee, put the flats of her feet on the seat and lifted her hips up towards him. His erection pointed at her vulva, so he gripped her under her buttocks and pushed himself deep into her.

June, using her arms did a crab to accommodate his length. He lifted her up against him as she yielded and did his will, her will, in her.

Satiated they cuddled together on the settee with their dressing gowns draped about them.

"I love you, Mrs Braun."

"I should hope so after the way you have just taken me. Does that mean I can come off the pill?"

"You mean you are still taking it?"

"Of course, I don't want to be permanently pregnant."

"So you haven't just conceived?"

"Of course not, silly! It takes a couple of weeks for my contraception to stop working, so that I am fertile and ready to receive your 'little men'."

"You mean I need to practise?"

"Of course, husband. Day after day after day!"

"Then I shall enjoy the practice for the next two weeks."

"Not just until I conceive, but also when I'm pregnant."

"Do it when you are pregnant?"

"Of course, I won't break!"

"But what about the baby?"

"She will be safe."

"She…?"

"Well, I'm hoping for a girl. The only time you need to stop making love to me is when I'm about seven months and lovemaking becomes awkward and uncomfortable, otherwise I invite you to fuck me as much as you like."

"Do you mean it?"

"Of course, lover."

"You didn't say so before."

"I didn't want to become pregnant before. Talking to Miranda, made me realise how lucky I am to have more children."

"You mean your motherhood thing?"

"Precisely!"

"O.K. I feel better. I'll wash up, I haven't done that for ages."

"That's because, as you always say, you are too stressed, but tonight you are relaxed."

"I thought you weren't interested in me any more."

"Don't be silly. See this. This is your fanny. Anytime you want it, just seduce me and I will be willing."

"I really am knackered now, I think the washing up is all I can manage."

A few minutes later, June appeared wearing a white silky baby doll and a matching satin negligee.

"Want me to dry up for you, darling," teased June.

"Come here."

He squeezed her buttocks and pushed her softness against him. He felt for her and to his delight she was knickerless. He took up the invitation and, with her back pushed up against the sink, he masturbated her until her fluids flowed and she had orgasm after orgasm, flooding the insides of her thighs. Her knees trembled and gave way. He reached down under her and bodily lay her back on the kitchen table and, before she knew it, penetrated her excited waiting wetness.

"Now bitch, take this!"

He became caveman like in his urgency as he folded her legs over her head and thrashed into her, banging her buttocks up and down on the table top in his urgency. He cried out like a wild animal as he spent his loins in the wife he loved.

Looking at him June became quite worried; he was as white as a sheet, all the blood having drained from his face. 'God you look awful', thought June.

Humphrey was gasping. "Come on, I'll help you to the settee."

He slumped down and immediately went into a deep and contented sleep. June covered him with his dressing gown and went to the bathroom to use the bidet for her necessary ablutions.

June watched the television and at eleven o'clock, with there being no sign of Humphrey stirring, turned off the television and went to bed dreaming of babies, especially girl babies.

At seven o'clock Johnathon awoke and cried to be changed and fed. June changed him, and he made happy noises giving his mother a big smile.

"Come on Johnathon, time for Weetabix and fresh milk."

In the kitchen the sound of a child laughing woke Humphrey up.

"What is it? Where am I? June? June, have I been here all night."

"Yes, darling. You did something naughty last night which made you exhausted, so I left you to sleep it off."

"Now I remember! Actually I feel really refreshed, June."

"Then we should do it more often, my lover."

"What's the time? Ten past seven! I need to wash and shave, quick!"

"Do you know something, toddler Johnathon, you are going to have a sister."

"Don't tell him that, wife, it may be a brother."

"I wasn't talking to you. You go and get showered and dressed like a good hubby."

Humphrey rushed a bowl of bran flakes and was in his Rover turbo diesel and was away by half past seven. Speeding through the country lanes Humphrey disturbed the early morning rabbits who ran along the roadside until they came to a run in the bank and shot inside. He felt no sign of urgency, instead he was really relaxed. He actually smiled to himself and started whistling, even braking for a pheasant that ran out in front of him. Usually he didn't look out for the wildlife, considering them an irritant if they were unfortunate to get in the way of his wheels, after all he was a Consultant Architect and animals shouldn't get in his way.

He arrived in the office in cheerful mood. He held the morning meeting at exactly a quarter past nine.

"O.K., get to it, time's money."

"You seem particularly cheerful today, Humphrey?" questioned Barbara, his Personal Assistant.

"Yes, I am."

"Some good news?"

"I may as well tell you, Barbara, I am planning to be a father again."

"Congratulations to you and Mrs Braun. Do you want a boy or a girl?"

"You know, I haven't thought about it. June wants a girl to dress in pretty clothes, but I really don't mind if it's another son."

"How are David and Johnathon, well?"

"Yes fine. David seems to like mathematics. I think I did the right thing sending him to André Laceys."

"André Laceys, Humphrey?"

"It's a school for gifted children."

"How old is David now? I only ask because the photograph you have of him on your desk is of a five-year-old."

"Yes, I must take a more recent photograph of him from home and bring it to the office."

"Has he changed much?"

"Yes, he is losing his baby looks and looking more like a youth, even though he is a Junior School pupil. He has lost some of his milk teeth; he has a double gap on his incisors, in fact, the central upper two."

"And Johnathon, how is he doing?"

"He's eighteen months now and learning to walk. He can push his walker along but forgets at times to balance and falls down. But he makes up for it by hanging onto all the furniture and making his way around the house. He has just discovered the stairs and climbs up on all fours. Luckily he comes down step by step on his backside."

"Perhaps you need to get a stair safety gate in case he falls."

"It just so happens, Barbara, June has put one across the kitchen doorway, because his latest trick is reaching up to the cooker to play with the shiny metal things."

"Yes, a safety gate on a kitchen doorway is a good idea. A kitchen, because of boiling water, a steam iron or sharp knives can be lethal."

"Not to mention, when June turned her back, Johnathon was in the kitchen under the sink, getting the coloured bottles out to play with, including bleach, so he is banned from the kitchen unless June is supervising."

"He sounds rather mischievous?"

"Just inquisitive, Barbara."

"Coffee, Humphrey?"

"Yes, please, while I read my mail."

There was a knock at the door.

"Enter!"

"Hello, Brian, what can I do for you?"

"As Chief Draughtsman, I must bring to your notice this Structural Engineer's report."

"Tell me the problem."

"The rectangular steel joists we are proposing to use on level two of the Bull Ring Shopping Centre, do not give sufficient load bearing."

"Show me."

"Strain gauges, under laboratory testing conditions, show crystal fractures in the steel above ten tonnes per square inch, so we need to recalculate."

"What do you suggest, as the quickest remedy, within budget?"

"Reinforced concrete joists with the R.S.Js set in the concrete."

"Will that take the level two roof loading?"

"With the engineer's specification of ten millimetres gauge of R.S.J. the load bearing should increase to twenty tonnes per square inch."

"Good, have the Physics Laboratory test the reinforced concrete joists to breaking point. I want a safety collapse limit of at least five tonnes per square inch."

"I'll see to it, Humphrey."

"Good. Have the Site Engineer call me straight away."

"Humphrey Braun."

"Hello, Humphrey, this is Dave Dickinson, Site Manager at the Bull Ring."

"Thanks for ringing. The R.S. Js for level two are not to be used. They failed under a loading test by the Structural Engineer."

"Good job you said. We are scheduled to start bolting them up to the roof skeleton today."

"Have you put any up yet?"

"No, but about to."

"Right, remove them from site. For safety reasons return them to steel stock. When my Chief Draughtsman, Brian, gives the green light, I'll let you know. Everything else going to plan?"

"All's fine, Humphrey. Anything else?"

"No. Carry on. Any structural problems call me straight away."

And Humphrey hung up.

"Anything exciting in the mail, Humphrey?"

"Yes. Newtown Football Club wants Braun & Partners to quote for a new football stadium."

"That is good news."

"You know the drill, Barbara. You have been my P.A. these last four years. We have to tender. And it's a long complicated process, because first we have to agree the plans that Newtown Football Club want. A letter of intention first, Barbara. Fetch your dictation pad. Then make an appointment for Brian, my Chief Draughtsman, to meet the Board of Directors of Newtown to make sure all agree on what they want."

"And budget, Humphrey?"

"The initial cost, which is preliminary, will have to be agreed between Newtown's Board of Directors and our Cost Engineer. Arrange a meeting for Bob Robertson, our Cost Engineer to meet with me and Brian in the Boardroom, on my next free day."

"Your diary is full until Thursday, 2.00pm."

"O.K. Thursday, 2.00 pm, it is. Barbara, no calls this morning, I have a lot of calculations to check and fine details to go over."

"Chief Draughtsman. Oh it's you, Humphrey. Something up?"

"No. Come into my office, I want to verify the next lot of drawings before they are approved and sent to the Site Engineer, Dave Dickinson."

"I'm your man, be right in."

"Right, Brian, I'm away for lunch."

"Barbara, come in please."

"Just a minute, Humphrey."

"Have you typed out my mail for today?"

"Just finished, Humphrey. Here, ready for your signature."

"Right, pass them across. There! Now, the reason I have called you in is to have a spot of lunch with me. Can you recommend somewhere?"

"Sure, Humphrey. I'll just get my jacket."

"Nice sunny day. I feel like some feminine company. Where are we going?"

"Chez's Wine Bar. They do great sandwiches and you can have a spritzig. That's if you like sparkling German wine."

"O.K., lead on, but I don't drink when I'm working."

"You can have it with soda so that you can still enjoy the taste but with a lot less alcohol."

"I'll stick to sparkling mineral water, thank you."

"Here we are."

"Down the stairs, it's in the basement."

"Below the National Westminster. I thought vaults were underground."

"Come on, you'll like it."

Inside Chez's Wine Bar the lighting was subdued, the air conditioning was pleasant and everybody was dressed for business.

"All right, Barbara, I'll let you off. I quite like the place. Why haven't you shown me the place before?"

"Because, Humphrey, you always ask me to order you a sandwich from the Sandwich Man, and you eat it in your office. Is this the start of something?"

"Taking lunch?"

"Going out for lunch, impromptu, on your own? I mean, when you don't have to go out to lunch because of a business meeting."

"My wife made me realise last night that I take life too seriously. People and family are more important than business, so I have decided today to take lunch. And I would like you to remind me of that each day from now on."

"All right, Humphrey. A break from the office is the right idea. Do you want to come to Chez's Wine Bar everyday?"

"No. I would like you, as a lady, to remind me how important my wife is in my life. I mean I work long hours, arrive home late every evening, and June is left on her own to bring up my children. I think, in recent years, I have taken her for granted. I would like you to introduce me to all your lunchtime watering holes."

"But, Humphrey, you said you didn't drink at lunchtime."

"I do, in moderation, but I like to have a clear head. Surely your hideaway bars do meals as well?"

"Of course, if you are sure, I will show you where the staff eat."

"I appreciate that, but now we have eaten it's time to return to the office."

Barbara went back to work. Humphrey nipped into his office and grabbed his briefcase with the plans in for the Bull Ring Shopping Centre.

"Taxi! Taxi!" hailed Humphrey.

"Where to gov'nor?"

"The Bull Ring Shopping Centre."

"You sure, sir, it's not built yet?"

"That's because I am building it."

"Oh, I see. You're a building contractor."

"Close. I am the Consultant Architect designing the Bull Ring. Braun and Partners."

"Beg your pardon, gov'nor. Of course your company's name is on the giant hoarding. There was a mention of the Bull Ring on the BBC news last night."

"That's interesting. What did it say?"

"It said it was futuristic and would provide employment for many people once built."

"Let's not forget the construction workers. There's engineers, surveyors, technicians, scaffolders, ground workers, plasterers and electricians, not to mention the business all the suppliers get from aggregates and concrete to reinforced safety glass."

"There you go, guv'nor. There already, less than five minutes. Eight pounds please."

"Here, a tenner."

"Thanks, guv'nor."

"Give me your card. I'll call you later when I need you, it's not so easy calling a taxi at a construction site."

"Right, guv'nor. Pick-up at the same point?"

"Fine, cabbie."

The taxi drove off and Humphrey walked across the perimeter onto the construction site proper.

"Hey you! You can't come onto here. This is a restricted access site. Personnel only. Sorry mate, you'll have to walk round like the rest, no short-cuts through here, health and safety rules."

"It's good you are health and safety conscious. What's your name?"

"Bert, I'm the Health and Safety Officer, I am doing my twice-daily check of the site. You would be surprised what some workers leave lying about for people to trip over."

"Well, Bert, I am pleased to meet you. Let me introduce myself. I am Humphrey Braun of Braun and Partners, Chartered Architects. This is my identity card and the design of the Bull Ring Shopping Centre is my responsibility."

"Oh sorry, Mr Braun, I've heard of you through Dave Dickinson, our Site Engineer, because I take my instructions from him, but I've never met you before, sir."

"That's O.K., Bert. Now show me your identity card."

"Here it is, sir."

"Fine, Bert, but where's your hard hat?"

"In the office, Mr Braun."

"You can accompany me to Dave Dickinson's office and collect your hard hat at the same time."

"Yes, Mr Braun, sir. I wasn't wearing my hard hat because I wasn't walking under any working areas, just inspecting the perimeter."

"No excuse, Bert. You are the Health and Safety Officer, you must set a good example of working practices. Now, I am going to report your laxity to Dave Dickinson. A spanner, a steel bolt even if it is small, if it falls from a great height can cause serious injury, surely you must know that."

"What about your own safety, sir?"

"As soon as I get to the changing hut I will put a hard hat on and a fluorescent jacket."

"But I have my own jacket on, it says Health and Safety Officer across the back."

"Which is good, Bert, but I cannot let you off not wearing a hard hat, whether on or off shift. I didn't have huge health and safety notices put up for you to ignore the rules. Look at it this way, if a fellow worker was injured by a projectile from overhead, and he wasn't wearing his hard hat, my company would have an injury claim against them, but you, as Health and Safety Officer would have to rule that the employee was negligent because he didn't wear his hard hat. What, Bert, would you tell the widow?"

"When you put it like that Mr Braun, I can see I have been negligent not wearing my safety hat. I apologise, sir, it won't happen again."

"Dead right, Bert, it won't happen again because if it does you will be fired. I cannot afford to have a negligent Health and Safety Officer on site. Now, out of all the Portakabins, which is Dave Dickinson's?"

"Follow me, Mr Braun, please, I'll lead the way."

"Why is there no safety rail to these steps, Bert?"

"I have already pointed this out to Dave Dickinson, he's instructed the steel erectors to build one this afternoon. These Portakabins were only stacked three high yesterday. We are pushed for space, sir, but I have put up the red hazard signs of 'warning of man falling', only this morning."

"Good, you seem to be on the ball. Don't let me catch you again without a hard hat."

The door to the Portakabin on level three had a brand new sign on it, 'Site Engineer'.

"Here we are, sir."

"All right, Dave, don't get up, I've arrived unannounced. Carry on."

"Right, Bert, show me the Site Engineer's Safety Incident Book."

Humphrey Braun wrote in it: 'you are cautioned today for not wearing your hard hat'. "Sign here and I'll sign next to you. You may go, Bert."

"Yes, sir."

The Section Engineer went back to his own Portakabin on level two.

"Hello, Humphrey."

They shook hands.

"Good to see you are busy, Dave. I have just disciplined your Health and Safety Officer for not wearing a hard hat. Are you ready for my site inspection?"

"Been expecting you. Here an engineer's hard hat for you."

"Ah! Mr Dickinson. My scaffolders are ready, where do you want a safety rail erecting?"

"Bert!"

"Yes, Mr Dickinson?"

"Show these lads where you want safety rails."

"Right away, sir."

"Are you boys sub-contractors?"

"I'm Jock, the foreman. Is there a problem, Bert?"

"Not a problem but an instruction. Health and Safety Rules say you cannot come on site without hard hats. Didn't the Site Manager stop you at the gate and tell you all visitors must wear a hard hat. Leave your tools on your truck and follow me."

"Mick! Mick! Where the hell is he?"

"I'm here, Bert. Is there a problem?"

"Yes, you weren't at your post. Where were you, you are supposed to police the gate twenty-four hours?"

"Bloody hell, can't a man go to the toilet?"

"Not without putting a security officer on the gate. These scaffolders gained access to the site in their vehicle without being checked or given hard hats. And, further more, the main man, Humphrey Braun is on site today, so you had better be alert."

"Who's Humphrey Braun?"

"He's the Consultant Architect in charge of the Bull Ring Shopping Centre, the top man."

"Sorry, Bert, won't happen again. Come on lads, this way. Here a hard hat each."

Humphrey and Dave Dickinson went outside. They both wore white hats, which were reserved for professionals as opposed to yellow or blue hats worn by technicians and tradesmen.

"How is the work progressing, Dave?"

"Everything is O.K. The main problem is space. Bert makes inspections twice a day, because you wouldn't believe the number of obstacles that sub-contractors leave lying around. He makes sure all walkways and driveways are kept clear. I only allow on site materials that can be used on the same day, otherwise we would be double-handling, which is a waste of man hours."

"Then is Bert good at his job?"

"Well, Humphrey, I couldn't manage without him, he's very conscientious. He insists on good work practice, you know, every man cleaning up after himself. And he makes sure all tools and equipment are locked up at night, and he instructs the men to immobilise all plant at night before they go off shift. As you know, the Site Manager on the gate has twenty-four hour security."

"What about the perimeter of the land beyond the construction area, you know, the access roads?"

"Well, Humphrey, we have consulted the Metropolitan Police on that and they have come up with an ingenious idea. Instead of building an ugly fence for security, plant a thick thorny hedge with plenty of deterrent spikes. They say even teenagers won't climb a thorny hedge, whereas they might attempt to scale a security fence."

"That's very good, Dave, and while a barrier and effective it looks aesthetic. I'll contact a landscaping company right away and instruct perimeter planting as soon as possible. That's one job an architect is not required for, except for overseeing the overall project."

"Shall we go up to level one, so that you can see what progress we have made."

Humphrey walked a full circle with Dave around the Bull Ring, as Dave pointed out how different projects were progressing. It took a full half hour.

"Right, Dave, second level."

"These are the glass panels that I have temporarily stopped work on because of the R.S.Js being supplied not being up to specification."

"The Structural Engineer was right to warn me. I have since upgraded the specification and the new joists will be ready as soon as possible. O.K., Dave, I am satisfied with what I have seen, let's go down. Any problems you want to tell me about?"

"Only minor accidents, which of course are recorded in the accident book, by Bert."

"Accidents? Such as?"

"A worker tripping over a couple of bricks, seriously spraining his ankle, that sort of thing."

"A good clean site, Dave. Can I keep the hard hat, it will be handy for coming on and off the site?"

"Sure. Goodbye now."

Humphrey went back to the office via the same taxi cabbie, who arrived in about ten minutes.

"Welcome back, Humphrey. The Bull Ring project shape-up?"

"Yes thanks, Barbara, a cup of coffee please while I write my report to the Board of Directors."

Humphrey made an effort to be away from the office earlier than usual.

"I'm away now, Barbara, switch the answering machine on to take any calls."

"O.K., Humphrey. It's only half past five, early for you."

"I know. It's my new routine to be home by seven o'clock. I have a wife waiting for me."

"Lucky Mrs Braun is all I can say."

"Don't you have a regular boyfriend? You never talk about one?"

"Nobody special. I seem to keep saying goodbye to my boyfriends."

"Afraid of a serious relationship?"

"Maybe. I don't feel old enough to marry and have children."

"You'll know when it's the right one. Goodnight."

"Goodnight, Humphrey, and good luck."

Humphrey joined the ranks of queuing cars. He didn't realise how difficult it was trying to leave the City of London at half past five.

"No wonder I normally drive home at six thirty after the rush hour. At this rate I'll be late again!" he fumed behind the steering wheel. He had satellite navigation but that didn't help much because the satellite always took you the most direct route, which meant using the motorways, which in turn were always chock-a-block. He switched his satellite navigator on and once he had crossed to the South Bank turned off the trunk route and tried a rat-run. Humphrey headed south not exactly sure where he was, but after a few miles the female voice cut in, 'turn right, turn right in five hundred yards, second exit at the roundabout'. He followed the instructions and after an hour came out on his home run heading for Lower Dale.

"Hello, darling, nice to see you home before eight o'clock," smiled Barbara.

"I know it's seven thirty, a bit earlier than usual but it's taken me two hours. I left at five thirty. I think tomorrow I'll try six o'clock and I bet I'll be home by the same time."

"Well I'm pleased, Humphrey. David likes to see you before he goes to bed, don't you, David?"

"Sure, father. Come and see what I have built in my bedroom."

"Just a minute, let me say hello to your mother."

They kissed and Humphrey tweaked her bottom.

"Later, darling, when David is in bed."

"O.K. sport, show me what you have made."

David had a large double bedroom to himself and in the middle of the room was a large old oak dining table to do his homework on.

"See, father, I have built a Technico Mecanno rocket with an astronaut lift to take the men up to the capsule with lights inside working off the same battery. Next I am going to build a tank with working motorised tracks. What do you think?"

"I think, David, maybe you have a designer's eye, same as your father. Do you think you could design buildings and bridges?"

"I wouldn't mind designing a suspension bridge, you know, like the Seven Suspension Bridge."

"Do you want to come downstairs for a bit to be with me and your mother while she cooks my tea?"

"O.K., father. I miss you a bit in the evenings. Are you going to come home earlier from now on? I mean, I know you are the boss, but surely your workers could do some of your work?"

"I'll try, but I, as the Consultant Architect, have certain responsibilities. I have to supervise all the work."

"I think when I grow up I'll be a boss, so that I don't have to do all the work."

"That won't be for some years yet, come on down son and enjoy being a boy."

"All right, father."

They sat on the settee side-by-side while June cooked the vegetables for Humphrey's tea.

While the boys were enjoying men's chat in front of the television, June nipped upstairs and changed into a seductive dress, adding a few discreet dabs of perfume to attract Humphrey just before she came down.

June called out from the kitchen, "Tea's on the dining room table!"

He went in leaving David to watch the television.

"Smells nice, June!? Where are you?"

"Here, darling," smiled June, making her entrance.

She had pinned her hair up and put on a bustier dress, which showed off her creamy neck and shoulders to her best advantage.

"God, you look seductive."

June just smiled.

"What's it in aid of?"

"You know what we talked about last night, well you are the sex machine. I need your little men to make a baby."

"Come here, sexpot. You've got knickers on!"

"Only while we have tea. David is in the lounge. You can take them off after dinner when David is tucked up in bed."

"David, eight o'clock, bedtime!"

"Oh, father, do I have to?"

"You can read in bed for thirty minutes but no longer."

"All right, father. Good nigh, mother."

"Don't I get a kiss?"

"You've dressed up for father. We do know about sex, we talk about it at school."

"You're not too old for a goodnight kiss, but too young to know about sex."

"Max says he knows his parents do it because he listens to them through his bedroom wall."

"Goodnight, mother."

"Get off to bed with you before I give you a clip around the ear," laughed Humphrey.

David ran up the stairs, shouting, "You'll have to catch me first," before he slammed his door.

June closed all the doors for privacy and sat down at the table opposite Humphrey.

Humphrey suddenly realised he was ravenous, having only eaten a single sandwich all day. He tucked into his tea.

June kicked her high heels off and slid her silken foot under the table, up Humphrey's leg to his crutch. He grabbed her foot and looked under the table. June was wearing her sexy suspender belt and stockings and, not only that, to tease and arouse Humphrey she opened her legs to reveal she was wearing open-crutch knickers.

"You sexy bitch!"

"I thought you might like them, I bought them for you as a special treat."

"You mean for you, to get yourself pregnant," smiled Humphrey.

"It's the same difference. Well do you approve?"

"Very much so, it's just that we are a married couple and you are already twice-over a mother, it doesn't seem appropriate somehow."

"You mean, because we have been together for nine years, we shouldn't have a naughty sex life like when we were courting?"

"I suppose so, but I approve of you being a sexpot. I mean, if I can't be sexy with my own wife who can I be sexy with?"

June only had a small portion as she was watching her figure, so she finished her meal quickly, cleared the table away on her side and stood on a dining chair. She lifted the hem of her skimpy dress up and exposed herself in full frontal view. Humphrey was so shocked he choked on a piece of meat.

June watched Humphrey's eyes as his desire was aroused. She turned round and bent over and gripped the back of the dining chair she was standing on to expose her pussy from the rear.

"You rude bitch! Get down you're like a dog on heat. How can a man eat his dinner?"

"Quickly is the answer while my Vesuvius is smouldering. I'll lie on the settee with my legs open waiting for you."

"You tease!"

It had the desired effect. June knew that anticipation was all part of making love and Humphrey was definitely aroused. He gobbled his tea down and went to his wife. He turned the light off so that he could only see his sexpot by the light of the fire.

"No, no! Don't touch me. You have to savour the moment. You must let me undress you."

She cheated. She dropped his trousers and underpants around his ankles so that he couldn't take even the smallest step and took him in her mouth. She licked him slowly and caressed his balls. He went tense and his knees started to tremble. She stopped, saving him for her. He groaned.

"Now take all your clothes off, so I can look at you for a change."

Humphrey felt foolish so to encourage him, June took off her dress and exposed herself in her skimpy underwear.

"Lie on your back on the fireside rug."

He did. She slid onto him, sitting bolt upright so he could watch her tits going up and down. He reached up for her.

"No, no! Don't touch! Stay where you are and take your punishment."

June got excited. Determined, she sat upright and gripped his length with her vaginal muscles and pulled long and hard driving him on. Then she called out and leant forward, throwing her brassier off all in one motion and gripped hold of Humphrey's shoulders. He responded in his urgency and took hold of her tits and sat her upright again as he exploded long and hard into her. He surprised himself at his virility as a married man.

Both gasping, she threw herself down on top of Humphrey and they cuddled together as their joint hearts thumped out a satisfied rhythm.

"I love you, Humphrey Braun."

"I should bloody well hope so, knackering a man like that."

"I need your little men if I am to make a baby, darling."

"I don't know about little men, that was more like a platoon of sergeants," laughed Humphrey.

"Yes, it was a bit like the Charge of The Light Brigade, lover."

"Well there are no reserve troops, that was the whole division."

"Stand easy, soldier, take five," smiled June. "It's nice you coming home earlier, we get to spend time together."

"It's nice but not every night because it will spoil that special moment."

"All right, Humphrey. I'll settle for twice during the week and Sunday mornings."

"You make it sound like an order."

"It's not an order, but to conceive we have to make love regularly."

Can I move now, the fire is starting to cook me?"

"Oh dear. And I was so comfortable."

"It's not your backside that is cooking."

"Oh dear, he's sulking now, you had better put him away."

"I will as soon as I put my clothes back on."

"No, don't do that, I'll fetch the dressing gowns from upstairs."

"Well, hurry up, I'll look pretty stupid if the doorbell rings."

"The front door isn't even locked."

"Bloody hell! You mean we made love with the door open?"

"Well, not exactly open, but it was unlocked."

"Humphrey went to the front door, locked it immediately and pulled the curtain across so that nobody could see his reflection through the frosted glass."

"Here you are Humphrey, put your dressing gown on, I'll put the washing on while I've got your shirt and pants."

"Bit late for washing, isn't it?"

"It's automatic darling, it washes and dries while we curl up together on the settee and watch the television."

"I'm glad I have you to look after me, June. I would be absolutely lost if I had to do housework."

"Well, when I have our next baby you will have to look after me now that our neighbour, old Mrs Johnson, has passed away. She looked after me when Johnathon was born."

"I wouldn't know what to do, all I can do is boil a kettle."

"Well, that's a start. Could you iron a shirt?"

"I've never tried. I'd probably burn holes in it. Couldn't you get a mother from your nursery and toddler group, to look after you?"

"They already have their hands full with their own small children."

"Then I'll hire a nurse for a week. She can sleep-in in the spare room and feed the baby during the night, which would give you a chance to catch up on your sleep and recuperate. What do you say?"

"Yes, actually that's not a bad idea. Where do I find one?"

"Yellow Pages, or ask at the local doctor's practice. Probably better if the local doctor recommends a nurse."

"O.K. I will," said June.

"You know it makes sense. Private nursing is on the increase these days. I don't mind paying, I can afford it."

"Thanks, Humphrey. I know it's in the future, but it's one less thing to think about, and anyway, if I'm being looked after it will give me time to look after you. I don't think you are the domesticated type."

Chapter Ten

Now, Robert and Miranda were packing for their Christmas holiday at Amos and Annette's villa, El Estancia in Seagull Cove, Atalia. Max Junior wanted to bring all his sports things and a fishing rod.

"For goodness sake, Max, you can't bring everything, there's not room on the aeroplane!"

"But I'll be bored without things to do!"

"Son, you can't put sports equipment in a suitcase, they simply won't fit. How about we divide your clothes between my suitcase and your mother's, and you have a backpack in which you can put your skateboard, a football and your new telescopic fishing rod?"

"Thank you, father, that's a good idea. Where's grandma and grandad?"

"I don't know. What did they agree in the end, Miranda?"

"They were going to come to Lower Dale and then we would all set off in Amos's estate car, but Annette said it would be a waste of time driving right across London when they live north of the city, not too far from Luton Airport, so they said they would meet us at the airport check-in."

"I hope we will be in time," said Miranda.

"Don't panic, I've allowed extra time, the M25 is always like this on a Friday afternoon."

"But the booking with Bi Baby said because of security checks we had to arrive at least two hours before check-in."

"I think the airline is scaremongering, we are going to Atalia in Spain not the Middle East. And anyway it's only a holiday flight, who is going to kidnap us?"

"They have terrorists, father, with guns, it says so on the television," blurted out Max Junior.

"You have a boy's imagination, Max, hijacks are very rare and, anyway, the reason we have to be early is for thorough security checks. The latest thing is screening suitcases as well as physically checking hand luggage and handbags."

"What about a small gun in your pocket, father? You know, like a James Bond secret agent. Or tucked in your socks?"

"They have a wand they pass over you if the metal detector door alerts to a metal object, so there won't be any guns, Max."

"This traffic, Robert, is hardly moving. Do you think we would be better with the satellite navigation?"

"No, darling, the tracker takes the most direct route and, anyway, trying to cut through the City of London on a Friday afternoon is suicidal. We would never get through in time."

The traffic on the M25, after what seemed to be ages, moved steadily, and the family made their way to Luton Airport.

Annette started fretting.

"I'll give Robert a ring and find out where he is?"

"Go on then, then perhaps you will settle down, you are getting on my nerves looking at your watch every five minutes," complained Amos.

"Get that, Max," said Robert as the car-phone rang.

Max didn't have to be told; he reached forward between the driver's seat and answered the phone, full of his self-importance.

"Max Junior Darling, who's calling please?"

"Hello, Max, this is grandma, I'm getting worried about the time. Where are you?"

"Oh, grandma, father is driving along the Luton Airport approach road."

"Pass the phone to your mother."

"Annette, this is Miranda, we will be at the check-in hall in about ten minutes, we are just heading to the car park."

"Thank goodness for that. I was getting worried because of the long queue at the check-in."

"Well, while there is a queue they will not go without you, so we have time to catch up. See you in ten minutes as soon as the shuttle bus picks us up."

"Right, we have arrived, let's get the suitcases across to the bus stop and stop Annette fussing."

"Hello, grandma, grandad!" greeted Max. "I have brought my own backpack and my fishing rod!"

"Hello, Max, you two."

"Why did you ring, mother, we have plenty of time?"

"Exactly!" said Amos. "Why do women panic?"

"Never mind now," said Robert, "let's join the queue."

The flight to Atalia, Spain, was just over two hours, which was enough time for Robert to relax and enjoy a drink with Amos. They were both indulging in German sparkling wine which made them both merry.

In the adjacent three seats sat Max, Miranda and Annette, with Max between the two ladies. Miranda, fortunately, sat immediately across the aisle from Robert which put, conveniently, thought Amos, Annette at a distance. Now Annette was afraid of flying and her continual nervousness and twitching got on Amos's nerves, so he was grateful for male company for a change. The bravest of the three in the middle seats was Max. He laughed and joked boyishly with his grandma while flying his model Boeing 373.

After two double gins, at Miranda's insistence, Annette managed to half relax and join in colouring-in Max's drawing book.

An hour into the flight and Robert and Amos became animated as they consumed three bottles of sparkling wine.

"That's enough, Robert!" called out Miranda, as she leant across the aisle. "You've had enough to drink."

"Just unwinding with Amos, I shan't be driving when we get to Atalia Airport."

"You won't?"

"No, I booked the car in your name, darling. You know the way to Seagull Cove a lot better than I do. And you're a safer driver."

"I don't know whether to be flattered or insulted," smiled Miranda.

"God you're beautiful when you smile. You remind me of when we first met, you were vulnerable and heart broken and I was a simple seaside, struggling artist."

"O.K. you can drink, but no more on this flight, promise?"

"Sure, poppet. When we get there we must go down to the beach restaurant to see if John and Linda are still there. It was only because of their restaurant that I sold my very first few paintings on a commission only basis."

"All right, Robert, I'll hold you to that. Have I told you lately that I love you?"

"Give us a kiss then."

"I can't reach with this seatbelt."

"Well, take it off. You don't have to wear it, it's only for landing and turbulence. And it's like a smooth mill pond, isn't it Amos?"

"Fine by me, I enjoy flying. Very civilised. All right, Annette?"

"I think so, Amos."

"Relax, we are already half way, we'll be at the airport in just under one hour."

"The sooner the better, Amos. I'm not taking my seatbelt off."

"That's O.K. Would you like another drink?"

"I'd better not or I'll be a bit tipsy."

"It's up to you, Annette. But remember today is the start of your Christmas holiday. Here comes the flight attendant."

"Could my wife have one more drink please? A single this time."

"What would she like, sir?"

"A gin and tonic, please."

"Coming right up. Shall I tell you something while I serve you?"

"Go on then," said Annette.

"When I qualified two years ago as a Flight Attendant, I was scared of flying. Would you believe it? But now it's just like taking a taxi."

"Well I never," replied Annette. "And now you're cured?"

"Absolutely! So you have nothing to worry about."

"Cheers!" called out Annette. "And thank you."

"You're very welcome," smiled the attendant as she disappeared down the aisle going about her duties.

Amos, much to his surprise found that, Robert, suddenly conjured up a pack of playing cards.

"Where did you get those from?"

"Aha! My jacket pocket and here is a pencil and paper."

"What's the game going to be?"

"101 and then out!"

"Now you're talking, I used to be quite good at 101."

"Shall we have a little bet?" asked Robert.

"I'm not as a rule a betting man. How about the loser buys the next round."

"Whisky?"

"O.K., I'll bet you whisky that you'll lose."

"Just play, we'll see how good you are," tested Robert.

It didn't take long for Amos to lose.

"You owe me a whisky. Call the attendants."

"Yes sir?"

"Two whiskies please, Amos will pay."

"This will be your last drink sir, the bar is now closed. We will commence our descent shortly."

"Cheers, Amos!" toasted Robert, enjoying his free bottle of miniature whisky.

"Ladies and gentlemen, in a few moments we will begin our descent to Atalia Airport, please return to your seats, fasten your seat belts and make sure your tables are in the upright closed position. Thank you."

"There we are, grandma. Told you we will soon be landing," chirped Max Junior.

"Oh, I hope we get down all right."

"Of course we will, grandma. You can hold my hand if you like?"

"Thanks, Max, I will."

"What about my hand, mother?" asked Miranda.

"Yes, yours as well. I know it's silly being afraid to fly when cars are more dangerous, I just can't help it."

"Never mind, mother, we will soon be down on the ground and I will be driving, which means you will be safe."

"Thank heavens for that. Amos and Robert are obviously in no fit state to drive. Look at them."

"They're just letting off steam. They both work long hours, it will do them good."

"I recognise that coastline," said Amos from his window seat. That's Seagull Cove down there, and that building on the cliff edge with the wall nearly all the way round is El Estancia."

"I forgot how close your villa is to Atalia Airport. From the air it seems like only next door."

"Not quite, about fifteen minutes drive."

"Well, I didn't know that, because when I lived in Atalia in my little terraced house, I used to walk everywhere, except when I caught the bus to the market at St Lucia's every Wednesday. It was your daughter, Miranda, who had the car and therefore did the driving."

"Yes, I remember, she was grieving over the loss of her new husband, Edward and, therefore to help her, I arranged for a hire car."

"You know, Amos, that red convertible was a godsend for carrying my large canvases to market. Before that I used to struggle on the bus. It was luckily, possible, because the locals would help me."

The aeroplane touched down with a bump as the undercarriage thumped into the tarmac and then lurched as the pilot applied the brakes.

Annette called out with fright. Quickly Miranda hugged Annette to her, which was the right thing to do, because next instant the pilot engaged reverse thrust and the Boeing 373 responded quickly as the fuselage shuddered slightly and the plane slowed considerably to a safe speed.

"Just touch-down, mother, it's quite normal; it's just the engines slowing down the plane," reassured, Miranda.

"Have we arrived?" asked an anxious Annette.

"Not yet, mother, we are taxiing down the runway to get us off the airfield. It's a bit like a taxi on the road looking for a parking space."

"Oh, that's all right then."

"Grandma, you are squashing my hand!"

"Oh, sorry, Max, I forgot. Silly of grandma to be nervous when a small boy is so brave."

"It's O.K., grandma, some of the boys at André Laceys are also afraid of flying."

"Are they? You mean it's not just me being silly?"

"No, grandma!" laughed Max Junior.

Then Annette laughed at herself. "I am a silly billy."

Amos called across the aisle from his window seat. "Nice sunny day Annette! Are you all right?"

"I am now, thank you, Amos. Brave Max has been looking after me."

The Boeing 373 docked at Atalia Airport, and inside the fuselage the passengers scrambled up eager to stretch their legs.

"Come on, Miranda, let's get off."

"Mother, we are near the rear of the aeroplane. The door hasn't been opened yet. It will be about fifteen minutes before it is our turn to get off. There are a hundred and eighty people in front of us."

"Well, how about getting the hand luggage down?"

Amos spoke up. "It won't take a minute, Annette. I can't get into the aisle yet."

"Allow me," said Robert, standing up from his aisle seat. "Here, Annette, your cardigan and handbag."

"Thank you, Robert."

"You won't need a cardigan on," said Amos, we're in Spain."

"May I remind you, husband, that it is December and if I want to wear a cardigan I will. You are a lot bigger than me and don't usually feel the cold."

"Take no notice of him, do your own thing," supported Robert.

"Would you please get my jacket down?" asked Miranda.

"O.K. everybody," said Robert, "we are on the move!"

"Yippee!" shouted out Max. "Can I have my rucksack down, father?"

"Of course, son. Let your mother get up first."

"Oh, Amos, I'm sorry I get frightened in the plane, I feel fine now we have landed."

The man in the seat behind Annette said, "I also get frightened when it's time to land."

"But you're such a big strong man, surely you don't get frightened?"

"Oh, I do."

"Then I'm not the only one on this plane, I thought it was just me being silly."

"Come on," said Amos. "Time to get off the plane, you're holding up the queue."

She turned to the big gentleman behind her.

"Thank you for telling me. I don't feel such a fool now."

"You're most welcome," was his reply.

"Goodbye," said Max. "Nice aeroplane!"

"You enjoy yourself," replied the flight attendant as Max departed.

Max Junior enjoyed his ride down the escalator to the custom's hall.

"Just a minute, sir, is this your son?"

"Yes, officer. Is there a problem?"

"Step this way, please."

"What's happening, Robert?" asked Miranda.

"Nothing to worry about madam, just a security check."

"Remove your son's backpack, please, and open it onto the table."

"Are you going to confiscate my skateboard?" asked an innocent Max Junior.

"The officer is just doing his job, son."

"Going fishing, sonny?"

"Yes, when I get to a jetty where there is deep water."

"What's in the football?" asked the suspicious officer.

"Nothing, my father pumped it up. It's a proper leather football, with a bladder. Bounce it if you like."

"I will," said the officer.

"See!" said Max, annoyed.

"Why have you picked on my son, officer?"

"Because, sir, smugglers and terrorists use children to get past airport security. I'm just doing my job to protect the public."

"Have a nice holiday, young man."

They went through passport control, and again their hand luggage was screened by X-ray machines.

"Put your backpack on the conveyor, son."

"They won't keep it, will they?"

"No. It's just routine screening."

The body scanner beeped when Robert went through.

"Just a minute, sir. Put all your valuables, coins and watch in this tray. All right, try again."

The alarm beeped again.

"Take your belt off, please, it may be the metal buckle. Try again."

This time it was fine.

"Come on, son, your turn."

The alarm sounded.

"Come over here, please," said the security officer.

"What's he doing dad?"

"Scanning with a hand held wand for metal objects."

"He's not having my aeroplane!"

The wand passed over Max's trouser pocket and the alarm sounded.

"Empty your pockets, please."

"It's my plane, my dad bought it for me, didn't you dad?"

"Just hand it to me, son. Now stand still."

"All right, young man, no need to worry, off you go now."

Adjacent to the exit there was a row of kiosks, one of which was Europa Car Hire.

"Hello there, you have a car reserved for me."

"Name please?"

"Miranda Darling."

"Bloody nerve of the man!" said an exasperated Annette. "Fancy picking on a boy!"

"I wasn't scared grandma. Was I grandad?"

"No, Max, you did well. He didn't get your model aeroplane, did he?"

"No he didn't, I jolly well told him my dad bought it for me."

"Your car sir, as requested is a convertible. It's a bright red Seat. Registration, AB 24 DH. It is parked in Bay 'A', just across the walkway. Have a nice day."

"I'm glad I don't have to drag a suitcase," said Max.

"I wish I was," said Annette.

"Porter, madam?" asked a young Spanish looking man, with a trolley.

"How much?" asked Amos.

"Just five Euros, sir. I'm a student working the Christmas holiday."

"All right, you're on."

The porter quickly stacked all four cases onto the luggage trolley.

"Where are you headed?"

"Bay 'A', for car hire."

"Very good, Senor, I know the way."

It was a good thing too. The concourse outside was undergoing modernisation and they had to walk there by circumnavigating hoardings.

"Which car, Senor?"

"The red Seat," said Robert.

The porter earned his five Euros; he put the suitcases in the boot.

"Thank you, Senor, have a nice day!"

"Nice car, Robert."

"Only the best for my wife. Should we have the roof down?"

"No no!" called out Annette. "I am in the back and will get wind-blown."

"It's stuffy in here, mother, because the car has been sitting in the sun with the windows closed. I'll put the air conditioning on that will freshen it up."

"Good idea," said Amos. "I fancy a bit of lunch."

"I was thinking the same thing, father. I'm going to drive directly to Sigma, to Sigma Taverna, instead of going east to Seagull Cove."

273

"That's the place where they have a village fountain, isn't it, Miranda?"

"Of course, Robert, you should know, Atalia is your home town."

"Sorry I was forgetting after all this time. I am more used to going to St Lucia, the market town, to take my paintings. Remember. I wonder if Pedro and Rosa Gonzalez will recognise us."

"I'm hungry!" said Max Junior.

"Nothing wrong with you then!" laughed Miranda.

They arrived at Sigma Taverna, and for a minute Miranda thought it was closed up for winter. She went indoors and, sitting at a table with a glass of wine and smoking a pungent cigarette, was Pedro, looking old.

"Hello, Pedro?"

"Welcome, senorita, you wish to eat?"

"I have my family outside, may we come in?"

"Of course."

"Rosa, we have guests!"

Miranda went outside into the sunlight.

"Pedro, this is my husband, Robert, and my son, Max Junior."

"You are Robert, Robert Darling the painter? You used to hang your paintings on my walls?"

"Yes, Pedro, how are you? I left eight years ago. You remember me?"

"Forgive an old man, my eyes are a bit slow nowadays. Welcome, welcome!"

"Rosa, Rosa, light the candles, open a bottle of best wine. Look who is here. It is Senorita Miranda and Senor Robert!"

"Bless you, Pedro. I am married now."

"Congratulations. Hello young man. What is your name?"

"Max Junior, sir."

"Come, give an old man a hug. You call me Pedro, all my friends call me Pedro."

"Senor Amos and your Senora?"

"This is Annette, Pedro, you haven't met her before, my wife."

"Pleased to meet you, Pedro."

"Have you come to live at villa El Estancia? Maria, the maid, still looks after the place."

"Pedro, we have come for two weeks holiday, for Christmas and the New Year."

"I'm glad you are here, Sigma, this time of the year is very quiet. We only get a few visitors from Atalia."

"Is Maria happy to look after El Estancia with it being locked up for winter?"

"Yes, yes, Maria, goes one day a week to air the place out and put the heating on to keep the damp away during the cold winter days. If you want to speak to her she is just next door with her mother, Meralda."

"I would like to buy Maria and her mother a drink to say thank you, for Maria's loyalty."

"Rosa! Bring Merlada round, tell her we have guests and she is invited by Senor Amos."

"Senor Amos is here?" asked Maria. "Is anything wrong?"

"No, no. He just wants to see you."

"Hello, Maria, are you well?"

"Yes, thank you, Senor Amos."

"Relax, come have a seat, and tell your mother also to join us. I would like to buy you a drink as a way of saying thank you for looking after El Estancia."

"I look after your villa, Senor Amos, because I enjoy having a little job and I need the money. You don't have to thank me."

"Yes, Maria, I do. If I didn't have you, I would have to go into Atalia and pay an unscrupulous management agent. I pay you, although I don't see you very often, because I trust you. Honesty is an important thing. Now what will you drink?"

"Mother and I can't afford the local red wine that the tourists order, so we have tea. But, as you are offering, I would like two glasses of red wine."

"Fine, Maria, fine."

"Pedro, another bottle of your finest red wine for Maria and Meralda, and fetch them chairs to our table."

"We are going to order lunch, Maria, so if you are hungry you are welcome to join us."

"Thank you, Senor Amos."

"Pedro, two more plates please, for Maria and Meralda, and some music."

"Spanish music?"

"*Si*. Flamenco music, play it quite loud."

"Now, Senor Amos, what would you like to order?"

"You're the host, Pedro, what do you recommend?"

"Well, we always keep in a good supply of local mussels, so I strongly recommend paella. I will cook it for you with plenty of sweet peppers and ripe tomatoes. Tomatoes from my own hot house. You like potatoes as well as rice?"

"Just put everything in, spiced up with black pepper," said Amos.

After a while, Rosa brought another bottle of red wine to the table and it was shared round.

"Your health ladies!" called out Amos.

"And your health, Senor Amos," said a widely smiling, Meralda.

"Just call me Amos, my lady," laughed Amos.

"How about a song, Miranda?" encouraged Robert.

"Oh, I don't know, it's been a long time."

"Miranda, you have a beautiful voice," supported Annette. "Go on, you used to sing."

"When you fell in love with me you sang, Miranda."

"That was eight years ago, husband."

"Max Junior, would you like to hear your mother sing?"

"Yes. Mother has a sweet voice, jolly good show. Go on, mother, show them."

"But, Max, I only sang at the school for the young children. These are adults, I would feel a fool."

"You sing for me at home at Rose Cottage."

"That's when your father is away at work, painting. The cottage doesn't seem so empty when I sing."

"So do you sing, Miranda?" questioned, Robert.

"Yes, but not when I have company."

"I sing also," said Maria, "when I dust El Estancia, it makes the villa feel lived in."

"Exactly!" said Miranda.

"Maria, why don't you sing with Miss Miranda?" suggested Meralda.

"You think we can?" queried Miranda.

"For heaven's sake, hurry up or I'll sing!" laughed Robert.

"Oh no you won't!" exclaimed Miranda, "you are dreadful, and what's more you are tone deaf."

"I'm not that bad!" protested, Robert.

"Afraid you are," said Amos.

"I'll second that," said Annette. "When you got off the plane you and Amos tried to sing. It was just a drunken slur."

"Oh come off it, Annette. Do you begrudge a man a drink?"

"Not if you are going to sing in a bar with a load of other drunks. This is Pedro and Rosa's restaurant."

Maria spoke to Pedro in Spanish and Pedro put some music on.

Pedro and Rosa sang quietly in the background. Maria picked up the tune and in English sang like a sweet bird. Next thing, Miranda joined in and the two ladies sung in harmony. When they finished everybody applauded loudly including Max Junior.

"See, father! Mother has a beautiful voice."

"I think from now on, wife, I would like to hear you singing around the house."

"Do you really think I am good, Robert?"

"Definitely! How some singers get a recording contract beats me."

"Senorita Miranda is most excellent," smiled Pedro.

"Now, I must go into the kitchen to see to the mixing of the paella, the rice and potatoes will be ready."

"Rosa, you look after our guests."

"Rosa, our hostess, more wine please," said Robert.

"I think we will have the wine down our end of the table," said Annette. "You men have had enough."

"Ladies drink up!" Maria and Meralda made the best of the freely flowing wine. "And, Rosa, come and sit with us, relax."

Everybody was laughing when Pedro arrived with a server piled high with steaming paella. He pushed the trolley up against Amos's table.

"Sit down, Pedro, rest. I will be mother," insisted Amos. "Come on, pass your plates down to the head of the table. It smells great."

"It is the fresh tomatoes and cloves of garlic I put in the paella," emphasised Pedro.

"I love garlic," said Miranda.

"That's what the Devil wears!" shouted up, Max.

"Nonsense, Max. Take no notice of silly stories!" insisted Annette.

"Have you ever met a devil, grandma?"

"Well, no actually."

"Hah! So you don't know whether devils wear garlic or not?"

"I think you have got the wrong end of the stick, Max. Devils are supposed to be scared away by garlic, not wear it."

"I bet, grandma, in that case it's because it stinks on your breath. Yuk!"

"Never mind, Max, are you hungry?" asked Robert.

"Of course, father!"

"No devils on you then. Eat up and well all stink together!" laughed, Robert.

On Christmas Eve all the preparations at El Estancia had long been done by Miranda, Annette and Maria and her mother Meralda. Maria, with her husband and so, had been invited for Christmas Day, as had Pedro and Rosa from Sigma Taverna. Pedro fussed as to how he was going to get to El Estancia with there being no buses on a Bank Holiday, but Miranda solved that.

"Ready, husband?" asked Miranda.

"Sure, let's go, they will be waiting for us."

At Sigma Taverna all the lights were switched off and the interior looked dark. Outside on the veranda, with a packed bag, were Pedro and Rosa.

"Merry Christmas!" called out Miranda.

"We were not sure whether you would come. We have never left the taverna before at Christmas," said Pedro.

"Relax, come and join the others at El Estancia."

"Thank you, Roberto, very kind of you," said Pedro.

The road down the mountainside snaked along empty as there was not a soul about. All the Christmas revellers were in the town of Atalia either doing last minute shopping or more likely holding up one of the many bars.

At El Estancia, as agreed between Amos and Annette, lunch was ready for Pedro and Rosa's arrival.

"Welcome, welcome!" shouted a tipsy Amos. "Please come in. Miranda, show them their room."

"All right, father."

"Come with me, Rosa, I will carry your bag for you."

"Beautiful! Absolutely beautiful! And a grand view of the sea. Maria said it was a big villa, but I didn't realise just how much!"

"I'm glad you like it. The cove down there Robert and I have named Seagull Cove, because of the seagulls that perch high up on the rocks, where they raise their chicks."

"I am pleased to have come, and such beautiful furniture."

"I'll leave you to unpack. Come down for a drink when you are ready."

Annette, Amos and Pedro were well into the port.

"Go down to the cellar, Miranda, and bring up two bottles of red wine. Make sure it's the good stuff."

"O.K., father."

Annette carved up a large roast chicken while Amos poured out wine into large cut-crystal glasses.

Miranda, bring the vegetables in, please, they are in the large tureens."

"Everybody sit down, please," said Robert. "I am going to light the scented candles."

"Come on, Robert, draw the curtains or the effect will be lost."

Amos stood up. "I give you Christmas cheer and good health! Drink up, Rosa and Pedro, remember you are stopping the night to enjoy Christmas with us. You have no driving to do, so enjoy yourselves. You are out of Taverna Sigma and on holiday."

After lunch Robert and Miranda went for a walk on the beach into Seagull Cove.

"Remember when we first met?" asked Robert.

"Yes, you were up in the cliffs painting and I was sat on this rock with Maria. You painted me and left the picture on the rock under a flat stone, where I found it. And the rest, as they say, is history."

"The rest, Miranda, is love. I loved you when I first met you, and I love you now."

"Robert, you are such a romantic."

"Come here. Merry Christmas!"

"That's not officially until tomorrow."

"Let's go into the cave."

"I know what you are thinking, Robert Darling."

"Come on, Mrs Darling, you are my wife, to have and to hold."

"Not on a full stomach, I'm not."

"You didn't have to eat everything, you should watch your figure."

"I don't need to with you watching it all the time. Anyway, tomorrow I will eat very little, except perhaps a few grapes. I don't believe in stuffing yourself on Christmas Day."

In the villa Amos and Pedro had fallen into a drunken stupor, which left Annette and Rosa to wash up. In the afternoon everybody went to bed for a siesta, which wasn't true of Robert and Miranda, they made love passionately.

The evening affair was a bit of a party atmosphere. Marco arrived with Maria and his son Sanchez, who was about Max Junior's age.

Amos poured the drinks liberally and Marco soon forgot he was a stranger and melted into the company. There was a surprise from Marco, he was a good singer.

"Everybody know, Silent Night?" he asked.

"Of course," said Miranda.

"When I was a boy my father used to sing to me while the family gathered around the Christmas tree. You would like to now, Senor Amos?"

"Of course," said Amos. "Everybody fill their glass and go out into the hallway and stand around the Christmas tree."

"I'll start," said Maria, "then you join in, Marco."

The first verse was sung in the beautiful sweet voices of Maria and Miranda, then the men joined in.

"Everybody sing!" shouted Amos.

Pedro and Rosa joined in.

"Come o, Sanchez, let's show them!" chirped Max.

The two boys sang their hearts out in a high falsetto. The combined sound was beautiful on old Pedro's ears to the extent that large tears rolled down his cheeks.

When they had finished Miranda went to Pedro.

"Are you all right, Pedro?"

"Forgive a silly old man. I was thinking back many years to when I was a boy and my father sang to me also around the Christmas tree. We were very poor, but my father gave me a lot of love."

"You're very sweet, Pedro."

"Come, Pedro, give your wife a cuddle."

"You know, Miranda, without Rosa, my life would be empty."

"I can see, even at your ages, you still love one another very much. How long have you been married?"

"Fifty-five years in May. A whole lifetime."

"Then I congratulate you."

Robert came across. "Merry Christmas, Pedro, Rosa!"

"You know, Robert, they have been married for almost fifty-five years."

"Gracious me! Will we still love one another after fifty-five years?"

"I don't see why not, based on love. But I am forty-five now. In another fifty-five years I will be one hundred!"

"Well, husband, do your best. I am thirty-one now and in fifty-five years I will be eighty-six. Will you still have a glint in your eye for me?"

"I will probably manage an admiring smile, while I totter on my Zimmer frame."

Everybody laughed, and they sang some more carols, Marco taking the lead.

Max Junior and Sanchez, excited by the thought of Christmas and all the presents Father Christmas would bring them tomorrow, got bored with singing and set off playing chase around the villa, in and out of the doors and around the considerable grounds. Outside were the stables, which provided shelter and fodder for two horses, Blitzer and Felicia. Blitzer was a gelding and Felicia a lovely old lady.

"Look, Sanchez, horses. I wonder if we are allowed to ride them?" queried, Max.

"Hello, boys, are you allowed out here?"

"Yes! This is my grandpa's villa. Who are you?"

"My name's Domingo. I look after the horses."

"Do you own them then?"

"No, young Max, they belong to Senor Amos."

"How do you know my name?" asked Max.

"Because I am a friend of your grandfather and he told me his grandson was staying for Christmas. Do you like horses?"

"I'm not sure. I have never ridden a horse. Am I allowed?"

"Your grandpa said you were curious and you would probably want to ride. Come and say hello to Blitzer because he is the most spirited, like you."

"Hello Blitzer, would you mind if I rode you?"

"Max, give him these carrots then he will be your friend," offered Domingo.

"What's the white one called?" asked Sanchez.

"She's an old lady, called Felicia. Very steady, you could put a baby on her and she would not come to any harm."

"If they are grandpa's horses why do you look after them?"

"Because, nosey Max, I look after them and in return I get to ride them for free to my smallholding and back every day."

"What's a smallholding?"

"A small farm for one or two people to look after. Or you could say, as in English, an allotment. That is a garden with an allotted amount of land. A sort of very big garden."

"Oh, I know what an allotment is. So you grow things?"

"Yes. Some out in the open and the other fruits and vegetables under polythene tunnels."

"My mother, Miranda, grows things in our back garden at home."

"Does she also keep horses?"

"Oh no, she just grows things, mostly to eat."

"O.K. You want to ride?"

"Sure. I'll have a go."

"O.K., come into the stable."

Domingo saddled up Blitzer for Max and Felicia for Sanchez, because Sanchez was obviously the quieter of the two boys.

"I'll lead him across to the mounting steps. Right, climb up. Put your feet in the stirrups."

"I can't reach!"

"That's because Blitzer is a man's horse. Let me shorten the straps for you. Now try."

"Take hold of the reins and I will lead him out with the yard rope. Let me have control. I will walk him round in a circle while you get used to the feel of the horse's movements."

After a few minutes Max was itching to try on his own.

"You sure, Max?"

"Take the rope off. I'll walk him round."

"O.K. Senor Max. To walk him kick his flanks gently, to stop pull back on his reins and say the command, whoa!"

"Let go, I'm ready."

"Giddy up," said Max, and kicked Blitzer's flanks. Obediently, Blitzer walked around the perimeter of the yard keeping close to the fences.

"Right, Sanchez, your turn. You have the old lady, Felicia, to ride on. Climb the steps and now sit up in the saddle. I will take hold of the reins at the bit while she gets used to you on her back."

Domingo walked Felicia around. "How do you feel, Sanchez?"

"O.K. can I have the reins now?"

"Sure, only don't rush her she's a grandma. She only has one speed – slow."

"Come on, Blitzer, giddy up!" Max kicked him hard in the flanks. Blitzer shot forward.

"Yippee! Look at me! I'm a cowboy!" shouted Max as Blitzer was given his head. Domingo can I take him outside the yard?"

"Sure, if you think you will be safe, but you must wear a hard hat in case you fall off."

"Do I have to?"

"If you want to go riding in the grounds it's the rules. It's for your own safety. A doctor can fix a broken arm but not a broken head."

"O.K. I'll do as you say."

"Good boy, you know it makes sense."

"Sanchez, do you want to go out into the grounds?"

"No thanks, walking the horse is fast enough for me."

There were jumps in the fields and Blitzer seemed to be let loose to enjoy the full scope of the grounds. As soon as Max commanded him, Blitzer took the jumps. Max Junior was elated, even though he was thrown about in the saddle.

"Hey! Domingo, look at me, now I really am a cowboy!" shouted, Max.

"Be careful, Max!" called across Domingo through cupped hands. But Max was in rapture. He had a big smile and wide excited eyes.

Domingo didn't hear Amos approach from the villa.

"So that's what they are up to?"

"Yes, Senor Amos, you said Max could ride if he wanted to."

"I did indeed, and I am glad. That boy is a natural."

Max pulled in the reins. "Whoa! Blitzer. Walk-on, good boy."

Amos went across to the gate, which gave entrance to the open grounds.

"Hello, Max, enjoying yourself?"

"Yes, thank you, grandpa. Can I have a horse?"

"I don't know about that, Max. It certainly can't be Blitzer because he's my horse and we can't take him home on an aeroplane."

"What about Felicia, grandpa?"

"No, no. She's too old to fly and, anyway, Felicia is a grand old girl your grandma rides."

"I didn't know you rode horses, grandpa?"

"When I was younger I used to ride in the woods but now it's only when I holiday in Spain, which is about three times a year, the autumn and spring mostly, when it is cooler in England."

"Could father buy me a horse? I mean there is a field behind the bottom of the garden at Rose Cottage."

"So this is where you have got to," said Robert.

"I'm riding Blitzer, father, aren't I grandpa?"

"Yes, Max, and you're doing very well."

"Time to come in, Max, it will soon be evening."

"Oh, father!"

"Your father is right, Max, the sun is setting."

"O.K. I'll come in."

"Hello boys, had a good time?" asked Miranda.

"Yes, thank you, mother, Sanchez and I have been riding, haven't we, Sanchez?"

"Yes, pa, we have."

"I didn't know you liked horses, Sanchez?" said a surprised, Marco.

"Well, they are O.K. as long as they don't go fast."

"Oh, Sanchez, I like them fast!" laughed Max.

"Never mind now, boys," said Miranda, "do you want anything to eat?"

"I'll have a sandwich, please," said 'hollow legs'.

"What about you, Sanchez?"

"I'm not hungry, thank you."

"Will you be sober to drive home, Marco?" asked Annette.

"I've had a few drinks but I'm O.K."

"I don't think so, Marco, put that drink down," insisted Maria.

"Sit him down in the kitchen, Maria. And you Amos, you need to sober up."

"Father, it's against the law to drink and drive," said a very serious Sanchez.

"You are too clever for your own good, son."

"Senor Marco, it is dangerous to drive the car after you have been drinking. I am right, father, aren't I?" said Max Junior, looking for support.

"Yes, son, you are right, as your mother always reminds me."

"Sorry, Marco, you are outvoted," laughed Robert.

"O.K. Maria, give me the coffee."

"I blame, Senor Amos," said Meralda. "He should know better a man of his age."

"Meralda, please, it is Christmas Eve, Marco is just enjoying himself. We will soon have him sobered up."

"Well, if he is still drunk when it is time to go I am not getting in the car with him!"

"Do you think, Annette, we could put Meralda up in the box room?" asked Amos.

"Me, stay the night? Yes, I would be happier about that."

"Then it's settled. Marco, your mother will not trouble you any more. She will stay with us tonight. Is that agreeable to you?"

"Hey! You don't know my mother. She still thinks I am a little boy and I have to be told what to do."

"Marco, you still like a woman to fuss over you, it makes you feel like the man of the house," pointed out Maria.

"It's true, Maria, that's why I love you."

"Don't embarrass me, Marco, in front of Senor Amos."

"I can't tell you I love you?"

"Drink your coffee and sober up, husband."

"Amos, sit down and drink some coffee, you also have had too much to drink," insisted Annette.

"This is my villa, woman, if I want to drink, I will."

"Papa, don't show yourself up. You can have another drink tonight after Marco has gone and the boys are tucked up in bed," pointed out Miranda.

"Max and Sanchez are staying?"

"I think Max has invited Sanchez all by himself."

"Where will he sleep, we have just offered the box room to Meralda, and Pedro and Rosa are in the guest room?"

"The boys have agreed to share Max's bed," said Miranda.

"Is there room?" asked Robert.

"I suppose so."

285

"Of course there is," said Annette. "There are five bedrooms, you think I don't know my own villa. Max's bed is a three-quarter double."

"You didn't tell me, Sanchez?" said Maria.

"Sorry, mother. Is it all right if I stay tonight with Max?"

"I suppose, Sanchez, but we will miss Christmas morning together."

"Don't worry, Maria and Marco, don't forget you are coming for Christmas dinner anyway. Why not come a little earlier, say midday, for before-dinner drinks?" suggested Amos.

"O.K., Sanchez, you can stay," said Maria.

"Yippee!" shouted Max and Sanchez, together.

About seven o'clock, after Marco and Maria had had tea, they set off home in their car back to Sigma.

"Do you realise, Maria, this will be the first night on our own since Sanchez was born eight years ago."

"And our first Christmas morning without Sanchez."

"Yes, Maria, in that case we should put the situation to our advantage."

"What are you getting at, Marco?"

"Well, if we aren't going to be interrupted in the morning, we can have a lie in."

"Oh I see. And there was me thinking I was going to get a treat."

"You are darling, me."

"Sex! You never change!"

"And, wife, we can not only have a late morning tomorrow, but I thought also an early evening."

"Twice in one day!"

"Well, it is Christmas, and the best thing is, we won't have your mother prowling about the house keeping an eye on us."

"O.K. Marco, you win."

Christmas morning, Marco was true to his word, and waking early in the half light of the rising sun filtering through the full lace curtains of their bedroom, made passionate love to his wife. Twice. Once when he woke up, and again just before they got up for a late breakfast.

"I love you, husband."

"I should think so, Merry Christmas! Now let me have a few minutes rest."

"All right, Marco, you have a lie-in, you have earned it. I'll make a Christmas surprise breakfast."

In the kitchen Maria poached some dry-cured smoked haddock, topped it with a poached egg and melted butter. She took it upstairs accompanied by a glass of brandy.

"Here you are, Marco, sit up!"

"Sorry? Oh, I feel asleep."

"Breakfast!"

"It smells nice. God, I'm knackered!"

"Serves you right, you randy goat. Last night and twice this morning. I didn't know you still had it in you," smiled Maria, dressed in an almost sheer nightie.

"Put some clothes on, woman, are you never satisfied?"

"It's been a long time, Marco, since you were like a young buck."

"Pass me the tray and get in bed."

"It's your favourite. Smoked haddock."

"Bless you, what's this?"

"Brandy."

"Brandy first thing in the morning?"

"It's Christmas and, anyway, you need to keep your strength up."

"Then thank you, wife. Merry Christmas!" and he downed it in one.

"Cheers, Marco!"

Like two courting lovebirds they fed each other smoked haddock on pieces of buttered toast. Then they lay down contented in each other's arms and nodded off. When they awoke it was midday.

"Oh hell, I promised Amos and Annette we would arrive for pre-dinner drinks," said Maria on awaking.

"Don't worry it's Christmas Day, everybody will be getting up late, then opening their presents. Will Sanchez's new bicycle fit in the back of the car?"

"I think so, first let me get shaved and dressed."

It was lovely sunny day, with a blue sky puffing small cotton wool clouds along on a fresh breeze.

"Nice day for a bicycle ride."

"At least, Marco, the land around Atalia is mostly flat so Sanchez will be able to ride his bicycle."

With the bicycle in the back, Marco drove down to El Estancia, arriving just before one o'clock. Meralda, who sat at the window waiting, was the first out when the car pulled up.

"Marco, you are late!"

"Mother, don't complain today, it's Christmas," said Maria, in her husband's defence.

Sanchez burst out of the door.

"Mother, mother, look what Max bought me for Christmas!"

"A red racing car, son. That's nice," said Marco.

"Happy Christmas, father!" and Sanchez gave his mother and father a kiss.

"Let me hold the racing car," said Maria.

"Come here, son. What do you think?" asked Marco as he got the bicycle out of the back of the car.

"For me, papa?!"

"Of course. Happy Christmas!"

"Thank you father. Just what I wanted!"

Sanchez jumped on and pedalled off down the road, it was a real junior's bicycle, a lot better than his infant's bicycle that he had grown out of. This new bike had five gears. He raced along, turned, and raced back.

At the news, Max came to the door and ran out into the street.

"Can I have a go, Sanchez?"

"Come with me, son," said Robert.

"Come on, Sanchez, put down your bicycle a minute and come and see Max's surprise Christmas present."

They went together: Robert, Max and Sanchez, to the stables at the back.

"Father, you have bought me a horse!" said an excited Max.

"No, son, go into the stable and see what is hidden there."

"Move over, Felicia."

"Father! A new bicycle!"

"Come on, Max, quick, I will race you on my bicycle."

Max pushed it round the side of the villa to the front street.

"They are the same!" exclaimed Sanchez.

Robert came to see the boys off.

"Thank you, father, brilliant!"

"Thank grandpa and grandma, they bought it for you."

But the words were lost. The two boys were tearing through the derailleur gears seeing who could get into fifth gear, top gear, first.

They pedalled flat out, reaching about thirty miles per hour as their top speed. Puffed they slowed down before braking to a halt.

"I could do with some lemonade," said Max.

"Race you back!" said Sanchez, and he immediately set off.

"Hey! You cheated, I wasn't ready!" shouted Max, pedalling like hell to catch Sanchez, up.

Meralda was sitting out the front in the porch enjoying the sun with a glass of port in her hand. She had just settled down when the boys came back at high speed. Sanchez, her grandson, was in the lead. She stood up, alarmed at their speed, but the bicycles quickly slowed to a halt as the brakes screeched and the tyres skidded on the tarmac surface.

"Hello, grandma, I won!"

"You cheated!" shouted Max. "You should have said, 'ready steady go'. It's not fair!"

"It was only a race, Max. I would like to be friends. Anyway, you're a better horse rider than me."

Max thought about it. "True. Friends it is."

"Mother, can we have some lemonade," asked Max. "Pedalling fast makes you thirsty."

"As it is Christmas Day, you may have wine with lemonade."

"Will I like it?"

"Of course, it's called a spritzer. Come inside."

"Happy Christmas, Sanchez!" they all greeted.

"Thank you, mother and father, for my new bicycle. Red is my favourite colour!"

"That's O.K., son, as long as you enjoy it."

"Yes, it's the same as mine," said Max Junior.

In the considerable lounge of Amos's villa the fire was burning brightly, the Christmas tree on the dining table was lit and Christmas music was playing through the quadraphonic speaker system of the cassette disc player and, on the lounge table, a game of Monopoly was underway.

"Can I join in, mother?" asked Max Junior.

"Well, you can, Max," replied Miranda, "but I am only a top hat."

"That's O.K. I don't mind which playing piece I share with you, because at least you have a hotel, and that I know generates a lot of rent."

"You're not daft are you, Max," said Robert. "Just because your mother has Mayfair."

"Father, mother may not have a lot of Monopoly money but a hotel in a prime spot in London is an excellent investment."

"What do they teach you at André Laceys? How to make money?"

"Yes, father, we are taught the rudiments of buy for one pound and sell for two."

"No wonder I am losing playing against a budding tycoon like you," said Robert.

"Never mind, Robert, have a whisky," said Amos who, being a Consultant Architect, was prospecting by spreading his net wide and buying up houses in a whole district in an investment area of London, so that he could collect top rents whenever another player came down his street.

Annette had the Electricity Company and the Water Works, which were, in their own rights, monopolies, but being nationalised industries only showed a small return for a huge investment which meant, in the future, a magnate could come together and privatise them. The result would be a licence to print money because, once owned a company with a national distribution network, could up its prices and watch the money roll in from the United Kingdom's sixty million population.

'Well it's great to dream', thought Annette.

Marco and Maria sat on the luxury leather settee with their son, and read to him from a Boy's Adventure Book, which Marco had bought him as a Christmas present. Both his parents were getting decidedly merry on Amos's red wine, a little of which Sanchez was allowed to share. Soon all three were contented and happy.

Amos landed on Miranda's hotels plot.

"Damn!"

"That will be a thousand pounds, please!" blurted out Miranda.

"I'll buy another hotel, please, banker."

"That will be one thousand two hundred pounds please," said a widely smiling Robert.

Robert and Annette took their turns.

Amos threw. "Damn! Only two?"

Amos landed on Miranda's second hotel.

"Huh! Just luck!"

"Pay up, Amos, that will be one thousand two hundred pounds, please!"

"You vixen, that will leave me almost broke!"

"Tough! Pay up or mortgage your houses to the bank?"

"Damn, damn. All right, I'll pay up. I'm not giving up my property, and I've worked hard to get where I am."

"Afraid that's life," said Robert.

The game went on for a while until Miranda had bought out both Robert and Annette, and she monopolised the board. Although, during the game Amos had faired better, it was too late now with Miranda owning so many streets in London. Eventually the rent got into thousands and Miranda made Amos totally bankrupt.

"O.K., you win. Who taught you to play like that?"

"Nobody. It's one of my hidden talents."

"Port, anybody?" asked Amos.

"Is very good," said Pedro.

Pedro and Rosa sat in the fireside chairs sharing a bottle of port between them.

"Can I have a drop, Pedro?" asked Amos, holding out his glass.

"Sure, Senor Amos. Very good."

"Mother, would you like another port?" asked Maria.

"I would, Maria. I was just thinking back to when your father was alive."

"He was a very good man, mama, but you have to think about yourself now and enjoy your grandchild."

"Sanchez!" called out Meralda, "come and give your grandmother a hug. It is Christmas and an old lady can be lonely even in a crowd."

"You look happy, grandma, I think port is good for your colour."

"Children, what do they know?"

"Mother, you have me and Marco as well."

"Yes, you are a good daughter. Marco, Merry Christmas! You are a very good son-in-law."

"I could do with some help in the kitchen to get the dinner ready," said Annette.

"Meralda will come and help, I don't want to be a useless old woman."

"No, no," said Annette.

"Mother, rest yourself, I will help," said Maria.

"But you are a guest," said Amos.

"But I would like to help," said Maria. "I like to feel useful."

"Father, if Maria would like to help, you should let her," put in Miranda.

"Go on, Maria, take no notice of my father. Mother will appreciate your help. I'll entertain the boys and your neighbours, Pedro and Rosa."

"You are a good woman, Miranda," said Maria.

"Tell me boys what would you like to do?"

"Play a game."

"Have you a game in mind?"

"Yes mother," said Max. "Charades. We play it at André Laceys."

"What is André Laceys?" asked Sanchez.

"Oh, you don't know do you Sanchez."

"What don't I know?"

"The name of my school. It is called André Laceys."

"Funny name for a school?"

"That's because it's a special school for gifted children. André Laceys was a physicist, you know, a scientist who deals with energy and matter. He came from a rich family and when he became famous for his physical theories he realised there were other children with talents but not so fortunate as himself, so he founded, by the legacy of his will upon his death, André Laceys School for Gifted Children."

"You mean if they were poor they could still go there to learn?"

"Exactly, Sanchez. The trust fund would nominate a gifted child from an ordinary school for a scholarship, so that his parents who were poor wouldn't have to pay for the school fees."

"So the poor boy can become recognised according to his genius?"

"That's right, but André Laceys is only for young boys. I hadn't given it a moments thought before now, but where do talented girls go?"

"Probably a special school for young ladies," said Robert.

"Anyway," said Max Junior, "who is going to play charades?"

"I'll join you," said Amos.

"And me," joined in Robert.

"I'll go first," said Max, "because it was my idea."

Now, Max was not only gifted, but crafty also. He made a circle with his arms.

"The whole thing!" blurted out Miranda.

Max encouraged his mother with a nod and a smile. He was doing the Poseidon Adventure. The ship that turned upside down in the ocean and there were only a few survivors who were saved by the rescue team cutting through the bottom of the hull with an oxy-acetylene torch.

Max acted a rough sea of a ship pitching and rolling a lot.

"A drunk!" shouted out Robert.

"The sea is rough!" said Sanchez.

Now Max couldn't speak because that wasn't allowed in charades, so he nodded and made encouraging movements with his hands, denoting, 'more, more'.

Max did an act of the whole thing turning over, one hundred and eighty degrees. Then he lay down on the carpet, first face up then rolled over and lay face down.

"Somebody drowning in the sea!" blurted out Sanchez.

Max sat up for a moment and encouraged Sanchez, with is hands again, motioning, 'more, more'.

Max stood up and mimed swimming.

"You're swimming!" said Robert.

Max climbed stairs, then some more stairs. He acted sweating as he climbed.

"You're climbing and it's hot!" said Miranda.

Max nodded to encourage his mother.

"You're climbing up a ships gangway because you have been rescued from nearly drowning and the sun's hot!"

Max motioned with his hands, 'sort of. More, more'.

Max banged on the roof of the upturned hull overhead and shouted, help, help!

"You're calling for help and your banging on a roof?" said Robert.

'Yes, yes', motioned Max.

"So you went upside down, swam, climbed stairs and banged on the roof to be rescued?" said Miranda.

Max smiled hugely and waved with his arms, 'Come on, come on'.

"I know," said Miranda, "it's the Poseidon Adventure!"

"Yes, mother, well done!"

"How the hell did you get that?!" fumed Robert.

"Because our Max is a brilliant actor."

"What's a Poseidon Adventure?" asked Sanchez.

"It's a film from the nineteen seventies when an ocean liner turns upside down and only a few passengers survive by banging on the upturned hull, and the rescuers cut through the thick steel of the hull with oxy-acetylene cutting gear."

"Oh, it's a film. Well, I have never heard of it," said Sanchez, "so it's not really fair."

"Never mind what's fair," said Annette, "Christmas dinner is ready to be served up. Where are Santa's Little Helpers?"

"I'll help," said Max Junior.

"And me," said Sanchez.

"What shall I carry?" asked Maria.

"You've helped me with the preparing and cooking the dinner," said Annette, "you can check the table settings."

"Amos, put the cut-glass crystal out, please, and don't drop any."

"Of course, wife, one to be obeyed. Don't worry I am not getting drunk, just merry."

"Can I do anything?" asked Marco.

"Yes, go and seat Rosa and Pedro at the dining table, the place settings all have names."

So Max and Sanchez helped to carry in the tureens. There were soup, sprouts, carrots and roast potato in the tureens, all-steaming hot.

"Make sure you carry them by the handles, boys, otherwise you will scald your hands."

"Miranda, take the soup bowls in please."

"What sort of soup is it, Annette?"

"Cream of leek and potato laced with white wine."

"That sounds tasty."

"Well it is Christmas. Not that Amos needs any alcohol."

"He's just enjoying his holiday. He's a good man, mother, cut him loose. I like him rather jolly, he's usually so straight laced."

"Your father, Miranda, believes in old fashioned values, and so do I."

"So do I, mother, and I love you both dearly. Robert is the best thing that has ever happened to me. It's a perfect family Christmas for me."

"Well it's family and friends, says Amos, that's why his generous heart has invited Meralda, Maria and Marco and Pedro and Rosa."

"Come on Annette, sit down, you have done enough. I'm pouring the champagne."

"Can we have some, grandpa?" asked Max.

"Go on, father, give Max and Sanchez a half glass each, it is Christmas," encouraged Miranda.

"Would everybody stand up, please," asked Amos.

"I toast my wife, Annette, and thank her for all the happiness she has given me over the years. Merry Christmas, darling. And I would like to wish our guests, Meralda and her family and Rosa and Pedro, a very happy Christmas."

Amos did the toast: "Raise your glasses, Merry Christmas everyone!"

"Merry Christmas everyone!" came the happy retort.

The soup was delicious.

"I'll take the bowls out," said Maria.

"Thank you, Maria."

"Amos, bring the turkey in, please, and carve while I heat the gravy."

"Here are the plates, Annette, hot from the oven."

"Thank you, Marco. You can pass the plates around as Amos carves, so that everything is still hot."

"Everybody help yourself from the tureens while the vegetables are hot."

"I'll pass the white wine down the table," said Amos. "Help yourself, but not you boys, you will have lemonade."

"Oh grandpa, that's not fair!" complained Max.

"Son," said Robert, "you will do as you are told. Boys of eight years do not drink alcohol."

"But Sanchez says his parents allow him to drink red wine at home."

"But," said Marco, "only one glass at a time and that's drunk with soda water."

"Well, father, could we have a spritzer then?"

"What do you say, Miranda?"

"I think, Robert, one glass, provided it is with soda, will be all right for Christmas," smiled Miranda.

"Thank you, mother."

"Now be quiet, Max Junior, and eat up your dinner, your grandmother has gone to a lot of trouble," said Miranda.

"Anybody for any more?" asked Amos.

"Yes please, grandpa," said Max.

"Nothing wrong with you is there, 'hollow legs'?" laughed Robert.

"We don't get turkey at André Laceys," said Max.

"Could I have some more, Senor Amos?" asked Sanchez.

"Of course, son."

"I've never had turkey before. We always have roast chicken for Christmas dinner."

"Always chicken?"

"Yes, papa catches one from the backyard, my grandmother looks after the chickens, and father plucks it the night before."

"That's right, Robert, the women are too squeamish to kill the chickens so it's my job."

"I should think so," said Amos. "Killing a chicken is a man's job."

"There you go, Sanchez, two large slices, that do you?"

"Yes thank you, Senor Amos."

"Good lad, eat up."

"Anybody else?" asked Amos.

"I'll have some more, Amos," said Marco. "For me it's a treat. Chicken is good, but turkey is tastier."

"If you're having seconds," said Robert, "then so shall I, I didn't want to appear a greedy pig."

"Nonsense, Robert, there is still half a breast left, it's best enjoyed hot. Can I persuade you all to eat up the rest of the turkey?"

"Not for me," said Miranda. "I have to watch my figure."

"And so do I," said Maria.

"Pedro, Rosa, you are our guests, don't be modest, you are welcome to second helpings."

"That's very kind of you, Senor Amos, that would be very nice," said Rosa.

"Come on then, pass your plates down."

"Robert, open some more wine and fill Pedro and Rosa's glasses."

"Sure. Anybody else for wine?"

"Please, Robert," said Miranda.

"And me," joined in Maria.

"Don't forget your mother-in-law, young man."

"As if I would, Annette," smiled Robert. "And thank you for a beautiful meal."

"It's not finished yet, Miranda, come give your mother a hand in the kitchen."

From the oven Annette turned out a huge Christmas pudding.

"Invert that on a plate and cut it up and put the portions in the dishes while I heat up the brandy sauce."

"Here you are," said Miranda carrying the dishes in.

"What no brandy?" asked Amos.

"Just wait a minute, father."

"There you go, husband. A large jug of brandy sauce, made with a lot of real brandy."

Amos sniffed it. "Smells heavenly."

"Well, don't hog it, pass it round while it's hot."

"It's delicious, Annette."

"Well, I know you like your brandy, husband."

"Thank you, darling."

"Hey, Sanchez, we are having brandy, like men!" laughed Max Junior.

"I've never tasted brandy before," said Sanchez.

"I should hope not, young man," said Amos. "Even men get drunk on brandy."

"I've tried it, father," said Max.

"When was that?" asked Robert.

"At André Laceys. One of the Senior School boys had a half bottle. We had to pay fifty pence to have a taste."

"And did you like it?"

"Oh no, father, it made me choke, it was like a fire in your throat, but the brandy sauce is in custard and sugar, that's different."

"So you won't go pinching any of grandpa Amos's brandy?"

"Definitely not, father. I am not a thief!" said an adamant Max, whose honour had been questioned.

"Marco, Pedro and Robert, shall we retire to the lounge with a quality brandy and leave the ladies to their cups of tea?"

"Now that's one thing I enjoy," said Pedro. "And a cigar."

"Sorry, Pedro, I haven't bought any cigars this Christmas."

"No problem, Senor Amos, here I have a present for you."

"Thank you, Pedro, what is it?"

"Open it and see," said Rosa.

"Ten Havana cigars! Why, thank you, Pedro."

"Cigar, Robert?"

"Why not, it's Christmas."

"You don't smoke, Robert," said Miranda.

"If you four are going to smoke those smelly things go out into the sun lounge at the back of the house and open the door to let the smoke out," said Annette, forcefully.

"O.K. love, I won't smoke your plants to death."

"You had better not, especially my beautiful cacti."

"Come on lads, let's go out the back."

"Grandpa, can we come?" asked Max.

"No, son, you help your grandmother wash up."

"That's not fair!"

"Son, do as your grandfather tells."

"Yes, father."

"Robert, the boys will probably break more than they wash up?" said Miranda.

"Boys, dry-up for your mother and don't break anything or grandma will be cross."

"O.K. father. Can we go out on our new bikes afterwards?"

"Of course, son, you can pedal off some of that turkey you have eaten."

"Come on Sanchez, let's do the drying up quickly then we can go out and play."

"Excuse me, Senor Amos."

"Hello, Meralda, have you come to join the men?"

"If you don't mind, I would like a brandy."

"That's great, Meralda! Come and have a man's drink. Please have my seat. Cigar?"

"How did you know I smoked?"

"The first time I met you I noticed smoke on your breath."

"I try to hide it from Marco and Maria, but Marco secretly buys me cigarettes now and again. I get lonely and smoking keeps me company."

"Have a Havana."

And Meralda did.

"Cigar cutter?" asked Meralda.

"I can see you're a seasoned cigar smoker," said an admiring, Amos.

Meralda took a deep breath and fully inhaled the cigar smoke, blowing it out of her nose a full five seconds later.

"Lovely. That's a wonderful cigar," said a smiling, Meralda.

"Mother-in-law, you smoke like a man," said Marco.

"I may be old," said Meralda, "but I'm no weak kneed woman."

"I believe you," said Amos, "I wouldn't want to cross swords with you."

"Robert, go pour Meralda a double brandy in a balloon glass."

"Here you are, Meralda."

"Thank you but such a small drink?"

"Robert, that's a British pub measure you have poured there, I meant a Spanish double measure."

"Give me your glass, Meralda, I will pour the brandy," offered Marco.

"On second thoughts," said Amos, "bring the bottle out."

"There you are, Meralda, pour whatever you like. Get drunk if you like," smiled Amos.

Meralda poured a very large measure.

"To you, Senor Amos, health and happiness!"

"Thank you, Meralda."

Happy, the men, including Meralda, passed the bottle round. The air was thick with clouds of blue smoke and brandy fumes.

"Hello Rosa, you drink brandy too?"

"If Meralda can, so can I," said Rosa.

"Do you smoke as well?"

"No, no, filthy habit. Pedro makes the house smell, I send him outside on the veranda to smoke."

"How are you men doing?" asked Annette.

"Ah! Now, my love, not just men but venerable old ladies as well, who also smoke."

"I do not smoke, filthy habit," said Rosa.

"And I am not so old," said Meralda. "I have a good few cigars left in me yet."

That comment cracked up Amos laughing 'til his sides split. His laughter was infectious and before long everybody was laughing.

"Well, it's nice to see you all so merry," smiled Annette.

"Did the boys help with the washing up?" asked Amos.

"Yes. They did it quickly, and now they are outside on their bicycles."

Maria came into the sun lounge.

"Mother you are smoking a cigar! And with the men."

"Yes, daughter," laughed Meralda through a gap-toothed smile, "and it is heavenly."

"Well, aren't you going to say something, Marco?"

"I say, Meralda, Merry Christmas!"

"Huh! Getting drunk. Men are no help."

"Miranda, take Maria and sit her by the fire and pour her some of my best port, that will relax her."

"I'll go join the other two," said Annette. "I can't do with all this smoke."

"Yes, love. Watch a Christmas film."

"But they are all in Spanish, Amos."

"We have a satellite dish, surely you can pick up one British programme?"

"The only English-speaking channel is BBC World News."

"What about a Spanish film with English subtitles?"

"I can't enjoy a film if I can't follow what's being said."

"O.K. dear, perhaps Miranda would like to get the card table out. You like a nice game of cards."

"I think, Amos, I would like a nice walk on the beach. Clear some of this smelly smoke from my head and from the villa."

"Good idea," said Robert. "Who wants to come with me?"

"Not us," said Pedro, "we are happy just sitting enjoying the sunshine in this beautiful sun lounge."

"O.K. Pedro and Rosa, I will leave you here with Meralda."

"I'll come, Robert, I have sat long enough, I need to work some of my meal off," said Marco.

"Come on, Maria, we are going for a walk on Senor Amos's private beach."

"It's a long time, Marco, since I walked on a beach."

Miranda went out in the road and called the boys in.

"We are going on the beach, do you want to come?"

"Can we bring our bicycles?"

"How are you going to get them down all the steps?"

"O.K. we'll walk, won't we, Sanchez?"

"Sure, friend Max."

So the eight of them, Miranda and Robert taking the lead, set off down the steps to the sandy beach below.

"Grandpa, can I take my bucket and spade?"

"If you want. Hurry up and fetch it, it's just in the porch."

Back in a flash, Max Junior and Sanchez raced down the steps, overtaking the grandparents and catching up Miranda and Robert.

"Where are we going, father?"

"Down to the sea and perhaps around the cove into the cavern."

"Come on, Sanchez, let's build a large sandcastle with a moat around it down by the water's edge. I'll dig a trench with my spade and you can make some sandcastles with the bucket, using your hands to scoop up the soft damp sand."

"O.K. race you!"

The boys flew ahead, screeching with delight as they went, scaring the seagulls clean off the beach.

Robert, hand-in-hand with his wife Miranda, walked into Seagull Cove, as Robert had aptly named it. Marco and Maria and, Amos and Annette, followed on likewise.

"You go ahead, Maria with Marco, we'll keep an eye on the boys," said Annette.

"Come on, Marco, it's a nice day."

"Where are we going?"

"Let's follow where Miranda is leading Robert," smiled Maria.

"Then we will have to get our feet wet."

"Why?" asked Maria.

"Because the tide is in and to follow Miranda and Robert into the cavern we'll have to take our shoes off."

"I don't mind, where's your sense of romance?"

He pinched her bum. Maria laughed and pulled her shoes off and ran excited through the shallows. Marco did likewise and chased after her. It was semi-dark in the cavern and it took a while for their eyes to adjust to the gloomy interior. There was no sign of Robert and Miranda so they lay down on the cool sand and canoodled like in their courting days.

They both felt like naughty children, but both unusually felt excited.

"What if the boys come in or Amos and Annette come looking for us?" said Maria.

"Don't be daft, Annette is not stupid, she is busy looking after the children, giving us private time together."

"You sure?"

"Of course. So let's be having you."

It was, after all, winter, even if it was sunny outside, so Marco took his jacket off and spread it on the soft sand.

"Now lie down and take what's coming to you."

Maria smiled, opened her soft creamy thighs and brought her knees up to accommodate her husband's ministrations. He entered her easily and she clung to him telling him how much she loved her husband. They were becoming highly aroused when they heard Miranda's voice calling out, "Yes, yes, yes!"

They smiled at one another a knowing smile and, realising they were not the only naughty couple, were encouraged. Marco instantly redoubled his efforts and he and Maria came together in a sand-shattering orgasm. In his excitement Marco had pulled the top of Maria's dress down and now her plump breasts were fully exposed. In his lust he sucked on them like a greedy suckling pig.

"I love you, wife!"

"Shh! Robert and Miranda might hear us."

Robert and Miranda did indeed hear them.

"Just wait five minutes, Robert, or they'll be embarrassed," whispered Miranda.

"It's all right for you, you're not laying on your back on the bloody cold sand."

"Well, we'll stand up for a couple of minutes but keep still so as not to disturb them."

Robert, now off the sand, felt warmer, so he hugged his wife to him enjoying the softness and warmth of her body.

"Come on, Marco, let's get up before Robert and Miranda find us," whispered Maria.

Marco stood up, brushed his jacket down as best he could and linked arms with Maria and walked back out into the welcome sunlight.

"Pa, pa, look what I have made!" shouted an excited Sanchez.

"We have made, Sanchez!" corrected Max Junior.

"Hold my jacket, Maria," said Marco.

"You boys call that a sandcastle, that's an anthill!"

"Come on, Robert, let's show these lads of ours how to build a fort."

Maria laughed with Miranda, "He's always been a big kid, and Marco has never grown up!"

Dads and sons started to dig in earnest. Robert and Marco gouged out big moats that ran down to the water's edge so that the sea could flow in. Between them they built up a defensive fort two foot high.

"There!" said Marco. "That's a man's castle! Not a kiddie castle."

"Look this way, you lot!" called out Amos. He took their picture with the camera Annette had bought him for Christmas.

The tide, not that it moved much on the Mediterranean, was going out.

"We need more water, chaps!" called out Robert.

"Come on, quick, help me build some channels down to the sea!"

Marco and Robert grabbed a sizeable sharp stone each and gouged out the underlying sand of the gently sloping beach until they were down to a level that allowed the sea water to pour into the dry, waiting moat, around the hill fort.

"Wow! Well done father!" said Max Junior, impressed.

"Your father is more than just a pretty face, son."

"Look at them, Maria, the original 'sand boys'," laughed Miranda.

"I don't know about you lot," said Miranda, "but Maria and I are getting cold in this winter breeze."

"All right, boys, time to go, your mother is right. I know the sun is out, but we are all getting wet and cold, after all it is December."

"Oh father! Do we have to go?"

"Yes, Max, we do. Your grandpa and grandma are also getting very cold in this breeze. Older people feel the cold a lot more than children."

"Well, grandpa could dig, that would make him warmer?" offered Max.

"Sorry, Max, I can't get down on my knees to dig at my age."

"Grandpa, couldn't you have a walking stick?"

"Don't be cheeky, Max! Do you want a clip round the ear?"

"Sorry, father, I thought grandpa might like to build sandcastles with me."

"Come on, boys, put your socks and shoes back on."

"But I've got sand in my toes, pa," said Sanchez.

"Watch me," said Max. "You brush your toes out with your socks, then put your shoes on."

"What about my toes?" asked Miranda.

"Look, wife, you have stockings on, so just brush your feet off."

"Spoil sport!"

"Come here, Maria, I'll do yours," said Marco.

"Everybody ready?" asked Amos.

"Ready, grandpa!"

"Come on then, let's go and see how Rosa and Pedro are getting along."

"And grandma, Meralda?" questioned Sanchez.

"I haven't forgotten, son," said Maria.

Back inside El Estancia, the three senior citizens were playing cards and all in a cheery mood with alcohol-infused red faces and contented smiles.

"Hello you three," said Amos. "Having a good time?"

"*Si*," said Pedro. "A Merry Christmas, Senor Amos."

"Cheers!" smiled Meralda, tipping back the last of the ruby port.

"No wonder they are happy," said Annette, nudging her husband's side with the elbow. "They have drunk all the port."

"Oh well, at least they are happy and there won't be any Christmas drink hanging around, which you usually complain about, Amos."

Robert had a clear head so he would drive Pedro and Rosa back to the village of Sigma. Meralda's family could all stop the night.

"Anybody want to come for a drive?"

"Me! Me!" shouted the boys.

"Come on then, lads, out to the car."

"Senor Robert, I want to sit in the back with Pedro and Rosa as they both are my friendly grandparents."

"That's fine, Sanchez, hop in."

Max sat up front with his father, feeling like a grown up.

The road back up into the hills was deserted, being Christmas Day, as everybody was either staying at home or had gone into the town of Atalia.

Pedro and Rosa thanked Robert for a lovely Christmas Day and said goodbye to Sanchez.

Boxing Day started with early morning sunshine and boys, being boys, were having a pillow fight in Max Junior's bedroom.

"What's all the squealing about?" asked Miranda, "it's only half past seven!"

"Just having a bit of fun, mother."

"Look at the mess, feathers flying everywhere!"

"Sorry, mother."

"Oh, I suppose its only feathers, but play quietly, your father is still asleep."

"I know, Max, let's make tea and toast."

"Tea and toast?"

"Yes, you know, for your parents in the morning."

"I don't normally make tea, mother does that."

"Come on, let's get dressed."

They put the kettle on and Max Junior made a pot of tea for Miranda and Robert. Sanchez put bread in the pop-up toaster.

"Sanchez! Turn it off, you're burning the bread!"

"Oh sorry. My mother usually makes the toast."

"Never mind. Scrape the black off into the rubbish bin and butter it."

"Now what do we do?"

"We'll get some cups, a jug of milk and a dish of sugar for the tea."

"Any butter, Max?"

"Yes, butter for the toast, and Marmite."

"Marmite?"

"Yes, grandfather always brings his own Marmite to El Estancia when he visits Spain."

"Shall we use this tray?" asked Sanchez.

"Yes, and a knife for the Marmite and a teaspoon for the sugar. Now, open the doors, I will carry the tray upstairs."

"O.K. Max."

Max went up the stairs very carefully so as not to overbalance the tray of breakfast things.

"Right, Sanchez, knock on the door."

"Yes, who is it?"

"Me, mother, Max. I have brought you breakfast."

"Oh! All right, come in!"

"Here you are, tea and toast."

"Robert." She shook Robert. "Robert, sit up!"

"What is it?"

"I have brought you tea and toast, father."

"What time is it?"

"Almost eight o'clock, Robert."

"Good God, it's supposed to be Christmas."

"Don't fuss, darling. I caught them at half past seven this morning having a pillow fight, so think yourself lucky you weren't woken earlier."

"Open the curtain, Sanchez, father is only half awake."

"You pests, well at least you have brought Marmite."

"And, Robert, they have wrapped the toast in serviettes the way I do to keep the toast warm."

"All right, son, put the tray down before you spill the tea. Well, you may as well pour the tea out now, now that you have my attention."

"I'm hungry, Max, let's go get ourselves some breakfast," suggested Sanchez.

"O.K. Mother, father, enjoy your breakfast."

Luckily, Max being tall for his eight years could reach the kitchen worktop and took the Cornflakes to the table.

"Sanchez, get the milk out of the refrigerator. Do you want sugar?"

"Yes, let's eat up and go out on our new bicycles."

"Good idea, they are all probably asleep. Let's go down onto the beach and pedal on the sand beside the sea."

"O.K., but we will have to push our bikes down all the steps."

"Coming back up will be a struggle," said Max, "but I'm strong. What about you?"

"Sure, I can do it, it's no big deal," replied Sanchez.

The boys, being boys, bumped their bicycles down the steps, using their brakes so that the bikes didn't run away.

Once on the compacted sand alongside the waterline they set off.

"Race you into the cove!" shouted out Max Junior.

"Let's go into the sea cavern!" said an excited Sanchez.

"But the tide is up?"

"It's only shallow, we can ride through that," encouraged Sanchez.

"O.K. I'm game if you are."

They pedalled on the bottom and headed into the cavern and were soon on dry sand.

"See! I told you it was only shallow," said Sanchez.

"There's nothing here?" said Max, "and it's gloomy and cold out of the sun. "I'll race you back to the beach!"

Max set off first, lifting his feet as the wheels sprayed through the water.

"Come on Sanchez! Slow coach!" shouted Max.

"Coming!" Sanchez pedalled flat out coming down the slope out of the cavern into the sea and hit a bump in the sandy shallows. He lost balance and fell into the seawater. He called out in alarm and Max looked back. He saw Sanchez sat in the shallows trying to lift his bike.

Max Junior thought Sanchez looked so comical that he burst out laughing.

"It's not funny, my shirt and shorts are soaking wet!"

"Come on, stand up!"

"I'm dripping wet and cold!"

"Come here onto the dry sand. Give me your shirt and shorts and I will wring them out."

"I'm cold now."

"Then let's go home. Here you can have my shirt because I have a vest on."

"Thanks. But I feel stupid in my underpants."

"Nobody is looking, we are the only people on the beach. Come on, pedal fast back to El Estancia, that way you will get warm."

They puffed and pushed their bicycles back up the steps.

"Come with me, Sanchez."

"Where are we going?"

"Never you mind, you go and get some dry underpants on, I'm going to make some hot tea."

"What are you doing, the washing?"

"No, silly, this is not a washing machine, it's called a tumble dryer, it's got your shirt and shorts inside. They will be dried in ten minutes because I have set it to hot."

"O.K. Good idea. My mother doesn't have a tumble dryer."

"That's probably because in Spain your mother gets lots of sunny days to dry her clothes on the line."

"Well, it's a jolly good idea. I can feel the hot air from here."

"Yes, you stand where it is warm while I make two cups of tea."

"There you go, dry shirt and shorts."

Sanchez put them on quickly. "Gosh they are warm! Thanks for the loan of your shirt."

"That's O.K., friends are supposed to help one another."

"What are you two up to?"

"Oh hello, mother. Sanchez got wet and I dried his shirt and shorts in the tumble dryer."

"That's why I came down. I heard the tumble dryer going round, through the ceiling. How did he get wet?"

"We went for a bike ride on the beach and Sanchez fell in."

"You went all the way down the steps to the beach?"

"Yes, mother, you were in bed with a sleepy-head father, so we went for a bike ride."

"I suppose that's O.K. but you should tell us in future if you are going out, so that we will know where you are."

"We weren't gone long, mother, anyway grandma and grandpa were fast asleep, so there was nobody to worry."

"What about Sanchez's mother, Maria, she may be worried?"

"My mother trusts me, Mrs Darling. Besides I was with Max, so I was all right."

"Would you like a cooked breakfast of bacon, eggs, beans and toast?"

"Oh, yes please, mother. That would be great, wouldn't it, Sanchez?"

"Yes, Mrs Darling, pedalling makes you hungry, and coming back up the steps is really hard work."

"Sit down then, and while I cook the breakfast I'll put some toast on. Marmite soldiers for my hungry little soldiers."

"Mother, father has the Marmite upstairs."

"Then go and fetch it and bring the tea things down."

There was a crash and a wallop, followed by, "ow!"

"Go and see what he has done, Sanchez?"

"O.K., Mrs Darling."

"Hah, hah, hah! Hah, hah, hah!" laughed Max Junior.

"I missed the step halfway down and the tray and tea things went flying, but nothing is broken."

Sanchez picked up the crockery from the carpet and put it back on the tray.

"Except my neck!" said Max.

"Let's have a look?"

"Ha, ha, ha! You have two tea bags down your shirt. Good job there was no tea left in the teapot or you would have got a soaking."

"What have you broken, Max?"

"Nothing, mother, I even caught the tea bags as the top flew off the teapot."

"If you've ruined the stair carpet with tea stains, grandma will be furious!"

"Honestly, mother, I didn't even mark the new wallpaper."

"Well, never mind, go tell your lazy father, breakfast is ready in two minutes."

"Somebody mention my name?"

"Morning, father."

"Good morning, Mr Darling. What got you up?"

"The smell of bacon cooking, my beloved."

"Don't try getting round me, you can make the tea, at least the teapot is in one piece after Max threw it down the stairs."

"Yes, I heard a calamity, but as it was just Max's voice I took no notice."

"What if he had been hurt?"

"Oh, come on, Miranda, boys will be boys."

"Did you break anything, Max?"

"No, father, absolutely nothing."

"There you go, Miranda, nothing to worry about."

"Men! Always stick together. He could have broken his arm, let alone a flaming teapot. Lot you care."

"Oh, mother, I'm fine. I'm sorry I fell down the stairs. It was an accident, I missed the step."

"See, darling, storm in a teapot."

"Oh ho, very funny. Actually it's a 'storm in a teacup'."

"I know that, where's your sense of humour this morning? I was only joking."

"Something wrong?" asked Marco. "I could hear raised voices?"

"Nothing for you to worry about, Marco, just that Max fell down the stairs."

"Good morning, Marco," said Max.

"Good morning, father," piped up Sanchez.

"Good morning, boys, you're obviously in one piece."

"Yes thank you, father, we went for a ride on the beach on our new bicycles."

"Did you indeed, and how did you get down the steps?"

"Easy, father, we rode down, using the brakes as we went. And then pushed them back up, it was really hard work."

"You haven't punctured the tyres, have you?"

"Oh no, we were very careful."

"No harm done. Marco, breakfast?"

"Yes please! What's on offer?"

"Eggs, bacon, beans and toast."

"Sounds good. I'll hurry up, Maria."

"Right, boys, sit at the table. You and Robert are the first."

"Maria, breakfast in ten minutes!"

"No need to shout. I am up. I just have to go for a wash."

"Wake your mother up Meralda, or she will miss breakfast."

"Mother is asleep, so I will leave her be. She needs her rest now she is starting to show more severe signs of old-age."

"O.K. Maria."

Marco went down to the kitchen.

"Any tea brewing, Miranda?"

"In the pot, help yourself, at least we still have a teapot after Max threw it down the stairs."

"Mother, it was just an accident."

"Take no notice, Max, your mother is pulling your leg," replied Robert.

"Good morning all!" called out Amos, with Annette in tow coming down the stairs. "Everybody sleep all right?"

"Morning, Amos, Maria and I slept very soundly. Your villa is absolutely quiet at night as you have no neighbours."

"Yes, Marco, I enjoy the peace and quiet, but it can be a solitary existence if you are here on your own. A villa, I believe, should have a family in it. Brings the building to life, gives it a homely atmosphere."

"I agree," said Maria coming down the stairs. "A house is just bricks and mortar, a home has people in it."

"O.K. boys, Robert, you have eaten, please vacate the table now for the others."

"Thank you, Miranda."

"That's O.K., Marco, sit down, and you two."

"We obey your commands o'daughter," saluted Amos.

"It's Boxing Day, so what are your plans for today?" asked Miranda.

"How about a drive in the mountains, it's a bright sunny morning?" suggested Amos.

"Fine by me," said Robert. "What about your mother, Maria?"

"I don't know. I'll have a word with her. Pour her a cup of tea, Robert, and I will take it up to her."

"Maria knocked on Meralda's door. There was no response, so Maria went in."

"Mother, mother, wake up! It's me, Maria, it's a lovely day!"

There was no response.

Maria, alarmed, drew back the curtains to let the sun in. Meralda was as white as a sheet. Maria shook her, felt for a pulse on her neck, and she jumped at her touch. She was stone cold.

"Marco! Marco, come quick. It's mother!" screamed Maria.

"Excuse me, Miranda, Maria wants me."

Marco bounded up the stairs two at a time.

"What is it, Maria?"

Marco could see what was wrong...

His wonderful mother-in-law was white as a sheet and her eyes were staring up at the ceiling. Maria flew into Marco's arms and broke down sobbing. "She's dead Marco. Mother's dead."

"Sit on the bed, I'll be back in a minute."

Marco closed Merlada's eyes and pulled the sheet over her face. He rushed downstairs.

"Have you some brandy, Amos, quickly?!"

"Yes, I heard what Maria called out. She's really dead?"

"Yes, must have happened during the night."

"Here, Maria, take this it will help fortify you."

"What is it?"

"Brandy, it's for your nerves, to help with the shock."

"Don't cover her up yet, Marco, I want to remember her just the way she was. Don't let the boys in here."

"I'll ring for the doctor," said Amos. "There must be a death certificate issued."

"What do we want a death certificate for?" asked a numb Maria.

"It's procedure, dear," said Marco. "I think you should come downstairs now."

"No, I want to stay with my mother until the doctor comes," sobbed Maria.

Not much later the doctor from Atalia arrived.

"Hello, Amos, I don't know whether it's appropriate to wish you a happy Christmas."

"Thank you for coming at short notice, I know you are really on holiday."

"A general practitioner is never really on holiday unless he can get away to far flung shores, out of reach."

"I'll come with you."

"Can I ask who you are?"

"I am Maria, this is my mother, Meralda, and this is my husband, Marco."

"Then I am sorry for you, but as you are immediate family, you may stay while I examine her."

"When you found her, were her eyes open or closed?"

"She was staring at the ceiling."

"Well, I have examined your mother, she died of a heart attack, and so that's what I'll put on the death certificate. I'll call the mortuary for you because your mother's body will have to be looked after while you organise the funeral. The mortuary is the best place because the Funeral Directors will be closed with it being a Public Holiday, while the General Hospital of Atalia never shuts."

"Thank you, doctor," said Marco.

"You have nothing to thank me for. I am just doing my duty. This is the Death Certificate. The van from the hospital mortuary will call this afternoon. I would advise that the two boys I saw downstairs are kept away from the body."

"It will be as you say, doctor. Let me show you out."

"Father, is it true grandma has died in bed?" asked Sanchez, unable to take it in.

"I'm afraid so, Sanchez, she was an old lady and she had a heart attack during her sleep. Elderly people sometimes die from heart attacks."

"Can I go and see her to say goodbye?"

"The doctor said you shouldn't because of the shock it may have on you."

"But, father, she was my grandmother and I loved her. I would like to say goodbye before somebody comes to take her away to the graveyard."

"All right. Come with me."

"Maria, Sanchez wants to see his grandmother to say goodbye."

"Come here, Sanchez. See grandmother appears to be asleep, but actually she has gone to heaven now."

"To the Holy Spirit?"

"Yes, Jesus has taken her spirit, this is just her body."

"Have a long sleep, Meralda, goodbye."

"Can I cover her up now, mother?"

"Yes, you can."

"Come on, Maria, come down now. You need a strong cup of tea with plenty of sugar in it," encouraged Marco.

Maria sat in the kitchen, just staring; she was in shock, very white.

"Drink this," said Amos.

"What is it?"

"Medicine, to help you."

Maria drank it like an automaton. She coughed a bit, then some colour appeared in her cheeks.

"A bit better now?"

"How did I get down here?"

"I brought you down, love," supported Marco.

"Perhaps," said Amos, "Maria would like to sit in the rocker on the veranda and relax in the sunshine while she remembers her mother's love."

Marco led Maria, out into the breezy sunshine.

"I'll go and sit with mother," offered Sanchez.

"You're a good boy, Sanchez."

"Meralda was my grandmother as well."

"What do I do next, Amos?" asked a feeling lost Marco.

"Wait for the mortuary van to come and then tomorrow ring the Funeral Directors so that Meralda's body can be placed in a Chapel of Rest, so that any relatives can pay their respects."

"Can I have a brandy, I think I need it?"

"Sure, Marco."

"Annette, take Marco into the lounge and sit with him."

"It helps to talk, Marco, to come to terms with shock, because initially it is unreal, but a little later it sinks in when reality strike home."

"Could you ask, Sanchez, to come and sit with me?"

"Sure, Marco."

"Annette, I think we should give Marco's family solitude, because they will want to grieve in peace. It's best if we go out, to give them 'room'," said Amos.

"Makes sense," said Robert.

"Come on, Max, get your jacket we are going for a drive," instructed Robert.

"Sanchez, you keep an eye on your mother. We will leave you in peace now," said Miranda.

So, Amos and Annette, Robert and Miranda with Max, set off for a day out.

They hadn't driven very far, when Max asked, why do people have to die.

"Everybody who is born has to die sometime, Max, usually when you are old. Meralda was over eighty, which is old, unfortunately her heart got tired and gave up. The doctor said she died peacefully in her sleep. It just happens when you get old."

"I'm never going to be old!" exclaimed Max.

"That's right, son, you are only eight years old, and you have many years to live yet. You have yet to grow up into a fine young man, meet a wife in later years and have, one day, children of your own."

"I don't know if I want children," said Max.

"That's good, Max. First you have to compete your education at André Laceys, that will keep you occupied for about another eight years."

"Eight years? Mother."

"That's right, son, you won't be leaving until you are at least sixteen, unless you stay on and study for 'A' Levels, to gain entry to university, in which case you will be eighteen by then."

"But I'll be a man at eighteen!"

"Spot on, Max, and you will be old enough to buy your father a pint in the local pub," laughed Robert.

"And, father, I will be old enough to vote, to decide who will be elected to Parliament."

"Surely, Max, you are not interested in government?"

"At André Laceys the Senior Boys talk about democracy and voting rights. Politicians have power. The Senior Boys say you are either a leader or a follower. I know what I want to be, a leader. I hate people telling me what to do!"

"I'm afraid, son, society has rules. You have to obey many ways to behave and several bylaws of the council in power, not to mention civil and criminal law enforcement of the Crown."

"The Crown?"

"Yes, Her Majesty's Government, which is made up of appointed Ministers selected from Members of Parliament. The Home Office is in charge of the laws of the United Kingdom."

"Then I think I'll be a law maker or a judge. I definitely don't want to be a policeman because all they do is uphold the law."

"What's wrong with that, clever clogs?"

"Officers just uphold the law, but the Crown Prosecution Service don't win many cases against criminals because they have clever Counsel."

"How do you know such things?"

"Some of my school mates' fathers are barristers and I get told all sorts of stories. There's one law for the rich, who can afford expensive Counsel to get Crown Prosecution's Service cases thrown out, and one law for the poor who cannot afford Counsel. The poor get told to plead guilty and are sent to prison."

"I would have thought the directions of Counsel are confidential. I'm surprised they tell their sons, Max?"

"Oh, I don't get to hear names or details, unless of course it is in the national newspapers. But, father, you get the picture."

"You are far too clever or knowledgeable for your age, son."

"I take after you, father, you are gifted and so is mother."

"But we don't discuss law and order. I paint and your mother is beautiful and famous because of her beauty. That's because Vogue Magazine and Estée Lauder chose your mother to model their products.

"Just enjoy the day out, Max. I have brought you out to take you away from thoughts of death. Sanchez has stayed behind because Meralda is his grandmother. Meralda is not your family and you hardly know her at all, so you don't need to feel sorry for her."

"But Sanchez is my friend, I feel sorry for him."

"Max, Sanchez is just a boy like you, he will soon get over it and go off to school and play football with his friends. But Maria is Meralda's daughter so she will grieve for a lost mother and so will, probably, Marco. They are a different family to us. Now think about us."

"Miranda, shall we stop for a walk on a mountainside trail?"

"Good idea. Max, is your kite still in the boot?"

"Yes, mother."

"Then let's go fly a kite up high," smiled Miranda.

It was breezy, as they were quite high up overlooking the sea far below, and as the wind direction was off the land the kite streamed out over the precipice.

"Don't go too near the edge, Max, I don't want an accident!" called out Robert.

The fresh air, sun and a soaring kite cheered Max up.

""Wow! Father, it's going out over the sea. Can you fetch the other ball of string from the boot of the car, please, father?"

Robert didn't argue, he wanted Max to forget about Meralda. Normally he would have said, 'Don't you think you have enough string out?' So he came back with the extra ball of string.

"I'm at the end of my kite winder now, father."

"Well, wind the string's end round your hand three times while I tie a good knot to the second ball of string."

"Ready, father?"

"Ready, son."

"Hold the ball, father, while I unwind the string from my hand."

"O.K., son, I have it."

"Let me unwind it, please, but you tie the end, when we get to it, to the kite winder."

Max's box kite, which was an old Royal Air Force signal kite that Robert bought from a car boot sale for a pound, was now a speck in the sky.

"Where is it, Max?"

"See where I am pointing?"

"I can't see it?"

"Follow the string up, see where it goes into infinity, there is a small orange speck, that's my kite."

"Blimey, son, sure it won't interfere with the air traffic coming out of Atalia Aero port?"

"I don't think so, but it will have to go a bit higher to get to the end of the ball of string, so I can tie it to the end of the winder."

"If the breeze gets any stronger, Max, it may snap the string."

"Well it makes no difference, it's pulling my arms out of their sockets and I can't see it anyway."

"Right, Max, make three turns around your hand while I tie the end securely to the kite winder. Got it!"

"I can't see it?"

"I can," said Miranda, "it's flying into the sun. It's just a black dot now it's so far away. Now I can't see it."

"I think you had better wind some length in now, Max. I can't see it either."

"Can you pull it down father, while I wind the string in, because it's pulling hard on my hands?"

Together they reeled in about a hundred yards, which was about halfway down the second ball of string, and then the orange kite came clearly into view.

"Can we go, Robert, it's all very well you two boys playing kites on a mountainside but I'm getting cold in this breeze," said Miranda.

"Just give us time to wind this kite down, love, and then we can stop at one of the little roadside cafés."

"Can I have something to eat?" asked Max.

"Something to eat?" asked Miranda. "You've only just had breakfast."

"That was ages ago, mother. I'm hungry. It's all this wind."

"What do you want?"

"A big pile of beans on toast."

"O.K., son, if that's what you want."

"I'm going to wait in the car, Robert, I'm getting cold."

"Right, Max, start winding faster, your mother's getting cold."

Miranda got back into the car, revved the engine up and put the heater fan on full blast.

"It's warm in here, Miranda."

"It's only just warming up, it's cold out there."

"Give us a cuddle, darling, I'll soon warm you up."

"Oh, father, don't be soppy, you're not going to start kissing her again?"

"Let's get one thing straight, young man, it is not soppy to show affection to someone you love very much, and I love your mother. One day, when you are a grown man, you too will have a girlfriend."

"Yuk! Girls are soppy!"

Robert let Miranda drive, it was after all her car, or rather Amos's rental car, but for Miranda's use.

They pulled up at a café with a Coca Cola sign swinging in the breeze, and though the sign squeaked on its rusty fittings nobody came to serve them.

"Father, it's closed."

"They have probably gone away for Christmas," said Robert.

"Go on, Miranda, drive on to the next café."

"O.K., darling, but it will be a while because this side of the mountain is in the shade, and during winter I want to be in the sun," smiled Miranda.

Now the breeze had almost stopped and around the next bend was a whitewashed building under a red tile roof where three cars were parked out front.

"This place is open, mother, pull in please."

They sat on the veranda and the waitress came across.

"Hello, young man, what can I get for you?" smiled a schoolgirl of about fourteen, wearing a waitress's pinafore and lace cap.

Max felt embarrassed with her yes boring into him and he flushed red, face and neck.

He blurted out, "Beans on toast!"

"Yes, sir, beans-on-toast, and to drink?"

"Coca Cola, please."

"You speak very good English, senorita?" queried Miranda.

"That's because I am not really a waitress, I am on holiday with my parents for Christmas."

"What do you do then?" asked Max.

"I am a student at a girls' school in London, England."

"Oh don't you like Spain then?"

"Oh no, I like Spain, but my parents want more for me than to just work in a café. I am going to be a lawyer when I grow up and I'll be successful and rich."

"You must be jolly clever."

"Well, actually I go to a special school for gifted children."

"Oh, so do I," said Max Junior. "I go to a boys' special school, called André Laceys."

"My school is the Convent of St Anne, of course just for girls, but the nuns are very clever and we have selected teachers who come in to teach music and drama."

"Lucky for you. Then I am pleased you are our waitress. What's your name?"

"My name is Suzy."

"That's a nice name, isn't it, mother?"

"Yes, son. Suzy, I would like a large cup of boiling hot coffee and a tea for Robert."

"Thank you, madam, straight away."

They sat out in the winter sun sheltered from the breeze.

"Lovely and warm now," said Miranda, taking her winter coat off.

"Well, some days winter in Spain can be cold."

"Not really, not on the Costa del Sol. It can be a little cool with, of course, rain on some days but rain is essential in the winter because in the summer millions of tourists flock to the tourist destinations and they all need water for the hotels."

"Where, father, does all the water come from in a hot summer?"

"Oh, that's ground water, Max. The ground has a natural water table, which is to say, there is an underground well of water between the top pervious layer of rock and the bottom impervious layer."

"So the rainwater from the interior mountains drains through the soft ground and is trapped by the hard rock beneath?"

"Spot on, Max, couldn't have put it better myself."

Max as usual had a Coke with a straw in a bottle and, as usual, he sucked the straw flat.

"Can I have another Coke, mother?"

"Of course, son, but ask for a glass, you make such a lot of slurping sounds with a straw."

"Hey, Suzy! Another Coke, please."

"Straight away, young sir."

Now Max, for the first time in his life, took notice of a girl. She had shiny hair, a smiley face and actually had breasts like his mother. She also had a short skirt and lovely slim tanned legs.

"My name's Max. Max Junior actually."

"Pleased to meet you, Max Junior," curtsied Suzy with a huge appreciative smile and a toss of her long auburn hair.

"I like you," said Max.

"Well thank you, young sir," teased Suzy.

Max became flustered, stood up, and took Suzy's hand and kissed it.

"I'm afraid, Max, tall as you are, and me short in stature, you're far too young to make eyes at me," smiled Suzy, kindly.

"Oh, er, all right, but I still like you."

Suzy laughed and went back inside to her parents.

"Mother, she laughed at me, I feel such a fool."

"Don't worry, Max, when you are older several girls may capture your heart. You're far too young to worry about such things.

Suzy is a teenager and teenagers flirt, it's part of growing up, becoming a woman."

"And boys becoming men, mother?"

"Yes and boys becoming men."

"Suzy is the first girl I have ever noticed."

"That's because you are far too young to notice girls, boys don't normally notice girls until puberty."

"What's puberty, mother?"

"Oh dear, you tell him, Robert."

Me?"

"Yes, you, you're his father."

"He's too young to know."

"What am I too young to know, father?"

"Sex, son. As you grow older you develop hormones in your blood which wakes up your sexuality, so you become interested in girls."

"Oh sex, I know what that is, yuk! It's how babies are made, all boys know that!"

"So you know about girls, Max?"

"Of course. I'm not a man yet, so I don't need to bother about girls."

"I'm glad, Max," said a relieved Robert.

"You got out of that one easily, darling."

"No help from you, I noticed."

"You, Robert, were doing so well on your own."

"Here, young sir," flirted Suzy, "a Coke in a man's glass." She laughed outrageously and threw her head back.

Max laughed with her. He didn't know what he laughed at but Suzy's whole demeanour was infectious, so he just laughed out loud, with much relief to both parents.

"That cheeky miss is having the time of her life," whispered Miranda into Robert's ear.

"She is going to break many a boy's heart," smiled Robert. "But she is likeable. I would like a daughter like her."

"Sorry, Robert, I have tried hard, as you know, I can't have any more children."

"I know, love, Christ knows I have enjoyed myself trying. I was just thinking out loud. How about adoption, I mean a girl like Suzy would be great to adopt."

"I haven't thought about it, but you can't just decide you want somebody else's child, Robert."

"They have Adoption Agencies, don't they?"

"Well, that's true, but I think you have to put your name down and wait to be selected. The agency chooses the parents not the other way round."

"But we could adopt a girl, a companion for Max?"

"Father, I am a boy. If you must adopt then it must be a brother for me. I would like a brother, he could be my best friend. We could play football together or cricket if he's a good bowler."

"I'll think about it, Max."

"Well, one thing, father, if you buy me a brother you won't have to do any more of that disgusting sex with mother."

"That's private, son, between your mother and me."

"Well, you are noisy sometimes, I can hear it through the bedroom wall, especially mother screaming."

Miranda blushed. "That's only because I love your father, Max. When a man and a woman get married it's not just for sex it's because they love one another. You'll understand when you are older."

"Can I have a packet of crisps, please?"

"Hungry again? Go and ask Suzy, you would like her as a friend, wouldn't you?"

"I feel embarrassed, she laughs at me."

"Not at you, but with you. She just enjoys being happy, so laugh with her, Max."

Max sat on a bench seat and shared his crisps with Suzy. She made him feel happy.

"Would you like an ice cream?" asked Max. "I have some pocket money. How much are they?"

"One Euro, fifty cents."

"That's O.K. That's about a Pound in English. Here, three Euros, fetch two please."

So Suzy and Max chatted on a bench in the sun while they ate their Cornettos. They waved their arms a lot, laughed a lot and swung their legs while they were sat.

"Well, thank you for talking to me, I have to go now, it was fun meeting you."

"You're a funny little man," said Suzy, she bent down and kissed him on the cheek.

Max flushed bright red.

"Goodbye, Max, have a nice day!" and she skipped indoors, back to her parents.

"Come on, Max, let's go before she asks you to marry her."

"She wouldn't dare!"

"Girls can be very grown up, Max, and very persuasive with their womanly ways." Robert winked at Miranda.

"Right, it's time we went," said Max, heading decisively for the car.

Miranda drove for a while in silence, just enjoying the scenery.

"Do you understand a bit about girls now, Max?" asked Robert.

"Yes, father, I think they use their bodies to get their own way with boys."

"Very smart of you, Max, you are learning quickly. So, as you grow up, watch out for girls' wily ways. They are a bit crafty. They usually get what they want by flaunting their womanly charms."

"Let's change the subject, Robert, Max is only a young school boy."

"Hey, mother, I am going on nine. I am a Junior School Boy now, like my name – Max Junior."

"Don't be in a hurry to grow up, adulthood brings responsibilities, and mostly they are about money and children. Money is all about working your backside off and the cost of living, the most expensive being the cost of a mortgage when you buy your first house, and children are all about setting moral codes of behaviour, to make sure they have a correct upbringing."

"When I get back to England after the holiday, I will go tree climbing with David Braun, my friend of Lower Dale and back at André Laceys School play football with Percy because, as you know, he's the captain of the Junior School Eleven. I'll have a jolly good time and I won't even see any soppy girls. Girls want to kiss you, yuk!"

"That's right, son you stick to your playmates. What will you do when you get back home?"

"Father, I think I'll go fishing in the woods with my friend David. Captain Percy will show me and David the best places to fish."

Amos and Annette had been quiet up to now, letting Max give free flow to his feelings so as not to dwell on the death of Meralda.

"I think, Miranda," said Amos, "we have been away a respectful amount of time, shouldn't we return?"

"Amos, I don't think three hours is long enough for Maria to have got over the initial shock. Marco and Maria need more time," said Robert. "So I propose we go into Atalia as a whole family and celebrate Christmas, after all, Meralda's family is not our family. They are, if truth be told, only strangers to us. We only know Meralda through Maria, and Maria is actually your maid, Amos."

"True, how about, grandson Max, we celebrate Boxing Day in Atalia with other happy children?"

"Good idea, grandpa!"

"That's more like it, Max, young boys should enjoy the Christmas holiday."

"Driver, to Atalia."

"Right away, father," smiled Miranda, and she made a mocking salute.

To their surprise Atalia was crowded with happy families. Children ran around outside roadside and pavement cafés and bars displaying their new Christmas presents. Children laughed, and grandparents were jolly. Loud Christmas music was playing and parents were drinking and whole families were singing along to the music.

The sales had also started so the big stores were busy with bargain hunters looking for the best discounts.

Outside a café bar a family stood up to leave their table.

"I like it here, Amos," said Annette. "Let's bag that table quickly."

"Yes!" exclaimed, Max. "They have ice cream!"

"Good evening, Senor, Senora, you would like to eat?"

"First of all, I would like a bottle of brandy and a bottle of your best Atalia red wine," said Amos.

"Are we celebrating?" asked Annette.

"Of course! It is the Christmas holidays after all."

"Thank you, father. But why brandy?"

"To fortify ourselves and to bring a glow to our cheeks."

"I don't really like brandy, father," said Miranda.

"In that case would you like it with sweet coffee?"

"Yes please, father."

"To us!"

Amos, Annette and Robert downed a good measure of brandy."

"That's better," said Amos.

"Perhaps you are right, Miranda, you are after all our driver, but you can have a couple of glasses of wine."

"What about me, grandfather?"

"Max, I will order you a large non-alcoholic cocktail, how's that?"

"Depends what it is?"

The waiter was opening the bottle of wine and listening in."

"I will bring the boy a surprise cocktail, with an umbrella, a straw and a stirrer."

"May I suggest," offered Amos, "a table spread with Spanish tappas? My treat!"

"That's the best idea you have had today, Amos!" congratulated Robert.

The waiter brought Spanish sausages, spiced meatballs, spicy chicken, minted lamb and garlic and spinach fillet steak.

"Would you like some vegetables, Senor?"

"Yes, two dishes of sauté potatoes and some lightly cooked courgettes, both lightly spiced with garlic. And another bottle of red wine."

"*Si*, Senor."

White Christmas was playing over the speakers:

"I'm dreaming of a White Christmas..." sang Amos, and Annette joined in.

"Come on you two, join in," urged Amos.

With the wine flowing, both Miranda and Robert were relaxed and so the rusty voice of Robert sang out, accompanied by the sweet soprano of Miranda,

Max just listened, a big smile spread across his face as he realised how lucky he was to have such loving parents and grandparents.

"Here you are, young man, a special cocktail."

"Wow!" A large glass with a curly straw in, a parrot-shaped stirrer and to top it a real live sparkler. It was coloured red with green and orange in the bottom like sandwich fillings.

"O.K. everybody, get stuck in!" said Amos.

"What about knives and forks?" asked Max.

"Use your fingers, Max, eat alfresco, Spanish style. Tuck in. Enjoy yourselves. Half of the fun is licking the tasty sauces off your fingers."

"O.K. grandpa."

Max made for the sausages and one followed the other. He wiped his fingers on the serviettes provided for the purpose.

"Hey! Hollow legs, don't pig all the sausages, eat some courgettes as well!" scolded Robert.

"Sorry, father, they are delicious. I'm going to try the spicy meatballs next," smiled, Max.

"Everything to your liking, Senor?" asked the waiter.

"Yes, splendid, but another portion of spicy sausages, please, for my grandson."

"He is a growing boy, eh, always hungry?"

"Yes, he takes a lot of filling up."

"I have also a son, about the same age as your grandson, he also is always hungry."

"Young man, your sausages will be five minutes, O.K.?"

"Thank you, they are very yummy."

"Now, Max, eat some potatoes, you can't have just meat, everything has to be shared."

"O.K. father. I like potatoes anyway."

"I think Max likes anything you can eat."

"No, father, actually, at André Laceys I don't like swede, it's disgusting! Or turnips."

"Well, I'm with you there, Max. I didn't like swede at school either. Have you tried sugar beet from a farmer's field, that's a slightly sweeter root crop?"

"No father, at André Laceys we are not allowed in the surrounding fields, they are out-of-bounds to all pupils."

"Oh well, I suppose in my day it wasn't seen as a crime to pinch a root crop from a farmer's field, but today with intensive farming things are different."

"I've had sweet potatoes at school, they are quite nice. The cook says they are very nutritious and come from Africa and South America where it's warmer."

Some more spicy sausages and meatballs arrived. Amos, Robert and Max dived on them.

"Anyone would think I didn't feed you," said Miranda.

"Boys will be boys," teased Annette. "Let them eat up, after all Amos said it was his treat."

"But they should eat more vegetables," said Miranda.

"Well, they have courgettes, but I don't think men are really into vegetables, whereas us ladies have to watch our figures," pointed out Annette.

"Amos eats vegetables," said Mirada. "I've watched him."

"True, but Amos didn't used to watch his diet until the doctor warned him about getting a fatty liver."

"How do you know he has a fatty liver?" asked Miranda.

"Because he went for his five year check-up and the doctor took a blood sample. The results showed he ate too much red meat and pastry and cakes, and his alcohol intake was too high. Now Amos has come off the whisky and brandy except at times of celebration, like now, but the doctor said he could have one to two glasses of red wine a day, because the wine contains antioxidants which are good for the blood."

"Do you hear that, Robert, cut out the spirits and keep to the wine," explained Miranda.

"And, young man, that means you can have half to one glass a day of red wine and no more, even if we allow you to have a spritzer. O.K.?"

"That's all right, mother, I don't drink alcohol, unless you give me a little," smiled Max, through a mouthful of spicy meatballs.

"You had better not, young man."

"Waiter, a bottle of soda water please."

"Right away, Senora!"

"There you are, Max, half a glass of red wine topped up with soda."

"Thank you, mother. But I still prefer Coca Cola."

The three men were like dogs bolting their food. It was like a race to see who could clean out the dishes the fastest.

"Lovely that," said Amos, wiping his sauce covered fingers on a napkin.

"I agree," supported Robert. "Just needs washing down with a glass or two of red wine."

"Burp! Sorry, mother, I've got wind."

"I'm not surprised, Max, the rate you ate at. Serves you right if you get severe indigestion."

"I'm fine, mother, but could I have another fruity cocktail, please?"

"You'll have to ask grandad, he's in charge of the ordering."

"No need to ask, Max. I don't mind you having a non-alcoholic cocktail, it's better for you than red wine."

"Thanks, grandpa."

Other customers around adjoining tables were in good voice singing Christmas songs. They were English well known tunes and some customers were singing in English and others in Spanish, but all understood and there was a general Christmas atmosphere of happiness and well-being.

Robert got up and invited Miranda to dance on the pavement. Amos and Annette did likewise. Both couples were applauded by the general assembly and then an announcement was made in English over the speakers inviting everybody to dance. Foreign tourists and Spanish holidaymakers alike rose from their tables and swayed to the soul of Frank Sinatra.

The café owner announced there was now a festival on the waterfront, if they would care to go down onto the promenade.

"What's a festival, father?" asked Max.

"I'm not sure," replied Robert, "but it's where people normally enjoy themselves. Let's go and see."

The crowds from the surrounding bars and cafés all congregated on the promenade. There was music and colourful dancers, followed by dramatic fire-eaters.

"Why doesn't the man burn, father. I mean he's covering his arms with flames?"

"He's a professional fire-eater, Max, he's clever. I don't want to see you attempting that it's dangerous."

"No way, I wouldn't do that!"

Then there was a whoosh, whoosh, whoosh, as rockets flew into the blackness of the night, followed by loud bangs as colours exploded into the heavens.

"Gosh, father, that's brilliant!"

Brilliant it was. All along the Bay of Atalia there were fireworks going off. The sky was momentarily lit by a whole prism of colours only to quit the black void before another volley of colours lit the night sky. The finale was a burning Merry Christmas display slung between two high lampposts.

There was a round of general applause, followed by an announcement:

"Senor, Senoras, ladies and gentlemen, please take your partners for the dancing. Merry Christmas!"

Everybody danced, even the children. A young girl, also English, asked Max to dance.

"I don't know if I can dance," said Max.

"Well, let's have a try," said Jenny. "It's quite easy really, just listen to the music."

"O.K. I'll try," said Max.

"Good, my name's Jenny, what's yours?"

"Just call me Max."

"I like that," said Jenny, "sounds like a real man's name."

"How old are you, Jenny?"

"Just turned ten. How about you?"

"Eight, well nearly nine actually."

"I though you were about ten or eleven. You are really big for just eight."

"Um, I'm nearly nine. You don't mind if I'm younger than you, do you?"

"Of course not. Everybody here is grown up, or just too young for me. You seem about right for me."

"Good, Jenny, we can be dancing friends."

"O.K., but I need a drink."

"Come with me, my grandad is good at drinks."

"Grandad Amos, this is my friend, Jenny. Could we have a drink please?"

At the back of the promenade the waterfront cafés were busy with waiters bringing drinks to the tables.

"Annette, we have a visitor, this young lady is dancing with our Max. They would like a drink, and therefore we had better bag a table."

"O.K. Amos."

"Grandad, can we have two of your special cocktails?"

"Would you like a cocktail, Jenny?"

"Yes please!"

"Waiter, two non-alcoholic cocktails for the children, with a sparkler in."

"Right away, Senor!"

"What about your parents, shouldn't you tell them where you are?"

"We'll go and tell them quickly, grandpa, won't we, Jenny?"

"Sure we will."

"Mummy, daddy, I'm having a cocktail at the table with my new friend Max, is that O.K.?"

"Sure, honey, we are keeping an eye on you, but don't go anywhere where we can't see you."

And so there was, during Amos's and Annette's Christmas vacation, Meralda's funeral and, Amos being the gentleman that he was, especially with Maria being in his employ, held the wake for a select few at El Estancia.

Max said goodbye to Sanchez, as he had to go back to his mother Maria's house in Sigma, and the holiday was soon over and Robert, Miranda and Max flew back to England, leaving Amos and Annette to holiday-on in Spain. It was, after all said and done, Amos's villa.

Chapter Eleven

The great metal bird hung lead grey in an early January sky as it descended towards the approach of Heathrow Airport. Then there were yards and yards of grey tarmac flashing by as the jet set down with a thump as the undercarriage made contact with the runway. The plane shuddered as the captain applied the reverse thrust of the huge Boeing engines. Then she was taxiing towards the terminal building.

"Oh, mother, what a miserable homecoming," sighed Max, looking out of his porthole at the wind driven rain.

Miranda looked out, the sky hung heavy with black foreboding thunder clouds and she saw the odd strike of fork lightning flash down from the dreary heavens.

"This is your captain speaking, welcome back to Heathrow, London, it's three degrees centigrade outside and there is a strong crosswind. Thank you for flying with us and have a nice day."

"Well, it was a reasonably smooth flight considering the winter weather we ran into," said Robert.

"What about the turbulence over the Pyrenees, Robert? I spilt my coffee," complained Miranda.

"That was just bad timing, and anyway most of it spilt into your food tray, so no harm done."

"I'll be glad to stand up and stretch my legs," said Robert.

"It was only a short haul flight, Robert. Just under two and a half hours."

"If we hadn't run into a stiff headwind it would have been two hours as scheduled. It's all right for you, you have spare legroom, I'm over six foot and my knees get squashed into the seat in front."

When they appeared pulling cases into the Arrivals Hall Max, Teddy Rosenburgh's chauffeur, met them.

"Welcome home, Robert, Miranda and young Max Junior!"

"What are you doing here, Max?"

"Sorry, Mr Darling, sir, Teddy Rosenburgh sent me, said I was to take you straight away to The Arch, he has a contract for you. My instructions are to take you straight there, and then take Mrs Darling, Max Junior and the luggage to The Block, so that you can settle in."

"He doesn't own me. Bloody cheek!"

"Mr Rosenburgh said you would be angry, so to show goodwill, he has given me this £10,000 advance for you."

"What the hell is he up to, he can't dictate my life?"

"Just following orders, Mr Darling, sir. Mr Rosenburgh said if you were not interested then he would not be offended if you gave the £10,000 back."

"£10,000, Robert, take it."

"Would you mind sleeping at The Block tonight?"

"Of course not, and it would be a first for Max Junior"

"How do you fancy sleeping in Knightsbridge tonight, Max Junior?"

"Cool, mother! I have never seen father's London studio."

"O.K., Max, you can tell your boss I'll be with him shortly."

Max phoned ahead. Teddy Rosenburgh was delighted.

"Teddy says, Mr Robert, sir, dinner tonight is on him in the West End, he's already booked a table."

"O.K. Max. Bloody cheek of the man."

"Let's get to the car," said Robert, "before I change my mind."

"I have a trolley right here, Mr Darling."

They got in the car and Max whisked them away.

"Did you have a nice Christmas holiday, Max Junior?"

"Yes thank you, Max. I had a new bright red bicycle for Christmas but of course I had to leave it behind."

"A bit big for an aeroplane seat, huh?"

"Oh, very funny. I could have put it in the cargo hold but father said that would make it an expensive bike and, anyway, how would I get it home in a car?"

"Good point, Max Junior, so you left it at your grandpa's house?"

"Sure, but how did you know?"

"A good chauffeur needs to know about his clients."

"Oh, I didn't know that."

It was a Friday evening and the traffic around Heathrow Airport was very busy but, Max, an expert driver in and out of London, made it look easy as he nipped in and out of lanes of traffic.

At traffic lights an illegal immigrant, a 'bucket boy', tried to wash Max's windscreen. Max laid on the horn and then slid the driver's window down silently and gave the unsuspecting young man a squirt with foaming de-icer. The immigrant swore, the lights changed and Max drove on, laughing.

"Do you get many of them?" asked Robert from the front passenger seat.

"They are getting more and more. Street immigrants now sell flowers, newspapers and drugs."

"Drugs, openly on the street?"

"Well, they are desperate if they do not have a work permit. The profits outweigh the risk of being caught by the police. I keep a can of de-icer handy whatever the weather."

"Are they dangerous?"

"Some are. They wait at traffic lights pretending to sell flowers and when the lights turn red a hammer suddenly appears from within the bunch of flowers, the passenger window is broken and the unsuspecting lady driver looses her handbag."

"And they get away with it?"

"When your car is trapped in a queue of traffic you can't follow the culprit. He is long gone before the shocked driver gets out of the car. And if she gets out she immediately causes a traffic jam and there are a lot of irate drivers behind you."

"Bloody hell, despicable criminals!" said an affronted Robert.

"I'm afraid it's a sign of the times. The gap between wealthy and poor is ever growing, and so the immigrants take a chance on getting rich quick."

At the roundabout exiting the access roads to and from Heathrow was a queue. A young black man suddenly appeared in front of the limousine. Max hit the horn and jerked the car forward, and the young black was almost run over. He jumped sideways spilling his half filthy bucket of water.

"Get out of the road!" shouted Max, and waved his fist at the culprit.

"Shouldn't be any more trouble now," said Max, "we are clear of the airport perimeter now."

"Why don't the police do something about it?"

"These young lads think on their feet, literally. By the time they have been reported by a motorist they are long gone. They are very elusive and, anyway, even if they are arrested they have no money so they can't pay any fines imposed by a magistrate."

"But bobbies on foot, on the beat, could catch them?"

"It's all about cost, Robert. Greater London has a population of ten million. The police have bigger fish to fry. For example, organised crime: gambling rackets, money laundering from the drugs trade and illegal prostitution, to name but a few."

"I didn't realise, Max, London was such a hot bed of vice."

"Afraid so, and with hundreds of thousands of migrants from the east, and large numbers of illegal immigrants, the problem is getting worse. Fortunately, affluent areas with a good reputation, like Knightsbridge and Kensington, are free of scrounging and illegal immigrants."

Max parked up outside The Arch, gallery in Teddy Rosenburgh's private space.

"O.K. Mr Darling, sir, this is your destination for now. Mr Rosenburgh will be waiting for you."

"What about Miranda and Max Junior?"

"I'll whisk them away to The Block where they will be safe and return for you later, Mr Robert, sir."

"See you later, darling."

"Bye Max, hope its something worth the trouble, dear."

"Hello, Robert, excuse Max hijacking you from Heathrow Airport, my instructions you understand."

"This had better be good?"

"Of course. I didn't want you disappearing to Rose Cottage in Lower Dale. I need you in Knightsbridge."

"What's on offer?"

"I have some influential Americans coming across the Atlantic in just under a week's time. They are big spenders, and I want at least two of your portraits of Miranda in The Arch. Could be up to a million."

"Pounds?"

"Sure. Pounds Sterling. So what do you say?"

"I'm interested, but what's in it for me?"

"That's what I like about you, Robert, always straight to the point. You paint and I display in my gallery works of top artists. As you know my terms are a straight twenty percent, and you could net anything from half a million to eight hundred thousand. Sound good?"

"I'm already a reasonably rich man, money doesn't interest me that much, I paint because it is my gift."

"But you will be promoting Miranda. You know, the kind of thing, 'Virgin's Blush' and the face of Vogue."

"Virgin's Blush is Miranda's private trademark, you cannot use that."

"Sorry, I am just pointing out the merchandising spin-offs from the gallery and the publicity in the national newspapers. Miranda is hot property, not just in London and Paris but across the pond in the United States of America."

"You mean, Miranda, is going international?"

"Sure. New York. If she can make it there then she can make it anywhere. New York is one of the fastest growing cities in the Western hemisphere. It will, in coming years, increase to a population of twenty million, that's a super city."

"How long have I got?"

"Just six days, commencing in the morning to produce two portraits. Can you do it?"

"It's physically possible but I'll have to work day and night and Miranda will have to pose for me for a lot of hours. What about Max Junior, what do I do with him?"

"I have thought about that, Max my chauffeur has two young sons, he is prepared to integrate Max Junior into his family. Is it a deal? I can make you a rich man, infamous as the husband of the Face of Vogue!"

"So Max will look after Max Junior during the day while Miranda poses for me and, in the evening while I am working, Miranda will have Max Junior?"

"Sure, we can crack two birds with one stone, and by Sunday the exhibition of my selected artists will be ready. On Monday you can go home to Lower Dale. Does it sound O.K. for a week of your undivided time?"

"All right I'll do it, but why couldn't you tell me on the phone?"

"Because I didn't want you to be swayed by your wife or child. As the artist it has to be your decision."

"Can I go home now?"

"Let's go for a drink first to celebrate the deal. Max will pick you up in the limousine later and take you to dinner at my expense."

The two men shook hands and minutes later Max arrived.

"Good evening, Mr Darling sir," said Yan Chong, the owner of The Red Lantern. "Your wife and child are waiting for you. Please follow me. May I take your coat?"

"I like it in here, father, these red lantern lights make it kind of mysterious."

"It's Chinese Max, it's a sushi restaurant. The big fish you see in the tanks and the giant lobsters scuttling around in the bottom are to be chosen for cooking."

"Are we ready to order?" asked Yan Chong. "Mr Rosenburgh says it is on the house, so you may choose whatever you like."

"What would you recommend, Yan?"

"Well, whole lobster is delicious, Mr Robert sir."

"Have you ever had lobster, Max?"

"I don't think so, father, but anything will be delicious, I'm starving."

"Fine, Yan, we will have lobster."

"Good choice, and while you are waiting a basket of prawn crackers made with real prawn sauce. I notice your son is hungry, would he like some soft noodles? While the chef is cooking your lobster I will see you have a dish each of chicken and sweet corn soup and a side order of bean sprouts and soft noodles."

"Thank you, Yan."

"May I recommend our Chinese wine, it is fermented from rice and diluted with fruit juice to give it a light, natural, refreshing taste, so it comes in fruit flavours. A little can be drunk by children because it is only 6-8% alcohol."

"Do you have lemon fruit Chinese wine?"

"Of course, Mr Robert, sir."

"Li Ching, lemon wine for our guests."

"At your service, Mr Chong."

"Would you like to taste first, sir?"

"Li Ching, relax, just call me Robert. This is my wife Miranda and my young son Max."

"Mr Robert, your wife is beautiful."

"Thank you, Li Ching," smiled Miranda. "You also are beautiful, are you married?"

"No, but I am making eyes at Yan Chong, he is a very nice man, most respectable. I would like him to be my husband."

"Yan Chong is not married?"

"He has two daughters from his marriage but he is now divorced. I hope to be lucky to be wife number two."

"Very nice wine, Li Ching, you may leave the bottle."

"No, I must pour, it is my duty to a man, otherwise Mr Chong will be angry with me."

"O.K. pour away, Li Ching."

The lobsters were delicious and, to finish off, Max had jelly and lemon flavour ice cream.

"Now, Robert, tell me what the urgency is with Teddy Rosenburgh at The Arch?"

"That's wonderful, Robert, for that money I'll pose standing on my head. And for just one week's work?"

"Yes, I only have six days. We start work in the morning and Max Junior, apparently, is going to be entertained by Max the chauffeur's two boys."

"Teddy Rosenburgh must be making a lot out of this?"

"Somewhere approaching two hundred thousand, apparently he has some billionaires flying in. Oil men from Texas, who are connoisseurs of oil paintings, especially nude portraits of the world's most beautiful women."

"Sounds like they cannot own all the beautiful women in the world, so they capture them on canvas so that they are always at their most alluring beauty."

"What the old fashioned call, dirty old men," laughed Robert.

"For a cool million pounds, I am prepared to pose for a nude portrait any week of the year."

"Oh no you are not, you are my wife. Let's keep this Teddy Rosenburgh contract strictly professional. You are for me only."

"Jealous husband?"

"Those tycoons may look at your portrait, but I, your husband am the only person who can look at you in the flesh."

"Protecting my virtue, darling?" teased Miranda.

"You have come a long way since our first meeting in Spain when you were a tender twenty-three, grieving widow and a bag of bones."

"Yes, darling, I know, and I love you for it. Shall we go?"

"Mr Robert, sir, Miranda, Mr Rosenburgh said I was to call Max to have you escorted home safely. I'll ring now," said Mr Chong.

"We can call a taxi, Yan, don't worry."

"No, no, no, I promised Mr Rosenburgh, Max would chauffeur you home, he considers you a valuable client, sir."

"Very well, Yan, may we have our coats, please?"

"Li Ching, coats please."

"Father, Max is here."

"Already?"

"Good night, Mr Robert, sir, thank you for patronising The Red Lantern. Madam, young sir."

"Right young man, bedtime, you've had a very long day, which started in Spain this morning."

"Oh, father, do I have to. Can't I look out your studio glass walls at the lights of London a bit longer?"

"No, Max Junior, you can't. If you are not prepared to behave yourself it's straight back to Lower Dale for you and no fun with chauffeur Max's boys tomorrow."

"Yes father, good night, mother."

"Drink, Miranda?"

"Chocolate night cap for me, no alcohol. If I am to pose for hours in the morning I want a really restful night's sleep."

"For me, an Irish coffee, it helps me sleep because it gives me a warm glow. Plenty of work in the morning. But first of all come here, wife."

"I know that glint in your eye."

"Oh, temple, I worship you."

"You're just a letch, darling."

"I don't hear you complaining, lover."

"What if Max walks in?"

"He's completely whacked, how he stayed awake to eight o'clock I don't know. He had an early start this morning. He won't disturb us."

"You rude bugger, I'm nearly naked."

"That's the idea. Just stand in front of the fire, while I admire you and caress you all over."

"You could at least undress yourself."

"No. I want you at a disadvantage, vulnerable, I enjoy you that way."

Robert took her bikini bottoms off and sucked her until she came.

"Come down her on the sheepskin."

"Now it's my turn to undress you. Come on get your shoes off and your trousers."

Miranda's body excited Robert that much was plain to see. He put her on top and lowered her down gently while she guided him in.

In front of the fire they made love. Robert found it more exciting on the lounge floor because he thought it was more daring.

They cuddled together enjoying the mutual afterglow of satisfying sex, until they felt cool and Robert had regained his steady breathing. Miranda cuddled up to his manly hairy chest and listened to the steady beat of his heart.

"Come on, darling, let's go to bed, we have an early start in the morning."

Max Junior slept soundly in the guest bedroom. He enjoyed the luxury of the double bed with its heavy winter goose-down quilt. He awoke full of beans and went down to the kitchen in the hunt for food. He found the tin opener and the bread. Even Max could manage beans on toast. He put the kettle on while his toast was cooking. He heated the beans in the microwave for a couple of minutes, and then had the brainwave to make his parents a cup of tea. He organised a tray of cups, milk and sugar. He nipped to the toilet but forgot about the toaster, it was strange one to him and he wasn't sure of the controls. He came back to the kitchen and blue smoke was pouring out of the toaster. He switched it off, but not in time because the smoke detector went off making a high pitched screaming noise.

The alarm alerted Robert and Miranda who thought the house was on fire. They dashed downstairs to find the kitchen half filled with smoke.

"Max! What's happening?"

"It's the toaster, the toast caught fire. I have turned it off but I don't know how to open the window."

Above the worktop Robert opened the extraction hood and switched the fan to full speed, the smoke was quickly drawn out and the smoke alarm stopped.

"Mother, you haven't got any clothes on!" shouted Max.

"Sorry, Max, I'll be back in a minute."

"And me, son, don't touch the toaster."

Max instead made a cup of tea.

"Why didn't you wait for us, Max?"

"I was hungry. I'm sorry I burnt the toast, mother."

"It doesn't matter. The important thing is there wasn't a real fire."

"At least the smoke detector works," said Robert. "Well done, Max, at least you kept your head and turned the toaster off. No harm done."

"You got us up, Max, that's a great alarm clock. Your father has to start painting this morning anyway and you, Max, are being collected by Max the chauffeur at nine o'clock."

"What time is it now, mother?"

"Quarter past eight."

"Then I had better get washed and shaved," said Robert.

"Sit down, Max, and I'll make some new toast."

"I've made the tea, mother."

"Good for you, Max. Have you washed yet?"

"Not yet, mother."

"Then go join your father in the bathroom and, if you are quick, your beans on toast will be ready."

At exactly nine o'clock, the intercom buzzed.

"Yes?"

"Max here, Miranda, I've come for Junior."

"Come on up, Max," and Miranda pushed the electric door release.

"Good morning, young man, ready?"

"Sure, Max, I've just had my breakfast. Beans on toast."

"Smells like, young man, somebody burnt the toast?"

"It was an accident, I'm not used to father's toaster's controls. I set the smoke alarm off but everything is O.K."

"Get your coat then, I'm parked on a double yellow. I've tipped the warden but she's a new one, and said, 'five minutes only, then it's a ticket'. So be quick."

"Bye, mother, father, see you later!"

"Where are we going, Max?"

"To my house, Junior, to meet my boys."

"Oh great!"

As usual, like an expert, Max weaved through the traffic until he was in Hammersmith. They passed beside Hammersmith Hospital and went down a side road and pulled in at a new looking apartment block.

"O.K., Junior, we are here."

Junior got out. "Gosh, is this your house, it must be a palace with many rooms?"

"No, no, young man, it's many small homes all in one block. I live in the top apartment. Let's go."

In the foyer, sat at a reception desk, was a security guard.

"Good morning, Max, who is the kid?"

"This is Max Junior, named after me. He is the son of a client of Teddy Rosenburgh. I have the honour of his pleasure for the day, Tommy."

"O.K., Max, have a nice day."

"Tommy, any messages for me?"

"Not so far, Max."

"Thanks, Tommy."

"Come on, Junior, let's go up."

The apartment block was obviously new because the lift was pristine, sparkling mirrors and a deep pile carpet. The lift was silent it whooshed to the top floor in seconds.

Max keyed the security pad on his apartment door and went in. The room, thought Junior, was actually quite large. The two boys wrestling on the floor jumped up when Max entered.

"I hope you two haven't broken anything while I have been out fetching Junior here?"

"No dad."

"Hi Junior, my name's Jack and this is my younger brother Bill."

"Hello, Jack, Bill. I'm Max Junior, my father named me after your dad's name."

"That's O.K. Max Junior is an interesting name. We have English names of Jack and Bill because father wants us to be British."

"That's right, Junior, I was born here so I don't think of myself as African any more."

"You a fighter, Max, this room looks a bit like a keep fit gymnasium?"

"I do some amateur boxing in the local Hammersmith Boxing Club."

"Yes, father fights for charity, he raises money for the Cancer Ward in the Hammersmith Hospital opposite."

Jack and Bill put on boxing gloves and started on the floor standing punch bag to make a point.

"Can I have a go?" Max Junior asked.

"Sure, but we haven't any gloves for you."

"Hey, Junior, try these," said Max.

Junior put on Max's gloves which were huge. Then he went to the punch bag and joined in with the others whacking it with all his strength. After a while he decided it hurt his knuckles.

"This is painful," said Junior. "How comes Jack's and Bill's don't hurt them, Max?"

They have kids' gloves with padding built in but my gloves are proper boxer's gloves. When I fight my trainer wraps my knuckles in tapes to protect them when I punch. How about we go out on the roof and pay basketball?"

"Right on, dad," said Jack. "Come on, Junior, I'll show you our basketball court."

"Wow! A playground on a roof, neat."

"Glad you like it, Junior, it was the boys' idea. I had the safety netting put up so the ball didn't bounce over the perimeter wall."

"Good idea, Max. Whose is the rooftop garden?"

"That's mine also, I rent the roof space. Well, my wife's actually."

"Where is your wife, Max?"

"In the hospital, she's a sister."

"A sister?"

"Not that kind of sister, Junior, a ward sister. She's a senior nurse in charge of Wendover Wing."

"Is that somebody's name?"

"Yes. Sir Nigel Wendover, he was a famous surgeon who operated on cancer patients. Wendover Wing is a cancer treatment wing, and when Sir Nigel Wendover died he left a large sum of money to buy a body scanner for the wing so that patients could be diagnosed early."

"Is that why Jack and Bill are being looked after by yourself? I mean your wife working."

"No, Sabrina, that's my wife, always works, her job is important. I have my boys off today to specially meet you, Junior."

"Oh, thanks, Max, that's kind of you, and because Teddy Rosenburgh suggested it?"

"You're a sly one, Junior. Yes, Mr Rosenburgh pulls the purse strings, after all he is my employer."

"My father says Mr Rosenburgh is a multi-millionaire. Is that true?"

"Yes, Max Junior, that is true, but let's play ball. You and me against Jack and Bill."

"O.K., Max, but I don't know the rules."

"No problem, just bounce the ball past Jack and Bill and shoot for the basket, O.K.?"

"O.K., Max."

"Just follow my example, you'll be O.K."

Now what Max didn't tell Junior was that Jack and Bill, being a little older at ten and nine years, respectively, were quite athletic and shot across the pitch in a few seconds and scored easily. Jack was a crack-shot at the basket.

"One! One to us!" called out Jack.

Now Max was a big man, but stripped down to his T-shirt he was solid muscle, no fat to be seen. He moved quickly, dribbling the ball by bouncing it at high speed across the pitch, turning his back to block his sons from getting the ball, and then springing up high to throw the basketball cleanly into the basket.

"That's one to us, Junior!"

"Father, let Junior do the throw-in, that's only fair, otherwise you will have the ball before we have had a chance to touch it."

So the three of them waited to pounce. Junior shouted out, "One, two, three!" and threw the ball in.

"Come on, Bill, quick, pass it to me," said Jack. Jack did a dummy, blocked his father, passed back to Bill and Bill successfully shot for the basket.

"Two to us!" shouted Bill.

"Come on, Junior, we're losing. Speed up a bit. That's it, bounce, pass! To me!"

Max got the ball and flipped it into the basket.

"Two all!" shouted out Max.

"How many, Jack?"

"First one to five, pa."

Meanwhile in Knightsbridge at The Block, Robert was furiously sketching away at a naked Miranda. He had made up his mind that half a day was enough time allotted to pencil drawing, but in truth he let her, for her modesty's sake, wear knickers, which he considered respectful being his wife.

"Sorry, darling, I can't hold this pose any longer, it's been three hours, surely you have finished by now?"

"Yes, perfect timing. Your pose has been good because you have been natural and relaxed."

"Never mind the pose, I need the toilet."

"Here's your robe. I'll turn the fire down a bit now it's getting a little too warm."

"For you maybe, you have a shirt and trousers on, I'm in my birthday suit."

"Just the way I like you."

Miranda came back into the room.

"How about something to eat, my artistic lover?"

"Probably a good idea. When I am creating I don't think about food."

"Well, my tummy is rumbling. What have you in the refrigerator?"

"I don't actually know, because Max brings in the shopping."

"Max? That Teddy Rosenburgh is a crafty sod, he's got you exactly where he wants you."

"I don't mind. Teddy gives me some brilliant commissions, for example up to a cool million for two portraits of you."

"Well, you have some salad in, so how about a tin of something?"

"Salad, I don't normally order salad from the local shop?"

"Well, I do, so your Teddy Rosenburgh has done his homework. I mean, he knows I am going to be here for the week. What have you got in the cupboard?"

"Loads of tins."

"Tins of what?"

"No idea, have a look."

"Well, there is plenty of pink salmon, so that will do. Any wine?"

"Whatever's in the wine rack. Help yourself."

"A five percent Chianti, that will do famously."

"I'll get the wine and the glasses, you do the salad."

"Sure, even I can manage that. And open a tin."

"Salad cream?"

"Top cupboard, beside the cooker."

While Miranda was making the salad, Robert put his arms around his wife and gently squeezed her breasts through the thin cotton of her housecoat.

"Behave yourself, this is a working lunch."

"Surely I can cuddle my own wife?"

"Leching after my breasts is more than a cuddle."

He kissed her neck and then nibbled her ears the way she liked it, and squeezed her bottom with one of his large manly hands.

"Hands off! You can wait till tonight."

"I don't know if I can wait."

"I'm surprised you're still interested today. I've been there in a reclined pose, stark naked, well apart from my knickers for three hours."

"When I'm painting or sketching I see the object or person with an artist's eye, not that of a red blooded man. It's the beauty I admire, the form and shape, light and shade and texture."

"Don't over do it, you are making me sound boring. Surely you must feel something for me?"

"Yes, an artist's model, but one thing you have is a natural beauty, you have the texture of silk, like a fine eggshell, perfect."

"Well, that's something you like about me, my skin. Tonight, when you have finished painting, you can massage me all over with baby oil, how does that sound?"

"Sounds interesting. Maybe I'll oblige, I like a silky finish."

"Sit at the table and I'll serve the salad. Come on, serve the wine and the tinned salmon."

Robert painted until the natural daylight lasted through his glass-walled studio. While he cleaned his brushes and palette knives, Miranda dressed ready for the evening.

At exactly five o'clock the intercom buzzed and on the CCTV monitor the familiar face of Max appeared. "Just returning, Max Junior."

"Thanks, Max, come on up."

"Here he is, safe and sound."

"Max, don't go, I have a favour to ask of you. How are you fixed this evening?"

"Nothing on, Mr Robert, sir. What's up?"

"Well, Max Junior should go home. I can't have him here tomorrow, I have a deadline to meet, so I've arranged with

Humphrey Braun at Lower Dale for Max Junior to stay with his friend David."

"Yippee!" shouted Max Junior. "We can go fishing!"

"You want me to go this evening, Mr Robert? It's a bit short notice?"

"I know, Max, that's why I'm prepared to pay you a hundred pounds for your trouble."

"In advance? Does Max Junior know the way to Lower Dale?"

"Sure I do, Max, I've made the journey dozens of times. Give us ten pounds and I'll be your navigator tonight."

"Max Junior! That's a bit mercenary."

"Mother, Max doesn't know the way without me, I'm just being the navigator."

"A hundred pounds in advance, Mr Robert?"

"Sure Max, just take me across to the cash machine."

"Max Junior, get your coat and give your mother a goodbye kiss."

"Bye, mother."

"Be back in a minute, love, just getting the cash for Max."

"Bye, father."

Sitting in the front of Teddy Rosenburgh's limousine Max Junior felt ten miles high, being chauffeured and sitting up front made him feel like an adult.

"Which way, Junior?" asked Max at the junction.

"Ten pounds in advance?"

"O.K., ten pounds in advance. Here."

"Thanks, Max. Turn right and head south."

"What's this Lower Dale, like?"

"Just a country village with a village shop, St Winifred's Church and the Black Bull on The Green, plus Dale Brook that goes through the woods. Captain Percy Lennox, a retired army officer, shows us where to fish for trout."

"Do you catch anything, Junior?"

"Not always, it depends on the weather. It's best when there is cloud cover, you know, on a dull day, and when the wind ripples the water's surface a bit because then the trout can't see us stalking them."

"Is there a trout farm nearby?"

"A trout farm, I don't think so?"

"Then where do the trout come from?"

"As far as I know, Max, they are wild brook trout."

"You know, when I was a boy a bit older than you, I would cycle miles into the countryside to go fishing."

"What did you catch?"

"It was a slow meandering river. I caught mostly roach, but occasionally I would reel the fish in and, before you knew it, a pike would snatch the roach off the hook biting clean through my fishing line."

"How many did you catch? Did you have a keep net?"

"Usually between ten and twenty, but of course I always let them go. You know, one time I was fishing, sitting on my tackle box, when there was a flash and a bang and I looked up and about fifteen feet in front of me on the opposite bank a lightning strike split a tree down the middle. It just separated as if a knife cutting butter, and then it smoked from the lightning strike."

"You were lucky the tree didn't fall on you."

"It happened so quick, Max, the tree sliced down the middle, then there was a tearing sound and then it dropped apart, it was all over in about three seconds."

"Weren't you scared, Junior?"

"I didn't have time to be scared it just happened. So I looked at the smoking split trunk and then carried on fishing."

"I think you were very brave. Do you like music, Max Junior?"

"Yes please. I like music from the sixties, you know, rock'n' roll and the Beatles."

"Good choice, Junior. Sit back and relax."

"That's David Braun's house, the one with the porch light on."

"You must be, Max. Please come in, my name's Humphrey, and this is my wife June."

"Pleased to meet you, Humphrey. You must be David's father?"

"David! Come down here, your friend Max Junior has arrived."

"Hello Max Junior, come on up, I'm making a model aeroplane."

"Which model is it?"

"It's a Second World War spitfire."

"Oh, cool!"

"How about a cup of tea before you drive back, Max?"

"Sure. A short break will do me good. Can I use your bathroom?"

"Of course, top of the stairs, first door you come to."

"Tea's ready Max."

"Thanks. If you don't mind I'll stand, I've been sitting behind the wheel most of the day."

"Sandwich?"

"I won't say no if you're offering."

"Cheese and tomato, O.K.?"

"That will be fine, Mrs Braun."

"June, please, only the vicar Reverend Thompson calls me Mrs Braun."

"I guess vicars can be a bit formal."

"Yes, they try too hard, not to be oversensitive."

"My local vicar is a good laugh, he leads a brass band and plays at the weekend at the Hammersmith Hospital in the Student's Union Hall."

"Does he charge admission?"

"Oh yes, the vicar charges between five and ten pounds. The events are well supported by the general public and patients' relatives. The students at the Hammersmith Hospital get in for five pounds by showing their Student's Union Membership Card. The public pay ten pounds, but nobody minds because the Reverend Jackson donates all the money to charity including the elderly retired or disabled parishioners of the church."

"Sandwich ready, please have a seat."

"Thanks, June."

"Here, a tip for you, for bringing Max Junior home at short notice."

"You don't have to."

"Its only ten pounds, Max, besides, my son David is very pleased Max Junior is back home. The two boys are best friends and they miss each other, so you have done me a favour, Max."

"Well, June, Humphrey, nice to meet you, I best get back to Hammersmith in case my employer, Teddy Rosenburgh, calls."

"Goodbye, Max, and thanks."

"You two come down here!" called out June.

"Now then, I need to know do you two want supper before I put you to bed?"

"Yes please, mother! Can we have it in my bedroom?"

"Yes and no. Yes you can have supper and no you cannot have supper in the bedroom."

"Oh mother!"

"Don't you, oh mother, me. The last time you had beans-on-toast in bed most of it ended up on the bed covers."

"Mrs Braun, can I have spaghetti?"

"O.K. Max. What about you, David, do you want your alphabet spaghetti?"

"That's for little kids, mother!"

"And you're a grown man all of a sudden?"

"Like Max, I'm nearly nine. I'm a junior now not an infant any more. I'll have beans-on-toast please, mother."

"Well, I'm not so fussy, June, I'll have David's alphabet spaghetti and sausages," said Humphrey.

"O.K. darling."

"Hey, mother, that's not fair, father is having sausages as well!"

"Well, that's because he's not a baby and doesn't complain about alphabet spaghetti. The sausages are for soaking up all the tasty tomato sauce in the Heinz Spaghetti."

"All right, mother, I'll have alphabet spaghetti with father, provided of course I get sausages as well."

"Don't give them too many sausages, June, because they are my treat."

"It's O.K. Humphrey, they're tinned sausages, small frankfurters. I have, luckily, two tins."

Chapter Twelve

Back at The Block the days passed quickly, one day blended into the next and, before Robert and Miranda knew it, it was Saturday afternoon.

The intercom buzzed while Robert was tidying up and cleaning his brushes.

"Hello, Max, come on up."

"Good afternoon, Mr Robert sir, Miss Miranda. Teddy Rosenburgh sent me. He wants to know if I can take the two portraits to The Arch."

"Sorry, Max, the oils are very wet, I won't be moving them 'til the morning. I can't put a cover over wet paint."

"What shall I tell, Mr Rosenburgh?"

"Tell him tonight I am going out for a drink and in the morning, about ten o'clock, I will bring, by black cab, my portrait paintings to be hung in the gallery. At the present moment the canvasses smell very strongly of linseed oil."

"I don't like going back empty-handed, Mr Robert, sir."

"Don't worry, Max, not your fault. The exhibition doesn't open 'til one o'clock and that's after invited guests have had lunch and pre-exhibition drinks, so they will be in a good relaxed mood."

"Right, Mr Robert, sir, I'll see you tomorrow about ten o'clock. I must say though, the portraits of Miranda are extraordinarily life-like."

"Thanks, Max, that's the idea. See you tomorrow."

Robert knew, with the central heating having a drying effect on his canvasses, that the 'initial set' of the paints would take place over night.

Now Teddy Rosenburgh, without telling Robert Darling, had invited the people who mattered in London, not just oil barons with cheque books bursting at the seams. Pauline, the Chief Editor of Vogue Magazine; Felicity Swanson, Marketing Director of Estée Lauder; Jake Higgins, Picture Reporter for the News of The World; Jacques Ferineaux, Clothes Designer from Paris; and Veronica Lawnswod, Literary Editor of the Sunday Times were invited also.

At ten past ten Teddy Rosenburgh was ready, his exhibition was ready except two reserved spaces on the gallery wall for Robert's portrait paintings.

Max was on the door as security officer, and Teddy Rosenburgh's hired hostesses were ready early inside the glass-walled and marble-floored gigantic foyer with tables full of reception wine. Actually quality bubbly to relax guests.

There was an air of anticipation because the whisper of a Teddy Rosenburgh private exhibition had gone round Knightsbridge, and so many newspaper photographers were gathering in the foyer photographing anybody who was anybody and hoping, after drinks, that they would be allowed in at one o'clock.

At half past ten a taxi pulled up. Eagle-eyed Max went immediately to the taxi door.

"Good morning, Robert sir, would you like a hand?"

"Yes, please, keep everybody away from me while I carry these canvasses in."

Robert, with covered portraits, walked swiftly through the foyer and Mr Rosenburgh let him into the main gallery. The photographers made a move for the door, but Max, 'brickhouse' that he was, let nobody through the door.

Inside Robert and Teddy Rosenburgh hung 'Miranda'.

"Brilliant! Absolutely brilliant! Your best work yet, Robert. I think I feel an auction coming on. A million pounds is the least I am going to accept."

"Sorry, Teddy, I am not stopping, I'm having lunch with Miranda."

"Where is Miranda?"

"Safe at The Block, away from cameras. I wish, as does Miranda, to keep a low profile until after one o'clock."

"After one o'clock?"

"Yes, you don't need me here. You have Miranda on canvas, which is what you were after?"

"But I want you and Miranda here for the publicity."

"Don't worry, we'll turn up. Have I ever let you down?"

"Well, no actually, Robert."

"There you go then, see you later."

Back at The Block Miranda and Robert relaxed on the sofa drinking wine.

"Ready for lunch, darling?"

"Sure. Can we go to The Red Lantern?"

"Good idea, take our minds off the exhibition. I don't like going to functions on an empty stomach it makes me nervous."

Robert phoned for a cab.

The intercom buzzed.

"Taxi for Mr Robert!"

"Be right down, cabbie."

"Hey! I know your face. You're not just Mr Robert, you're Robert Darling, your photograph is in today's paper. You're that famous artist."

"Let me see that. No wonder there was a load of photographers this morning at The Arch. Teddy Rosenburgh loves publicity."

"I won't tell anyone gov'nor. Where to?"

"The Red Lantern and take a round-about route, I don't want any photographers following me."

"Right away, gov'nor."

The cabbie circumnavigated a few blocks before pulling up outside The Red Lantern.

"Here, cabbie, a twenty, now you haven't seen us, O.K.?"

"Sure, Mr Darling sir."

"May I help you, sir?"

Robert took his shades off.

"Oh, it's you Mr Darling and behind the dark glasses is your wife, the beautiful Miranda?" asked Yan.

"That's right, Mr Chong, the headscarf is to hide behind. Can we have a discreet corner?"

"Of course, Mr Robert, sir, follow me."

"Thank you Yan, this will be fine."

"What would you like to order?"

"The chicken and sweet corn soup, followed by lobster."

"And to drink?"

"Just sparkling mineral water, I want to keep a clear head. I have an exhibition today."

"Yes, sir, I know, but if anybody asks, I haven't seen you."

"Good man, Yan."

They enjoyed their meal and lingered until gone one o'clock to let the hullabaloo die down at The Arch.

"Mr Yan, call me a taxi please."

"Right away, Mr Robert."

Inside the entrance, photographers were jostling one another for entrance to the main doors to the gallery. Max, in uniform and cap, had one door firmly bolted and the other door he blocked with a table and his bulk.

"Sorry, nobody gets in unless they have a ticket! That means no uninvited photographers!"

"Hell, what's going on here!?" asked a big man with a sun-tanned face and a ten-gallon hat.

"Who are you, sir?" asked a newspaper photographer.

"Sonny, I'm an oil magnate," said Hagman through a cloud of cigar smoke. His two companions though as tall were not as broad, but they both also wore ten-gallon hats.

"You in charge here, boy?"

"Yes, sir, name's Max. Have you a ticket?"

"Sure have. What are all these people doing hanging around the door."

"Trying to get in without a ticket, sir."

"Hey, you know the rules, no ticket, no entry!" shouted Hagman. He spread his bulk against the door, blocking its entrance. "Now move back a bit and let this man do his job!"

The photographers, seeing that the three oilmen were guests, gathered in front of them and took their photographs.

"Welcome sir, Mr Hagman. I'm afraid cigars are not allowed in the exhibition because smoke and ash from smoking can affect the surface of the pictures," said Max.

"Hey boy! I can appreciate that. You have the cigar. This is Langley and Blackthorn, friends of mine."

"Can I see their invitations please?"

"Sure boy. Show him lads."

"Please go in," said Max, and he quickly re-locked the door.

"Hagman, over here!" called out Teddy Rosenburgh.

"Hi, Money Bags, how goes it?"

"Fine, Hagman, fine, who are your friends?"

"They are both from Houston, owners of oil wells. This is Langley an easygoing man, and this is Blackthorn who likes to get his own way. If it's desirable and it has a price, then it's for sale, that's Blackthorn's maxim."

"For the News of The World, can I have your names please gentlemen?" asked Jake Higgins.

"Sure, kid, fire away."

"Now, Teddy, what the hell did you bring us across the pond for, something about an irresistible woman?"

Miranda stepped out of the taxi as if dressed for a film set in a sexy little white number. She had plenty of cleavage and a whole lot of leg showing. She walked into the foyer and posed against the glass wall. Every photographer, for a short while that is, went quiet, as they concentrated on photographing the beautiful Miranda.

Shutters clicked, flash bulbs lit up the foyer and reflected spectacularly off Miranda's fine satin white dress. One reporter said, "She looks like a bride."

Miranda replied, "That's my 'Virgin's Blush', darling,"

Then Robert, in dark shades, moved Miranda quickly towards the gallery's main door.

The reporters rushed forward, but Max made a gangway just wide enough for Robert and Miranda to squeeze through, then he quickly re-locked the door behind them.

"Thank you for coming, Miranda!" boomed Teddy Rosenburgh.

"Aha! The lady in the flesh. And you must be the painter husband, Robert Darling?" asked Hagman, removing his ten gallon hat.

"And you are?"

"Hagman, Oil Baron from Houston, Texas. Can I have your autograph, that is the one in the portrait, just to verify who you say you are? Wouldn't want to bid for a forgery."

"You want to buy?"

"That's what I'm here for son. Teddy here tipped me off that there would be something special in his exhibition this time. And yes, sir, this sure as hell is the lady Miranda in the portrait."

"Have you an autograph book, Mr Hagman?"

"No, Mister, just Hagman. Sure I have, always carry it with me."

He removed from his inside jacket pocket a genuine solid gold case inside of which was an autograph book.

"There you go."

"What would you like me to write?"

"How about, 'at The Arch, Knightsbridge, regards Robert Darling'?"

"O.K."

Robert autographed Hagman's book.

"Now you, pretty lady."

'Love, Miranda Darling', signed Miranda.

Langley and Blackthorn were looking at the pair of nude portraits of Miranda.

"Hey! Teddy Rosenburgh, how about business?"

"That's what we are here for, boys."

"You have some good paintings here, Teddy, but Miranda knocks spots off the rest."

"It can't be shipped for seven days because the oil is too wet, it's only just been finished. When it has dried we will pack it and crate it in a special container so that it doesn't come to any harm."

"What about air transport? If it's specially crated it could go safely in a plane's cargo hold."

"Whatever, Hagman. Which portrait do you want, 'Miranda Posing' or 'Miranda Reclining'?"

"I don't mind, they are a pair. Maybe, if the price is right, I'll buy both."

"I'll take 'Miranda Reclining', that's the one I fancy," said Blackthorn. "How much, Teddy?"

"At least a million."

"Bucks?"

"No, pounds Sterling."

"Hell, that's nearly two million bucks!"

"Name your price, Blackthorn," said Hagman.

"One million, five hundred thousand bucks."

"Sorry gentlemen, for that price it stays in the gallery or I may refuse to sell it and place it in my own home," said Teddy.

"Come off it, Teddy, everything has a price," said Hagman.

"Well, name your price?"

"One million pounds!" said Hagman forcibly.

Now the room had gone deathly quiet as the other guests crowded round the oilmen, straining to hear every word. Jake

Higgins, the reporter from The News of The World, was scribbling furiously in his notebook. Veronica Lawnswood, Literary Editor of the Sunday Times was talking to her Dictaphone.

Langley, cut in, "Stop pissing about you two. Two million pounds!"

"Three million," said a relaxed Hagman.

"Four million," said Blackthorn.

There were gasps amongst the guests.

"How much as a pair?" asked Teddy Rosenburgh.

"Five million the pair!" said Hagman.

"Six million the pair," said Langley.

"I thought we were friends?" said Hagman.

"Not when it comes to desirable beauty," said Blackthorn.

"Do I hear any advance on six million, gentlemen, or the rare pair of canvases goes to Langley."

"Eight million," said Hagman, and that's my last word."

"In that case, I'll go ten million the pair," said Blackthorn with a winner's smile.

"Any more bids, gentlemen? No? Sold to Blackthorn for ten million the pair. Congratulations!"

"Thank you, young man," said Blackthorn, shaking Robert's hand, "that's what I call a bargain. Miranda will hang in my private gallery, which I had built onto my ranch on the outskirts of Houston."

All the chatter started again, and now Pauline of Vogue and Felicity of Estée Lauder moved in on Miranda.

"Can we have the rights to your full photograph on the cover of Vogue?" asked Pauline.

"As I am Miranda's Agent or Manager, or whatever you want to call it, you have to have my permission. First of all, for my copyright of the originals of my oil paintings of 'Miranda Posing' and 'Miranda Reclining' and then, a contract for the right to publish," pointed out Robert.

"I knew you would want paying, Robert, for Miranda's picture on the cover of Vogue, so I brought along a contract for you to read and sign now," said Pauline.

Once that was settled, Jacques Ferineaux, the famous French fashion designer from Paris, begged Miranda to model his latest fashion collection at the next Paris Fashion Show scheduled for the Spring.

"Jacques, I would be delighted to model for you in Paris the 'J. Ferineaux' label.

The News of The World splashed across the front page, 'Miranda Reclining', with her private area censored to make it acceptable to the decency of publishing.

Miranda was in the news: being talked about on the radio and all the television channels as more stations picked the story up.

Luckily it was Monday morning and David and Max Junior would be at André Laceys, so they wouldn't know about Miranda 'til the early evening when June dropped them off.

Chapter Thirteen

On that same morning Humphrey went off to work to his office as a Consultant Architect in the opposite direction to Robert and Miranda.

June strapped infant Johnathon, now four-and-a-half years, into his child safety seat and set off for André Laceys with Max and David.

It was early morning and the lane through Lower Dale was deserted except for the postman and the milkman. There was a morning mist that hovered, magically, just above ground level, exposing roadside verges and winter-brown ploughed fields, but obscuring hedges with a smudged white blanket. In the window view, where the low level watery sun broke through the suspended curtain, wildlife could be seen scampering about: rooks attacking carrion squashed onto the road; hedgehogs pulling at worms that had exposed themselves overnight; and rabbits enjoying a run on the grassy banks in the first daylight.

"Why couldn't I sit in the back with Max, mother, it's not fair!" complained David.

"Because Johnathon is only four-and-a-half, and he has to be in his booster seat now he is older, and because it's the law. It's for Johnathon's safety."

"But when Miranda takes us, we sit in the back seat together, always."

"Don't argue, David, or I will tell your father you have been belligerent. And, further more, Max's mother is called Mrs Darling to you, not Miranda, so mind your manners."

"Sorry, mother. I forgot it's your turn to drive us."

"I should think so, I don't enjoy driving as much as Miranda. And I should really take Johnathon to nursery school."

"Couldn't Max's mum have Johnathon before we set off for André Laceys?"

"She could but I don't want to impose on her because as it is, she already has her hands full helping out in the Infant School. When Johnathon's five then he can go with Max's mum."

"Mrs Braun, I wouldn't mind looking after Johnathon, he's no trouble now that he is a bit older," said Max.

"Thank you, Max, but in the morning you have to be off to André Laceys."

At that moment a pheasant rushed out of the beech woods to their left and dashed across the lane, but as there was no escape into the hedgerow to their right it turned back again, and at that moment was struck by the front wheels of the car.

"Stop, mother!" shouted out David. "You have run it over."

"I couldn't help it, David, it stopped in the middle of the road."

David got out; the pheasant was lying on the road. He picked it up and took it to his mother.

"Is it dead, mother?" asked David.

"June got out the car and examined it."

"Sorry, David, its neck is broken. Let's leave him in the woods so that another car doesn't run him over."

"All right, mother. Can I take two tail feathers to remember him by?"

"I suppose so."

"One for me and one for Max, because he is my friend."

"Now put him in the beech woods."

"Thanks, David, a fabulous feather."

"Put your seatbelt on, David, I don't want you in an accident as well."

June drove on, heading towards the Surrey-Sussex border. The mist cleared as they headed south, but as they crossed The Downs the sky clouded over and a drizzle started, which made driving hazardous because of reduced visibility.

The woods gave way to grazing meadows and then fields as they descended off The Downs. June turned off The Dalesway and headed along a minor lane, following the black and white painted road sign pointing to André Laceys. The concrete-surfaced lane was hemmed in on both sides by a prodigious growth of rhododendrons, which in the summer gave a proliferate display of pinks and reds.

As if on cue, as they approached the imposing gateway to André Laceys, the rain stopped and a fresh breeze drove the clouds away, allowing the sun once again to shine.

June's car tyres crunched on the gravel as they arrived at the dropping-off area in front of the school.

"Thank you, mother," said David.

"Yes, thanks, Mrs Braun, see you at four o'clock!" called out Max as he jumped out.

"Right, Johnathon, it's just you and me now. Let's go home."

"Mummy, when I am a bit older will I go to David's school?"

"I don't think so, Johnathon. You're more suited to the local school."

"You mean the Infant School, where Max's mummy teaches?"

"Yes darling, Miranda's school."

"Good, I like that school it's smaller, not big like David's school."

"Would you like some music, Johnathon, while we ride back to Lower Dale?"

"I don't mind, mummy. I like to look out of the windows."

"What do you like to see, Johnathon?"

"Farms. Pigs, sheep, cows and horses."

"Oh, animals."

"Yes, daddy takes me sometimes to see the horses in Farmer Brown's field."

"I didn't know that you liked horses?"

"Well, daddy talks to Farmer Brown over the fence. He gives me a carrot to feed the horse. He's called Dobbin, mummy."

"Which horse is that?"

"The big white one. Daddy says it's a Shire Horse which farmers use for pulling a plough."

"Well, that's true, Johnathon, Shire Horses used to pull a plough, but Farmer Brown now has a tractor."

"Yes, a big red one. It's noisy and smokes."

"Don't you like tractors?"

"No, mummy. Animal's quiet but Farmer Brown smokes. Smoke smells."

"You mean, Johnathon, his tractor smokes?"

"No, mummy. Farmer Brown has a big smelly pipe."

"Oh, he smokes a pipe!"

"Yes, daddy says smoking makes your breath bad and gives you brown teeth."

"Daddy is right, smoking is bad for you, and you have lovely white milk teeth."

"O.K., Johnathon, some cows in the next field."

"Moo! Moo! Black and white cows."

They are called Friesians."

"Are they cold, then?"

"Cold? Oh, not freezing as in very cold. It's their name, Friesians, like Johnathon is a name for a boy."

"Do cows have names then?"

"It's a breed of cows, like different names for dogs, like terriers and collies. The brown cows that live near us are called Jerseys. The black and white ones are called Friesians from Friesland and they produce large quantities of low-fat milk."

"Does our milkman get his milk from our cows?"

"Yes, the milk comes from the Friesian cows, but actually they are Farmer Brown's cows."

"Does Farmer Brown give it to the milkman?"

"Well, all the milk goes to the dairy, a place where all the farmer's milk is put into clean bottles. Farmer Brown sells all his milk to the dairy, then the milkman sells it in pint bottles to mummy and daddy."

"And me?"

"Yes, milk for you as well, but mummy buys it for you and, David and daddy."

"I like milk on my Rice Crispies because they go snap, crackle and pop. Does Max Darling have milk as well?"

"Yes, because our milkman, Joe, delivers to all the houses along Dale Lane, including Rose Cottage, Max's home. Satisfied now?"

"I think when I am bigger I would like a horse."

"I think you mean a pony."

"What's a pony?"

"A small horse, ideal for a child to ride."

"Then I would like a pony to ride. A brown one."

"Johnathon, wouldn't you prefer a bicycle. How about David's bicycle, which is too small for him now?"

"No. Tyre's flat."

"Daddy can fix tyres. All he has to do is buy new inner tubes and pump the tyres up."

"I don't want a bicycle, I want a pony. Brown pony for a friend."

"When daddy comes home from his London office we can ask him."

"When daddy comes home I have to go to bed. Never see daddy after tea-time!"

"Tonight, I promise, before you go to bed, daddy will come and see you about a pony."

"Yippee! John John is going to have a pony!"

"Now Johnathon, it's not up to me, it's up to daddy, because a pony has to have a field, a stable and someone to look after it, and that costs money."

"David my big brother can look after a pony, mummy."

"Johnathon, David is only eight years old, only just old enough for a pony himself."

"John John ask David after school."

"Ready boys?"

"Thanks Mrs Braun, we played cricket with Captain Percy today in the Junior School Eleven. I scored forty runs and David took three wickets!" bragged Max Junior.

"Is that good, David?"

"Brilliant, mother! Forty runs is jolly good."

"David, John John wants a pony."

"Johnathon don't use baby talk, you're nearly five years old now."

"Mummy said I could have a pony."

"Johnatho, don't tell lies or you'll get a smacked bottom. I said we will ask daddy and, if you're really good, perhaps David would look after your pony."

"Mother, if Johnathon has a pony it will have to be a small one and, anyway, if he can have one, so can I."

"Now look what you have done, Johnathon."

"Mrs Braun, when I was in Spain at grandad's villa I rode a horse and made it gallop."

"Gosh, you were brave, Max," said David.

"Do you like horses then, Max?"

"Yes Mrs Braun, they are good fun."

"In that case, Max, if David's father agrees to buy David a pony, would you help him look after it?"

"Sure, Mrs Braun. David could keep it in the field behind my garden. I bet Farmer Brown would be pleased to rent us a field, I mean a pony will have to have a field for all the grass they need to eat, and a shelter from winter weather if it snows or there is a heavy downpour."

"Thanks, Max, I think two of you could more easily look after a pony. I'll ask Humphrey, tonight."

"Come on let's play I-Spy!" spoke up David.

"O.K. David."

"I'll go first because I thought of it. I-Spy with my little eye something beginning with 'H'."

"House!" shouted Max.

"No, not house."

"Hedge!" called out June.

"I can't see anything else beginning with 'H'," said Max.

"Give up?"

"O.K. David, give up."

"Horse, silly!"

"Where's the horse?"

"In that field back there."

"Hey! That's cheating, we passed it ages ago. When you say I-Spy, we have to be able to see it, that's the rules."

"All right, I'll pick something we can see now. I-Spy with my little eye something beginning with 'C'."

"Car!" said Johnathon.

"No, Johnathon, not car."

"Clouds!" said June.

"No mother, not clouds, and anyway this is just a boy's game."

"Spoil sport, can't a mother have a go?"

"It's just between me and Max, mother."

"I know," said Max. "It's crows, because they keep flying down from the trees to the hedgerow."

"No, Max, it's not crows."

"Then I give up. What is it?"

"You'll never get it in a month of Sundays. It's cable."

"Cable!?"

"Yes, beside the road, the cables between the telegraph poles."

"That's cheating. That's telegraph poles or power lines!"

"Mother, I am not cheating am I? Father said between the telegraph poles there were strung power cables."

"Afraid, Max, David is right, they are power cables. I know it is a bit of a tricky one, but David didn't actually cheat."

"O.K. In that case he should have said, I-Spy with my little eye something beginning with 'P.C'. That's two words for power cables."

"That David is technical I-Spy."

"Come on you two, I-Spy is just a bit of fun, don't take it too seriously," pointed out June.

When they arrived back home at Rose Cottage in Lower Dale, all three jumped out of the car.

"Hey! Where are you all going?"

"Mother, Max says we can go and ask Farmer Brown if he will let us use his field for a pony."

"If you're going to play at Max's house at least have the manners to tell me."

"Hello, June, was the drive back O.K.?"

"Sure, Miranda. Is it all right if you have all three for a while?"

"No problem, June, they can have tea with me. I'll bring David and Johnathon home a bit later."

"Thanks, see you later."

"Come on you three, I suppose as usual you are starving?"

"Mrs Darling, can we have strawberry jam sandwiches?" asked David.

"If that's what you want. Go to the bathroom and wash your hands and I will make some sandwiches."

"Yummy tummy!" said Max, "I like strawberries!"

All three rushed to the bathroom to use the basin. Two pairs of hands fighting for the soap and the hot water tap and a small pair of hands on the front edge of the basin trying to squeeze in.

"I've done," said Max.

"Come on, Johnathon, reach across to the taps."

"He can't, David, he's not tall enough. Put him on the step stool. Come on Johnathon, put your hands in the water, rub, now dry them."

"I hope you three are not dirtying my clean white towels!" called, Miranda, from the kitchen.

"No mother!" lied Max Junior, because Johnathon's hands left marks on the towel.

"My father is going to buy me a pony," said David.

"Don't tell lies, David, your mother said she would ask your father."

"Pony is for me," said Johnathon.

"Are you sure, Johnathon? You're not five years old yet, surely you are too small for a pony."

"Well, mother, we discussed it with Mrs Braun in the car, and David and me thought we could share a pony. What do you think?"

"Well, Max, you did ride a horse at El Estancia in Spain, so I suppose you would be safe, but what about David and Johnathon?"

"Mrs Darling, I'll be all right," said David, "but I don't know about Johnathon."

"I think," said Max, "if I am in control of the pony and have the reins, David could sit behind me and Johnathon could sit on my lap. I would hold onto him. I mean I would be careful and go slow."

"That's very considerate of you, Max. Thank you."

"But when I ride on my own I will go fast over the jumps."

"We haven't got any jumps, Max."

"I think, Mr Braun, could buy us some."

"And I think for now this is enough talk of ponies because it's all news to me. Until David's parents actually buy a pony it's pure conjecture."

"What's conjecture, mother?"

"Max, it is making decisions about what's going to happen without any concrete facts. In other words, it's just pie in the sky."

"Oh," said Max. "In that case can we go and play in the garden?"

"Yes, off you go and, Max, take care of Johnathon."

"Come on, Johnathon, now you are a bit older you can come and play in my tree house."

"You go up first, David, and be ready to pull Johnathon up when he gets to the platform."

"O.K., Johnathon, your turn. You go up in front of me and then I can catch you if you fall."

In Max's tree house there was a secret horde of biscuits, which he kept in a plastic box with an airtight seal to keep then fresh.

Inside Rose Cottage it was still a dream because up until then she had been occupied with the children, but now they were outside playing. Miranda couldn't believe the size of the Banker's Draft Robert held in his hand.

"You sure that's genuine, Robert, or is it just a piece of worthless paper?"

"I'll tell you again, Blackthorn pays Teddy Rosenburgh ten million pounds on a banker's draft, he takes twenty percent commission, that's two million for himself, and then he makes out a banker's draft for eight million, 'Payable to Robert Darling'."

"You mean it's real. We have another eight million pounds?"

"Yes, darling, as soon as I pay this into the H.S.B.C. our account will swell by another eight million pounds."

"Yippee! We are millionaires!"

"Hello, June, come to collect the boys. I see you brought them home safely from André Laceys."

"Yes, safe, but Max Junior is very excited."

"What's he excited about?"

"A pony?"

"Yes, mother, we are going to have a pony."

"Who says so?" asked Miranda.

"It's the boys' idea. Coming home in the car from school, Johnathon said he wanted a pony, then Max said he could ride a horse and, before you know it, between them they have decided to buy a pony."

"I said, we will ask David's father and see what he thinks, because a pony needs a field and exercising and looking after, which will all cost money," pointed out June.

"But, mother, Farmer Brown has a field, we can keep it there. David and Johnathon could ride with me. I'll be careful, so what do you say, mother?" pleaded Max.

"I have some good news for you, June and the boys. Come in, don't let's discuss it on the doorstep. I have been very successful in London. I have just sold two oil paintings for eight million pounds," laughed Robert.

"Hey, David, my dad is rich!" laughed Max.

"So you see, June, I'll buy a field off Farmer Brown then we won't have to rent it, and I'll buy three ponies and have a stable built."

"Yippee!" shouted Max and David together, "we are going to be cowboys!"

It was Tuesday evening, and Robert, at his good fortune, had invited Humphrey and June round to celebrate at Rose Cottage.

"Mrs Burns, are you sure you will be all right with David and Johnathon?" asked June.

"I am pleased to baby sit, it's company for me, and it gets me away from the Village Shop and, further more, twenty pounds is much appreciated."

"Now, David, eight o'clock bed and you, Johnathon, seven o'clock and no arguing with Mrs Burns, or she will not read you a bed-time story."

"We'll be good, mother."

"See you later, Mrs Burns. Bye boys."

It was February and, though dry, a cold wind was blowing, so June wrapped herself in a full-length coat and a scarf. Humphrey had a thick jumper on and a tweed jacket. It was only a hundred yards along Dale Lane to Rose Cottage but it was evening and cold. There were only two street lamps and they only gave out a half-light, so they walked quickly to keep warm.

The porch light at Rose Cottage was welcoming. Humphrey knocked with the brass lion's head, and the outer door was opened almost immediately.

"We have anticipated your arrival and, therefore, placed champagne on ice half an hour ago, so it should be ready now."

"Come on in, you two," said Robert. "Let me take your coats. Wow! That's a very sexy dress, June. You had better keep a hold on your wife, Humphrey, I could fancy her tonight!"

"Yes, she's a little cracker when she's a mind to," smiled Humphrey.

"More importantly, a winter stiffener, Humphrey?"

"Please."

"Double brandy?"

"That will be splendid, Robert."

"June, vodka?"

"Yes please, large one. Vodka and orange."

"Cheers!" said Robert. "I drink to the health of the four of us."

"Congratulations, Robert, on your success!" replied Humphrey.

"Come to my bedroom, June, I have something to show you," said Miranda.

"Oh that's beautiful. It's very lifelike, Miranda, it captures your bust and your face exactly."

"I didn't know you had a portrait of yourself in Rose Cottage, when did Robert paint it?"

"Oh, a while ago, in Spain. We brought it back from Atalia when we first moved into The Block. It hung in the Knightsbridge studio in pride of place because it reminded Robert of when he first met me. Robert said it was special and definitely not for sale, so he decided to bring it home. Home is where it belongs and, according to Robert, above the marriage bed is the right place."

"What are you two up to?" asked Humphrey, coming into the bedroom.

"None of your business," said June.

"That's beautiful, Miranda, you look so natural and so vulnerable.

"Oh, hello, Robert, I hope you don't mind me looking at your wife on canvas. You are very talented."

"It's a natural gift I have, Humphrey, but because I love Miranda so deeply she inspires me. I love her more today than when I met her eight years ago."

"Can we come out of my bedroom, please," said Miranda, "you are invading my privacy."

"Sorry, Miranda, you have a good point. It's my fault, let's get back to the lounge."

"Robert, how about painting a portrait of June? I mean I would pay you for it."

"It depends on June, whether she wants to see herself as others see her."

"How do you feel about it, June?" asked Robert.

"I would be flattered, being painted by the now famous Robert Darling, but not my breasts because having two children has affected my figure. I would like head and shoulders though."

"There you go, Robert, June is keen, but how much would it cost?" asked Humphrey.

"It would be a work of love. Let's face it, I can afford to paint for free now."

"That's settled then, June, you just have to make a date with the Maestro here."

"Come on you two, you're here to help me celebrate," smiled Robert. "Let me pour you some ice-cold champagne."

"That's rather a lot for four people, Robert," said June.

"Just a standard magnum, you know, two regular bottles, so you will have to drink up."

"I think I should eat something first?" said June.

"Come into the dining room and feast your eyes."

Miranda opened the door into the dining room.

"Wow! What a spread!"

"Do you like it, including smoked Scottish salmon and fresh cream cakes?"

"Just the ticket. Can we start now, I'm starving," said Humphrey.

"Sure, pull out a chair and help yourself."

It was a feast that Miranda organised via the Yellow Pages, by letting her fingers do the walking to Party Caterers. Humphrey refilled his plate three times before he felt replete.

"That's better, it's a long day working in London and I only had a sandwich at lunch time."

"Shouldn't you have a proper meal if you are working long hours?" questioned Miranda.

"My Personal Assistant makes sure I stop for lunch and takes me to different sandwich bars where I have a sparkling mineral water and a bite to eat. Otherwise I would fall back into my old ways and eat at my desk with a bought-in sandwich."

"Good, I'm glad you and Robert have had a good feed because us girls, though we can indulge, still have to watch our figures. However, June and I have left room for a cream cake. Naughty, but nice."

"Come on girls, drink up, this is a celebration, this magnum is still half full. You are allowed, and even expected, to get a little drunk. It's not every week I sell two portraits for eight million pounds."

"Darling, it was actually ten million but Teddy Rosenburgh took twenty percent," smiled Miranda.

"The man got two million for being your agent? That's some commission!" said Humphrey.

"Well, without Teddy Rosenburgh's contacts and the right to display in his gallery, The Arch, I wouldn't have got a penny."

"That's not true, Robert, if you had sold your work at a public auction room for fine arts you still would have got a sale."

"True, but I may have only got about a hundred thousand pounds."

"Still good wages, Robert," said Humphrey.

"Yes, but wages only once in a blue moon. Did you know, some of the artists I met in Spain lived a life of poverty; only after their deaths were their paintings sold for any realistic amount."

"True, Robert, I am fortunate that I am an established Consultant Architect with a solid reliable income plus consultancy fees. The busier I am the more I make."

"You, Humphrey, deserve your rewards, you studied for many years before you were established," supported June.

"We do quite well, both Robert and I. I receive good fees for modelling and, Estée Lauder and Vogue bring me in a good commission."

"You're right, Miranda, commissions are the best way to be paid. The bigger the contract the greater the fee," said Humphrey. "I'm not fabulously wealthy like you, Robert, but I net over four thousand a month, which is a good professional income."

"I am very proud of you darling," said June. "I couldn't imagine life without you now."

"What will you do, June, once Johnathon starts school full time?" asked Miranda.

"I haven't given it any serious consideration. I have to make a choice: another child or a vocation."

"Another child, darling?" queried Humphrey.

"Sorry, Humphrey, it's just that when Miranda told me she couldn't have any more children, I realised the gift of motherhood is precious, so I have been feeling broody lately."

"If you want another child, I don't mind, really I don't."

"Thank you, darling, I would like a girl to dress in pretty clothes and watch her growing up and becoming a young lady. I suppose one day, Humphrey, I will become a grandma."

"Blimey! That's a long way off. I think you need some more champagne, June. This is Robert's celebration party, so live for the moment and leave people like the vicar to think about hereafters."

Chapter Fourteen

By the summer, with further fame of Robert Darling and the beautiful Miranda, known not only for her gorgeous looks on the front cover of Vogue on both sides of the Atlantic, and her promotion of Estée Lauder 'Virgin's Blush' in all leading women's magazines and on main channel television, both had achieved celebrity status.

They were the talk of Lower Dale in Mrs Burns' Village Shop, Sam Smith's Black Bull and the Village Hall, particularly in the Village Hall where the retired folk gathered for their daily events, Miranda was looked on as something of a sex goddess. She was admired and held in awe, but not everybody saw her that way. Some said posing nude was not art but pornography. These were, in the main, pensioners who were steeped in the life of Reverend Thompson's teaching at St. Winifred's Church. They were dry old sticks who, in their day, considered showing an ankle was provocative.

But, nevertheless, when it came to the Grand Opening of the Annual Lower Dale Summer Fete, Reverend Thompson selected Miranda to do the honours.

"I shall be pleased," said Miranda, "to open the fete. My pleasure."

"Thank you, Miranda, the church funds need every penny we can raise, and having celebrity status on our programme will attract people from the surrounding district. I have taken Robert's advice and advertised this year, with him being my benefactor, in the Dales Times. I know it usually pays to advertise but, until I had Robert's backing, the Church Council simply couldn't afford it."

"How are the arrangements going, vicar?"

"Well, now that business people know that 'The Face of Estée Lauder' and 'Miranda Reclining' by the famous portrait artist, Robert Darling are supporting the Summer Fete, there is more interest this year than there has ever been. I have had to ask Farmer Brown if we could have a second field to use, because with there being greater interest we expect a lot of cars wanting to park in Lower Dale. Captain Percy Lennox has agreed to man the car park, at two pounds a car, and Mrs Burns is selling advance programmes from the Village Shop at a pound a time."

"I can see you have your business hat on, vicar," encouraged Miranda.

"Not only that, traders and entertainers are clamouring for space to erect stalls."

"Entertainers?"

"I use the word loosely, Miranda. You know, fairground traders with rides and swings. I also have a band booked. I took the Church Council's advice on that, they said music was important to create a happy atmosphere. Happy people spend more money apparently."

"How about things on the gymkhana side, you know, competitions and displays?"

"Well, we will have the jumps for the children's ponies and the dog competition. Also the traditional tug-of-war between the team from the Black Bull and the guest team, plus the majorette marching band by The Starlets."

"Sounds good this year, vicar. Well, see you later."

It was a sunny July day and the Church Council, together with the help of the Ladies Circle, had done well. The second field, given over for the use as a car park by Farmer Brown, was completely full. The village was decorated with bunting and there was a general carnival atmosphere.

Around the perimeter of the gymkhana display ground there were several horseboxes. Their owners, parents with children, were grooming their equine friends and dressing them up with ribbons. There were two categories for children's ponies: riders four to six years, and seven to eleven years. In charge of the pony displays was Humphrey Braun.

"Well, boys, you've had since February to practise over the jumps, how do you feel?"

"Easy, father," said David. "I can control Rupert to do anything, even sit."

"All right, don't show off, how about you, Max Junior?"

"Mr Braun…"

"Call me Humphrey, Max, we are friends today, all boys together."

"Humphrey, I am going to win because I am going to do my standing up trick."

"Is that allowed, Max, in a display of pony competence?"

"I don't know, I don't even care, it's advanced horsemanship."

"You sure, Trigger will allow you to stand on his back in front of spectators?"

"Sure, Humphrey, Trigger is my friend. Anyway, he knows if he's a good boy he gets a carrot."

"You're not daft, Max, I'll give you that."

"Father, what about me?" asked Johnathon.

"You're on later in the miniature class. All you have to do is ride around the display area, keeping control of Goldy. Just remember to smile and keep your riding hat on in case you should fall."

"What about the race, father?"

"You've done lots of runs in Farmer Brown's fields, so the run in a straight line inside the display area and back again will be easy for you. Just remember your practice sessions with Goldy."

"I know, father, pull on the reins, stop Goldy, then turn his head and run back again. I can do that."

"Good for you, Johnathon. As long as you sit properly in your saddle nothing will go wrong.

"And we'll cheer you on, won't we, Max," said David.

"Would all riders in the seven to eleven years group please go to the arena!" was announced over the Tannoy.

"There you go, David and Max, it's your turn now."

"Would all owners and parents please lead their mounts out and wait at the start for Mr Humphrey Braun's attention."

"That's me, lads. Now there are six of you entered for the event."

"Everybody ready? Right, you know the course. You have five minutes to complete the circuit. David, you have been drawn first. Are you ready?"

"Yes, sir."

"Right, off you go!"

David, on Rupert, went steady round the jumps. Rupert knocked down only one rail, then completed the circuit.

"Well done, David, not bad," said Humphrey.

"Rupert caught one rail, father."

The circuit marshal replaced the fallen rail and signalled to Humphrey that he was ready for the next rider.

Humphrey set them off one at a time: - a young lad who failed one jump and three girls, older than Max and David, who all had a clear round.

"Well, you've seen the competition, Max Junior, so it's up to you and Trigger, now."

"Mr Braun, Trigger is one of the largest ponies and a good jumper. Just watch me," said a confident Max.

"Ready, Max?"

"Yes, sir."

"Off you go, good luck!"

"Come on, Trigger, these are babies' jumps, you can jump a five bar gate. Let's show the cissies what we can do."

Max patted Trigger's head, gave him free reins and kicked his flanks.

"Come on boy, giddy-up there!"

Trigger responded by flying over the jumps with plenty of clearance and was back to the start in just under four minutes.

"Well done, Max!" congratulated Humphrey as Trigger came back to the start.

"Watch me, David!" called out Max.

He climbed carefully onto Trigger's back and then stood up, standing sideways, so that he had one foot on the saddle and the other on Trigger's back.

"Good boy, Trigger, walk on!" commanded, Max.

Max went right around the perimeter of the arena facing the crowd with a big smile on his face. There was spontaneous applause as he went round.

"Well, ladies and gentlemen, we weren't expecting this display of horsemanship but Max on Trigger not only had a clear round with no faults, he was also the fastest, and this extra activity off his own back, so to speak, makes him a clear winner in his section," said the announcer.

Once Trigger had completed a circuit Max called out, "Stop boy, good boy!" and he was again back at the start.

"Here I am, Humphrey, how did I do?"

"Top marks, Max, you won!"

"I won?!" But what about the older girls, surely they were better?"

"Four of you had a clear round within the five minutes of allotted time, but you were only three minutes fifty-five seconds, the fastest, so you are the winner."

"Hooray! Did you hear that, David, we won!"

"You won, Max."

"No, we won, because we are friends. I'll share the cup with you."

"You'll share with me? Well thanks, Max."

"It's only fair because it was Johnathon who got me interested in ponies. I'll have the cup on my parent's mantelpiece one month and the following month you can display it in your house. What do you say?"

"That's jolly decent of you, Max. I'm glad you're my friend."

It was time for the miniature ponies.

"All right, Johnathon," said Humphrey, "time to get on Goldy."

Several parents entered their infants for the four to six years' class. The course marshal held one end of the tape and Humphrey the other.

"Ready, go!" said Humphrey, as the tape was quickly lifted head high.

"Come on, Goldy," said Johnathon as the miniature ponies trotted forward.

For safety, Humphrey followed them to the end of the display arena making sure they all turned safely. A young lad called Jimmy seemed to have the nimblest Shetland pony, unlike Goldy, who thought a quick walk was top speed. Jimmy on Bumper trotted back while the others, including Goldy, thought it was O.K. to stroll along.

"Come on, Johnathon, hurry Goldy up!" shouted David and Max Junior.

But it was encouragement too late; Bumper trotted home a clear winner. The other miniatures also walked home nonchalantly to anxiously waiting parents.

"Winner!" shouted Max as Jimmy returned to the home rail.

"Right, young Jimmy," said Humphrey. "Lap of honour."

"Well done, Jimmy!" encouraged Mrs Smallbridge, Jimmy's mother.

"I'll lead him round, Humphrey."

"You've a proud mother there, Jimmy."

"Bumper is a good boy," said a five-year-old Jimmy.

At the end of the gymkhana, after the majorettes, The Starlets, had marched by, the announcer called over the Tannoy system: "Would all competitors please go to the steward's tent for presentation of the prizes."

On a rostrum, especially constructed for the purpose, just in front of the steward's tent, was a table set with prizes.

The marshal, Terry Higgingbottom, made the presentation speeches and Miranda presented the rosettes to the first, second and third places. Max Junior, being the winner for the seven to eleven year's class, received the Lower Dale Junior's Cup.

And so, over the years, Max, David and Johnathon started a long association with riding, ponies and horses. And Johnathon even took his new pony, Moonshine, with him when he left home.

Chapter Fifteen

At the age of sixteen, David and Max Junior graduated from André Laceys with very good grades. Johnathon, at the age of twelve, moved up from the infant's school to the junior school at Lower Dale and took after his mother's side. He was gentle, loved animals and was very kind to others. Johnathon had also discovered, through his own efforts, God the Holy Spirit.

At St. Winifred's Church the Reverend Thompson was very pleased with Johnathon's choice to seek out the spiritual life and encouraged him all he could.

"June, I feel strongly, that Johnathon's disposition suits him very well to join the clergy. I, therefore, propose sending him to St. Benedict's Monastery, where boys can go from the age of twelve to a monastic school for a full time education."

"Have you discussed this, vicar, with Johnathon?" asked an incredulous June.

"Yes, I have and, young as he is, he seems very mature in his approach to the Kingdom of God. He knows how to pray, how to give his own spirit to meet with the Holy Spirit. He truly believes and has already started writing his own Spiritual Journal, which is not unusual for a young man who feels the calling of God."

"Gosh, this is all new to me, vicar. I knew he prayed and that he was not to be disturbed when he prayed but I didn't realise the strength of his commitment or his calling to God."

"I shall call back this evening. I have told Humphrey to expect me at seven o'clock. This is the most important step in Johnathon's life.

"Johnathon himself is very keen for me to tell you."

"I'll prepare Humphrey's tea a little early. See you at seven, vicar."

Humphrey was intrigued by Reverend Thompson when he said that he wanted to discuss Johnathon's career, so he promised to be home to Lower Dale by six o'clock.

"Hello, darling, is Reverend Thompson still coming?"

"Yes, and it's going to be a surprise for you. The vicar came to see me today to lay down the framework. Apparently Johnathon wants to join the church full time, you know, become a member of the clergy."

"You mean become a vicar?"

"I suppose, I'm not sure. You had better have your tea and be ready for the Reverend Thompson."

"Where is Johnathon? Or don't I have to ask?"

"Don't ask. He's out the back in the stable grooming his pony. I'm sure he thinks more of Moonshine than he does of people," said June.

"He's just a sensitive lad, he'll grow out of it," assured Humphrey.

"I don't think so, Humphrey, he's a truly feeling young man, and you have to realise he has grown out of his boyhood and is seeking out the meaning of life."

At exactly seven o'clock Reverend Thompson knocked on Humphrey Braun's door.

"I'll get it," said June. "You go and fetch Johnathon in from the stable."

"Good evening, your reverence, do come in," said June. My husband has just gone to fetch Johnathon."

"Hello, Johnathon, how are you?" asked the vicar.

"Fine, sir, thank you for coming. It's best if you tell my parents."

"Tell your parents what?" asked Humphrey.

"I have asked you to see me," said Reverend Thompson, "because your son here, Johnathon, wants to join the clergy."

"You do, Johnathon, you didn't tell me?" questioned Humphrey.

"Oh yes, father, more than anything."

"Now I need your consent to send Johnathon for a full time education to St. Benedict's Monastery."

"A monastery? But isn't that a dramatic step?" queried Humphrey.

"Not if your son wants to go and feels the calling. He will be well educated and indoctrinated into the teaching of The Church of England. Initially he will be on a year's probation as a novice. This is for him to find his feet in his journey seeking out God and decide how he feels about his own commitment."

"Have you discussed this, Johnathon, with Reverend Thompson?"

"Yes sir, in depth, and that's why in recent months I have joined the Church Choir and wore the vestments, and assisted at Holy Communion."

"You assist at Holy Communion, I didn't know that?"

"That's because, father, it's at seven o'clock on Sunday morning, long before you attend the Family Service at ten thirty."

"Your son, Mr Braun, has found God, he wishes to dedicate his life to the ways of The Church of England."

"Well, Johnathon, I am surprised and feel I didn't realise your own strength of feelings. If you are sure you want to leave Lower Dale Junior School for a monastery then I shall back you a hundred percent."

"Thank you, father."

"Will Johnathon be a boarder then, vicar?"

"Oh more than that. It's a way of life. He will have his own cell. The training of a monk is a strict life based on obedience and prayer. It is a life dedicated to the teachings of Our Lord Jesus Christ and service to God The Holy Spirit. He will be trained and well fed, he will also work, learning cooking, carpentry, farming and stone masonry until, at the age of sixteen, when he must choose the life he wants, to become a full time monk or leave and become a vicar-in-training attached to a church. In all this time he will become a scholar."

"When will we see him?"

"Only for three weeks in a year, two during the summer and one week at Christmas when we encourage all novices to be reunited with their family."

"It sounds a harsh life, Johnathon, you sure you want to go to St. Benedict's Monastery?"

"Yes, father, I do. Please sign the papers."

"Do you have the consent forms, vicar?"

"Yes, in my briefcase."

"Then let's do it."

"Oh, Humphrey, I will miss Johnathon," said June.

"Mother, this is my choice. I am not your little boy any more, I have grown up. You have to let me go."

"Will you write to me, Johnathon?"

"Of course I will, mother, as often as I am allowed."

"As often as you are allowed?"

"Mrs Braun, it's part of the discipline, a cutting-off from the material world. Johnathon is going on a spiritual journey, it is his destiny. To aid that end Johnathon will only have a very limited contact with the outside world. He is allowed to contact his friends and family once a month, and no telephone calls."

"Oh, Johnathon, only once a month. It will seem ages before I hear from you."

"I shan't be alone, I will have Moonshine."

"You mean, Reverend Thompson, horses are allowed?"

"Yes, when he goes to St. Benedict's Monastery you may tow behind your car a horsebox, because they have stables. All things to do with nature are encouraged, all fauna and flora."

"So you see, mother, I won't be alone if I have Moonshine. I can go riding in the grounds."

"Yes, between chores, work, scripture and prayers, Johnathon is allowed an hour a day of free-time, that's when he can go riding."

"Sounds like a hard life, son, but if it's what you want then I support you."

It was eight o'clock before the Reverend Thompson left; they had been talking for a whole hour before both Johnathon's parents signed the consent forms.

"I think I need a drink," said Humphrey.

"I'll make tea, father," said Johnathon.

"I was thinking of something a bit stronger, son."

"You know, father, I don't approve of strong drink: it causes an unclear mind."

"I'll have tea please, Johnathon," said June.

"I'll have whisky, it's not everyday I lose a son," said Humphrey.

At André Laceys, Robert and Miranda were in the headmaster's office, along with Humphrey and June Braun.

"Well," said Peter Davidson, "you know why you are here. Both Max and David are extremely gifted and also inseparable. Further to our preliminary discussions I have been in touch with the Dean of Faculties at Oxford University, and the Registrar has agreed to enrol both boys onto undergraduate courses even though they are only sixteen. This is because the Registrar and myself, agree that it would serve no purpose for Max and David to stay on at André

Laceys as Senior Boys until they are eighteen and then go to university. They are ready now.

In line with their wishes David is to read for a BSc in Architecture, following in his father's footsteps, and Max Junior is going to read for a BA in Sports Studies. I'm not sure whether Max is going to play rugby for England but, one thing is for certain, André Laceys in the Sports Department cannot help him any further; he is naturally talented and needs a University Sports Club to stretch his abilities."

"Thank you, headmaster," said Humphrey Braun. "I am pleased because some of the designs David comes home with are really impressive. He is chomping at the bit to apply himself to the real world. He says he would like to design and build a spaceship, but I have told him repeatedly he will have to solve the problem of gravity, that is, build an anti-gravity power unit."

"And as for Max, with him being a good all rounder, I didn't know which way he would go. I didn't realise that sport can be a career. Yes, but he's a big lad now, six foot three and all solid muscle. He gets injuries at André Laceys but he wears them like trophies. They call him at school by his nickname The Refrigerator."

So, at the mature age of sixteen, Max Junior Darling and David Braun go up to Oxford, Max to read Sport Studies and David, Architecture.

It was the Freshman's Ball and David and Max met up with Pamela and Sonia, also only sixteen. They were both at Gabriel College for Ladies and lived in the Female Hall of Residence on campus, so the foursome only met up at weekends. With them all being gifted to varying degrees, study came before pleasure, but it didn't stop them from drinking in the Student's Union Bar.

Now, strange as it may seem, David and Max had similar tastes in women, for both Pamela and Sonia were redheads with green eyes and small, but perfectly formed figures, being size ten to twelve. They both had long hair surrounding a heart-shaped face with pouting lips. Max thought it was something to do with the portrait painter in him on his father's side. David just accepted it was a coincidence, though both Max's and David's mothers were beautiful. The only real difference was that Pamela was about five foot four, suiting David's height of only five foot six, while Sonia was not only slim but also tallish at five foot nine, which suited Max, being a rugby prop forward at six foot three.

"Come on, Sonia, drink up, you're two pints behind me," laughed Max.

"It's all right for you, my hero, you weigh about nineteen stone, just about twice my size. I can only manage halves of lager."

"Another drink, David?"

"I'm O.K. Max, thanks."

"Load of softies. Barman, another pint please."

"Sure, Max, but that's five you've had now."

"Don't nag, it's the Freshman's Ball. Come on, Sonia, they're playing sixties rock'n'roll. Let's show them how to dance."

Now Sonia was sexy and she knew it. She was wearing a flared skirt which, when she spun round, completely showed her thighs, bottom and knickers and she knew it. Her breasts were full but small and the dress she was wearing hardly concealed her womanhood.

Buddy Holly was playing, and he was one of Max's favourites. Max threw Sonia about like a willing rag doll, much to the appreciation of the student audience. He laid her across one hip and then the other, then flicked her head over heels before finishing by bringing her through his legs and lifting her above his head, bringing her down and giving her a big kiss.

"Wow! That was exhilarating!" cried out Sonia. "I love you!"

The room had gone quiet, and then there was a burst of spontaneous applause from all his fellow students, for Max had already made a name for himself in his first month on the rugby field.

"Bravo Max! Bravo!"

Max with Sonia left the dance floor and went and joined his lifelong friend, David, with Pamela.

"You were great, Max. I bet many a girl is jealous of Sonia. You two go together well."

"Thanks, David, that means a lot to me. I am strictly a one woman man. Isn't that right, Sonia?"

"It had better be, Max Junior Darling, or I'll dump you."

"You shouldn't make threats like that, it spoils a relationship."

"Just joking."

"You sure?"

"Now you are starting to frighten me."

"Then be careful what you wish for because I am a faithful person," said Max.

"Sorry, darling, of course I don't doubt you, it's just that I don't want to lose you."

"Then you must bend to my will and please me."

"Of course I will, Max."

One of the subjects that Max found very interesting in his Major was Sport Psychology. He had to learn about interactions between players and, between rival supporters. Yobbish behaviour and fans rioting after a football match was an act of catharsis, that is acting out an individual's feelings: frustration, rage or disappointment and resentment because their team lost. Similarly, supporters of a winning team act out their exuberance by going on a drinking orgy.

The difference between non-contact sports like professional football and American football and rugby, where there is a lot of contact, is that during a contact sport the game is acted out and, therefore, at the end of the game there is not a lot of pent up anger either between players or between the opposing fans.

Max came to realise that whole families came to watch rugby because it was considered a lot safer and friendlier than football. He also realised why he felt better after a good rugby match. He felt renewed, relieved of all his male aggressive hormones. His team-mates in the showers after a match, whether they won the game or lost, became comrades.

"There's one thing for sure, David, you won't get any injuries working over a drawing board."

"Why should I? I don't play rugby but I enjoy a game of cricket."

"Cricket suits you, David, it's a game of fractions: bowling, striking, throwing and catching."

"Injuries don't seem to bother you, Max."

"That's because I am studying Sports Injuries, which means I know what to be aware of on the rugby field. Most damage is done in the shoulder area in the full frontal tackle."

"How do you know?"

"Because in a scrum when two teams oppose one another there is a combined force of considerable pressure. My Sports Injuries Physiotherapist looks after the Oxford University Rugby Team.

He's very knowledgeable and he has a private practice but, luckily for me, being on the team I get free treatment on campus."

"I'm glad I don't play rugby. I would be a physical wreck by the end of the game."

"Yes, you're probably right, you're not built for rugby, but the bigger players look out for the smaller men in the team. But enough about my studies, how is the School of Architecture doing?"

"Going all right, but it's a good thing I enjoy mathematics because being an architect means being a physicist, mathematician and engineer. I didn't realise it takes seven years study to become a fully qualified architect. The university degree is just a beginning; it is followed by four years of practical application.

There was a difference between David and Max. David was saving himself for when he qualified as a Chartered Architect, some seven years in the future. And then he decided he had to be well established in a company of architects, and then, and only then would he go with a woman. He thought it right that he should be a virgin when he married.

However, Max had no such reservations as Sonia soon found out when she fell in love with him. Max and Sonia both used contraception but when she was halfway through her final year at Gabriel College she fell pregnant.

"I think it's great!" said Max

"Typical man, all he cares about is himself and sex!" exclaimed Sonia. "How about how I feel?"

"How do you feel?"

"Well I think I will have to drop out of college."

"I don't see why, you're only just pregnant. You won't be more than four to five months pregnant in May-June when you take your finals."

"I suppose that's true. But what about after the baby is born. How will I cope?"

"Mother, you are going to be a grandmother," said Max, on the phone.

"Did I hear you right, Max?"

"Yes, mother, I am going to marry Sonia and have our baby."

"Marry, Max, but you're not nineteen yet, surely you haven't thought it through."

"How young were you when you first married?"

"I wasn't a teenager, though I admit I was widowed at twenty-three, but then I met your father and was soon married."

"Why did you marry father?"

"Because I loved him. I still love him."

"Well, I love Sonia, and as soon as we have completed our finals we are going to be married."

"If you have made up your mind, I suppose I had better say congratulations. When will you be home again?"

"I'll be home for the Easter Holidays and I'll bring Sonia with me."

"Hello, Sonia, I am pleased to have you in my home instead of your usual flying visits with Max. Max has told his mother over the phone that you two wish to marry?"

"Yes, Mr Braun, we have been together ever since we met at Oxford University, two and a half years ago. We love each other."

"Please, Sonia, call me Humphrey."

"How are you going to support a family, Max?"

"Now I'll give you my very good news," smiled Max, very full of himself. "I have been selected for the England Under 21 Rugby Team."

"Wow! Max, why didn't you tell me?"

"Because I wanted my father to be the first to know."

"Congratulations, Max! When do you play?"

"After the summer vacation, in September. I'll be professional rugby player just before Bobby is born."

"Bobby?" said Sonia and Miranda, together.

"It'll be a boy, mother. I'm sure of it with all my testosterone."

"Why Bobby?"

"I like the name. I thought about calling him Robert after you, father, but he would get the nickname Bobby, so I have decided on Bobby."

"Don't I get a say?" said Sonia.

"Yes, darling, of course you do. What is your choice?"

"If it's a girl, because your mother is both famous and beautiful, I shall call her Miranda."

"That's very kind of you, Sonia, I am honoured," said Miranda.